ELLA MILES

SAVAGE LOVE

PROLOGUE

VICTORIA

My heart flutters in my chest as Mark leans against the locker next to mine with a grin on his face. I try to focus on putting my books into my locker and packing up my backpack to go home, but I can't focus. I have a feeling I know what he's here to ask me and an unsettling feeling pulls at my stomach every second that passes.

"I have a question I'd like to ask you," Mark says.

I grin as I pile the rest of the books into my locker, not bothering to organize them at all. I turn to give him my full attention. "Ask away." Please don't let it be that he wants to invite me over to study for geometry again. I loved spending time with him the last time, but I want to be more than just his tutor.

He glances down as he rubs his neck.

I sigh. Mark is great. He plays soccer, he gets good grades, he's good looking. He's not exactly in the popular crowd, but he is definitely high on the social ladder. And every sign points to him being interested in me.

"How did your geometry test go?" I ask, breaking the awkward silence.

"Good, thanks to you."

"Have any plans for this weekend?" I ask at the same time he asks, "Will you go to prom with me?"

I stop breathing and my cheeks flush. He asked me. He finally asked me.

He smiles at my reaction. "So will you?"

I open my mouth to say yes, when my brother, Logan, walks up between us and his jerk of a friend, Carter, throws his arm over my shoulder.

"You ready to go?" Logan asks, looking from me to Mark.

"Can you give us a minute?" I ask glaring at my brother to leave me alone for five minutes so that I can say yes without having to be teased about it the rest of the night.

"Can't do that. We have to get home, have a busy afternoon planned," Carter says, staring at Mark as he pulls me tighter into his chest. I don't know why he's acting like this. He loves to tease me and torture me, but he's not interested in me. I can tell from the way that Mark is looking at him and then to me that he thinks we are together. We aren't.

"I should go. I have practice. I'll catch you later Victoria," Mark says, turning around and jogging quickly in the opposite direction.

"Mark wait," I shout as I run after him, but Logan steps in front of me blocking my path and Mark doesn't turn around or hesitate for a second.

"What are you doing?" I ask, crossing my arms over my chest.

"Mark Wagner really? You want to date Mark Wagner? You do realize that guy has slept with half of the girls in this school and that all he wants to do is get in your pants," Logan says.

I frown. "So? Maybe I want to sleep with him."

"No, you don't," Carter says from behind me.

I turn and glare at him too. "You guys can't tell me who I can and can't date."

Logan sighs. "Come on, Carter promised his mom he'd be home early today to babysit the new foster kids."

I grab my backpack off the hook and then slam my locker shut.

I'll argue with Logan later once we drop off Carter. Once we are home and I'm alone I can call Mark to tell him yes.

"Here let me help you," Carter says grabbing my backpack out of my hands.

He swings my backpack over his shoulder along with his own as all three of us start walking down the hallway toward the parking lot where Logan's 1994 Buick LeSabre sits.

I raise an eyebrow at Carter not understanding at all why he's offering to carry my backpack. That is something nice people do or boys do when they are dating someone. It's not something that Carter does.

"I can carry my own bag, thanks," I say reaching out to grab my backpack back but Carter grips it tighter.

I exhale deeply and give up. It's not worth the fight anyway. I'm just glad that he's going to be at home tonight instead of over at our house like usual. I could use a break from him.

We get to the Buick, Logan climbs into the driver's seat while Carter opens the back door for me. I climb in giving him an *what the hell has gotten into you* stare. He hands me my backpack before closing the door and climbing in the front seat. Logan puts the key in the ignition and we all cross our fingers while we wait for the engine to purr to life. When it does, we all sigh in relief that we don't have to spend the afternoon walking the five miles home.

Carter turns the radio on to some hip-hop station. Neither Logan nor I like hip hop but it helps Carter relax, which is what he's going to need if he's going to survive an entire night at home. We all sit in relative silence, the music the only thing keeping us company until Logan pulls up in front of Carter's trailer and turns the car off. Carter stares at the front door, but doesn't move to jump out.

Our home life isn't great, but Carter's is far, far worse. He became a foster child when he was six. His foster parents have basically treated him as free labor and a welfare check ever since. He rarely stays at home, usually sleeping on our couch or in Logan's bedroom. Today is one of the rare occasions when he's required to be home. He's supposed to babysit his foster siblings.

Carter exchanges a glance with Logan and then opens the door and climbs out of the car. He doesn't say anything and we don't either. We don't say good luck dodging his foster father's beatings. We don't say keep your cool while the people that are supposed to be your parents throw all their money away on the slots instead of providing food and clothes for you. We don't say anything because despite not having to worry about getting beat, our life isn't much better. So we just watch Carter walk up to the door and disappear inside.

Logan doesn't start the car up again. Instead, we just sit outside and hope that Carter comes back. Even I, who hates Carter's guts and wishes I had some time to myself without having to worry about what stupid pranks he and my brother are going to pull on me, would rather have him here than getting beat.

"Why did you and Carter try to get between me and Mark?" I ask as I climb into the front seat.

"You're too young to date," Logan says ignoring me and staring at the door. He seems more worried than usual about his friend.

"I'm fifteen! That's plenty old enough. You started dating way before that."

"Yea and I shouldn't have. You don't want to end up like Amber, do you?"

I frown. "I'm not stupid enough to get pregnant in high school like my sister did."

He finally looks at me. "You're not having sex or dating until you're in college."

"You can't tell me what to do. You're not my father. You're only two years older than me."

He sighs and runs his hand through his hair. We both realize that it's time to go. That Carter is stuck inside for the night and there is nothing we can do to protect him. Not tonight anyway.

"I can't tell you what to do. Date Mark if that's what you want.

Just be careful, you're the only one of us that has a chance at breaking free of this shitty town."

I smile a little as I twist my frizzy hair around my finger and put my feet up on the dashboard.

Logan starts the car and begins speeding off toward our house. He glances in the rearview mirror and suddenly steps on the breaks.

"What the hell?" I say as my body is thrust forward and then back abruptly.

Logan continues to stare in the rearview mirror as his face goes white. I turn around scared to glance behind me when I see Carter running toward our car. He throws the backdoor open and jumps in. Logan immediately steps on the gas as soon as Carter is safely inside. I see Carter's face out of the corner of my eye. His eye and cheek is black and blue.

We don't ask questions. We don't have to. And Carter offers up no explanation of what happened. We just drive to our house and pretend that this isn't our life. That we are normal kids that don't have to worry about problems like this.

Logan parks the car in the driveway to our house. It isn't much, just a little over a thousand square feet in total. We don't have a garage and the lawn has never been taken care of so it is mostly weeds at this point. We walk up the sidewalk that has large cracks in it and throw open the front door that no one ever bothers to lock. It's not like there is anything worth stealing inside anyway.

We all head to the kitchen. We're starving and food is the only thing that will make Carter forget about what just happened. Logan throws open the fridge and finds it empty. He opens the freezer and finds one bag of peas which he hands to Carter. He puts it to his face.

"Mom! We are out of food," I yell as I walk into the living room.

I fold my arms across my chest when I find our mother in her usual position, passed out on the couch from drinking. She works the night shift at a convenience store and then spends her days drinking or smoking. I don't even know why we bother calling her Mom, it's not like she is one. We are basically on our own, always have been, always will be.

I walk over to her because I can't take her crap today. I shake her shoulder until she finally stirs enough that she opens her eyes.

"What?" she barks at me, her voice sharp with plenty of bite at being awoken from her drunken state.

"We are out of food. And I need money to buy a prom dress." I know Logan and Carter are listening to me from the kitchen, but I don't care. I know Logan is just trying to protect me, but he isn't actually protecting me. I can take care of myself. And Carter is just being his usual self. If he isn't happy, then no one should be happy.

Mom sighs and closes her eyes again. "Take the cash in my purse to buy some food for tonight. And you don't need a prom dress. No one has asked you."

"Mark Wagner asked me."

She half chuckles and half chokes on her saliva. "I didn't think any boy would ask out a girl as flat chested as you."

My head falls back and my eyes close tight trying to block out the disgusting woman in front of me. Her words mean nothing to me.

"What are we going to do about a dress?" I ask. I don't bother asking about getting my hair done or buying some half decent makeup for the occasion because I know the answer to that is a no.

She yawns. "Wear one of Amber's old ones or get a job and pay for one yourself."

My heart sinks. I only have a few days until prom. I won't have time to find a job, let alone make enough to afford a dress. And Amber was much curvier in high school than I am. Her old dresses will never fit me, not without some serious help.

I'm not going to let it deter me though. Good things don't happen to me very often. And I'm not going to let my brother, his best friend, or even my mother from preventing me from having a good time at prom like every other normal teenager.

I storm into the kitchen and find her purse lying on the kitchen counter. While Logan and Carter both stare at me, I reach into it hoping for a miracle that there is actually money in here.

I pull out the wallet, open it, and pull out the single bill that sits inside. A five dollar bill. It couldn't even be a twenty. With a twenty we could buy enough real food for us to last for days. Instead, we will have to settle on ramen noodles for the week.

I start walking out of the cramped kitchen and thrust the five dollar bill into Logan's hand as I walk by. He can go figure out what to do to prevent us from starving tonight. I can't deal right now.

I storm upstairs to my bedroom that I used to share with Amber. I throw open the sliding closet door that is barely hanging on. I start digging through the closet to the very back where I know Amber kept her prom dress. I pull out the single dress. It is light pink with some silver sparkles at the bodice. It's strapless and flows out at the waist. There is no way it will fit me. I have no boobs.

I walk over to the landline because we can't even afford cell phones. I dial Amber's number.

"Hey sis," she says.

"Hey, I need your help. A boy asked me to prom and I don't have anything to wear. Mom said I could wear your dress, but there is no way it will fit me."

"I'm sorry Victoria, I wish I could help." I hear the baby crying in the background and I know there is nothing she could do to help. She has much more important troubles.

"I shouldn't bother you with my stupid problems. How is Sailor doing?"

"She's fussy and misses her Aunt."

I smile. "I miss her too. I'll have to come visit soon."

We hang up and I realize what I already knew, but had to try anyway, that my sister can't even help me. If I want to go to prom with Mark, I'm going to have to figure it out myself.

I start removing my t-shirt and jeans. I might as well try on the dress and see what hope I have of making it fit by this weekend. When I'm down to my bra and underwear, I pull the dress up my body and zip up the back. I let go of the dress to walk to the bathroom and look at myself in the mirror but the dress instantly falls to the ground at my feet. I have no curves anywhere on my body to hold the dress up.

I sigh and reach down and pick up the dress holding it up to my body while I walk to the bathroom. I step inside, turning the light on as I see just how big the dress really is.

I grab all the tissue paper we have and start stuffing my bra, hoping that if I can stuff it enough and maybe pin it slightly in the back, I can get it to stay up.

I hear a chuckle and I freeze, realizing that I didn't shut the door. I was too focused on the dress.

"I don't think there is enough tissue paper in the world to make you have tits big enough to hold up that dress," Carter says as he leans on the doorframe.

I glare at him. "No one asked you."

He shrugs and steps inside the bathroom behind me. He grabs the back of the dress around my waist and pulls it tightly until the front is flush to my skin.

My breathing stops at his touch. His touch is not a feeling I'm used to. I feel an electricity tingling from my fingertips to my toes when he touches me.

"There, that's better," he says, his eyes devouring my body in the mirror.

I narrow my eyes and remind myself to breathe. *He doesn't like you*, I remind myself. *And I hate him.*

"Know how to sew?" I ask.

"Nope," he responds.

I exhale deeply.

"Put some clothes on and come to Logan's room," he says.

"Did you guys get dinner?"

He shrugs. "We got alcohol."

I turn and walk out of the bathroom, but not before Carter's hands crawl across my lower back, sending chills down my back. I shake my head as I walk to my bedroom. I don't know what is wrong with me right now, but I need to remind my body that he's the enemy. Even when he tries to be nice once or twice a year, it's only to make the pain that much worse when he eventually hurts me again.

I shut my bedroom door and then find my baggiest sweatpants and sweatshirt. A shield of sorts to keep Carter from hitting on me.

I step into Logan's tiny bedroom that barely fits his queen sized bed. I find Logan lying back on the bed, while Carter is sitting on the floor leaning against the opposite wall. Both hold a beer in their hands.

"Here," Carter says, holding out a beer to me.

I walk to Carter while I look at Logan, waiting for him to say that I can't have the beer. He doesn't say anything though. I've had a few beers before, but I've never drank with Logan. He never lets me. I don't know why today is any different, but if we aren't going to get to eat then we might as well get drunk to pass the time.

I take the beer from Carter and watch as he pats the floor beside him. I take a seat next to him despite my better judgment.

Logan starts playing some music on his radio and we all just sit there listening to the music while thinking about our shitty lives. Logan finishes his beer and then gets up, leaving Carter and me alone. I don't know where Logan is going, but neither of us ask or care.

Carter downs his beer while I continue to sip mine. "Want another?" he asks.

I finish mine and then nod, handing him my empty can. He takes it from me and tosses them both in the corner of the room before grabbing two more cans from the box sitting on the floor at the foot of Logan's bed. He hands one to me as he takes a seat next to me again.

"So who are you taking to prom?" I ask. I'm sure he's going. Logan's going with Michelle, a girl he's been seeing recently. And Carter wouldn't miss an opportunity to get a girl in his bed, or more likely my bed, while I end up sleeping on the couch.

He shrugs. "Haven't decided yet."

I raise an eyebrow. "Every girl you asked so far has turned you down," I joke even though I know it isn't true. No girl in our high school would turn down Carter. He's far too good looking. No one can resist his charming smile. When he wants someone, he gets them.

"Don't say yes to Mark," he says.

I frown. "Don't start that again."

He fingers trace across my forearm as tiny goosebumps raise up and down my arm.

I pull my arm away and try to change the subject.

"What are you going to tell your teachers tomorrow when you come in with a black eye?" I ask.

He shrugs. "I'll come up with something."

"I have some makeup you can use. It's not the best but it might help."

He looks at me as a slow smile creeps up his face. "Do your worst."

I jump up and run to my bedroom to grab my small bag of makeup before walking back to Logan's bedroom. I feel the strange flutters in my stomach again as I take a seat next to Carter again. Logan is back on the bed drinking another beer, and Carter sets his down next to him as he looks at me.

I pull out my concealer and foundation and begin applying it around his eyes over the red and purple bruise that has formed on his face. I try to focus on the bruise instead of on his eyes but it's difficult when he's staring at me so intently. I've never seen him look at me this way.

I swallow hard and put down the makeup brush. "There, much better."

He doesn't respond or ask to look at himself in the mirror. I'll have to apply more in the morning, but I think it will work well enough that most people won't notice.

He reaches forward and tucks a strand of hair behind my ear. My heart stops, along with my breathing, and every other cell in my body. I don't know what that was. But it felt like something I never expected to feel from him. It felt like he cared. Like adoration. Maybe even more.

"You're beautiful, Tori," he says so quietly that I'm not sure I even heard him say it.

But his words are what I play over and over in my head as I fall asleep. They are what I think about when I decide to wait to call Mark and tell him I'll go to prom with him. They are what make me think that Carter wants to go to prom with me.

MY HEART RACES in my chest as Logan drives the three of us to school the next morning. Butterflies flip in my stomach throughout the day, until they become giant piranhas eating up my insides with nerves as the day ends and I know that I will see Carter again.

He's driven me crazy my whole life, but deep down I've always felt something for him. I've always wished that when he was with the other girls, it was me he was kissing instead. I just never thought he would feel the same way about me. I never thought he would call me beautiful. I never thought he'd choose me.

I've been avoiding Mark all day, but as the school day comes to a close there's no way for me to avoid him. He walks up to my locker just like he did the day before. Except this time, he barely looks at me and doesn't smile at me when I look at him.

I bite my lip trying to decide what I should do. Mark is great. He's been nothing but nice to me, but Carter...Carter brings me alive like nothing I've ever felt before.

I glance past Mark, and see Carter walking down the hallway to me.

'No' he mouths to me while nodding toward Mark.

I know he wants me to tell Mark no. I'm just not sure why.

I look at Mark and say words I never thought I'd say to him, "I'm sorry Mark, someone else already asked me to prom."

"Oh, okay Victoria. I'll see you around then." His eyes widen a little and then he walks away in shock.

I smile brightly at Carter who is walking toward me. This is it. He's going to ask me now that I turned Mark down.

He keeps walking toward me when a blonde woman grabs onto his waist. He stops and smiles at her before he leans down and kisses her on the lips.

My mouth drops open at what I'm seeing. How could I be so stupid to think that Carter would ask me to prom?

I turn back to my locker to keep the tears from falling. I'll cry later in my room. Alone. But not here.

"Hey Tori, you ready to go?" Carter asks.

I nod as I close my locker and place my backpack over my shoulder. He doesn't offer to carry my backpack like he did yesterday. Instead, he holds onto her like he's been waiting his whole life for her.

"I'm Lily," the blonde says.

"Victoria, Logan's sister," I say.

She smiles. "That's so cool that you're gay. I've never met a gay woman before. Have you found a girl to go to prom with you?"

My eyes flutter at her words. "What?"

Carter takes over for her. "No, Victoria hasn't found a girl to take her to prom. Maybe next year."

He pulls her in and kisses her again right in front of me while my heart is breaking. Carter has done some messed up shit, but this might be the worst. I've suffered plenty of physical pain because of him. But never heartbreak like this.

And it's not over. I'm never going to find a boyfriend, let alone a date, the rest of my high school career. Carter made sure of that with his stupid rumor that he started. Even though it isn't true, the whole school will believe him over me.

I've felt plenty of pain in my life. But my brittle heart has never been so hurt by a man that I thought behind all the bullshit he actually cared about me. I was wrong. A man like Carter could never truly care about me, because he doesn't have a heart.

1 VICTORIA

Ten Years Later

"YOU'RE FIRED," my boss, Will, says.

My mouth falls open a little. He's got to be kidding. He can't fire me. I'm his best employee. The company wouldn't survive without me.

"This is a joke, right?"

Will gets up from his large oak desk and walks around to my side. He sits on the edge of his desk as he looks at me with sad eyes.

He's not joking. That much is clear.

"I wish I were joking."

He crosses his arms over his chest as he looks even more distressed. I don't care how he feels right now. He's the one who made the decision to fire me.

"Are you sure? I mean...I thought I was doing a good job here."

I thought I was doing the best job here. I've worked at the company less than a year, but I am already heading three different PR projects. When I take over a project, I live and breathe for my clients, making sure that no obstacle goes unnoticed. I'm completely prepared for every negative aspect of every situation and know exactly how to spin it in a positive light.

"You were, Victoria. It's really not about your job performance."

"Then, why am *I* getting fired?" My whole body shakes as I speak much too loudly for this office.

I glance behind me at the glass doors that look into Will's office. The office was built for transparency so that we could all feel close, like a family. I used to enjoy how open the office felt, how light and airy it was. But, now that I'm getting fired and the entire office is staring at me, I wish it looked more like a dungeon I could hide in.

Will rubs the back of his neck. "Because the company is struggling. Decisions that were made long before you came here have left the company failing. We have to lay someone off, it's the only way we can afford to keep running."

I nod. I understand the need for layoffs. "That still doesn't explain, why me? I bring in more income than most of your employees, combined."

Will smiles a little at me. "You do. You're terrific. But being as good as you are also comes with a price. You negotiated the highest salary. And you were our last hire. Those two things mean you are the first one out."

I bite my lip to keep from saying what I really want to say. I want to chew him out. I want to say that it doesn't even make sense to let me go if I'm the best. But I don't. I just keep my mouth shut. I learned long ago that saying what I want to say usually just makes things worse.

"I'm sorry, Victoria."

I glare up at him. He doesn't get to be sorry. He's the one who can't lead a competent team. He's the one who doesn't make enough money so that he doesn't have to fire his employees to keep the company afloat.

"Are we done then?" I snap. I can't be in here any longer.

When I was first hired, I thought all my dreams were coming

true. I got my dream job, in my dream city. But, now, I know it was too good to be true.

"Yes."

I get up and turn to walk out.

"But just know, Victoria"—Will lowers his voice—"that this is really for your benefit. Unless a miracle happens, the company won't survive the year. When this company goes down in flames, you will already be working your way up the ladder at your next company."

I stop at the door and smirk. "You're an idiot, Will, because you just lost your last chance to save your company. Because I was that miracle. I would have stepped up and started working a hundred hours a week or more for the same pay to ensure that this company survived. I would have done anything because I believed in this company. I liked my coworkers. I loved my job. But, instead of reaching out for help, you're getting rid of the only shot you had left. But you're right about one thing. I will already be at a more successful company while your company is ripped apart and sold piece by piece to try to give something to your investors."

I push the glass door open and walk out with my head held high to my desk. I keep a large fake smile plastered on my face as I glide across the room, pretending like I just quit instead of getting fired. I gather my laptop and things into my briefcase. And then I walk out, like my life is fine.

But, instead, my world just fell apart. I don't even make it to my car before the tears drop. Tears I would never let anyone else ever see, but in the darkness of the parking garage, they descend.

This was the absolute worst day for me to get fired. I just bought a new house last week. There are still boxes everywhere. My sister, niece, and I haven't even fully moved in yet. Putting down the down payment practically emptied my savings. I need a new job and fast.

I hit the steering wheel over and over, trying to get my frustration and pain out. This is the third time I've been fired in five years. None of them were my fault. I'm good at fixing people's problems. Everyone's, except for mine.

BY THE TIME I get to the house, the house that I thought we would live in for years to come but is now threatened, I have lost the tears and returned the fake smile to my face. I won't let them know that I just got fired. I can't. I won't let them worry. Ever.

I open the door, and before I even get inside, I'm tackled by two dogs and my ten-year-old niece.

I laugh as we all fall to the floor while I try not to bump into any of the boxes that are piled high everywhere.

"You're home!" Sailor squeals. "I thought you weren't supposed to be home until five."

I tightly hug her, loving that the second she's in my arms, I feel ten times better—but ten times worse at the same time. I try to focus on the happy feeling of getting to spend more time with my niece today.

"I got my work done quickly so that I could come be with you this week."

"Yay! Does that mean we can go to the beach?" Sailor's little eyes light up as her blonde curls hang down around her cheeks.

I smile. I'm not sure I could ever tell her no. I'd do anything for her. I'll do everything I can to make sure that she is taken care of. This is her home now, and I will make sure it remains her home, including flipping burgers, waitressing, or serving coffee. Anything. Let's just hope I don't have to resort to that.

I'm a generally positive person. But I do know how long it took me to find my last position. Six months. I had been offered several jobs before the last one, but none of them paid enough. None gave me the flexibility that I needed.

I look back at Sailor. I'll figure it out though. I don't have six months to make something happen. I have about a month of savings. I can find a job that fast in the San Francisco area, no problem.

"Absolutely! Let's go see if your mom wants to go."

Sailor's face brightens. "Good. I'm tired of being cooped up in this house."

I laugh. "You've been cooped up for a total of four hours."

She shrugs. "But it was a long four hours!"

"Your mom upstairs?" I ask, already knowing the answer.

Sailor nods.

"Go get changed into your swimsuit, and I'll go see if your mom wants to go."

Sailor shoots up the stairs to her bedroom while I go check to see if my sister, Amber, is out of bed yet. I knock on the door before I slowly enter her bedroom. She's still in bed, like I expected.

I go over to the window and open the blinds.

"It's a beautiful day, Amber."

My sister groans and covers her head with the thick comforter. I want to be angry. I want to yell at my sister to get up and go take care of her daughter. To get a job. Or, at the very least, spend time with Sailor. But I know that would be the opposite of helpful. Tough love never works with Amber.

We are different like that. Amber needs soft encouragement while I need tough love.

Amber has gorgeous, long blonde hair, just like her daughter, while my auburn hair makes it so that you wouldn't even know that Amber and I were related from our looks.

"I'm taking Sailor to the beach. You up for joining us? We would really like that."

"No."

I take a deep breath, needing to remain calm.

"You sure, Amb? It's a beautiful day out. You don't have to swim if you don't want to. Just come enjoy the day with us."

"No."

I walk over to the bed and sit on the edge while I rub her back, trying to encourage her to come. But we've been through this before. She had postpartum depression after Sailor was born. And despite trying to get her help, she's never gotten better. Losing her job and apartment didn't help. She's at one of her lowest places. And there is not much I can do to help her when she is like this but make sure she is taking her medications and going to therapy while letting her know I'm here for her when she finally makes it through the fog.

"Do you need anything before I go?"

"No."

I lean down and kiss her on the cheek. I wish there were more I could do, but depression is hard to fight. It's not something I can fix, no matter how much I want to.

"I love you, sis," I say, getting up before getting ready and heading to the beach.

I COULD LIVE my life at the beach and never get enough of it. Sailor is the same way. She was meant to live in the water. Sometimes, I wonder if she was meant to be my daughter instead of Amber's. But then she does something that reminds me completely of my sister, and I know she is hers. And, when Amber is healthy, she makes an amazing mother. It's just hard when she is in one of her depressed places. Hard for her to keep a job, hard for her to take care of her daughter, hard for her to even get out of bed.

That's why I have to have a job. I have to take care of Sailor when Amber can't. That's what family does. We pick each other up and handle things when others can't take care of themselves. If only I could convince my mother and brother of that, then maybe it wouldn't fall on me all the time.

Who am I kidding? I like the responsibility. I like being in control of the family. I like taking care of them. I just hoped life would go my way for once in my damn life.

My phone buzzes, and I don't have to look at the screen to know who it is. My mother, who recently married a wealthy doctor and now thinks she is mother of the year. At least she doesn't get drunk as often anymore. I consider not answering. I don't want to tell her that

I got fired, but I'm not the best liar. She will know. But, if I don't answer, she will just keep calling all day long until I finally do.

"Hello?" I answer, trying to sound chipper.

"What's wrong?" my mother asks.

I frown. "Nothing's wrong."

"I know you. Something is wrong."

"What did you call me for, Mom?"

"Is it your sister again? What did she do now? I told you it was a bad idea to buy a house for her and Sailor. You are a successful businesswoman. You should have a nice penthouse downtown. Not throw all of your money away on a house in the suburbs where it takes you an hour to drive to work every day."

"Amber's fine. And I wanted to buy the house. It's a good investment, and I like being close to Amber and Sailor."

"Boyfriend trouble then? You are too young to worry about dating. You should just focus on your career. You're in your twenties. You'll have plenty of time for boys later."

I sigh. I wish it were boyfriend trouble. I haven't had a date since graduating from college. No one wants to take on a woman who spends all her time working or with her niece.

"No, it's not boyfriend trouble."

I can feel my mother's scowl on the other end of the phone.

"It has to be your sister then. I told you she would take you down. That—"

"I got fired."

There's a pause.

"That can't be. You're awesome at your job."

I sigh. "I know, but that's why they let me go. They couldn't afford to keep paying me what I'm worth."

"Well, it's their loss then. But it's actually perfect timing."

Ugh. I don't want to hear whatever nonsense my mother is going to say next. This isn't good timing. This is the worst timing. If they had fired me even six months from now, I wouldn't feel so lost. So desperate.

"Why is it good timing?"

"You remember Lily Taylor?"

"Yes."

How could I forget Lily? She was the most popular girl in school. Smart, beautiful. My brother was obsessed with her even though she dated his best friend and my archenemy, Carter Woods, for most of high school.

"Well, she is in need of a fixer."

I smile. "Really? And how do you know that?" I regret the words the second I ask.

"Cathy told Cindy who told Melissa. Have I told you about Melissa's botched Botox job yet? It looks hideous. I don't know what she was thinking or who she went to, but—"

"Mom, I don't care about Melissa. I care about Lily and why she needs good PR right now."

"Oh, sorry, sweetie. Lily was engaged to Phillip. But it turns out, she had been cheating on him the whole time."

"Why does that matter?"

"Because she's running for Senate. It wouldn't matter that much, but her law firm also just got accused of several immoral acts. I don't think she was directly involved, but it's not looking good for her. She's currently shopping for a good PR firm."

"There's just one problem. I don't run a PR firm."

My mother sighs. "So, start one. You can do anything you want sweetie. Go convince her to hire you. You know she will pay well, and if you can help her win, you'll have clients lining up for you."

I smile. She's right. I can fix my own problems by helping Lily fix hers. I just have to get to her quickly. Companies will be lining up for a chance to work for Lily Taylor.

2 CARTER

My mouth drops as I stare at the television screen, watching the mess unfold before my eyes. I've never seen anyone fall apart so completely, so quickly, and I'm in the crisis business. I've seen my fair share of meltdowns. In fact, I've created plenty of chaos before. But I never thought I would see Lily Taylor fuck up her whole life in a matter of seconds in a single interview. I just didn't think it was possible.

I've known Lily most of my life. She's smart and beautiful. Her family had money, and she went to the best schools. I even dated her for a year in high school. I was probably stupid for letting her go. I always knew that Lily was going to make something of herself someday. She could be anything she wanted. She had everything going for her. Intelligence, money, and good looks.

She's decided to go into politics. To become a senator and then make a presidential run.

But, from the look on Lily's face right now as she stares wide-eyed at the talk-show host, she thinks those dreams are squashed. Over. Gone.

And, if she were any other candidate, she would be. She fucked up, and she knows it. But, lucky for her, I can fix all of her problems.

That's what I do. I fix people's problems and turn them into something amazing that works in their favor. I own a PR firm that only takes on the biggest problems with the highest-profile clients. Over the past five years, I have turned the company into the best PR firm in the country. No one does it better than Carter Woods.

But Lily is going to be a challenge. First, I'll have to convince her that her dreams haven't completely been destroyed. That she can still become a senator from North Carolina. And that I can get her there. But it comes with a price. I'm not cheap, but Lily can afford the best. If she really wants this, then she won't even bat an eyelash.

The interview is finally over, and I close the lid on my computer before picking up the phone.

"Ruby, can you come in here, please?"

"Be right there, Carter," my assistant answers.

A second later, Ruby bursts through my door with a large smile on her face. Her body is practically jumping up and down with excitement as she stands inside my office. She clasps her hands together to keep from exploding.

I raise an eyebrow at her. She's always a positive woman who is usually happy, but this is on a different level.

"Spill, Ruby," I say.

"You finally watched the Lily Taylor interview, didn't you?"

I nod, although I don't know why she says *finally*; it aired only a half hour earlier. And it doesn't explain her bubbliness.

She turns, ducking out of my office for a second, before returning with a thick file that she throws onto my desk. "This is everything I have on Lily Taylor. I cleared your schedule to make sure you have time to focus just on her for the next month. I have a flight for you this evening to Charlotte, North Carolina, and I booked a hotel room, although I'm sure you would rather stay with Logan. Just let me know, and I can cancel. I'm just so excited for you," Ruby squeals.

I narrow my eyes, not understanding why Ruby is so thrilled. "It will be a big account. If we succeed, we will have clients lining up, wanting to work with us, but I'm not sure why you are this enthusiastic about it, Ruby."

Her cheeks flush as she takes a step forward to my desk and begins flipping through the thick manila folder lying on top. She stops when she gets to a picture and points at it. My eyes drift down to the picture of Lily and me wearing our homecoming crowns after winning King and Queen. We were a perfect couple. If we had met later in life, maybe we would still be together, but we were far too young then for it to last.

I look back up at Ruby, who still has the goofiest smile I've ever seen on her face. "We used to date. So?"

"So? So, she is flawless. Just look at her! She's beautiful, smart, ambitious. She's your perfect match! This could turn into a romantic love story. You go save her reputation and career, all the while falling in love with your high school sweetheart. How awesome!" she squeals.

I look down at the picture of a woman I haven't thought about in years. She would be ideal for me. My career has always come first and will always come first. That's who I am. But, if I found a woman who was just as ambitious as I was, then maybe it would work. I would finally have a woman who understood me. Who wouldn't complain when I was at the office for far too long because she was, too. A woman who didn't care if we had kids. And, if we did, she'd agree that a nanny was the best person to raise them. Lily could be that person.

I smile, still holding the picture. "Thanks, Ruby."

She grins and leaves me alone. I grab my cell phone and call up Logan. He knows me better than anyone. He lives in Charlotte and won't have a problem with me crashing at his place. And he'll be the perfect wingman to help me get Lily.

I KNOCK at the same time I throw the door open to Logan's apartment. I've been down a handful of times but not as much as I would like. North Carolina is a nice place to get away to when I need to relax, but I prefer the hustle and bustle of a big city like New York. And Logan is a bartender. Not exactly bringing in the big bucks, so he usually comes up to New York when he wants to have a good time.

"The fun has arrived!" I holler as I step into his apartment.

Logan gives me a bro hug when he sees me, slapping me hard on the back.

"I didn't expect to see you back here after last time," Logan says with a chuckle.

I frown, thinking about the last time I stayed here and how it took my chiropractor a month to fix my back after sleeping on his horrible futon. "I couldn't miss an opportunity to see you. But, if you haven't bought an actual bed for your guest room yet, then I'm turning around and getting you one right now. I'm not sleeping on that twenty-year-old futon again."

"Relax. My sisters already beat you to it and bought me a mattress for Christmas last year."

Images of Victoria and Amber pop into my head. Amber is older than Logan and me, and she wasn't around much. But Victoria...she was the annoying little sister that I never had. Logan and I loved torturing her. I haven't seen her in years, and the few times I've been back to see Logan, we have both been too drunk to talk about how his family is doing.

"How is Tori doing?" I ask.

Logan smiles. "She's been better. Just lost her job. But I wouldn't call her Tori. She hates that nickname."

Tori never did have the career ambitions. She's probably back at her mother's house now, living the good life on the beach in California, until she finally decides she needs a little cash, like her brother, and gets a bartending job or something.

"Trust me, I don't plan on seeing her anytime soon, so you don't have to worry about me calling her Tori." I pick up my suitcase. "You working tonight, or do you have time to go grab a drink?"

Logan glances at his watch. "I'm already five minutes late to work. I should go, although I'd really rather be here."

"Don't worry; I'll be here for at least a couple of weeks. We will have plenty of time to grab a drink and hang out."

Logan grins as he walks backward toward the door, still looking at me. "I'm not worried about having time for us to hang out. I'm just disappointed that I'm going to miss the fight."

"Fight?"

Logan just continues to grin like the bastard that he is. "Have a good night. You might need to call a chiropractor for tomorrow. The couch is worse than the futon—or so I've been told."

Logan leaves me standing alone in the living room. I eye the couch; it looks ancient. A large indentation is on the cushion on one end; it's clear that Logan sits there every single time. The other end is scratched up from where his dog used to sleep. There is no way I'm sleeping on that couch. I don't know why I would anyway if there is a perfectly good bed just down the hallway.

I prepare myself for what is waiting for me down the hall. I know my friend too well. We always pulled pranks on each other as kids. So, I'm sure he did something stupid to the bed after I complained about my back last time. If the bed is unusable, I'll just buy a new one.

I carry my bag down the hallway, trying to think of what I would do to him if I wanted to prank him. Pour beer in his bed. Put books under one corner of his bed, so it's crooked. Just remove the mattress completely.

I reach for the handle of the door just as it turns.

I frown.

The door swings open, and the last person I expected to see is standing in the doorway.

Tori.

Except this woman can't be Tori. Tori is an awkward high

schooler with braces, frizzy hair, and oversized clothes that don't fit her body. The person standing before me is all woman. Her dark jeans make her legs look long as they hug over her curvy hips. Her gray V-neck accentuates her waist and cleavage, which shows just how much she has grown up since the last time I saw her. And her auburn hair shines as it frames her face, which is no longer covered in freckles and instead looks smooth and flawless.

Tori frowns when she sees me. "What are you doing here?"

I smirk. "I could ask you the same question."

"I'm here to see my brother." She places her hands on her hips, and her breasts automatically push up against her shirt.

My cock twitches at the sight.

I force my eyes to look into her deep brown eyes instead of at her breasts. I never thought that I would have that problem when it came to Tori. She's my best friend's little sister. We used to make her life miserable. I can't fuck her and then leave her. Logan would kill me.

"Same."

Her eyes darken as she glares at me and then down at the bag I'm carrying. "You'd better be taking that to a hotel."

"I'm not staying at a hotel. I'm staying here. That way, I can get plenty of time to see Logan and torture you, just like old times."

She narrows her eyes and steps forward, trying to intimidate me even though she is only half my size. "Then, you can sleep on the couch. And, as far as torturing me goes, that won't be happening. I'm not the scrawny teenage girl I was before."

I laugh as I look her up and down. "You might have filled out a little since the last time I saw you, but you still barely come up to my chest. I can torture you as much as I want, and you won't be able to do a thing about it."

Her nostrils flare, and her face turns bright red.

"I have an important meeting I need to get to in the morning. I really need to go to sleep. Give me the bedroom tonight, and maybe we can work something out tomorrow." I wink at her.

Her eyes deepen, and I think I see a vein popping out of her head. She's so angry with me.

"This is my room!"

"Who is the one who has to get up to go to work in the morning? From what I heard, it sure isn't you. You can nap in my bed while I'm at work."

"No. I'm not sleeping on the couch. You are."

I laugh. "Oh, come on, Tori. You're tiny. You can easily fit on the couch."

"My name is Victoria, not Tori."

I cock my head to the side and stare at her breasts. She's right, a cute nickname like Tori just doesn't cut it. "I can see that."

She frowns but doesn't cross her arms over her chest, like I expected. She doesn't hide and cover her body. She points her finger toward the living room. "Enjoy the couch. I've heard it will give you one wicked neck- and backache in the morning."

She turns and walks back into the bedroom. She grabs the door to slam it shut, but I grab it, stopping it just before it reaches the frame.

I push it back open and take a step forward so that I'm standing in the doorway, and my face is inches from hers. I watch as her breathing picks up. I watch her lick her lips, like she is preparing for me to kiss her. I watch her eyes deepen at the thought of what my body could do to her.

Victoria wants me. Badly. I always thought that she secretly had a crush on me when we were kids. She used to try to hide it, but I knew. But, now, she isn't hiding it. Despite how much she hates me, she wants my body with the same passion.

Torturing her is going to be more fun than when we were kids.

"We could always share the bed." I wink again.

The spell she's under quickly breaks. "Out. Now."

"No."

"Out."

"No."

"Don't make me slam your hand in this door."

I laugh. "You couldn't if you wanted to."

She starts trying to push the door shut on my hand, but the door barely moves.

I raise an eyebrow, and she huffs but stops. In that second, I can see the adorable little girl she used to be.

I grin.

"Can't you be a gentleman for once in your life and let me sleep in the bed?"

"Really? You're going to play the *I'm a woman, so I deserve the bed* card."

"No, I'm playing the *I was here first; I have equally important things that I need to be up for in the morning; yes, I'm a woman, so I'm held to a different standard than you; and I don't want to have circles under my eyes from lack of sleep* card."

I pretend to consider what she is saying for a second. "Sorry, life ain't fair."

I step completely inside as she stumbles backward.

"Are you going to take your stuff and get out, or do we have to do this the hard way?" I ask.

"I'm not going anywhere."

I grin. "Hard way it is."

I scoop up her duffel bag and throw it over my shoulder, and then I turn my attention to Victoria. She's standing at the foot of the bed with her arms crossed over her chest. Her eyebrows are raised, like she doesn't believe I will actually force her out of this room. She's forgotten what I'm like if she thinks I'm not going to do anything.

"You wouldn't."

I walk over to her, bend down, and grab her ankles as I toss her over my shoulder.

Victoria screams and beats at my back as I carry her over my shoulder.

"Put me down! This is ridiculous!"

I don't put her down. I carry her down the hallway, loving how it feels to control her like this and have her so close to me. She smells like the ocean. I can smell the salt in her hair as I hold her.

I toss her down onto the couch and drop her duffel bag next to her.

"You're an asshole!"

I nod. "I'm an asshole who is about to get a very good night of sleep."

She huffs. "You haven't changed."

I shrug. "Why mess with perfection?"

She shakes her head as she sits on the couch. I turn to walk back to the bedroom, but I already know what she's going to do. She's not going to give up this easily. At least the Tori I used to know wouldn't.

I can hear her running after me, but I'm much faster than her. I always have been. I run into the bedroom before she even makes it to me. I stand in the doorway, marking my claim, as she stands in the hallway, breathing hard.

I smirk. "You'll never win, Tori. You might as well give up."

She sighs. "Fine. You win." She throws up her hands in the air and starts walking back to the living room.

I watch her ass sway back and forth and then shut the door, happy with my victory. I don't know why it's so fun to tease Victoria, but it is. I love making her miserable. But I do really need to get a good night's sleep so that I'm fresh for tomorrow.

I turn to grab my bag when I realize that I left it in the hallway. I open the door to get it and then freeze. My bag is no longer in the hallway.

I shake my head and smile just a little. I should have known that Victoria would pull something like this.

I walk down the hallway and find her standing in the only bathroom with the door open, her makeup and hair crap already spread all over the bathroom vanity, as she begins to tie her hair up into a ponytail.

"What did you do with my bag?"

"You lost your bag? That sucks."

I frown. "No, I didn't lose it. You took it."

She purses her lips and scrunches her face, like she's thinking real hard. "Nope. I don't remember any bag. Sorry."

She slams the bathroom door in my face before I have a chance to argue with her any further. I sigh. The apartment is tiny. Just two bedrooms, one bathroom, and an area that functions as the living room, kitchen, and dining room—combined. It can't be that hard to find where she hid my bag.

But, after searching for twenty minutes, I can't find it. And, now, I'm mad.

Victoria finally comes out of the bathroom. The makeup is gone from her face, her hair is up, and she is wearing flannel bottoms with a tank top and no bra. My eyes are glued to her hard nipples, which are pushing against the thin purple shirt.

She clears her throat, and I look up at her.

"Where is my bag, Tori? This is getting old."

She smiles. "Give up the bed, and I'll show you where your bag is."

I laugh. "That's not how this works. Tell me where my bag is."

She smirks and brushes past me. "Good night, Carter."

My bag has to be in the bathroom. I step inside and search for it, but I can't find it. I take a deep breath as I step back out. It's fine. Logan and I are close to the same size. I'll just borrow a suit from him for tomorrow, and then I'll find my bag after my meeting. I'm not going to let her get to me.

I find a spare toothbrush and brush my teeth, and then I head to bed. I remove my clothes and then climb into the queen-size bed. My body melts into the bed after a long day of traveling. She thinks she's won by taking my clothes, but I would take this soft bed any day over that damn couch. *Who cares that I don't have any clothes?*

Music starts blaring loudly down the hallway.

I groan. *Really? That's what she's going to try?*

She can't sleep, so she's going to try to keep me from sleeping as well. I laugh. The joke's on her because I can sleep through anything. It's a talent really.

I roll over and throw the covers over my head, knowing that I will be asleep in a few seconds—as soon as I can get Victoria out of my head. She's started a war that I can't wait to finish. She thinks I was cruel to her before. Well, she hasn't seen anything yet. Because, now, I know her real weakness.

Me.

She wants my body. She wants me to fuck her. And I know exactly how to torture her and win this war.

3 VICTORIA

I smile sweetly at Lily as I hold back a yawn. I might be completely exhausted after staying up all night, preparing for this meeting, but it was worth it. I'm killing this meeting.

When I first arrived at her doorstep, Lily wasn't sure that she should even continue to try to run for the Senate, but in the last hour that I've been here, I've seen her skepticism slowly turn into optimism. I'm going to get this job.

The only thing standing in my way is Carter.

I was shocked to see him standing in my doorway when I opened the door at Logan's. I'll have to remember to kill my brother later for not telling me that Carter would be staying with him as well. But I shouldn't have been that shocked. I know what Carter does for a living. I should have known he'd be all over Lily, trying to get this job. He didn't fool me with his *I'm here to see my best friend* speech. He's here to get this job.

He just doesn't have a clue that I'm here for the same reason.

That's why I moved my meeting up earlier. I knew I would need to get to Lily first to have a chance at competing with Carter. I know he has a lot more experience than I do, but that doesn't mean he is the best person for the job.

I just wish I could have been there this morning when he realized that I turned off his alarm and that his clothes were all covered in beer. I would have loved to see the expression on his face. He thinks he can win this fight, but he's wrong. I have years of pent-up frustration from all the times he and my brother teased me. Now, it's time for payback. And nothing is going to be sweeter than me landing this once-in-a-lifetime job instead of Carter.

Although it was incredibly fun to sneak into his room and turn off his alarm, carrying in his beer-soaked suitcase. My cheeks flush when I think about him lying naked from the waist up in bed. He was always good-looking, but now he's a buff man. A man who, from what I've heard, has dated his fair share of women. He's a man who most women would die to have. He has the body of an athlete, the money of a prince, and the wit of a jester. And, when I saw him lying naked in the bed, all I could think about was how badly I wanted to slip in next to him. Not how angry I was at him for taking that bed away from me.

"Victoria, are you okay?" Lily asks.

I clear my throat and drink a sip of water, trying to get my cheeks to stop flushing and my mind to move away from Carter.

"Sorry. So, what do you think of my ideas?"

Lily smiles, looking back at the plans I have laid out of how I think she can manage to still keep the public on her side and make a real run for the Senate.

"You certainly have given me a lot to think about. I thought I was done when..."

I nod. She can't even speak about what happened. I'm not sure I would be able to either if a sex tape of me with a man who wasn't my fiancé was exposed on national TV.

"I would love to work for you, Lily. I think, together, we would make a great team. I know you think that things look bleak right now, but I promise, come election time, no one will even remember this. I'll make sure of that."

Lily smiles sweetly at me and nods. I haven't convinced her. Not yet at least. I want to stay here all day, talking with her until she's persuaded. But I can't. I've made the best argument I can, and now, it's up to her to decide what she wants to do next.

"I would love to work with you, too, Victoria. From what you've presented here today, it's clear that you are one of the best, and I have no doubt that, with you by my side, we could conquer the world. I'm just not sure if my heart is in it anymore."

I nod. "I understand. But I don't think you should give up on your dreams because of one hiccup. You can do this, Lily. We can do this together."

I take Lily's hand and give it a squeeze. Through my years in this business, I've learned that the best way to connect with a client is to connect with them emotionally. I have to gain their trust, and the best way to do that is to treat them like a friend, not like a client. She needs to trust me completely if we are going to work together. She has to be able to tell me anything.

"Thank you for coming. I don't have too many friends in this world right now, and it's been nice to just talk to someone and to realize that my life isn't over."

"It definitely isn't."

We both stand, and I give her a quick hug.

"I'll call you tomorrow and see where your head is at. Unfortunately, this is something you need to decide on quickly, so we can start spinning the news in your favor before the public has totally made up their minds about you. But, even if you decide that this is not what you want, you can always count on me being here for you as a friend."

I pick up my oversized purse that functions as my briefcase, and I turn and walk out the door of her second-floor office where she works as a lawyer, which is situated in a larger building that contains several offices.

I haven't walked far when I bump into a hard chest. I should step back, giving the man some space, but I linger, keeping my face against his chest as I breathe in the manly scent of his aftershave. My body tingles as his hands go to my waist. He hesitates for a second as well, not sure if he wants to pull me closer or push me away. Finally, he gently pushes me away from him.

I look up, hoping to find a sexy stranger standing in front of me, who I can ask out for a drink, hopefully leading to dirty things later tonight. I could use the distraction and an actual bed to sleep in tonight. And, if his smell and firm grip on my body are any indication, I would love to get in his bed.

My heart immediately hardens to that idea when I realize who is standing in front of me.

Carter.

His eyes widen when he sees me. "What are you doing here? Trying to sabotage my meeting?"

I smile. "No, despite what you think, my life isn't all about you."

He smirks. "It should be."

I resist the urge to punch him in his chiseled, alluring face and wipe the smug expression off his face. But, man, does he look good with a cocky expression and a tailored dark gray suit. If he wasn't such an asshole, he would be exactly my type. Ambitious, confident, good-looking. The bad boy I shouldn't want because I know he will burn me in the end. That's exactly who he is, and even forgetting our history together, his bad boy reputation is the reason I shouldn't want him. If only I could figure out how to turn off the button inside me that finds him far too attractive for what is healthy for me.

The way Carter is looking at me isn't helping either. His eyes are searing into my body as he studies my black stilettos, my dark gray pencil skirt, and my purple blouse. He doesn't hide the fact that he is imagining what it would be like to remove each item of clothing from my body. He stares for far too long, lingering over what he finds sexiest—my legs and breasts.

I bite my lip, and his eyes immediately go to my lips.

Please suck on my lip, I think.

No, what am I thinking? He's the devil.

The devil who is amazing in bed—or so I heard from half of my high school.

"I think you have ketchup on your lip." His thumb brushes against my lip before I can stop him.

He stares at the red liquid on his thumb, smells it, and then tastes it. "Nope. It's blood from you biting your lip so hard to keep from kissing me."

I glare at him. "I don't want to kiss you."

He laughs. "You should tell your body that."

I roll my eyes. *I'm not going to let him goad me.*

He cocks his head to the side. "I never thought I'd see you in a dress. You look good, Tori."

"Victoria. And it's a business skirt, not a dress."

He nods. "I thought you hated dressing up."

"No, I hated dressing up because you always ruined whatever I was wearing. So, what was the point?"

He looks from me to Lily's office behind me. "So, you hoping that Lily can help you get a job?"

I smirk. "Something like that."

He studies my eyes for a second. "You can't seriously think that you can come in here and get the crisis PR job to fix all of her problems, do you? Lily's life is a mess right now; she needs an expert. Not someone who just got fired and has zero work experience."

"I was laid off, not fired. And I am an expert. Just because I don't have a flashy business card and my own business doesn't mean that I don't know what I'm doing. I've been doing this for almost as long as you. I know what Lily needs and how to solve her problems. We just had a great discussion. She and I will be working together."

Carter laughs. "Not after I talk to her."

I narrow my eyes. "Oh, that's right; I forgot. You plan on sleeping with her to get the job. Lily's better than that. It won't work."

"I don't need to sleep with anyone to get the job. I actually make

38

a living from doing this. I have an entire company that relies on me. I have employees. What do you have?"

"I'm getting this job."

He steps closer to me until his face is inches in front of me. My breathing picks up. I don't know whether I want to slap him or kiss him. Maybe both.

He grins. "We'll see."

I grin, too, because I know, if Lily picks anyone, it's going to be me. I'm more prepared than Carter. I'm better than him. I laid out a superior plan. And I'm more trustworthy than Carter. It's not a fight between the two of us; it's a fight to convince Lily to continue to pursue her career.

"And, as far as fucking someone goes, it looks like you are the one in need of a good fuck," he says, glancing down at my nipples, which are hard because of him.

I roll my eyes. "It's cold in here."

"Sure it is."

I glance down at where his cock is straining against the zipper. "I could say the same about you."

"I'm always down for a good fuck, Victoria. Just name the time and place."

I shiver when he says my name. Partly because I'm so used to him calling me Tori and partly because I love how he says it. I really need to find the off button on my hormones, or he is going to have the upper hand and take advantage of my ridiculous body that I can't control.

He wants me, too. He acts like he is in charge, but I know that control will vanish as soon as I show up, naked, in his bed.

I hate him. I can't really fuck him. I can't give him the satisfaction of winning.

But I can make him pay for all the pain he has caused me. Carter doesn't seem like the type who falls in love easily. So, it would be next to impossible to make him fall in love with me, only to rip out his heart. But I can make him *lust* after me. I can drive him wild with my body while denying him the one thing he wants.

I can destroy his career.

I can wreck his friendships.

I can drive him mad as he waits for a fuck that will never happen.

The door behind me opens, and Carter's attention immediately goes from me to Lily. I watch Carter as he takes in Lily. While I'm all business, albeit in a sexy business dress, Lily exudes beauty without even trying. He forgets I'm even here as he stares only at her.

I thought he wanted me, but from how he is looking at Lily, it's clear now that it's not me he wants. It's her. It only makes me want to hurt him more. I want to get this job and destroy everything he's worked so hard to get.

4 CARTER

The second Lily appears, I give her my complete attention. Partially because she needs to know that this is the type of attention I would give her if she became my client and also because, if I keep looking at Victoria, I'm going to throw her over my shoulder and go fuck her in the restroom. And, as much as I want to forget about my job and just fuck Victoria, I won't. My career always comes first. Always.

My dick will get plenty of action later. It just won't be touching Victoria. Logan would kill me, and she's not my type anyway. Lily's my type. I should focus on fucking Lily, but first, I need to land the job. It should be easy if Victoria is my only competition.

"Lily, it's great to see you again," I say, walking over to her and kissing her on the cheek.

She smiles sweetly, and her eyes light up. "It's great to see you, too. Although I wish it were under better circumstances."

I shrug. "I've seen worse. It's nothing I can't fix."

She laughs. "Trying to sell me before we even get into my office?"

"Is it working?" I ask with my most mischievous grin.

She shakes her head but says, "Maybe. Come on in."

I follow her inside, glancing back to get one last glimpse of Victoria. But she's already gone. I ignored her, and she vanished.

I take a seat at the table, next to Lily. The room is more of a meeting room than an office, although it seems like it functions as both to Lily.

"It really is good to see you, Lily. I know your personal and work life aren't going exactly as you planned, but I'm happy that I'm here. It's been far too long."

"I missed you, too, Carter. I thought about calling you dozens of times in college."

I laugh. "Good thing you didn't. You wouldn't have liked college me."

She laughs. "Too much of a bad boy?"

"Something like that."

Lily blushes.

"So, tell me what you want now, Lily? What future do you want for yourself?"

She looks down at her hands.

I grab her chin to get her to look at me. "There is no wrong answer, Lily. Do you still want to be a senator? Do you want to change the world or not?"

"I don't know."

I narrow my eyes, studying her. I wasn't expecting that. The Lily I used to know was fearless and would have said *yes* without hesitation. I sit back in my chair.

"Well, I can't help you until you figure out what you want. If you want the world, I can give it to you. But I need to know that is what you want."

"Victoria said the same thing."

I sit up in my seat. "Victoria hasn't been doing this nearly as long as I have. If you want this, I'm your guy. I'm the one who can make it happen. Victoria is a sweet girl with good intentions, but she doesn't have the experience for a job like this."

"Because I fucked up my chances. There is no coming back from this."

"No, because you are an amazing woman who deserves the best. And I'm the best."

Lily smiles weakly.

"So, what do you want, Lily?" I take her hands in mine, forcing her to look at me and stop turning away.

She has to stop running from her problems. Even if she doesn't want to be a senator anymore, she still needs me to help her rebuild her image. She needs to face her troubles head-on. But I can't help her if she doesn't know what she wants.

"Do I have to answer now?"

"Yes. I'm not letting you run away from this. You need to decide what you want. And then I can help you."

She swallows hard.

"What do you want, Lily?"

"I want to be the next senator from North Carolina."

I grin. "Good girl."

She smiles brightly, finally showing me the confident girl I used to know.

"Today's a Sunday; it's not the best day to get your team caught up on everything or to do any interviews, so I'll spend today getting a plan together. Then, I'll have my team get your team up to speed, and we will start working on this tomorrow."

"Thank you, Carter. I'm not sure what I would do without you."

I hug her. "You would be just fine. But I'm going to make this a lot easier for you." I kiss her cheek. "Get some rest. You have a busy day tomorrow. But don't worry; I'll take care of everything."

"SO, I see that you won the bedroom argument last night," Logan says as I take a seat at the bar next to him.

"Yeah, I did. But your sister won the clothes fight. I had to take all my clothes to the dry cleaners today for them to attempt to get the beer out of them."

Logan laughs.

"It's not funny. Your sister is annoying as hell."

"And you aren't?"

"When is she leaving anyway?"

Logan takes a drink of his beer. "Not sure. Probably when whatever job she came here for is finished."

I grin and sip my own beer.

"What's so funny?" Logan asks.

"I got the job that she came here for. So, my guess is, she won't be staying much longer."

Logan raises an eyebrow. "Victoria didn't get the job?"

I shake my head.

Logan frowns as he stares intently at his beer.

I slap him on the back. "Relax. I'm sure she will find something back in California."

Logan shakes his head as he stares at me with wide eyes. "You don't know Victoria at all, do you?"

"Of course I do. She's the same girl we used to pick on all those years ago when we were young."

Logan laughs. "She's not the awkward tomboy you used to know. And she's not going to just let you push her around and not fight back anymore."

"Well, it doesn't matter. Lily made her decision, and she chose me, not Victoria. She can fight all she wants, but the decision has already been made."

"Maybe. I don't want to get in the middle of things between my sister and my best friend. But, if I were to bet, I wouldn't count out my sister."

"Whatever. Let's just celebrate my victory tonight and forget about Tori."

I lift my beer, and Logan clinks his against mine. I take a sip.

Logan raises the glass to his lips and then grins, lowering it and looking at something behind me.

I don't have to turn around to know who's standing behind me.

"Hello, Tori," I say, using the nickname that apparently drives her crazy.

"Hey, Logan," Victoria says, ignoring me to walk over to Logan.

They hug, and then Victoria takes a seat next to Logan at the bar.

"What can I get you to drink?" the bartender asks her.

"I'll take a beer," Victoria says. "And they will each take another beer as well." She slaps the cash down on the bar to pay for all of our beers.

I narrow my eyes at her as she slides my beer over to me.

"What's this for?"

She eyes me. "We are celebrating."

She lifts her glass, as do Logan and I.

"Did you find a new job back in California?" I ask.

She smirks. "No, Lily gave me the job."

I chuckle.

"What's so funny?"

"That you think Lily offered you a job."

"Well, she did."

"You must be mistaken because she offered me the job before I even left her office this morning."

"Then, you must be the one who misunderstood because I just got off the phone with her. I start tomorrow morning, bright and early."

I shake my head. "I don't want to embarrass you, Tori, but she offered me the job." I pull my phone out of my pocket. "But we can settle this once and for all."

I dial Lily's number and wait for her to pick up.

"Hey, Carter. What's up?" Lily asks.

"I just ran into Tori."

"Who?"

"Victoria. She says that you just offered her the job of handling your PR. I just need you to verbally tell her that it isn't happening and that I'm the guy who will be handling everything."

There is a moment of silence and then, "Actually...I just hired her."

"What?"

"I hired both of you. I loved both of your approaches, and this is a big enough project that I thought hiring two PR firms would be worth my investment. She can loop you into her ideas tomorrow. I'm sure you will work well together."

I stare at Victoria as she smiles slyly at me. I don't know what she did to convince Lily that she needs both of us, but whatever it is, I'll change Lily's mind tomorrow. Tonight, I need to work on Victoria.

"We will meet you at seven at your office. Get some sleep, Lily. We have a lot of work to do tomorrow."

I end the call and then glare at Victoria. "What did you do?" I ask.

She sips her beer. "I got the job, didn't I?"

"No, you didn't."

"Then, why are you so upset?"

"Because she hired both of us."

Victoria's eyes widen as she looks at Logan, like he is going to be able to do something about the situation. "What did you do?" she asks her brother.

"Nothing. I haven't talked to Lily since high school, same as you."

"Logan Grant, don't you dare lie to me. I know you enjoy watching me and Carter fight. Is this some kind of sick joke to force us to work together? What. Did. You. Do?" Victoria stands, towering over Logan, grabbing on to the neck of his shirt. She's a tiny woman who shouldn't be able to threaten a man like Logan with anything, but right now, the rage building inside her gives me no doubt that she would be able to take on Logan or any other man.

"Lily and I had lunch today," Logan says.

Victoria releases him. "I knew it. What did you tell her?"

"I told her I wasn't going to get in the middle of this. She asked me for advice on deciding who she should choose and what she should do, and I told her I couldn't help her. That either of you would be able to do the job. That it was up to her."

"Some friend you are," I say at the same time Victoria says, "Some brother you are."

We glare at each other for a second before turning our anger back on Logan.

"This isn't a game, Logan. I'm not some teenager you get to play with for your amusement. This is my career you are messing with."

Logan stands up and grabs Victoria's arms. "That's why I didn't say anything. I didn't do anything. Maybe I should have reminded Lily that you two didn't get along, but I never thought she would choose both of you. I promise. I would never do anything to hurt you. Not anymore."

Victoria takes a deep breath. "I know." She looks at me. "I guess we will be working together."

"Or you could quit," I say, taking a drink of my beer.

She takes a seat back on the barstool. "I'm not quitting. I don't care how miserable you try to make my life while we work together. I'm not quitting. This is my chance to start my own company. This is my big break, and I'm not letting you jeopardize that."

I shake my head and push down the fury building inside me. Lily needs my help, and Victoria is just going to get in the way.

"You're jeopardizing your career by staying."

"You can't scare me off, Carter. I'm a different person than I used to be. I'm done taking your crap."

"Yes, you are definitely done taking my crap. That's why I got the bed last night."

"And your clothes were drenched in beer."

"Nothing a little dry cleaning can't fix."

I gulp down the rest of my beer before walking over to her. "Thanks for the beer, Tori. I'll see you at seven sharp. Make sure to get lots of rest on that couch. I have a lot planned for tomorrow."

"You'd better look sharp because I plan on blowing Lily away with my ideas, and I doubt she will want to keep you around. You'll be out on the streets, looking for a new job, so you'd better look good for your job interview."

I smirk. "I think I like the old Tori better."

She turns and pushes her breasts out. My eyes immediately go to her cleavage. I want to bury my face in her chest and taste her smooth skin. I want to flick my tongue over her hardening nipple. I want to hear her scream my name when I push my dick inside her. I want—

"Your dick seems to like the new me."

"My dick is happy with any woman with breasts and a nice body. But it knows better than to get involved with trouble like you."

She rolls her eyes. "I don't doubt that. I think you should just fuck Lily and leave me to handle the crisis."

"Oh, don't worry, Tori; I can multitask just fine."

I brush a strand of her hair behind her ear and watch as her face fights between flushing with anger or blushing with lust. I might not get to fuck Victoria, but she sure is fun to play with in other more torturous ways. She'll break. She can't stand me. I give her eight hours of working with me tomorrow and trying to put up with my crap before she quits and leaves the job to me.

5 VICTORIA

I needed a plan.

And that's exactly what I spent all night doing. Coming up with a plan to knock Lily's socks off to ensure that Carter will get sent home. While he was sleeping in the comfortable bed, I was working. All night long.

That's two nights in a row without any sleep. But it will be worth it to watch Carter's smug smile being kicked off his face.

I yawn for the millionth time this morning.

Thank God I was able to find the biggest coffee that Starbucks makes to keep me awake all day.

"Good morning, Lily," I say as brightly as I can as I enter her office.

"Morning, Victoria," Lily says.

She looks happy and beautiful in her red dress while I look like a hot mess. I'm wearing a business suit, my hair is up in a bun, and I barely had time to apply any makeup.

"I'm excited to see what you and Carter come up with. Two days ago, I thought my life was over, and then both of you came into my life and showed me that my career wasn't over. I just need to regenerate it."

"I'd be happy to get started on showing you some of my new plans while we wait for Carter," I say, trying not to add anything snarky at the end.

"We should probably wait. That way, you don't have to share your plans twice."

I sigh. So much for blowing her so out of the water with my ideas that she doesn't even remember that Carter is coming.

A knock rattles on the door before it is thrown open. Carter walks in, dressed in a dark blue suit. Lily's and my eyes both go to the hot man standing in the meeting room. A man who is equally handsome and awful at the same time.

He prances into the room, with a gleam in his eyes. He very clearly got plenty of sleep last night.

I grab my coffee, trying to ignore him, and stifle a yawn. As the coffee cup reaches my lips, Carter smacks me hard on the back.

"Good morning, Tori," he says as the coffee spills all over myself.

"Morning," I say through clenched teeth, trying not to scream from the pain all over my body.

"Oh goodness, did I do that?" Carter says sarcastically, looking at the coffee now dripping all over my face, arms, jacket, and pants.

"Yes, but it's not a problem. No need to cry over spilled coffee," I say, wiping off my face with the back of my jacket sleeve. I won't let him know that he is getting to me. I'll just pay back the favor later.

I stand up to take my jacket off and see what I should do with my pants.

"Here, let me help you," Carter says, grabbing my jacket.

Lily looks straight at me with a giant smile on her face. So, as much as I want to knee Carter in the balls for spilling scorching hot coffee all over me, I don't. I pretend to smile and let Carter remove my jacket.

My hands wrap around my bare arms as I feel the pain of the burn all over. I should have worn a long-sleeved blouse instead of one without any sleeves. Maybe it would have protected me better from the burns.

"Oh my God! Victoria, are you all right? Your face and arms are bright red," Lily says from across the table.

"I'm fine."

I feel Carter's hand touch my shoulder, and I jump. He moves his hand away for a second and then touches me softer, moving me to look at him. When he sees what I'm sure is my bright pink face and arms, he darts out of the room.

"Do you want me to get you a change of clothes or something?" Lily asks.

"No, I'm fine. Really. It's just a little spilled coffee."

Lily eyes my arms though, and I know it looks bad. But the pain is already subsiding, so it can't actually be that bad.

Carter returns with a bowl of water and a washcloth. He sets the bowl on the table. "Put your wrist in the water."

I roll my eyes. "I'm fine," I say again, hating the attention I'm getting.

He ignores me and grabs my wrist. He sticks my wrist and forearm into the cool water. The burn on my arm soothes immediately. I voluntarily stick my other arm in. When I look down I realize that my arm is redder than I expected.

"Look at me," Carter says.

I do.

His eyes narrow as he studies my face. He quickly puts the washcloth into the water, wrings it out, and then places it against my cheek. I wince and pull away from the cool water. He places his hand under my chin and gently turns it back toward him as he cautiously places the washcloth on my face.

I close my eyes at the initial sting and then open them as the cool cloth starts to calm my burn.

Carter intensely stares at me while he holds the washcloth to my face and then slowly pulls it away. I remove my hands from the water and shake them off.

"I'm sorry. I didn't mean to hurt you."

I shake my head. "I'm fine. No damage done."

He tucks a strand of hair behind my ear.

I swallow hard, trying to push any feelings that are creeping up, the more he takes care of me.

"I'm fine," I say for the millionth time, trying to convince myself more than him. "It barely hurt. My skin is just sensitive."

I turn away from him before he does anything else to make my heart flutter. It's just an act. He doesn't really care if he hurt me. He never has before.

"Here's some ointment to put on your burns, Victoria," Lily says, handing me a tube.

"Thank you. Let's get started with the meeting though," I say, taking it from her.

Lily and Carter both look at me, still concerned. Lily rubs her ear while she exchanges glances with Carter like she is secretly passing a message to him that I don't get to know.

I sigh. "I'm fine. I promise."

I glance down at my phone to check the time. "I was hoping to share with you my thoughts on the plans first, but I suspect that our savior himself is here."

Lily looks at me with wide eyes, and Carter just stares.

I get up and run out into the hall. I sigh with relief when I see him waiting for me.

"You came."

Phillip, Lily's ex-fiancé, nods. "You were very persistent that I get here. Are you okay?"

I bite my lip to keep from screaming. "Yes. Just a hot mess, as usual. Come on, let's go inside, and I can share the plans with everyone."

I grab his arm because I'm afraid he is going to run, and I lead him into the meeting room.

"Oh my God! Phillip, what are you doing here?" Lily says as she runs over and throws her arms around his neck.

To my surprise, Phillip hugs her back. I stand to the side, smiling, as I clasp my hands together and watch their reunion. I wasn't sure that my crazy plan was going to work, but seeing how happy they are to see each other reassures me.

A knot in my stomach forms when I look over at Carter, though, who is unfazed by the interaction. I thought he would be concerned that I just won Lily over. But he doesn't seem concerned; in fact, he seems amused.

"I came to help you. Victoria convinced me that you needed my help, so here I am," Phillip says.

Lily has tears in her eyes, which makes me tear up a little as I see them reunite. Phillip has no reason to forgive Lily or to help her in any way. They were engaged when she cheated on him. But, despite all the pain she caused him, he still loves her. I know it. And this proves it.

Phillip links his fingers with Lily's, and I about lose it. Such a simple gesture, but it's beautiful to observe the two of them together.

"I'm so sorry," Lily whispers.

As much as I want to stay and continue to grow envious as they reclaim their love for each other, I know I shouldn't. I motion with my head for Carter to follow me out and give them some privacy, and to my surprise, he does without protest.

I grin and sink into the couch in the lobby, down the hallway from Lily's office, as Carter leans against the wall.

"So, my plan is going even better than I thought."

He frowns as he walks over and sits next to me. "What is your plan exactly?"

"My plan is to give Lily and Phillip a chance to make up for real and then put them on every TV show, radio show, and newspaper, showing the love they have for each other. Lily won't hide her error, but she will make it clear that it was a mistake. Phillip will show forgiveness, and Lily will show her humility. They are a normal couple with real problems, just like everyone else."

"Your plan won't work."

"Are you crazy? Did you not see the two of them together? Their love is infectious."

"No, Phillip is too nice. He's not strong enough. He's a school-teacher, not a powerful businessman. He's not seen as an equal to her. And, because of that, their love will never be seen as real. It will be clear that the only reason he's forgiven her is because she is way out of his league. Everyone will suspect that she is sleeping with hotter, more attractive men behind Phillip's back."

"You're wrong. You're just upset that Lily is going to love my plan, and you are going to be out of a job soon." I fold my arms across my chest and wince when I hit my burns a little too hard.

"Are you okay?"

I nod.

Carter takes my hand that has a burn on top of it. He lowers his lips and softly kisses the burn.

My eyes widen, and my breathing stops. It's just a stupid kiss on the hand, but it's one of the sweetest things a man has ever done for me. I don't understand how he could be so cruel one second and then so sweet the next.

He grins. "You don't trust me, do you?"

I shake my head.

"You shouldn't. Just like the people of North Carolina wouldn't trust Lily if she went back to her fiancé."

I frown. "You and Lily are different. You're an ass, and she's..."

He laughs. "She's a bitch."

I freeze when he calls Lily that. "I thought you liked her."

"Of course I like her. Lily and I are a lot alike, which is how I know your plan will never work."

He grins, and I know he has something up his sleeve. Something he isn't telling me.

I jump as a loud thump happens down the hallway.

"What was that?" I ask.

Carter frowns as he looks toward Lily's office. He starts jogging down the hallway, and I follow, not having a clue as to what is going on.

"Oh my God," I say and cover my mouth with my hands when I see two men fighting, covered in blood.

Lily is screaming for them to stop, and Carter is trying to figure out how to break them up without getting hurt himself.

Finally, Carter grabs hold of Phillip and pulls him away from the other man.

"What is going on?" I ask, looking from Phillip to the other man before it becomes clear who the other man is. I recognize the other man from the sex tape with Lily.

"What are you doing here?" Lily asks Jacob.

"I'm here for you. Your PR team asked me to come, so here I am. I'll do whatever you want to make this easier on you," Jacob says.

I turn to Carter, who is still holding Phillip back, realizing what he did. I brought Phillip, and he brought Jacob. We couldn't have fucked this up more if we had tried.

"Get the fuck out of here, you asshole! Lily is my fiancée!" Phillip shouts.

Jacob laughs. "I think that ended the second she got into my bed and agreed to be filmed."

Phillip tries to break free of Carter's arms, but he holds him back.

"Tell him to leave, Lily!" Phillip shouts.

But Lily can't say anything right now. Her tears are flowing down her cheeks, but otherwise, she's frozen. She has no idea how to handle this. This is the exact situation that Carter and I were hired to avoid.

"Escort Phillip out, Carter," I say.

Carter begins walking Phillip out of the building while I grab onto Jacob's arm and guide him out the back exit. I can hear Phillip fighting with Carter behind me, but to my surprise, Jacob doesn't fight me.

When I get him all the way outside, I ask, "What are you really doing here? You don't want to be involved in this, do you?"

Jacob shrugs. "Carter made me an offer I couldn't refuse."

"Money?"

"Something like that."

"Leave Lily alone."

"You don't have to worry about me. I get paid either way."

I frown and sulk back inside. That was a disaster. I walk back into the meeting room, just behind Carter.

"I'm so sorry, Lily. Victoria and I should have talked before we took action, and—"

"Shut your mouth," Lily says firmly.

I freeze, and so does Carter, who is sitting at the table in front of me.

"You two fucked up! Now, there is no way Phillip will take me back, and Jacob is too worked up to do anything you ask. I'm going to go get a massage and have lunch with a friend to try to get over my heartbreak at what just happened. You two have until I get back to come up with a plan together to fix this, or you're both fired." Lily walks calmly out of the room, leaving Carter and me alone.

I take a deep breath. *This is not my fault*, I repeat to myself over and over again. *This is Carter's fault.*

My eyes dart to him sitting calmly at the table. It doesn't matter whose fault it is. I'm going to be out of a job if I don't fix this.

I walk over and sit down on the opposite side of the table. I need to keep Carter at a distance if I'm going to have any control over the situation.

"You're mad," Carter says.

"Yeah, I'm mad. What were you thinking?"

He smirks. "I was thinking that I had years of experience in fixing people's problems, and I made a good living from doing it, so I should be the one who made the decisions."

I raise an eyebrow. "And you think that I don't have experience?"

"I know you don't have experience."

"I've been working in this industry, same as you."

"And what do you have to show for it? You lost your job; you didn't get promoted."

I frown. I hate him. I should just quit. But I won't give him the satisfaction of winning.

"Let's just figure out a solution to the mess you created."

He holds up a finger and then walks out without saying anything to me. It's annoying that he doesn't tell me what he is doing. But it gives me a chance to compose myself and calm down. We won't be any good to Lily if we spend the whole time arguing. I have to find a way to push through my feelings and be civil with him. No more fighting.

Carter walks back in a few minutes later, carrying a large coffee cup in his hand. I glare at him for getting himself a coffee after he spilled mine all over me.

I realize what I'm doing and close my eyes. *He's just goading you. Don't let him do it.*

I open my eyes, and he isn't standing across the table from me. He's leaning over me as he places the coffee cup in front of me.

"A peace offering," he says before sitting in the seat next to me.

I smile. "Let's get to work."

He holds my gaze for far too long before he says, "Where do you want to start?"

I don't know why he's being so nice to me. It's either from guilt from spilling coffee on me or ruining my plans for Lily, but whatever the reason, I'm not going to waste the moment.

6 CARTER

I fucked up.

Not by convincing Jacob to come here today. I know that my instincts were correct. That Jacob would have been the best way to get the public back on Lily's side.

I fucked up by letting myself feel anything toward Victoria. I don't have feelings. Ever. I'm ruthless and uncaring. It's why I'm so good at my job. I never care about my clients. I just do what's best for them even if they hate me at the time. They always thank me afterward.

And, now that I've let myself care about Victoria, I don't know how to shut it off. I don't even feel anything that loving. I just feel guilt and concern. I've hurt Victoria countless times. But today was the first time that I didn't like it. I didn't like seeing her in physical pain. I didn't like the emotions it evoked in either of us.

"Carter, are you listening to me?"

I blink, trying to come back to the real world instead of the world of torture I have created for myself in my head. A world where I want Victoria, but I can't have her.

"To every word."

She frowns. "Then, what was I saying?"

"You said, 'Carter, are you listening to me?'"

She can't stifle the tiniest of grins from her lips. It makes me happy to see her smile.

"Before that."

"That you feel the best way to move forward is to show Lily as a strong, independent woman who doesn't need a man by her side. Don't paint the men as monsters but not as saints either. Just do one interview with another strong, independent woman who will want to address the sex tape but then will focus on the issues that Lily wants to tackle as a senator instead of doing dozens of interviews, like the plan was before."

She clears her throat. "You were listening."

"I have an impeccable memory. Anything I hear or see, I will remember."

She sips her coffee to keep from yawning. I know she stayed up all night, preparing for this. She's smarter than I gave her credit for. Most of her ideas are spot-on, and she has a backup in mind for every scenario. If we didn't hate each other so much, I would offer her a job. But her exhaustion is going to lead to mistakes. She might think she has the same level of experience as me, but having to spend all night formulating a plan shows me just how little experience she actually has. She's talented, but she needs someone to harness that talent.

"What do you think?"

I lean forward in my chair until I'm close enough to smell the coffee mixed with her perfume. "I don't think you care what I think."

She leans forward in her chair as well. "What do you think?"

"I think your ideas are good."

"Just good?"

I grin. "Better than good. But you have some flaws that you still need to work out."

"Yeah? And what are those?"

"You haven't slept in two days, so you aren't thinking clearly."

"What are the flaws in my plan?"

"You'll figure them out after a good night's rest."

She rolls her eyes. "Tell me now. We already screwed up once with Lily. We can't do that again. We are supposed to be working together to ensure that we don't mess this up anymore. That means, there can't be any secrets. We have to tell each other everything."

I lean back in my chair as I rub the back of my neck. She watches me.

"I'll make sure that we don't fuck up again. My reputation is on the line, too. But I want to help you grow. And you will never grow if I just tell you what you fucked up. I'll guide you, but you have to figure it out for yourself."

"Why are you trying to help me?"

I get up out of my chair and walk over to get my laptop. Then, I plug the projector into it. I'm trying to help her because I don't know how to turn my emotions off now that I've turned them on. I don't know why, but I actually enjoy listening to her voice. She talks so confidently about what she wants. It's nice, hearing her. It's nice, being near her.

"It's because you feel guilty for spilling coffee on me, isn't it?"

"No, it's because, when I see someone with talent, I can't help but nourish that talent."

"Was that a compliment?"

Victoria bites her lip, and I ache to have that lip in my mouth. I don't know what's come over me, but right now, my brain is obsessed with her.

Lily chooses that moment to walk back into the room. I knew she was coming back soon. She's been gone for hours, and I have an instinct when it comes to clients. This isn't the first time a client has walked out on me.

"Do you have a plan, or am I firing you both?" Lily asks. She folds her arms across her chest, and her face is stiff and rigid. Gone are the tears from earlier. Gone is the anger. She's all business now.

I can feel the nerves oozing off of Victoria as she sits at the table.

She has a thorough plan, but I know it makes her nervous not to have visuals and a written plan for Lily. She wants to look as professional as she can. She thought she would have more time.

I click on the projector, and my plan pops up on the screen. I should be nice and let Victoria talk about the plan while I show the visuals. Our plans are similar enough that it doesn't really matter anyway. But I'm not nice. And the longer I pretend to be nice to Victoria, the more likely it is that she is going to get hurt later on. I'm the kind of person who would fuck her and leave her without a second glance.

Victoria doesn't deserve that. She doesn't deserve that kind of pain. Being an ass to her now is the only way to keep me from breaking her heart later on. She needs to hate me. So, I'll make her detest me by presenting our ideas as my own, by myself. And then she'll hate me.

✳

MY PLAN WORKS. Victoria hates me.

I can feel it from the second she walks into Logan's apartment.

"Where is he?" I hear her ask Logan in the living room from where I'm sitting on the bed with my laptop on my lap.

She's angry, and she should be. I don't hear Logan's answer, but I'm sure that he's pointed her in my direction because I can hear her stomping down the hallway toward me.

"What the hell was that?" she yells, throwing my bedroom door open.

"I did my job. You can't hate me for that."

"No, you weren't doing your job. You stole my ideas and claimed them as your own."

I fold my arms across my chest, amused at how worked up she gets. I think that's why I like teasing her so much. She's adorable like this.

"I didn't steal your ideas."

"Yes, you did! I told you every single idea, and then you shared them with Lily. Now, she thinks they were all your ideas."

"I didn't steal your ideas," I say again.

The look she gives me is beyond anger. Her nostrils are flared, and her face is red, but her eyes suddenly stop on my bare chest.

"Are you naked?" she asks, changing the subject.

"Does it matter if I am?"

Her eyes drop to the sheets covering me from the waist down. "Yes. You shouldn't be naked."

"Why? Because you won't be able to control yourself if I am?" I smirk.

"No...because, um...because I want to have a serious conversation with you, and I can't do that if you're trying to distract me with your body."

I grab the top of the sheets and slowly push them down. Her eyes stay glued to them as I reveal my boxers beneath them.

"Put some clothes on."

"I have clothes on. This is my room. You entered without knocking. I can wear whatever I want."

She huffs. "Why did you steal my ideas?"

"I. Didn't. Steal. Your. Ideas."

She glares at me.

"If you recall, I had all the same ideas already written down on my laptop before you started blabbing them to me. I came up with those ideas yesterday and wrote them down as a backup plan because I figured you would somehow mess up my original plan."

She places her hands on her curvy hips while pushing her breasts out at the same time. "You messed up my plan."

I nod and smirk, which only angers her more and makes my cock desperate to fuck her. I love her pouty mouth. I love how she stands confidently in my bedroom, still in her coffee-covered outfit instead of changing. I love how she hates me.

"So, what did you talk to Lily about after I left?" I ask.

"Wouldn't you like to know?"

I raise an eyebrow. "I thought we were a team, that we needed to share everything with each other, so we don't fuck up Lily's life again."

She casually runs her hand across the footboard of the bed. "I realized my first flaw."

"Oh, and what is that?"

"That I thought we could ever be a team. You don't have a heart. Whatever niceness you showed toward me was all an act."

I nod. "You're learning."

She flicks her shoes off into the corner of the room.

"Now, get out of my bed," she says.

I laugh. "This isn't your bed; it's mine."

"No, tonight, it's mine. And don't even think about throwing me over your shoulder again and carrying me out. You wouldn't dare do that, not with Logan here."

She's right. I wouldn't. Logan would kick my ass if he saw me doing anything to hurt her. But he also wouldn't get in the middle of this.

"I'm not going anywhere."

"Fine. Be a stubborn ass."

She walks to the door and throws it shut. I cock my head, confused at what she is doing.

She turns and begins undoing the buttons on her blouse, swiftly moving down until all the buttons are undone.

"What are you doing?"

She throws her shirt off onto the floor. "I'm going to bed."

She quickly undoes the button and zipper on her pants and pushes them down.

I know I'm sitting here, gaping at her hot body, giving her exactly what she wants, but I don't care. I can't help myself. No man could stop from getting turned on by watching her. I'm shocked that she doesn't have a boyfriend or fiancé or husband.

She walks over to my side of the bed. She puts her finger under my chin and lifts it up, closing my jaw.

"It's not polite to stare, you know."

She tries to move away, but I grab her wrist.

"It's not polite to tease."

"Who said I was teasing?"

I narrow my eyes at her.

She reaches behind her with her free hand and undoes her black lace bra. She slides one arm out of it, and I immediately release her other hand to watch her bra fall to the floor.

I watch her bite her lip out of the corner of my eye, but I can't take my eyes off her breasts. Her nipples are hard, begging for me to take them into my mouth. I grip my hands to keep from feeling the fullness and softness of her breasts.

She clears her throat, and I look up at her. She thinks she's won this fight. That, if I show her how badly I want to fuck her, she will have the upper hand. So, I do the only thing I can to keep my power.

I pull her onto the bed. I toss her over me onto the bed next to me, and I climb on top of her, pinning her to the bed beneath me. Our faces are millimeters apart as we both breathe fast. She licks her bottom lip, anticipating a kiss that I'm desperate to give her.

In all our years together, growing up, I never thought to taste her lips. I never thought to date her. To make out with her. To get her naked. Fuck her. But then the girl I used to know would never have dared to get naked in front of me just so she could win a fight.

I move just a little closer, taking every second of this in because this is the closest I will ever get to her. I won't fuck her. Even if I wanted to, she hates me too much to let me touch her. This is just a game to her.

"Good night, Tori." I roll off of her, rolling away from her to turn off the light.

She growls lightly in her throat.

"Disappointed, Tori?"

"No, just shocked that you are able to resist me."

I roll back over and throw my arms around her, pressing my dick against her ass. "You want me to be nice and caring and do what's right, right?"

She nods.

"This is me doing that."

I pull her tighter to me, showing her just how badly I want her. My cock pushes harder against her. And, if she listens closely, she will be able to hear my heart beating as fast as hers.

"Comfortable?" I ask, knowing that she won't say no. She's too stubborn, just like me.

"Perfect."

I grin.

"Good night, Victoria."

She sucks in a breath, and despite how exhausted she is, I know she isn't going to be able to sleep a wink. I wish I had the same problem. I would love to remember every second of holding her tonight. I want to remember every curve, every smell, every sound. I want to hear her restlessness at the fact that I'm so close to her. I want to hear her gasp when my hand accidentally brushes against her breast. I want to know when she regrets ever undressing in front of me.

But I can't. I won't be able to stay awake. I know my body too well. I know that the second it realizes it doesn't get to fuck her, I'll be out, and I'll miss all the moments I'm desperate to remember.

7 VICTORIA

Damn it.

How stupid could I be to think I could win a fight with Carter Woods?

He's had years of practice in winning fights while I've just barely started learning how to fight back. And, now, I'm more exhausted than ever before. I'm not sure I slept more than an hour or two all night. Either his arms or his legs were wrapped tightly around me, even when he was fast asleep. His cock pushed hard against me, driving me mad. I've fucked plenty of men, but I've rarely slept all night in the bed with them. I'm used to sleeping on my own, and Carter made it impossible for me to sleep.

I didn't think he would have the strength to resist me, not when I was naked in his bed. I'm not sure if I would have actually let him fuck me or just taunted him to prove my point.

But it doesn't matter now. He's proven yet again that he can win any game. I just have to learn to win when he doesn't realize we are playing the game.

"Sleep well, Victoria?" he asks, stretching after getting a full night's sleep, releasing me for the first time all night.

I don't know whether to hate or love that his arms are no longer wrapped around me.

I give him a dirty look because I know he will know if I'm lying to him.

He smirks as his eyes drop down to my breasts. There's a gleam there I've found in his usual stare when he looks at me.

I don't cover my body. I let him see what he missed. I gave him plenty of chances to apologize. To have sex with me. Now, he needs to know how much of a mistake not fucking me was.

"I'm going to shower," I say, walking to the door so that he can stare at my ass.

"Don't use all the hot water!" he shouts when I open the door and walk out.

I sigh. I don't know what it's going to take to break him. I threw myself at him, naked, and he still didn't take the bait. He's winning, and I'm not sure how to stop him.

"Please put some clothes on, sis," Logan says as he walks down the hallway, shielding his eyes.

I grab a towel from the bathroom and cover up. "Sorry, I forgot you were here."

His eyes look at me and then the door to the guest bedroom that I left open. "Wait," he says, looking back and forth again. "You and Carter?" He looks to the bedroom door. "I'm going to kill him."

Logan starts storming down the hallway to give Carter a piece of his mind.

I bite my lip. I should say something. Let him know that Carter didn't fuck me. He just slept with me naked in his bed while he tortured me with his unrelenting touch and hotness. I might not be able to win against Carter, but at least Logan can chew him out.

⁂

I STEP into the office with a fake smile on my face when I realize that Carter is already here. I don't know how he got here so fast since

I occupied the only bathroom until the last possible second before I needed to leave to get here on time. But, somehow, he looks clean and completely put together, as he always does.

"Good morning, Lily," I say, ignoring Carter.

He stares me down as I enter.

"Good morning," Lily says, seeming relaxed, which is good since she has the television interview this evening.

Her phone buzzes, and she answers.

I turn my attention to Carter. "You look surprisingly clean and well dressed for someone who didn't have access to a bathroom this morning."

He leans back in his chair while I take a seat next to him.

"I used Logan's neighbor's bathroom. Katherine didn't mind me using her place in exchange for getting my company."

I raise an eyebrow. "So, you offered to sleep with her in exchange for using a bathroom? How desperate are you?"

He leans close to me. "Not as desperate as you are to have sex with me."

I push him away from me. He falls back in his chair with a thump, but it's not enough. I want to slap him in the face. I shouldn't feel that way. He's not mine. If he wants to sleep with the hot neighbor, he can. But I'm tired of him taunting me about it.

"Did Logan let you have it?" I ask, knowing that will at least push his buttons a little.

"Logan doesn't know what he's talking about," Carter says, staring off into space.

I sigh. "I should have told him that you didn't fuck me last night. But it was too fun for me to let him yell at you first."

"He knows I didn't fuck you," Carter says with a seriousness in his voice I wasn't expecting, turning back to me.

I tuck a strand of my hair behind my ear. "Then, what was all the yelling about?"

Carter swallows. "He thinks I'm going to hurt you."

I laugh. "You already have—about a million times. Nothing you do now can really hurt me." I sigh, running my hand through my hair, pulling out the few curls that I have. "Don't worry. I'll talk to Logan when I get back. You'll still be best friends."

"I'm not worried about my relationship with Logan."

My heart stops when I see how Carter is looking at me. I'm not sure what to think. I see the lust that was there last night, but I also see something else that I don't understand. There's a kindness that I haven't seen before, especially when he's looking at me.

"Sorry about that," Lily says, hanging up the phone.

I swallow and turn to give my full attention to Lily. If I'm going to beat Carter, then I have to focus everything I have on this job.

"So, prepare me for this interview," Lily says with a large smile on her face that looks as fake as my warm feelings toward Carter.

"I have a list of questions that they will most likely ask you. How about we start with me just reading through them and you answering honestly? Then, we will go from there."

Lily twists her bracelet around her wrist as she swallows. "Sure."

She's nervous. Everything in her body is screaming just how terrified she is about this interview. I never thought that Lily would be terrified of an interview. She loves the camera. But I guess, after what happened the last time she did an interview, I don't blame her. But it's going to take all day to get her feeling comfortable again.

I eye Carter out of the corner of my eye. I'm ready for him to argue with me, saying that my plan isn't the best way to start our preparations. But he doesn't say anything. Maybe he will actually behave today.

I pull out my notes with the questions that I wrote up. "Let's start with some easy questions. Why do you want to be a senator?"

"Because I want to make a difference. I'm tired of always being the pretty girl who is just meant to marry the attractive guy, and that's it. I want my life to be more than just some hot body that men ogle. My passion is helping children. I want to make sure that no child ever has to go a day hungry. I want to make sure that all children have access to the best education. I want to make sure that all children can get the medical care they need. And I want to be a role model to little girls everywhere, showing that they can grow up and become a powerful woman who can bring about change in the world."

I smile. Her answer isn't perfect, but it doesn't need to be. The way she spoke with such sincerity—that's what is important here.

"Don't mention yourself as a role model to girls. It's going to trigger too many questions about how you could be a role model for girls when you made a sex tape. You also need to dig deeper," Carter says.

I glare at him. He's going to make her lose what little confidence she has on the first question. She's going to be a mess by the end of our session if he keeps nitpicking her like this.

"Actually, I think you were amazing, Lily. I wouldn't change anything. Let's just go through all the questions, and then we can discuss how to make the most important answers better," I say.

Lily's eyes dart back and forth between the two of us.

Carter turns to me with his own devilish glare, his face tense, and I can tell he is doing everything he can to hold back his anger. "I know you don't have a ton of experience in preparing people for interviews, but if we let her practice wrong, that is what she is going to remember when she gets asked questions in the actual interview."

He turns to Lily. "I'm not going to coddle you, like Tori wants to. You're better than that."

I can't hold back my anger and frustration with him. I thought we could be civil, for Lily's sake, but I guess I was wrong.

"Next question. What is the status of your relationship with your fiancé?"

Lily freezes as the tension rises. She's unsure of who to answer or what to say. We are making this worse. If she can survive the day with the two of us arguing, she will be able to survive any stupid interview questions thrown her way. I'm just not sure if I can put up with Carter for an entire day without killing him.

"I CAN'T HANDLE THIS ANYMORE!" Lily screams, grabbing her head.

Carter and I both freeze, staring at her. We've spent the better half of the morning arguing about how she should answer each question. Every single question came with an argument. Every. Single. One.

I'm not surprised to see Lily breaking like this. She deserves better than what we are giving her.

"This was a mistake," she says, standing up and pacing back and forth in front of the table in the room we have been cooped up in.

I stand up and walk over to her. "I'm sorry, Lily. We will take it down a notch. You're doing great. If you can put up with us drilling you now, then you will do a great job tonight at your interview."

Her eyes widen, and I see the true fear and anger come out in one look.

"No." She strides over to her chair, grabbing her jacket and her purse.

Carter stands up, blocking her way to the door. He grabs on to her shoulders. "Relax, Lily. You got this."

She laughs. "I'm not worried about myself. I've done interviews countless times. I know what to say and what not to say. I know how to say charming things to distract the audience from what they should be worrying about. How do you think I got this far? But what I can't put up with is you two bickering. I thought I was being smart when I hired both of you, but now, I realize just how much of a mistake that was."

She takes a deep breath and then looks back to me. "I'm going to the salon to get my hair colored and get my nails done. Give me the interview questions."

I slowly walk over, handing her my notebook of questions.

She snatches them out of my hand. "I'll prepare for the interview on my own. And, when I get back, you two had better have worked out whatever shit is going on between the two of you. And, if I hear one more stupid argument, then I'm going to fire you both. I don't need this stress right now." She looks at Carter, who is still blocking her path to the exit. "Now, move."

He opens his mouth to say something but thinks better of it and steps out of her way. She stomps out of the room, leaving Carter and me alone in the meeting room.

"Great job," Carter says, snarky.

"You're an ass," I say, gathering my things.

I take Lily's lead and walk out. I know it is going to do nothing to solve our current predicament, but I can't let myself stay trapped in the same room with him for another second.

I march quickly out of the building, not caring that, by doing so, I'm probably losing yet another job and my best shot at starting my own firm. My head is already spinning with how I can salvage this, but my ideas all start with me strangling Carter to death because he is the root of all my problems. Every problem I've ever had started with him.

"Tori, wait," I hear Carter yell behind me as I continue down the sidewalk to my rental car.

I freeze. *Don't engage him. Just walk away. Give up. Let him deal with Lily. I can find a new job. I don't need this one client in order to start my career. That's what I should do. Just get in my rental, go back to Logan's, pack up my things, and get on the first flight back to California.*

But I can't give up so easily. I'm too stubborn for that.

I turn around. "What did you just call me?"

He cocks his arrogant head to the side. "You aren't running away, are you, Tori?"

I can't control myself anymore. I stomp over to where Carter is standing on the sidewalk, and I slap him. Hard. Across the face.

It's not one of my better moments as far as judgment goes, but I can't let him just get away with being the biggest jerk on the planet anymore. I'm tired of him hurting me even though I should be used to it by now.

He doesn't seem shocked that I hit him. In fact, he seems like that is exactly what he wanted. "I thought I couldn't hurt you anymore."

My nostrils flare, and my face turns bright red as I try to keep my breathing even and cold. "I lied."

He nods, putting his hands into his pockets, as he walks closer to me. "I know."

I take a step back. I don't want him anywhere near me.

"I'm sorry."

I pause at his words before walking backward, and he takes another step forward, gaining on me.

"You aren't capable of being sorry. At least, not toward me."

He nods. "You're right. I probably don't deserve your forgiveness, but does it make you feel any better to know that the past two hours have just been me goading you, trying to get you to break, so that I could prove to you that I'm still capable of hurting you?"

"No, it doesn't make me feel any better that you purposefully hurt me to prove a point."

He bites his lip, and I find myself staring far too intently at his damn lips. *How can I find a man I hate so sexy?* It shouldn't be possible.

He takes another step toward me until he's only a foot away from me. "I needed to know."

"Why?" I throw my hands up. "Why did you need to know that you could still hurt me?"

He reaches his hand out and lightly touches me on my bottom lip. "Because, believe it or not, I care about you."

I laugh. "You can't care about me. It's not possible."

His hand goes to the back of my neck before I realize what he is doing. He pulls me hard toward him. Our lips crash together in a hungry kiss. My eyes close the second our lips touch. My hands wrap around his neck, and my body responds to his. The kiss makes me forget about all the pain he's caused me. It makes me want him. It makes me ache for him. He takes complete control over my body with just one single kiss.

"No," I say, pushing him away from me. "I won't let you control me. You don't get to just kiss me and make everything better."

"How am I controlling you if this is what you want?"

"You think I want this?" I motion between us.

"I know you do. You can't kiss me like that and not want this."

I laugh. "I can. You can kiss me a million times, and I will never want anything more. There is nothing you can do to make up for the past. Nothing."

He narrows his eyes. "Even this?"

He scoops me back into his arms and kisses me again. My breathing stops as he kisses me. His tongue pushes deep into my mouth, begging me to let go of our past. To let him in.

I shouldn't. I know that, if I do, nothing but pain will follow. But, with his hand tangled in my hair, my body in his arms, his lips kissing me like I've wanted him to since the second I saw him again, I forget about the pain.

He gently pulls away, looking deep into my eyes, now asking for permission for a kiss that he just took from me again.

I slap him across the face again, but he doesn't let go of me. He just holds me tighter.

"I'm not yours. You don't get to control me. No one controls me."

I push his arms off of me, and I start walking down the sidewalk again although not as fast as before. I need to get out of here before I agree to do something stupid that would only leave me more broken than ever before.

He runs after me until he catches up with me. I expect him to grab my arm again and force me to stop, but he doesn't. He just walks next to me. Maybe he's tired of getting slapped.

"I'm sorry."

"Sorry isn't good enough."

"Why not? I know you want this as much as I do. I'm not saying that you should marry me. Just give me a clean slate to start over. Let me take you on a date. Let me fuck you. Give me a chance."

"You want to date me? Seriously?"

"Maybe."

I shake my head. "Why would I let go of everything that you have done to me when you give me no confidence that this is even what you want?"

"Because we can't keep doing this. Whatever is going on between us, it has to stop. We are destroying Lily and hurting our careers, all so that we can deny this sexual tension. If nothing else, at least maybe we should just fuck whatever this is out of our systems, and then we can move on and finally do our jobs."

"Fucking you won't get the time you cut my pigtails in kindergarten out of my system," I say, stopping as I glare at him. "Fucking you won't get the time you convinced my brother that girls were gross and wouldn't let him talk to me for a year even though I needed him." I take a step toward him as I let my anger through.

He doesn't take a step back even though I'm more than likely going to slap him again.

"Fucking you won't take away the time you shoved me off the playground and broke my arm."

He stands frozen, taking it all. Every horrible thing he has ever done to me hits him.

"Fucking you won't take away the time you said you would drive me home when it was freezing cold outside, and instead, slept with some girl while I had to walk home in a snowstorm without a coat."

I let all the horrible things he's ever done to me out. Every single one. Except one. I keep the worst for myself. If I told him, he would realize how much I cared about him when we were teenagers. If I tell him the worst thing that he's ever done to me, then he might try to ask for forgiveness. I might let go of the pain and actually forgive him. And I can't do that. He doesn't deserve my forgiveness.

"Are you finished?"

I cross my arms over my chest. "Why? You want to do something else to hurt me?"

"No, I want to tell you how truly sorry I am. I was fucked up as a kid. I had my own problems to deal with, but rather than deal with them, I took them out on you. Can you forgive me for what I did as a kid?"

"Yes, but I can't forgive you for what you've done as a man."

He swallows and looks like I slapped him even though I didn't.

"You're right. You shouldn't forgive me for hurting you now."

I nod, hating how silky and deep his voice sounds when he speaks. Because, if I listen to his voice too long, I will do anything he says.

I look into his damn eyes before I realize that it's a trap. His eyes are full of sincerity and lust. A deadly combination.

"What do you want, Victoria?"

And then he has to say my real name.

"Do you want me to let you have this job? Do you want me to go away and never see you again? Do you want me down on my knees, begging you for forgiveness for the rest of my life? What do you want?"

I bite my lip. I don't know what I expected to happen, but I never expected this. I could ask him to let me have Lily as a client. It would make my career if I did. But I won't. Unlike him, I want to win the job fair and square. I don't want to know that my whole career was made because Carter let me have it.

"Kiss me," I say.

His eyes search mine for just a second, as he's not sure if he actually heard the words that fell from my lips.

"Fuck it out of me. Fuck away all the pain. All the sexual tension. Fuck it all away."

8 CARTER

Victoria just told me to fuck her.

It's what I've been wanting to hear since the moment I saw her again. But, somehow, it feels like both the biggest mistake I could ever make and the best thing that I could ever do.

I gave her a chance to choose her career over me, and she chose me. She's putting her trust in me. A man who has hurt her more than any other person on this planet. I could use this to finish her for good or make her mine forever.

Or I could just fuck her. No emotions. No promises of anything more. Give her the best sex of her life. That's how I want her to remember me when this is all over. The best damn sex of her life. That's what I can give her.

I grab her face as I press my lips against hers. Her lips are the softest lips I've ever felt. When her tongue tangles with mine and her body presses against me, I know I just made the best damn decision of my life.

She's beautiful. But then she's always been beautiful. She's more than that now. She's hot. Her body fit and curvy. She's smart and stubborn. She's ambitious and ruthless. She's exactly what I want.

She pulls away, and I can feel her slipping away again. I can't handle not having her.

"What are you doing?"

"Trying to compose myself so that I don't let you fuck me right here, on the sidewalk."

I kiss her again, pulling her lip back into my mouth, as she moans. "I think you would like it if I fucked you right here."

She blushes. "You're probably right. But then we would both get arrested for indecent exposure, Lily would fuck up her interview, and we would both get fired, our careers over."

I raise an eyebrow. "It would be worth it, don't you think?"

She cocks her head to the side as she stares at me.

"Fine. We'll find a more suitable place to fuck."

"Thank you," she says, happy with her win.

I can see the wheels turning in her head. She grabs my hand and begins pulling me down the sidewalk, desperately trying to get to wherever we are going as fast as possible.

But she isn't the only one with ideas.

I let her lead me down one block before I can't take it any longer.

I grab her hips, and I push her against the brick building while I kiss her again.

"We. Have. To. Keep. Going," she says, kissing me between every word.

"No, we don't."

"We do if we are going to get to my car," she says as I kiss her neck.

I laugh. "We are not going to make it to your car."

She tangles her hands in my hair as she nibbles on my lip.

"Sure we are."

I kiss down her neck again and listen as she gasps.

"There is no way you will make it the two blocks to our cars," I whisper into her ear as my fingers dip inside her pants and beneath her panties to find her pussy already dripping for me. "You will come before I even get inside you. And I can't have that happen."

I pull my fingers back out and lick them while she breathes heavily.

"Fuck me. Now," she breathes.

I grin. I grab her hand, pulling her to the next door. She grabs my face as soon as we enter the building, and her lips kiss me. She can't get enough of me, and I can't get enough of her. She thinks one fuck is going to be enough to get whatever is going on between us out of our systems, but she is wrong.

It's going to take more than one fuck.

It's going to take more than one day.

More than one night.

I'm not sure if I can fuck her enough to get over her.

I keep kissing her as we walk. My hands do naughty things to her body. One hand grabs her ass, and the other pushes her shirt up, needing to feel her smooth skin. We are ridiculous. At least half a dozen people see us as we walk, but neither of us cares.

We continue to act like horny teenagers until we get to the elevators. I press the button, and the doors open automatically. I push Victoria inside and then stop a man who tries to walk onto the elevator with us.

"You don't want to be on this elevator with us, trust me," I say with a wink before the doors close.

I turn to Victoria, expecting her to be blushing from embarrassment but her eyes only deepen.

"Fuck me, Carter."

I press the emergency stop button on the elevator. "I plan to."

I walk toward her, taking my time, while she breathes in and out, in and out. She's terrified—that's what her breathing tells me—but she wants this anyway. She's willing to take the chance. And I'm going to make it more than worth the risk she feels she's taking.

I stop just as my body touches her. She's leaning against the elevator wall for support, like she can't even stand another second on her own.

"I won't hurt you."

She shakes her head. "You can't keep that promise."

"Sure I can."

"No, because I haven't even had you yet, and I already know that it's going to hurt like hell to have to stop."

"Then, we won't stop."

I grab her arms and push them high over her head as I kiss her against the wall, holding nothing back. She doesn't either. Whatever fear she has disappears the second I kiss her again.

She clutches my jacket and pushes it off my shoulders. I shake it off to the floor. I grab her blouse and rip it open, watching as the buttons pull apart.

"You owe me a shirt."

I laugh. "I think I owe you a lot more than that."

I lower my mouth to her breasts, which are peeking out of her red-hot bra. I kiss over the soft mounds as she pulls at my shirt. She rips my shirt apart, making it known that she is going to fight back with everything she has.

I reach my hands under her damn skirt, find her panties, and tear them down. She grabs my belt, undoes it and my pants, and roughly pushes them down.

Her eyes devour my cock while she licks her lips in anticipation.

"Like what you see?"

Her eyes burn into mine. "I'll like it better when you're fucking me with it."

I grin. "My pleasure."

I grab her bra with my teeth and rip the thin piece of material in the middle of her breasts before I take her newly freed nipple into my mouth.

"Damn it, Carter," she moans as I tease her nipple with my tongue. "That was my favorite bra."

"It might just be my favorite, too," I say before I take her other nipple into my mouth.

She arches her back. Her skin tastes salty from the sweat of being trapped in a tiny elevator with me.

I reach into the back of my pants and pull out a condom. I roll it onto my cock while I continue to tease her. The second I have the condom on, she jumps into my arms, wrapping her legs around my waist while she bites my neck.

I growl as she bites hard, paying me back for the pain I've caused her. I push her hard against the wall as my cock rests at her entrance.

She pulls her head back, so she can look me in the eye as I push my cock just a little into her pussy.

"More," she demands. "Please, God, more."

"I'll give you more than you can ever imagine."

I bury my cock deep inside her as her nails dig into my back.

I growl.

She grins and digs in further. Her mouth grabs my lip and pulls it into her mouth as I fuck her. Her eyes are devious with a gleam of how bad she knows this is but doesn't care. I could stare into her eyes all day if it wasn't for the rest of her body trying to fight for my attention.

Her skin glistens with sweat. Her breasts are swollen, and her nipples peaked. Her stomach is hard, and her pussy is tight as I fuck her.

I try to move slower so that this can last longer, but I can't. Because, every time I do, her moans beg me to move faster. Her nails dig into my back harder. Her pussy pulls me in deeper.

I can't slow down, but I'm going to make this the best sex she's ever had.

I push her harder against the wall as I fuck her.

She gasps before biting her lip.

She doesn't get to hold anything back.

"Let go," I say against her lips before I kiss her again, taking what little air she has away from her.

I kiss her.

She kisses me back harder.

I grab her breasts.

She claws my neck.

I thrust my cock inside her.

She pulls me in deeper.

I tease her clit.

She groans, taunting me with how much I want her in every possible way.

Her eyes sear into mine, and I know she feels it, too. Whatever this is between us, it's more than just sex. But neither of us can speak as to what it is right now.

"Let go of everything," I say, fucking her harder.

She doesn't move her gaze from mine as she begins to come undone. I've never seen a woman come so unashamedly and so passionately as when Victoria comes. Her whole face changes, becoming alive in a way I've never experienced.

She doesn't call out my name. She doesn't say anything. She doesn't need to. Her body says everything. That she hates me. That she forgives me. That she wants me. And that she wants to push me away.

I'm so focused on her that my own orgasm sneaks up on me out of nowhere. It radiates throughout my whole body as I take what I want from Victoria. I explode inside her, releasing everything that I have ever felt for her. Letting go of everything but what I'm feeling right now. A need to have Victoria in my bed every damn night.

"Fuck, Victoria," I growl.

I gently kiss her again, needing to feel her lips more desperately now than before I fucked her.

We stop the kiss at the same time. We stare deep into each other's eyes, trying to figure out what the hell just happened. But neither of us has a clue.

"You should probably put me down," Victoria finally says.

"I don't want to."

She bites her lip and then glances at the doors behind me. "I don't either, but I also don't want an employee to figure out how to open the elevator doors, only to see your bare ass."

I grin. "Why not? I have a fabulous ass."

She blushes. "I'm sure you do, but right now, no one gets to look at your ass but me," she says, winking at me.

I slowly place her on the ground, but I can't take my hands off her. I need to touch her. I need to have her again. I need to be near her. I need her to be mine.

One fuck was not enough. I don't know if I can fuck her enough.

She reaches down and picks up her bra and shirt off the floor. She puts the shirt on and then holds it closed since the buttons no longer work.

I pull my pants back up and pick up my shirt and jacket. I put my shirt on but don't bother trying with the buttons. Then, I entwine our fingers together as I walk to the elevator and start it again before pressing the button for the tenth floor.

"Where are we going?" she asks.

The elevator doors open, and a man is standing on the other side. He smirks when he sees us.

I glare at him as I pull Victoria behind me, trying my best to block his view of my girl.

Except she isn't yours, my stupid mind reminds me.

I glance back at Victoria, who raises an eyebrow at me. I pull her down the hallway and then reach into my pants and pull out the hotel key.

"Wait...you've had a hotel room this whole time?" Victoria says, stopping just outside the door.

I wince. "Yes."

"The entire time? You could have just come here instead of sleeping at Logan's?"

I nod.

"We could have had sex in an actual bed instead of in an elevator?"

"Well, what fun would that have been though?"

She sighs and walks into the hotel room that my assistant got for me just in case. I met my assistant at a coffee shop before I went to Logan's to get the key, but I knew that I wouldn't use it for anything except bringing women here. I just never imagined I would be bringing Victoria here. Now, I can't imagine wanting anything more than fucking her again.

She glances at the clock in the room. "We should clean ourselves up and find some new clothes before we get back to Lily. She should be back soon, and I don't want to get fired for the second time in a month."

I put my hands in my pockets as I watch her try to pretend like we didn't just have sex in an elevator.

"I'll let you shower first while I try to call Logan and see if he can bring us some clothes."

She frowns as she takes a seat on the edge of the bed.

"But then he'd be suspicious of what happened. Let me call around to some local stores first and see if they can bring us some clothes. You shower, and I'll get clothes. Then, we can try to figure out some way to be civil with each other in front of Lily."

With my hands in my pockets, I continue to just stare at her, waiting to see what she will do.

"Why aren't you moving? Shower now. We don't have time for this."

I take a step toward where she is sitting on the bed with her phone, ready to get to work, like she always is. She's a fixer. She fixes things, but sometimes, things don't need to be fixed.

"What are you doing?" she asks, annoyed.

I hold out my hand to her without saying a word. I'm not going to let her push what just happened under the rug. I'm not going to let her push me away.

She folds her arms across her chest. I love her fight, but despite her behavior, I can see in her eyes that she wants to touch my hand again.

"Come with me."

She glances down at my hand but doesn't budge. "Why?"

"Because I want you to."

Her breathing quickens as she looks into my eyes and realizes what I want. That I'm not through with her yet. I'm not sure I'll ever be through with her.

"I..."

"I want you, Victoria. Once was not enough."

I can't see her heart beating wildly in her chest, but I know it is. Her body is flushed, her breathing is fast, and I now know what my body does to her. The same that hers does to me. And I'm not going to spend the rest of the day with her without being able to touch her.

"We don't have time for whatever your deranged mind is thinking."

I lick my lips and watch as her eyes intensely hold their gaze on my lips. She might think she is hiding her feelings well, but I can read her like an open book.

"So, time is the problem?"

She nods slowly.

I pull out my phone and dial my assistant. "Ruby, I need you to get me and Victoria new clothes. Work professional and have them delivered to my hotel room in thirty minutes." I hang up the phone. "Clothes are taken care of."

She swallows hard, realizing that I'm going to win.

"Anything else I need to take care of for you to ensure that we have plenty of time?"

"We don't have time to have sex again. We both need to shower and get ready." She straightens the clothes she is wearing, fighting her grip on her blouse, trying to keep it closed so that I can't see even an inch of her skin.

I hold my hand out again. "Then, we will shower together."

She stares into my eyes and then places her soft hand into mine.

I grab her hand and pull her up from the bed until she is pressed against my body.

"What did you do to me?" she whispers.

I smirk. "I'm making you want me more than you hate me."

I grab her face and kiss her. Hard. This is what she needs to remember how badly she wants me.

Her tongue immediately pushes into my mouth, her hands grab the nape of my neck, and she moans when I stop the kiss.

"That's all you've got?" she teases.

"How did I never notice you before?"

I tuck her messy hair behind her ear even though it's about to get even messier.

"Because you're an idiot."

I grin and grab her hand again. I lead her into the bathroom, hoping to God the shower is big enough to hold both of us.

It is.

I need to remember to give Ruby, my assistant, a raise for getting me this hotel room with a large shower.

As soon as we get into the bathroom, Victoria attacks me. She kisses me like she thinks this is the last time she ever will again. That can't happen.

She rips my shirt off my shoulders and then jumps back, shocked.

"What's wrong?" I ask.

She holds her hands over her mouth as she stares at the mirror behind me. I glance over my shoulder and see the blood dripping down my back.

She spins me around and gingerly touches me on the back. "Did I do that?"

I chuckle. "Yes."

"I'm so sorry. I didn't—"

I turn around and grab her wrists, forcing her to stop touching me. "Don't apologize. You don't get to be sorry for showing me how badly you wanted me. I'm sure I deserved it anyway."

She grimaces, and I know she is still thinking about the wounds she caused on my back. Funny how, a few minutes earlier, she would have been more than happy to give me scars like that on my back. She wanted to rip me apart, but now, she wants to apologize. I think I prefer her wanting to rip me apart.

I lift her up as she squeals in my arms.

"What are you doing?"

I carry her into the shower and turn on the water; it's freezing cold.

She squeals louder. "Carter, stop!"

"No."

I kiss her as the cold water slowly starts to warm up as it pours over our still partially clothed bodies. But it quickly shuts her up, and she forgets about being sorry.

I link our fingers together as we kiss, nibble, lick. The water turns warm, and I kiss down her body, needing to touch every single place on her skin. Her grip on my hands tightens as I take her nipple into my mouth.

"Yes," she moans as I swirl my tongue around her nipple.

I turn her around and push her skirt down her body. I grab on to her ass. Her hands grab on to the shower wall.

I reach into my back pocket and pull out my last condom. *Damn it*. I should have told Ruby to get me more condoms as well.

Victoria reaches back, pulling at my pants, wanting me. Now.

I grin. "Touch yourself."

I don't have to tell her twice. I watch as her hand slips down her body. Little whimpers leave her body as she turns herself on. I'm not sure whether I want to turn her around to get a better view or fuck her right now.

I push my pants down and slide the condom on as the noises she makes get louder and louder.

"You'd better fuck me now, or I'm going to come without you," she says in a snarky voice.

God, this woman.

I grab her hips and push my cock into her pussy as the water continues to pour down on top of us.

"Finally," she moans loudly.

I used to think her voice was annoying. Now, I think it is the most fantastic sound in the world. And her voice gets even better when she is moaning because of me.

"What do you want, beautiful?" I ask, needing to hear more of her voice.

"Fuck me. Hard."

I do. I fuck her harder. She might hate being controlled in the boardroom, but here, she loves when I take over the control. She's begging for a man who can equal her during the day and then take over at night. She needs a man like me, and my dick can't imagine a life without her.

I fuck her until we both come. Until we are both completely exhausted. Yet we haven't had our fill. Too bad we are out of condoms and out of time.

"Can you hand me the shampoo?" Victoria asks.

I take the shampoo bottle behind me, and instead of handing it to her, I squeeze some on top of her head and then massage it into her hair.

"That's not what I asked you to do," she says, trying to sound annoyed.

I don't believe her. She likes me taking care of her.

"You didn't ask me to do this either." I take the washcloth and cover it with soap before I begin to wash her body. I run it over her arms, across her chest, and down her stomach before she grabs my wrist, stopping me.

"Don't."

I smirk. "Why not?"

"Because we will both get turned on, and we don't have time to fuck again."

"We are out of condoms, too," I groan.

She smiles as she rips the washcloth out of my hand and finishes washing herself. "See, the universe doesn't think it's a good idea either."

She steps back and rinses the shampoo and soap off her body. She steps out of the shower while my eyes follow her tight ass.

"I think the universe is wrong then."

She laughs as she wraps herself in a towel. I wash quickly and then rinse off. I turn the water off before stepping out and grabbing the remaining towel. I can see the hint of disappointment in her eyes as I wrap the towel around me.

"How are we going to handle Lily? We can't keep fighting in front of her, or we are both going to get fired. And I'm tired of getting fired."

"Really? Back to work, just like that?"

She nods. "This was a quick break to try to release some of the tension we were both feeling. That's it. We got it all out of our systems, and now, it's back to work."

I nod. "You're right. That wasn't the hottest sex that either of us has had. That didn't just heighten the sexual tension between us. We are just two people trying to work together. Nothing more."

"Right."

I tuck a strand of her wet hair behind her ear, and her eyes close at my touch as she revels in the feeling. It's the last touch, according to her.

"I won't argue with you anymore."

She raises an eyebrow.

"Fine. I won't argue with you in front of Lily anymore. You can be the lead on the interview since it seems that Lily cares more about what she looks like than what she should say."

Victoria frowns. "And I will let you be the lead on making sure she gets her coffee in the morning."

I smirk but don't argue with her. She wants to be the lead. I'll let her lead. I couldn't care less about Lily anymore. All I care about is finding a way to get Victoria undressed again as quickly as possible. And, if letting her have control over what happens with Lily does that, then so be it.

9 VICTORIA

"Wow, Lily, you look nice," I say as Lily walks back into her office.

"Just nice?" Lily asks, looking from me to Carter.

"You look beautiful," Carter says.

"Definitely beautiful," I say, hating how Carter is looking at Lily a little too much.

But then he looks at me and winks before his hand brushes against my thigh.

I suck in a breath. *Damn it.* This is going to be harder than I thought. I thought we would fuck once and then be done. Carter clearly has different ideas.

I cross my legs away from him and turn my attention back to Lily as I adjust the jacket that Carter's assistant sent for me. It fits well— almost too well. I don't even understand how she knew what size to bring me. I wait for Lily to ask why we are wearing different clothes than when we left, but she doesn't.

"Do you two have your crap together now?"

We both nod.

"Then, let's prepare for the interview."

"Great. Do you have any questions about the interview questions you read through or the direction we want you to try to guide the interview?"

"Nope. Seems pretty clear. I just need to figure out which dress I should wear."

Out of the corner of my eye, I see Carter give me an *I told you so* look. I roll my eyes back at him. Just because he's right doesn't mean he has to be arrogant.

"Well, let's see the choices," I say, hoping I can get some question prep in as she shows me the dresses.

"Yes, I'd love to see you in the different dress options," Carter says, obviously trying to make me jealous by giving Lily attention.

It's working.

I'm ridiculously jealous. It's stupid. I shouldn't be jealous. For one, it's clear he is into me, not Lily. He just fucked me, not her. And, two, I'm not into him. It was a one-time thing. Okay, two-time thing. I shouldn't feel jealous or anything toward him.

I look over at his cocky grin. The only problem is, I don't know how to tell my body that.

"YOU LOOK BEAUTIFUL," I hear Carter's voice say from behind me.

"Thanks—" I say and then stop as I turn around and realize that Carter isn't talking to me. He's talking to Lily.

I plaster a fake smile on my face. "Absolutely gorgeous."

Lily lights up as she stands just offstage in her dark green dress. She decided on the green one after Carter said it brought out the green in her eyes. I have to agree. She looks gorgeous in it, and it's perfect for the occasion. Just enough sex appeal without looking too sexy.

"You ready?" I ask Lily.

"Of course," she responds.

She looks at Carter like she wants to eat him up. Of course she does. He's hot. Even more so now that he's trying to make me jealous by giving Lily extra attention.

"Good. You're going to do great," I say.

"We are ready for you, Lily," one of the assistants says.

Carter leans forward and whispers something in her ear before kissing her on the cheek.

My heart stops as I watch him with another woman. Even doing something as innocent as kissing her on the cheek. I glare at him as he walks over to where I am, so we can watch Lily on the monitors together.

"I know we aren't together, and you aren't the type of guy who does relationships, but you could at least wait twenty-four hours before you start flirting with another woman in front of me."

His fingers brush against mine. "Someone's jealous."

I roll my eyes. I shouldn't have started this conversation with him.

"Let's just do our jobs and make sure that Lily's interview goes well."

He moves behind me, rubbing my shoulders. "Relax. It's out of our hands now. Now, it's up to Lily."

I fold my arms across my chest as I stare intently while Lily walks out to the couch across from Phoebe. I will not think about Carter again until the interview is over. And, even then, I will only think of him professionally. I will not have sex with him again. The sex might be amazing, but it's not worth the pain I would definitely experience afterward.

The interview starts out pleasantly enough. But then Phoebe turns her questions in a harsher direction, like I was expecting.

"Are you and Phillip still together?" Phoebe asks.

"No, we aren't," Lily says.

I nod. *Come on, you can do this, Lily.*

"So, you are with Jacob?"

"No, I'm alone," Lily says.

I wince when she says *alone*. She's supposed to be coming across as a strong, independent woman. Not weak. Not a woman in need of a man.

"Alone? You don't seem like the type of woman who likes to be alone. You were with two men at the same time after all. I don't believe that there is no special someone in your life right now."

Lily freezes.

I turn to Carter. "She's fucked," I say.

He nods, grabbing the nape of his neck while he watches the disaster begin to unfold.

Think, I say to myself, pacing.

There has to be a way to fix this. That is what I do. Maybe I can find a way to turn the power off and shut down the whole production. Maybe this won't actually air. I might have to sleep with someone, but I can convince them to air an old episode instead of this one.

As I walk, Carter's eyes stay fixed on the screen. Same goes for the backstage crew. Except for the women. Most of the women are either blatantly staring at Carter or sneaking a look. He's attractive. One of the most attractive men I've ever seen. And he clearly has the attention of everyone in the room.

I wanted Lily to have her chance to do this on her own. But she fucked that up the second she wouldn't prepare with me. So, now, she's going to have to do this with a man by her side.

"Carter," I hiss.

He turns toward me with a grin. He clearly thinks I think we should just sneak off and have sex somewhere since Lily is such a lost cause.

"Take off your jacket," I say.

His grin brightens as he takes it off.

I undo the top couple of buttons on his shirt.

"You know I want you, Victoria, but I think we should go somewhere more private before you undress me completely," he says with a wink.

I ignore him as I spit in my hand and then fluff his hair, making it a little messier.

"Roll up your sleeves."

"Why?" he asks, realizing that I'm no longer doing this for sex.

"Because you are about to go on camera."

His eyes widen, but I don't give him time to fight me.

I run over to the production assistant. "Have them go to commercial. We have Lily's boyfriend, and he's willing to go on camera after the break."

The PA's eyes light up as she signals to go to commercial.

"I am not pretending to be her boyfriend," Carter says to me as the hair and makeup team swarm him. "And I'm definitely not going on camera, looking like a slob," he says as the team rolls up his sleeves, like I told him to do earlier.

I shake my head, staring at him with a smile in my eyes. "You are going on camera. You put me in charge of the interview, remember?"

He glares at me. "I am not doing this."

"Yes, you are."

"How is this going to make anything better? How is her fucking three men better than her fucking two men?"

"Because you are going to go on and be charming. You are going to provide a hot distraction for the audience. You are going to say that you used to date Lily in high school. You went your separate ways in college, but you have wanted her ever since. She felt the same way, but you had a girlfriend, and she had a fiancé. But she wasn't happy because the true love of her life was with another woman. She hated herself for not fighting harder for you. But, after everything happened, you realized how much you loved her. You're going to go on and say that everything that Lily did was because she had lost her true love. And, now, you are back in her life. You're going to say that true love conquers all."

Carter searches my eyes. He knows I'm right. He knows that my plan will work. But it doesn't stop him from hating this plan.

He's shoved onstage before he gets a chance to stop it from happening.

I walk back to the monitors to watch. He's charming, attractive, and smart. He offers the distraction that is needed to make people forget about all the bad things Lily did. Clearly, if she got Carter to fall for her, she can't be that bad. The host even falls for Carter. Everyone does.

It doesn't take Lily long to figure out the plan and go along with it. She holds his hand and flirts with him like she really wants him. She probably does. Everyone else watching wants him.

I want him. I just can't have him. I've just sealed my fate by making him publicly pretend to be in love with another woman. He's going to have to pretend to be with her for at least a year until she gets elected. Maybe even for the duration of her term.

I'm not going to be able to do this. I'm not going to be able to watch him pretend to be in love with another woman. It's only a matter of time until the pretending becomes real anyway.

I can't watch this. Not when I'm falling for a man I can never have. I need to get out of here. So, that's what I do. I leave.

10 CARTER

I throw the door open to Logan's apartment, pissed. I spent the last few hours trapped in a world I never wanted to be in. My assistant, Ruby, thought this is what I wanted. And maybe, for a split second, I thought this was exactly what I wanted. But I was wrong. It was complete torture. And my wants have changed.

I take a step inside and slam the door shut. I head down the hallway to find Victoria.

Logan steps in front of me with a deep grimace, folding his arms across his chest. "What did you do?" he asks.

"What did *I* do? Are you serious? This is your sister's fault."

"I know my sister, and I know you. What did you do?"

"Move, Logan."

"No, not until you talk to me. What happened?"

The bedroom door cracks open, and Victoria stands there, staring at me with wide eyes and a smirk on her flawless face.

I cock my head to the side as I look at Victoria, not Logan. "Victoria decided to make me Lily's new boy toy by pushing me onstage to appear on national TV to discuss a nonexistent relationship with her, effectively deciding what my relationship status will be for at least a year, most likely longer, all so that she could fix Lily's problems after our client didn't listen to us."

Logan turns and looks at Victoria, who confirms my story with the light in her eyes.

I pull out the hotel key card and hold it out to Logan. "Pack a bag, and go stay in my hotel room tonight. It's on me."

Logan looks from me to Victoria.

"You're not going anywhere, Logan. This is your apartment. You are staying here," Victoria says.

I grab Logan's arm, getting his attention again, and I press the card into the palm of his hand. "You owe me, Logan."

Logan frowns. "I don't owe either of you anything. It's more like you both owe me plenty."

Victoria stands next to him, pulling his attention back to her. "I'm your sister. Do what I say, and stay here. Please."

Logan sighs.

"The hotel is the nicest in the city. You can bring the hottest women back to that room. They will think you are a millionaire. Please."

Logan ignores both of us and walks to his bedroom.

I grab the nape of my neck in frustration.

"Some friend you are!" I shout in his direction.

Victoria takes the moment as a win and turns to head back to the guest bedroom. She thinks that, if Logan is here, then we won't fight. That I'll just let her be. But she's very, very wrong.

I go after her just as Logan opens the door to his bedroom with a bag over his shoulder.

I grin.

Victoria's mouth drops open. "What are you doing?" she asks.

"I'm going to stay in Carter's hotel room."

"Why?"

"Because I think you two have a lot of things to work out. I've

97

been in the middle of you two for far too long, and I won't keep doing it."

Logan leans toward Victoria's ear and whispers something that I don't hear before softly kissing her on the cheek. He glares at me as he walks past me, and then I wait until I hear the front door slam behind him before I turn my attention to Victoria. As much as Logan says that he's not picking sides, it sure does seem like he might be picking mine from the way he gave in to my demands.

Victoria crosses her arms and pops her hip out to one side. "Let's hear it. I don't have all day. I need to get to work to revamp our entire plan for Lily, and unlike you, I don't have an assistant I can call to do all my dirty work."

I smirk. "Don't blame me for doing good enough work that allows me to afford an assistant."

She shakes her head. "Don't even act like you do better work than me. I saved us in there."

"*You* saved us?" I run my hand through my hair to keep from strangling her. "You have got to be kidding! You threw me out in front of the cameras because you couldn't come up with anything better. I did all the work. I came up with the stories about Lily and me being together on the spot. I charmed the crowd. I spent all evening pretending to care about a woman. I did all of the real work."

"Fine. You did all of the real work. I'm just taking credit for that work. Just like you did to me earlier."

I hate her. But I also want her. I hate how she's exactly like me. I don't remember her always being like this, but I also love that she is. I'm afraid I've ruined her, turning her heart cold like mine, but maybe I made her that much better.

"I want to fuck you."

She laughs. "I'm not fucking you."

I take a step forward until I can tuck a strand of her hair behind her ear. "You sure about that? I'm pretty sure you've said that before, and it's ended in me giving you the best sex of your life."

"It wasn't the best sex of my life."

"No? Who was better?"

Her eyes dart to the side as she thinks about it. Running names through her head, trying to come up with an answer.

"Andrew. Andrew was better."

"When did you date Andrew?"

"Two years ago."

"Why was he the best sex of your life?"

I see the fight in her eyes. She's not going to give in to me.

"I'm not talking about my sex life with you."

"Because it isn't true. I'm the best sex of your life."

Victoria's face blushes bright red. "Because he loved me. That's why he was the best sex of my life. We were in love."

My heart drops at her honesty. I know I'm the best sex she has ever had. Except for Andrew. Even if he was horrible in bed. Even if he had no idea how to kiss her, how to move her body, how to make her forget about everything. Even if he was horrible, he loved her, and that apparently makes all the difference.

"Well, give me a chance to change your mind. I'm sure you gave Andrew plenty of chances."

Victoria walks past me to the kitchen. She opens the fridge and stares inside at the contents. She starts pulling out a carton of eggs and some bread.

"I'm not talking to you about having sex again. A momentary lack of judgment led to it in the first place. It was just us trying to release our frustrations with each other. That's it. We should talk about what you pretending to be Lily's boyfriend now means."

She turns, and I'm standing right in her way.

She gasps, and I grin.

"What are you doing?" I ask, looking down at her supplies.

"Making dinner."

I grab the carton of eggs and bread out of her hands. "Eggs and toast aren't dinner. It's barely enough food to make breakfast."

She snatches the food back out of my hands. "I'm not that hungry, and Logan doesn't have much food in the fridge."

I grin.

"Will you please move?" she says, clearly annoyed with me.

"You don't know how to cook."

"I do, too. I just don't want to spend time cooking when there are other more important things to do, and like I said, Logan doesn't keep much food in the house."

I nod and smugly walk over to the fridge. I quickly scan it before pulling out some chicken, brussels sprouts, lettuce, and carrots. I move to the pantry and pull out some potatoes. Then, I lay them on the counter.

"Prove it then."

She puts her hands on her hips, like she always does when she is mad and wants to make a point. "No. I don't have to prove anything to you."

"Prove to me that you can cook a simple meal, and I'll stop talking about fucking you. Cook me dinner, and I'll be a good boy and discuss what your crazy plan is now that I'm pretending to date Lily."

She grins. "Fine. What do you want me to make you?"

"Anything that you want with the ingredients in front of you."

She stares at them with wide eyes, not having a clue what to do.

I laugh. "How about some grilled chicken with mashed potatoes, roasted brussels sprouts, and a salad with carrots?"

She nods and then starts opening drawers, pulling out a tiny knife and a cutting board. I take a seat at a bar stool opposite her.

I hold back a laugh as she pulls out the carrots and begins attempting to chop them without peeling off the skin. Each chop requires the full force of her knife in order to make a slice in the carrot.

I laugh. I can't help it.

I get up and walk behind her, placing my hands on hers. "First, you need to peel the carrots."

I reach into the drawer next to her and pull out a peeler. I replace the knife in her hand with the peeler. My hands stay on her hands as

I show her how to move the peeler down the carrot. I feel her suck in a breath as I move my head next to hers under the pretext of looking at the carrot.

I reach back into the drawer and pull out a chef's knife. I take the peeler out of her hand and replace it with the knife.

"Then, you can cut the carrot into pieces." My hand glides over hers as I show her how to properly cut it. I can feel her pulse beating faster in her wrist.

I take a step back and let her continue by herself. She takes a deep breath as she adjusts to the emptiness.

"So, what is your grand plan for Lily now?" I ask, leaning on the bar behind her so that I can stare at her body without her judging eyes.

"Um...what?"

I grin. She can act like I don't affect her at all, but it's a lie.

"Nothing," I say, happy not to talk about work right now. It will only make me angry, remembering exactly what she did to me. "You should probably start on the chicken if you want to eat tonight."

She gives me a dirty look over her shoulder.

"Do you want some help?" I ask, crossing my arms.

"No."

She takes the chicken and plops it into a grill pan before putting it on the stove and turning the stove on high.

She walks back over to her cutting board, and after pulling the brussels sprouts out, she cluelessly stares at them.

She takes her knife and chops down hard. The brussels sprout goes flying away from her.

I chuckle.

"I don't like brussels sprouts anyway. Let's just stick to every-thing else."

I grin and nod while I resist helping her again.

She takes the potatoes, puts them into a pot, covers them with water, and then places it on the stove.

I snicker.

"What?"

"It's going to take hours to boil the potatoes if you don't cut them up first."

"I knew that."

She takes the pot back over to the counter. She pulls the soaking wet potatoes out of the pot and places one on the chopping board. She starts cutting and chops it into tiny pieces.

I shake my head. She's one of the smartest, strongest women I've ever met. *How does she not have a clue as to how to cook?*

I walk behind her again, and she freezes, already anticipating my touch.

"Need some help?" I ask, keeping my distance.

"No," she says stubbornly. She walks to the fridge, searching for something. When she finally finds what she has been looking for, she smiles and pulls it out. "Cheese makes everything better."

I shake my head at her as she pulls out some shredded cheese and pops it into her mouth. She's avoiding my touch, which just makes me want to touch her more.

I have a dairy intolerance, but I'll deal with some stomach cramps in order to get what I want.

I walk over to her and reach into the bag she's holding. I eat some of the cheese as she watches me with large eyes.

She tries to walk around me, but I make sure our hands brush against each other.

She goes back to the cutting board and starts angrily cutting the potatoes again.

"Ouch!" she yells.

I'm behind her in two seconds. My arms are around her body as I take her cut finger into my hands. She's bleeding pretty badly. I pull her hand over to the sink where I turn on the faucet, running cold water, and I begin washing the wound, trying to get the bleeding to stop.

It takes a few minutes, but it finally stops. I turn the water off, and then I lean down and gently kiss her finger.

"All better. I should get a Band-Aid for that," I say, trying to ignore her beating heart and how she looks at me like I just saved her life instead of just healing her finger that would have healed without my assistance.

I sweep past her, but she grabs on to my shirt, stopping me.

She narrows her gorgeous eyes at me as she peers into mine. I don't know what she's doing. I don't know what she's thinking. Her hand moves slowly up my body until it reaches my neck, and then she pulls my neck down until she cautiously kisses me on the lips.

My hands grab her face as I deepen the kiss. Her kisses say so much that I know she would never tell me with her words. They say, *You were right.* They say, *I'm sorry.* They say, *Thank you.*

She pulls away, realizing what she just did, as she wipes her mouth on the back of her hand. She doesn't say anything. She just stands there, looking at me.

"I'll go get a Band-Aid," I say, keeping my promise not to talk about having sex with her again.

I walk quickly to the bathroom, and after searching for a couple of minutes, I come back with a Band-Aid in hand.

"Found one," I say as I return to her in the kitchen.

She hasn't moved an inch since I left. She's clearly lost in her own thoughts when I walk back over to her.

I open the Band-Aid and then take her hand in mine. I place the Band-Aid on her finger.

I lean my head down to kiss her finger again because I can't pass up that opportunity when she grabs my face and kisses me hard again with a force I wasn't expecting.

I stutter backward as I wrap her in my arms and kiss her back.

"I hate you," she says, breaking from the kiss.

"I know." I pull her bottom lip into my mouth, needing this more than she knows.

"And you hate me."

I nod.

"Good. Just so we understand that this changes nothing."

I grin. She's very, very wrong about that. This changes every-thing. If the first time was a mistake and the second time was a bigger mistake, then the third time is a choice. It means that, despite how mad she is at me, she wants this more.

She grabs my shirt, ripping it open, just like I did to her earlier. Her eyes devour my hard body.

"Damn it," she says.

"What?"

"Why does your body have to be so hot? I've spent a week with you, and I haven't seen you work out once. You shouldn't be this good-looking."

I give her my sexiest grin before I kiss her neck. I grab the hem of her shirt and lift it over her head.

I take a step back to really look at her body. "Talk about hot bodies."

She blushes, and I love it.

"You've been a naughty girl," I say, grabbing her hips and pulling her back toward me.

"Yeah? How?" She moans against my lips as her soft lips kiss me again.

I grab the sweatpants that she changed into and push them down her body. I turn her around and slap her hard on the ass. "You forced me to pretend to date a woman who isn't you."

I slap her again, and she yelps.

She turns her face toward me as she bites her lip. "Does that mean that I have to be punished?"

My eyes deepen with that thought. "Yes."

She bites her lip harder but I realize it's not because I turn her on. It's because she is stifling a laugh.

"You think it's funny that I want to punish you?"

She turns around and swallows as she takes a step away. "Yes."

We both make our move at the same time. She runs, and I chase after her.

She doesn't make it far before I grab her body, pulling her back to me. She grabs the cheese and begins throwing it at me, trying to get me to let her go. I grab her hand and eat the cheese out of it to get her to stop. I suck each of her fingers into my mouth, and she melts.

I should punish her. Make her pay for hurting me. But that would mean not having sex with her. And that would punish me.

Instead, I reach around her back and undo her bra, watching as her plump breasts show themselves to me again. She grabs her panties and pushes them down, and then she's naked, standing in the kitchen.

I groan at the sight of her. Her body is glorious. Her skin is smooth, her boobs are delicious, and her smooth stomach leads down to the tightest pussy.

Her entire body distracts me with thoughts of what I can do with her. Fuck her on the counter, in the living room, or in a bed. Claim her mouth, her pussy, her ass. I want it all.

I look into her eyes though, and I see something there that I didn't see before. Fear.

"Why?" I ask, wanting to know why she pushed me into Lily.

She sucks in a breath as I slowly undo my pants and remove them along with my boxers and shirt.

"Because I was scared."

I grab her and lift her onto the counter, needing her here and now. I need to look into her eyes when she comes. I need to understand everything about her.

My cock hardens as I kiss her. I push against her and then stop, resting my hands on her thighs.

She grabs my face, trying to pull me to her again.

"I need to go get a condom," I say, hating myself for not having a ready stash on hand.

"No, you don't."

My eyes light up at the thought of fucking her without a condom.

I grab on to her and start kissing her again as I push my cock at her entrance. She swats me away.

"What?" I ask.

She looks in the direction of her sweatpants. I grin as I reach down and pick them up off the floor. I dig through the pockets and find a condom, holding it up to her lips.

"Now, tell me, why do you have a condom in your sweatpants? You weren't planning on seducing me when I got home, were you?"

She bites her lip. "No."

I rip the condom open, roll it onto my cock, and then thrust inside her.

"Liar."

Her nails dig roughly into my back as I thrust. I just can't figure out if she is pulling me closer or pushing me away as I fuck her.

She wants this, but she won't ever admit it to herself, let alone me.

I kiss down her neck. I kiss every inch of her breasts, all while fucking her with everything I have.

She moans and groans as she fights with herself, trying to decide if she should hold back or tell me how she really feels.

I'm not going to let her have a choice. I need the truth. Now.

I fuck her faster, pulling more groans from her strong body.

"Why are you afraid?" I ask without having to mention what specifically I'm talking about. We both know I'm talking about Lily.

I grab her hips, pushing harder into her slick opening.

Her eyes shoot wide, looking at me with terror. She doesn't want to tell me. Or maybe she doesn't want to admit the truth to herself, but I need to know.

"What are you so scared of?"

I push harder, holding on to her, not letting her go until I get an answer. I watch her breathing quicken. Her heart is racing, and her whole body is so alive that I know one flick of my tongue over her nipple would be enough to make her come. But I won't let her, not until she answers me.

She fiercely looks back at me, trying to come on her own without my help. Her hand goes to her breast, ready to get herself off.

I grab her wrist, stopping her before she has the chance. She glares at me, but it's just a mask for the fear.

"What are you afraid of?"

"You," she says.

She moves her hips forward to rub her clit against me. It's enough. I feel her pussy clenching against my cock. She growls deep in her throat as her orgasm rolls through her body.

I let go and fuck her hard until my own orgasm pulses through my body. She wants it to be a distraction. She wants me to forget her answer, but there is no way I can forget it.

We both come down, breathing quickly as we stare into each other's eyes.

"Why are you afraid of me?"

"Because you've hurt me so many times before. But those times would be nothing if I let myself fall in love with you. You would break my heart."

I open my mouth, but she kisses me, keeping any words from leaving my mouth.

"Don't make promises you can't keep. You would break my heart. Now that you are with Lily, it can't happen."

The smoke detector starts blaring loudly. Victoria jumps off the counter and races over to where the chicken is burning on the stovetop while I fan the smoke away from the smoke detector.

She thinks I would hurt her. She's right. I've made too many mistakes in the past when it comes to Victoria to be given a second chance. One big mistake comes to mind. When she finds out about it, she will never forgive me. But there would be nothing to forgive if she never found out.

We could start over. This could be our fresh start. It will be complicated with the whole Lily situation, but I've never wanted a woman more than I want Victoria.

"So, I lied. I can't cook," Victoria says, dumping the pan into the sink.

I grin before softly kissing her on the lips. "You are an amazing woman with plenty of skills, but no, cooking isn't one of them. Good thing I can cook."

She smiles, oblivious to my plan. She's already mine, and she doesn't even know it yet. I won't ever hurt her again. I just have to find a way to prove it.

11 VICTORIA

I step out of the bathroom after a long night of sex with Carter. Sex in the kitchen. Sex in the living room. Sex in the bedroom. Followed by sleeping hard in his arms. It was a night I would love to repeat over and over again till the end of time.

I can't though. Today, it has to stop.

I walk into the kitchen to make coffee and a piece of toast, but I quickly change my plans when I see Carter standing in the kitchen with a large grin on his face. I just need to get out of here as fast as possible and grab breakfast on the way.

I walk around the island to grab my briefcase before heading out, but Carter blocks my way.

"Really? This is your genius plan—block my path out of here so that I have to talk to you?"

He smirks and pulls out the barstool at the counter. "My plan is to feed you a real breakfast while I convince you that this can work."

I glance over at the plate. The smells hit my nostrils all at once. Pancakes, bacon, and eggs. I've never eaten so much food for breakfast at one time. But he went all out.

I sigh as I take a seat and begin to dig into the food that Carter prepared for me.

"How is it?"

"Delicious," I say, annoyed that he can cook so well. *It's just pancakes*, I remind myself. But they are the best pancakes I've ever had.

"Good."

I shovel another bite into my mouth. "So, your plan is to cook delicious food for me so that I'll forget about everything else and do everything you want?"

He shrugs.

"It's working," I say with a sigh.

He grins as he takes his fork and tries to get a bite off my plate. I stab his hand with my fork.

"Ow."

"This is mine."

He laughs and leans back. "Fine. But you're mine."

I almost choke on the food in my mouth. I swallow quickly and take a drink of coffee to wash down the rest.

"I'm not your anything, Carter. I'm your coworker; that's it."

"A coworker who has had sex with me how many times now?" he says with his grin that makes me want to do anything for him.

"We can't keep doing this."

"Why not?" He folds his arms across his chest.

"Because of Lily."

"You do realize that what Lily and I have is fake. It's not real. We are just acting to save her career, which was your idea."

"I know. But we can't because, if we got caught together, it would ruin Lily's career."

"We won't get caught. Trust me."

I don't answer. I just keep eating my pancakes.

"What are your other problems with us?"

I push the pancake around with my fork, trying to avoid talking about this.

"I know you like me. The sex is amazing. We could be incredible together. Just give us a shot."

"As I told you before, I don't trust you not to hurt me. We haven't even gone on a real date. All we've done is have sex or fight. You can't build a relationship on that."

He grins, leaning on the counter over my food. "Go out with me tonight."

I shake my head. "We can't. If we got caught—"

"If anyone saw us together, we would just play it off as two consultants on Lily's team, discussing our plan over dinner, nothing more."

I search his eyes, trying to find the asshole that I know is in there somewhere.

"Give me one chance. Go out with me on one date. If you still think us being together is a bad idea, then I'll leave you alone. But, if you enjoy yourself, then we can talk about a plan for us to continue dating. Do we have a deal?"

I try to think about what the cons are to agreeing to such a deal. But I can't, not when he's smiling at me with such hope. I want to go out with him. I want to go out on a date with this fun man. I want to go out with the man who could change my whole world.

"Okay. Just one date."

⸙

"YOU SHOULDN'T WALK in with me," I hiss to Carter as we walk into the building where Lily's office is.

"Why not?" Carter says, grabbing my hand.

I pull my hand out of his. "Because we can't look like a couple."

He laughs. "You think anyone is paying attention to us? They are all wrapped up in their own lives; they won't notice two people they don't even know."

A young woman comes up to Carter. "Oh my God! Are you Carter Woods? I saw you with Lily on TV last night. I had no idea the two of you were a couple. And that story you told about how you fell in love? It was beautiful."

"I'm glad you enjoyed our story," Carter says, darting his worried gaze toward me.

"I'm Jillian, I'm one of the paralegals for Lily," the woman says, holding out her hand to Carter.

Carter shakes her hand. "It's nice to meet you, Jillian."

"Lily is already in her office, but if you are looking for a place to be alone, there is a restroom on the top floor that nobody ever uses." She winks at him.

Carter smiles. "Thanks for the tip."

I start walking to Lily's office, and Carter jogs after me seconds later.

"Hold up, Victoria."

I slow because I know he will make a bigger scene if I don't walk with him.

"We can't do this. A random stranger from Lily's office noticed you, and we are barely even inside the building. We will get caught if we go on a date."

Carter stops in front of me. "You promised. One date. I will take you to the most hidden restaurant I can find. No one will know. Okay?"

I nod, hoping that something will happen between now and then that will not let me go on that date. Because I know, if I go, he's going to be charming and wonderful and perfect. He's going to buy me flowers and hold my hand. He's going to tell me all the lovely reasons he likes me. He's going to give me his jacket when I get cold and then turn into an animal who kisses me and then fucks me in the cab on the way home. And, after a date like that, I'm going to fall. Completely and fully in love with him because I've wanted him since we were kids. I've wanted nothing more than to make him fall desperately in love with me, but he was always with someone else.

I can't let myself fall in love with him. Because, as much as I want to think that he has changed, I know he hasn't. One day, he will flip the switch again and turn back into the monster I know he has hidden deep inside.

We walk upstairs to Lily's office. I knock before entering. I walk in with Carter close behind.

Then, Lily attacks Carter.

Lily's arms wrap around his neck as she launches at him. And then she presses her lips against his and kisses him. Not a chaste kiss. Not a *thank you so much for saving my butt yesterday* kiss. A real *I want you right here, and I don't care who is watching* kiss.

My mouth falls open at the sight, but I quickly recover. I twirl my hair around my finger, trying to distract myself. I try to force my eyes away from the two of them kissing. But, even if I could manage to somehow tear my eyes away, I could never stop seeing the two of them together over and over in my head.

I knew that sleeping with Carter was going to result in agony. And I was right. I can tell by the look on Carter's face that he is just as shocked as I am about the kiss, that this isn't what he wants. But it doesn't matter. This is our life now. He has to pretend to date Lily. That's the job. And it's going to be the worst pain I've ever felt, watching him with another woman. It doesn't matter that it's pretend to Carter. It's clearly not pretend to Lily.

Carter slowly pushes her back from his lips, and he stares at her with wide eyes. He wipes his lips. "Um...it's good to see you, too," Carter says, backing up toward the door like he wants to run.

I want him to run, too. Forget about this stupid job and just run. I'll chase after him. It can be just like when we were kids, and he chased me all over the playground. Except, this time, when I catch him, he won't push me down. He'll fuck me.

Lily's face lights up. "It's a very, very good day, Carter. The best day in fact."

Carter rubs the back of his neck. "And why is it the best day?"

"Because I have the most amazing boyfriend ever."

"I'm not your—"

A knock on the door stops Carter from speaking.

"Yes?" Lily asks.

"I have a DVD from last night for you," says a small, petite woman when she pokes her head inside.

"Thank you," Lily says, holding her hand out to take the DVD.

Before she begins to walk out of the room, the woman eyes Carter like he's the most delicious man she's ever seen. Lily walks over and takes his arm. She takes the arm of *my* man. I tightly grip my hands together to keep from attacking Lily and claiming Carter as my own. But it's clear that Lily is just as jealous, except she's jealous of a woman who wasn't doing anything other than looking.

When the woman leaves, Lily walks over to the door and closes it. She glares at Carter, still ignoring that I'm even in the room.

"You can't talk like that! There are plenty of people in this office who would head straight to the first reporter if given the chance. If we are going to do this, we have to make it believable. I get in trouble when I don't." She drapes her arm around Carter again. "Plus, I think, after you see this"—she holds up the DVD—"you are going to remember just how good we are together, and we won't have to pretend anymore."

My eyes widen. I glance over at Carter, giving him a *this bitch is crazy* look, as Lily fumbles with the DVD player.

I'll handle it, Carter mouths to me.

I roll my eyes. There is no way he is going to figure a way out of this. Whatever I missed last night made Lily completely smitten with Carter. He was either too good of an actor or...I can't think of the alternative. As much as I thought I could stop this before I had any true feelings for Carter, it's impossible. I've had feelings since we were kids. Kissing Carter, letting him touch me, fuck me made my feelings that much stronger.

"There," Lily says, proud of herself, as the video begins playing. She quickly fast-forwards through the part of the interview where she fell apart.

I should have let the bitch burn out there, I think as I keep my distance. I don't want to see her pretend to be dating my boyfriend.

Boyfriend.

He's not my boyfriend. Not even close. But, right now, I want nothing more than to walk across this room, grab his neck, and show Lily what a real kiss looks like between two people who actually care about each other.

She presses play as she holds out her hand to Carter. I watch his hand. I watch him hesitate for the tiniest of milliseconds, considering holding her hand. It's unfair of me to judge him so closely. I probably even made it up. I'm just torturing myself.

Carter takes a seat at the table near the TV that one of Lily's assistants must have brought in, but he doesn't take her hand. Lily drops her hand with a hint of disappointment on her pursed lips as she leans against the table, ensuring that she can be as close to Carter as humanly possible. I stay standing near the door. I might as well not even be here.

I try to pretend like I don't care. That whatever happens on the TV won't affect me. I know who Carter really wants. Me. Nothing else matters.

But, as they begin speaking, telling stories from high school that I know to be true, it feels less like pretend and more like a real thing between them.

"Give her a kiss," the host says.

My heart sinks. It's just a kiss, but it's a kiss before millions of people on national TV. Something that I can never have. At least, not anytime soon.

I find my legs bringing me forward to watch what is happening on the screen as the crowd eggs them on, wanting them to show their affection in front of them. I walk until I'm standing only a foot from the TV.

I watch as the host asks again for them to kiss, knowing that she's given the crowd enough time to get excited about the two of them. I watch as Carter leans over to Lily and kisses her. I watch his eyes close. I watch his tongue push into her mouth. I watch his hands tangle in her hair. I watch him kiss her like I don't exist.

I don't. It was a lie. I just thought Lily and the world were the ones being lied to, not me.

"That was a genuine kiss, wasn't it, Victoria?" Lily asks.

I nod because my throat is far too dry to speak.

"See? Victoria agrees. We should be together, Carter. Look at us on the screen. We look great together. If I remember correctly, the sex was amazing," Lily says, inching her way toward Carter.

I can't listen to this anymore, or I'm going to vomit or scream or wring both of their necks for letting me get involved in this mess between the two of them.

"I'm going to give you two a minute to figure out whatever is going on between you. I'll be back in a half hour or so to figure out what the plan is," I say, walking toward the door.

Carter pops up, running until he beats me to the door. "Stay."

I shake my head. "You two have plenty that you need to work out."

"Victoria," he says my name.

One word, but I can tell everything he is feeling. Pain, scared, need, lust, sorry. All the feelings I need him to feel.

I scoot past him, walking out the door, telling him how I feel without a word. Betrayed.

I keep walking until I exit the building, until fresh air hits my face. I take a deep breath as I stand outside, able to really think for the first time all day. *I'll take a walk. Just circle the block a couple of times. Give Carter a chance to talk to Lily.*

And then, when I come back, he can talk to me.

I walk briskly, trying to get as much of my frustration and pain out as possible. But walking quickly doesn't help.

I try to reason with myself. I convince myself that their kiss meant nothing. It was just Carter acting, that he wants me, not Lily.

I try distracting myself. I think about Sailor, Amber, my mom. I have hardly talked to any of them since coming here.

I pull out my phone and dial Amber's cell. Sailor isn't out of school yet, but I can call and just check on my sister. I'll call Sailor later in the day.

"Hi," Sailor's meek voice answers the phone.

"Sailor, what are you doing home from school? Are you sick or playing hooky?" I tease, happy. Whatever reason my niece is home, it means I get to talk to her for a few minutes, lighting up my day.

"Amber didn't drive me to school."

My heart sinks. "What do you mean? Sailor, can you put Amber on the phone? I'll talk to you again in a second, I promise. I have a funny story to tell you about an old high school friend of mine."

"I can't. She's asleep."

My heart stops. All my worst fears start flying through my head. That something happened to Amber. She committed suicide. She overdosed. She finally gave up.

"Okay, Sailor. I need to hang up a minute to call Grandma, and then I'll call you right back, okay?"

"Okay."

I reluctantly end the call and dial my mom's number. I give her all the details, and she promises to call 911 and get over there ASAP. But I have to sit here, hopeless. Because I can fix everyone's problems but my own family's.

I shake my head. I can fix my family's problems. I just can't fix my own problems.

I pull up an airline website on my phone and book the next one home. I start walking back to my rental car when Carter ducks out of the building, grabbing on to me.

"I have to talk to you," Carter says.

"I need to talk to you, too," I say even though I don't have time for this conversation. "But it needs to wait."

Carter puts his finger to my lips. "No, it can't wait. I need you to know how incredibly sorry I am. Both of those kisses back there meant nothing. I feel nothing for Lily. Not even the tiniest of sparks compared to what I feel with you."

I smile weakly, trying to pretend I care about his words right now when all I can think about is Sailor and Amber.

"Are you listening to me? I want you, not Lily. I want you, Victoria. I'm sorry about all this mess, but I'm not really dating Lily. It's all a lie. It's all pretend. Lily understands that now. That all we will ever do is hold hands and pretend to be in love and occasionally kiss, although I will try to prevent that at all costs. That woman kisses like I imagine a lizard would."

I zone him out. I can't hear his words. Only focusing on the fact that my family needs me.

"Victoria?"

I don't answer. I just think about if I have time to stop by Logan's to pack or if I should go straight to the airport.

"Victoria?"

I probably should just go straight to the airport.

Carter grabs my neck and waist as he kisses me. I'm caught off guard, but he's desperate to give me everything with this kiss, and slowly, I let him into my world of pain. I let him know how scared I am. As our tongues dance together, I tell him that I like him, too.

He slowly breaks away. "What's wrong?" he asks.

I shake my head and stay in his arms for a second longer. If I tell him what's going on, I'll start crying, and then he'll insist on coming with me. But he can't. He needs to stay here, and I have to go.

"I just have to go. Tell Lily that I quit. That a family thing came up."

And then I walk away from what I know is a man I could love with every fiber of my being. I just don't know if he will still be waiting for me when I get back from fixing my family.

12 CARTER

I should have run after Victoria.

I should have chased her down and forced her to talk to me. Or just followed her until she was ready to tell me what was going on.

But I didn't.

I let her go. And, now, I don't know what's going on. *Is this the end? Is she coming back?*

The hug and kiss she gave me before she left sure didn't feel like the end. It felt like the beginning. It felt like she needed me, but then she just left.

The door to the apartment opens, and I jump off the couch I've been sitting on most of the afternoon, waiting for Victoria to come back. All of her stuff is still here, so she must be coming back soon.

"Victoria, I'm sorry," I say, running to the door.

Logan raises an eyebrow at me as he enters. "Why are you apologizing to my sister?"

I rub the back of my neck. "Because I fucked up."

Logan walks past me toward the kitchen. He opens the fridge, staring at it.

"Aren't you going to kill me for hurting your sister?" I ask reluctantly.

He slams the door shut with anger and rage I was expecting. I know he is going to hit me, and I deserve it. I should never have agreed to date Lily while being with Victoria. Even on a pretend basis. I knew it would eventually hurt her.

"No."

"No?"

He shakes his head. "You might have fucked up, but I've always thought you and Victoria were meant for each other. I think you would make each other better."

I frown. "I hurt her pretty bad. I deserve to be punched or at least thrown out of your apartment or something."

"You're probably right. But, lucky for you, I'm not looking for a fight today."

That's when I realize that the look on Logan's face isn't just rage and anger. It's fear and sadness. Victoria had a similar look before she left.

"What's going on? Victoria just upped and left today, and I have no idea where she is going or when she's coming back."

"She's not coming back."

"Then, where is she? I'll go to her."

Logan's head drops. "Come get a drink with me. I don't have shit in this apartment. Then, maybe I won't end up killing you."

†

"SO, what did you do to piss off my sister?" Logan asks after the bartender gives us our beers.

"I made a kiss between me and my pretend girlfriend a little too believable."

Logan laughs. "I really should kick your ass."

I shrug and take a drink of my beer.

"I would, but I don't think Victoria is mad at you because of that."

I raise an eyebrow.

"Okay, I'm sure she isn't happy that you kissed another woman even though it was needed to pull off her stupid scheme. I just mean that she has a lot more important things going on right now."

"And that is?"

"Our sister, Amber, is sick. She has depression. But our idiot mother made it worse by giving her some of her prescription pain killers. Amber overdosed."

"I'm sorry."

Logan takes another long drink of his beer. "Thanks. I just wish I could do more. I can't take off work. I'm horrible with kids. Well, beyond the fun play stuff, I don't know how to actually take care of a kid."

I remember now that Amber has a daughter. I've only met her a couple of times when she was a baby.

"Sailor's amazing, and Amber is great with her when she's well. When the depression takes over again, Victoria always comes in and saves the day. She's lost jobs because of it. Between losing her jobs and getting fired for things out of her control, Victoria has had a hard time with living the life she wants. She usually has to pick up other random jobs just to pay the bills. Her last company made me think it was finally going to make her life work, but then they fired her for no reason. She just can't catch a break."

Realization hits me of where I factor in all of this. I didn't realize what I was doing. I didn't realize I was hurting Victoria. But, now, my problems with Lily seem small.

"What are Victoria's plans now?"

"She checked Amber into a place to help her heal. It will take a few months at least. Our mother isn't much help. So, Victoria will probably stay with Sailor in San Francisco and try to find another job. She'll survive, just like she always does. I'll fly there any chance I can get and send any extra money I make to help out, but it's never really much help."

"What about her stuff? What about her job?"

"I'll ship her stuff. And job? I thought she said she quit."

"She told me to tell Lily that she quit. I didn't tell her though. I just said she was sick and needed to go home. I told Lily I had some other work things I needed to address and then got out of there as soon as I could to wait for Victoria."

"You need to tell Lily that Victoria quit. She won't come back. She won't pull Sailor out of school or take her away from Amber. She will stay in San Francisco even if she can't find another PR job. She will do everything that she can to fix our family's problems."

I think for a minute, hating that I have to be so far away from Victoria. I don't know when I will be able to see her again. And I know one thing; I can't live without her. I love her. I think I've always been in love with her. I just thought I couldn't love her. That she was all wrong for me.

My mind flashes back to my favorite memory of her. We must have been twelve, maybe thirteen.

"*LOGAN,*" *I hiss, poking him in the ribs.*

His hand swats me. "Go away. I'm sleeping."

I sigh. It's not even ten o'clock on a Saturday. There is no way he is sleeping. And I can't fall asleep.

I get up from the couch in the basement and head upstairs. Maybe his mom made some food. I walk into the kitchen and open the fridge, but there is no food.

I sigh. So much for that plan.

Music? My ears perk up at the sound of music coming from upstairs.

I creep up the stairs as I listen to the music getting louder along with Tori's voice. I haven't ever heard her sing before, and maybe she will offer me some level of entertainment.

I walk to her door and listen as she belts out Spice Girls. She's horrible, but I don't care. It's amusing actually, how she can sing so confidently. I guess it's because she doesn't think anyone is here.

I throw the door open, planning on embarrassing her. But she doesn't get embarrassed. Her cheeks don't flush, and she doesn't scream in fear.

Instead, she just rolls her eyes at me and keeps on singing into her hairbrush.

I frown. So much for entertainment.

"Sing with me," she says, tossing me a hairbrush.

"No. It's stupid, and you're horrible."

"So? It's fun."

She keeps singing and dancing around the room like a crazy person while I stand, frozen in my spot, with wide eyes.

"You're crazy."

"You're boring."

She walks over to me until she is standing inches away from me. She lowers her hairbrush and says, "Sing and dance with me, or I'm going to kiss you."

"What? Why?"

"Because you don't want me to kiss you. Now, sing and dance with me."

I frown. "I don't know the words."

"Then, make them up." She grabs my hand and pulls me into the center of her bedroom.

She starts dancing again, and I start flapping my arms around.

She smiles. "See? That isn't so hard."

She grabs my hands and spins us around as we dance. As we spin, my world changes. The way she smiles and makes me smile changes everything. Because, for a split second, I wish I had taken the other option. Or at least said both. Because, right now, there is nothing more I want to do than kiss Tori.

I DIDN'T LET myself love her because I thought there was no way that she'd ever love me in return. Not after all the cruel things I had done to her. What I did just a few weeks ago is the most savage thing I have ever done. She's going to hate me.

But maybe I'll have a chance if she's already in love with me. Maybe I'll have a chance if I can find a way to fix all the problems I've caused.

"What if she doesn't have to quit?" I ask with a grin.

13 VICTORIA

It's three p.m. I need to leave to pick Sailor up from school. But the bills lying on the kitchen table are overwhelming me. Bills for the house. Bills for electricity and water. Bills to cover Amber's treatment. And that doesn't even include basic things like food and clothes for me and Sailor.

All I can see are bills. And no way to pay them.

What was I thinking, quitting?

I was thinking I needed to be here for my adorable ten-year-old niece. I was thinking that was what was most important. But it was stupid. My mom could have taken care of her for a couple of weeks. Because I can't take care of Sailor if I don't have any money to feed her.

I hear the doorbell ring, but I don't move from my spot. I can't deal with any more nosy neighbors coming to figure out what happened to Amber. I have to find a way to fix my problems. I have to find a way to make a lot of money and fast.

The doorbell rings again and then again.

I sigh. It's probably an annoying kid. I run my hand through my hair. I can feel the tangled knots throughout my head. I haven't showered in three days. I've either been at the hospital with Amber or on the phone, finding a treatment place for her, all while trying to distract Sailor from everything. Basic hygiene hasn't been high on my list.

The doorbell rings again, and I finally force myself up from the table. I need to get up anyway to go pick up Sailor. I trudge to the door, not wanting to deal with any other humans today other than Sailor.

I open the door and fold my arms over my chest, ready to chew out whatever kid is there.

"Carter?" I ask, like I don't know it is him standing in my doorway.

"What are you doing here?" I ask, hating that I'm in sweatpants and an old, ratty shirt. *Why didn't I shower today? Or at the very least, run a brush through my hair or apply some makeup?*

"I'm here because I missed you," he says, carefully choosing his words.

"I missed you, too," I say without thinking, because it's true. I missed him desperately. I missed the obnoxious way that he held me in bed. I missed the way his arms felt while wrapped around me. I even missed arguing with him about everything.

He grins. "Can we talk?"

My phone buzzes in my pocket. The alarm I set to go get Sailor is going off.

"Actually, I have to go pick up my niece."

"Mind if I tag along?"

"Sure," I say, even though I'm not sure at all.

Sailor will ask a million questions about Carter that I'm not ready to answer.

I step outside, closing the door behind me. I lead Carter down to where my car is parked a few feet away.

I climb into the driver's seat, and Carter climbs in next to me. I start driving while Carter stares at me.

"What?" I ask, assuming he is looking at all my flaws and is about to criticize me.

"You look beautiful."

I blush. "Stop it. I do not. I look like a mess."

He tucks a strand of hair, which I'm sure is covered in grease, behind my ear. "You look beautiful because I've never seen you stronger."

I bite my lip. I can't believe he just said that.

"It's true. I never realized how driven you were, how powerful you were, until recently. I'm sorry for that."

I swallow and try to focus on the road. I can't have him saying things like that to me right now. Our life is far too complicated. He has to pretend he is with Lily, and my life needs me here right now. We are on opposite coasts. Anything between us could never work.

"Stop analyzing this."

"I'm not."

He chuckles. "You are because you don't know how this could work. But you've seen my work. You know I'm one of the best fixers in the world. Just one other person might be better."

I laugh. "I'm not a fixer. I can't even fix my own problems."

"I don't know about that. I think you've been doing a fine job so far, but only because you keep putting yourself last instead of first."

I exhale deeply, trying to stay calm. Trying not to get my hopes up that something magical is about to happen. Because that's not my life. My life is one problem after the other. My life isn't easily fixed. My life is a broken mess.

I pull the car over to the curb outside the school to wait for Sailor to come out. Once she gets into the car, then I'll be safe. Carter won't do anything with Sailor in the car.

"Victoria."

One word, and my heart already betrays me. It starts beating for him. Begging me to let him in.

I look at him. His eyes look deep into mine.

"I love you, Victoria. I've always loved you. Since the moment I saw you singing Spice Girls in your bedroom and made me join you. To years later when I realized how many times I'd hurt you. To the moment I saw you again after way too long. There has never been another woman. Only you. I love you."

Everything in my world stops when he says that he loves me. It's something I've secretly wanted since we were kids. Even when he was torturing me, I still wanted him. There was a connection I didn't understand.

I feel a tear slipping down my cheek. I'm literally crying because this man just told me that he loves me. I'm ridiculous.

"Aren't you going to say *I love you* back?" I hear Sailor's voice from behind me.

I didn't even hear her get into the car.

I quickly wipe my tear and turn to Sailor. "How was your day, sweetheart?"

She folds her tough arms across her chest. "I want to hear if you love him first. My day sucked. I could use some good news. I could use another uncle."

I laugh and turn back to Carter. "I love you, too."

He grins as he leans forward and softly kisses me on the lips.

I compose myself before I start driving back home.

"I'm Carter," he says, holding out his hand to Sailor.

"Uncle Carter, you mean," Sailor says, shaking his hand.

I bite my lip to keep from laughing at her sassiness today.

Carter catches my eye. "Definitely Uncle Carter," he says, giving me a wink.

I roll my eyes at him. She can call him whatever she wants, but we are nowhere near ready to make him a real uncle to Sailor.

"So, I have a proposition for you, Sailor," Carter says as he turns around in his seat so that he is looking straight at Sailor.

I raise my eyebrow at him, but I'm not sure that he sees me.

"I'm listening," Sailor says in her sweet voice.

"Your aunt Victoria here has a job in North Carolina. Do you know where that is?"

"Yep! That's where Uncle Logan lives."

"That's right. She has a job that she needs to go back to North Carolina to finish for a couple of weeks."

I furrow my brows, confused as to what Carter is talking about. I quit my job.

"How would you like to go to North Carolina and live with your uncle Logan, Victoria, and me for a couple of weeks?"

"Carter," I say sternly, trying to end this conversation without saying too much in front of Sailor.

"What do you think?" Carter asks, ignoring me.

"I think that would be awesome!"

I look in my rearview mirror at Sailor. "Sailor, you don't need to say yes. It's not fair to you. You would miss school here and go to a different school there for a couple of weeks until I finished working."

"I want to go to a different school."

I frown. "Why do you want to go to a different school?"

"Because there's this boy—his name is Jack—who picks on me all the time. I hate him."

I glare over at Carter.

"What? It wasn't me," he says.

I give him another evil glare, letting him know that, till the end of time, I will blame him for other boys who treat Sailor badly.

"We can talk to your teacher and make sure that doesn't happen anymore."

"No, I need a vacation. I want to go to North Carolina."

I sigh. "Sailor, you need to understand, this wouldn't be a vacation. You would still need to go to school."

"Whatever. It beats being here."

I exhale deeply, trying to remain calm because my world just got thrown on its head. Apparently, I have a job still. I'm pretty sure I have a boyfriend, whom I can't really date in public, and I'm moving back to North Carolina. I don't understand how any of this came to be or why it's happening. But now isn't the time for questions.

Carter holds out his hand to me, and I take it. I might not be able to fix everything in my life, but I have Carter. Maybe that's enough.

"Now, about that date you promised me," Carter says.

I sigh. "You can take me out when we get back."

I SAID yes to the date just like I said yes to bringing Sailor back to North Carolina with me a few days ago. Now I just have to figure out how to help Amber and I might finally have a chance at fixing my life.

I've spent hours getting ready for our date tonight. I shouldn't have spent five minutes on it since he made it perfectly clear after he showed up at my house in San Francisco that he wouldn't care what I wore or how I did my hair. But I'm making an effort because I'm not sure how many of these dates we are going to get to go on publicly until we figure out a plan to undo my stupid idea of making Carter Lily's boyfriend instead of mine.

I take out my red lipstick and apply it to my lips. I take a look in the mirror. I don't even look like myself. I have so much makeup on. My hair is curled, and I'm wearing a black dress with a few sparkles and heels. Even if anyone recognizes Carter, they won't recognize me.

I hear a knock on the door, and my heart starts racing. I shouldn't react this way to a simple knock, but I do when I know who's behind the door.

I take my time in walking over to the bedroom door—partially because I want to make Carter sweat a little and partially because I have to take time not to topple over in my heels. I open the door while biting my lip.

Carter's eyes light up like he's never seen me before. It's not an expression I'm used to seeing on his face. But it's definitely a look I would like to get used to.

"What do you think?" I ask, popping my hip out.

His eyes travel up and down my body, but he doesn't speak.

"Carter?" I ask, grinning because it's clear from his body that he thinks I look hot.

Sailor pokes her head out from around Carter. "You look hot!"

I laugh. "Thank you, Sailor." I walk around Carter, who is still standing in my doorway with his tongue hanging out. "You going to be okay staying here with Logan tonight while we go out?"

"As long as he's not cooking."

I laugh again. "You're ordering pizza."

"Actually, I made your favorite," Carter says.

I look at him with one eyebrow raised. "You know what her favorite food is?"

"Of course. It's sushi."

"Wow, you do know Sailor's favorite food. But do you really know how to make sushi?" I ask, skeptical.

Carter jogs toward the kitchen. Sailor and I follow. When we enter the kitchen, Carter opens the fridge and pulls out a plate of food.

"No way! You bought that at the store," I say, not believing that he made the perfectly sculpted rolls.

Logan gets up from the living room and walks over. He takes one off the tray and pops it into his mouth.

"How is it?" I ask.

"Delicious. He definitely made them. I was sitting here, watching him make them."

I take one, and so does Sailor.

"Oh my God," Sailor and I say at the same time.

"How did you learn to cook so well?" I ask.

Carter shrugs. "I'm just naturally good at everything."

I playfully hit him on the arm. "Uh-huh."

"Come on. We have a date to get to."

I grin. "That we do."

I bend down and kiss Sailor on the cheek before hugging her. "Make sure Logan doesn't get into too much trouble," I tell her.

She grins. "We are eating sushi and watching *Keeping Up With The Kardashians* all night."

I grin. *Such a mini Amber already.*

Carter's fingers interlink with mine. I glance down to look at our intertwined hands. I will never get used to that.

Carter leads me outside.

"So, where are we going?" I ask.

Carter stops and reaches his hand up to caress my neck as his lips kiss me. My whole body comes alive as we kiss. His lips are all it takes to make me forget about everything other than him.

The kiss ends all too soon.

I laugh when I see his face.

"What?" he asks.

"You have red lipstick..." I run my thumb across his lip to get rid of the lipstick.

He grabs my hand again and pulls me to a limo.

"A limo? Really? Don't you think it will make our relationship more obvious instead of trying to get us to blend in?"

The limo driver opens the door for me, and I climb into the shiny black car. I immediately regret saying anything negative about the limo. I've never ridden in one, and this thing is beautiful. Leather seats, tons of room, and I can have Carter all to myself instead of him being distracted with driving.

Carter slides in next to me. "Want some champagne?" he asks, his voice sounding nervous.

"I'm not really a champagne person."

"Me neither, but it's what you are supposed to drink in a limo."

Carter moves over to the limo's built-in bar. His body looks yummy in his dark suit that somehow looks nicer than the ones he wears for work. He quickly comes back with two glasses and a bottle.

The driver begins driving without a word as Carter pours us each a glass of champagne. I should look out the window to see where we are going, but I don't want to do anything but be here with Carter.

We might not get too many other dates like this for a long time, and I'm going to make the most of it.

I hold up my glass to Carter.

He does the same. "To the best night of our lives."

I grin and clink my glass with his. I take a drink.

Carter rubs my earlobe as he studies me.

"What are you thinking?"

"I'm thinking, I'm going to fuck up all my plans for tonight."

"Maybe you should tell me what your plans are, and then I can tell you if they are crap or not."

The limo takes a hard turn, and Carter falls into my lap, losing his drink. Our lips are close together as the electricity between us comes alive. One hand caresses my neck while his other hand is gripping my ass.

I grin because I do know one thing that I definitely want right now. "Fuck me."

Carter's eyes light up at that. He crawls up my body, kissing every inch of bare skin that he can find as he works his way up to my lips.

"You're a naughty girl," he says against my lips.

"A naughty girl who's yours," I say. Every fiber in my body aches for him. Every breath I breathe is because I want to consume his breath. Everything inside me draws me closer to him, wanting him like no man I've ever known before.

He kisses me, and I know it's true. I'm his. I don't want any other man's lips on me.

And Carter is mine. I don't know how to tell him, but there is no way I'm going to be okay with watching him and Lily kiss again. They can pretend to date, hold hands even, but I don't think I can handle anything more than that.

His lips move to my neck, kissing every inch of my skin, while his hand tangles in my hair, undoing all of my hard work.

I groan, loving the combination of rough and soft kisses on my neck and earlobes.

"You have to be quiet," Carter whispers against my neck before he nibbles on my earlobe.

I feel the excitement grow deep in my belly. A feeling that there is no way of containing.

I bite my lip, trying to keep from screaming, but I can't. I moan louder than I did the first time when his lips devour my neck again.

I feel his grin against my skin.

"You're not very good at obeying me, are you?"

I exhale deeply. "You wouldn't be with me if I were."

His fingers travel down my neck and over my cleavage before he grabs my breast. I suck in a deep breath.

"You're right. I want a strong woman who will challenge me on everything."

His hands grab the top of my dress, and I know what's coming.

"Don't you dare," I pant.

He gives me a wicked grin. And then he rips the dress apart, exposing my black lace bra and panties.

"You're going to pay for that."

He sits back on my lap, staring at me. "Oh, I plan on it."

He grabs my hips, and in one motion, he flips me until I'm straddling his lap. I grab his button-down shirt and rip it apart.

He grins. "I figured you would do that. That's why I wore one of Logan's."

I shake my head as I kiss his hard chest.

He groans, and his thick cock hardens beneath me with every kiss.

"This," he says, pointing to my bra, which is extra lacy and sexy compared to my other bras, "I don't want to destroy."

His mouth pushes the bra down, and his lips take my nipple into his mouth.

I dig my nails into his shoulders, careful not to grip him so tightly that I cause him to bleed like before. But he makes it almost impossible for me not to with the way his tongue expertly glides over my nipple and the way his teeth bite with just the right amount of pressure.

He comes up for air, giving me a second to recover, before he kisses me, pushing his tongue deep inside my mouth.

"You can dig your nails in as hard as you want. You can fight with me or love me. It doesn't matter. I love all of you."

I smile. "I don't understand what happened. I don't understand how I can love someone I used to hate with everything inside me, but I do."

He tangles his hand in my hair again and pulls my bare neck to him, kissing me hard. "It's the sex. I'm way too good at fucking for you not to fall in love with me."

I bite my lip as warm liquid pools between my legs with every kiss. The sex is amazing, and it's definitely something I will never get enough of, but it's not the only reason I love him. It's his charm. The way he takes care of me. The way I know that how hard he used to fight with me is the same fight I know he's going to use to protect me. It's sexy as hell to know that is how badly he wants me.

I grab the waistband of his pants, needing his cock. Now. He's teased me enough. I need to feel him thrusting and pounding inside me. I need to feel fully and completely his.

I push his pants and underwear down, and his hard cock springs free. Carter pushes my panties down while I search in his pockets for a condom. Instead, I find a box. A box I know I wasn't meant to find.

He grins when I hold out the box to him. He takes it from me. It takes me a second to understand what he is doing because it's so crazy that I don't even think of it as a possibility, but when I realize what he's doing, I gasp.

He takes my hand in his. "Victoria, I know this is crazy. I know we've hated each other most of our lives. I know we have gone on a total of one date and that we are currently on it. I know you have your family problems, and I have Lily to deal with.

"But I don't care about any of that. I don't care that everyone else will tell us this is stupid. That we don't even know each other. We already know more than most people do about each other when they get married. And, what we don't know, we will learn. I feel like I've waited all my life for a woman like you, not even realizing that you were that woman all along.

"Forgive me for being stupid, and marry me?"

I bite my lip to keep myself from spitting out an answer that is rushed and not what I actually want. I'm a planner. I plan everything in my life and then watch as all my plans get thrown out the window when reality hits. I didn't plan on Carter. Or any of this. But that doesn't mean I shouldn't say yes.

He opens the box, but I can't look at it. I can't process anything that is happening. This is too fast. Or maybe it's not fast enough, considering we've known each other all our lives. Whatever it is, my mind is too one track focused for me to think about anything other than needing his cock inside me.

I don't have time to look for a condom. I'm on the pill, and he'd better be clean, or I'll kill him later. I grab on to his shoulders as I lower myself onto his cock.

"Fuck me," I whimper against his lips as I look deep into his eyes, letting him know that what I need right now is him. We can talk marriage later.

I move up and down as his hands grasp on to my hips and ass, moving me harder.

"I love you, Victoria," he says as he fucks me harder.

I stare into his eyes, trying to remember this moment forever, as he fucks me harder and harder. Because, no matter what our future holds, this is a beautiful, unplanned moment that we can never repeat. We aren't just fucking. We are changing our future together. No matter if I say yes or no, this moment, right now, will remain with me forever.

"I love you," I say in a whimper as he brings me close to the brink.

"Come, Victoria."

I don't want to come. I want this moment to last forever.

But forevers don't last. Forevers are not infinite. Forevers are only as long as we pretend that our problems don't really exist.

"Come, Victoria. Marry me. Be mine forever."

I dig my nails into his back. I bite my lip. And then I come, pulsing hard around his thick cock, as I let out, "Yes, Carter. Yes."

14 CARTER

She said yes. Of course, she said yes while my cock was deep inside her as she was coming, but it still counts. And, now, she's passed out against my chest, still almost completely naked.

I don't want to wake her—ever. I want her here, in my arms, forever. Especially if she's naked.

But the driver is going to stop soon, and we need to get dressed.

I lean down and softly kiss her on the forehead. "Victoria, you need to wake up."

She moans and wraps her arms tighter around me in the cutest way possible.

My lips hover over her ear. "If you wake up, we might have time to fuck again before we get there."

Her eyes shoot open.

I grin.

"You're lying," she says, hitting my chest.

"Yes, sorry. You need to get dressed. We will be stopping soon."

"What am I supposed to wear? You ripped my dress, remember?" she says, yawning and stretching.

I point to a bag sitting on the floor toward the front. "I brought a couple of your other dresses for you to change into."

"You knew you were going to rip my dress off me?"

I shrug. "I hoped. It was so fun the first time."

She gets off my lap and grabs the bag. She begins digging through it to find another dress to put on. "You are going to owe me, like, a million dresses by the end of this, aren't you?"

I kiss her on the lips. "More than a million. And there is no *end of this*."

She nods. "You're right. We should be optimistic."

She pulls out a white dress that I was hoping she would choose and begins putting it on. She looks gorgeous in white, and if I can find some sort of wedding chapel, maybe I can convince her to elope tonight and not wait any longer.

Now that she's said yes, I don't want to wait. I'm a man who knows what he wants and doesn't doubt himself. I know I want Victoria. Forever. And forever needs to start as soon as possible. Tonight, if I get my way.

She pulls a dark blue shirt out of the bag and tosses it to me. We both get dressed while the limo continues driving to our destination.

Victoria runs her hands through her hair. "I look like I was just fucked."

"And is that a problem?"

"It is if anyone sees us together and puts two and two together."

"Let's not worry about Lily or any of our other problems tonight. Let's just enjoy tonight."

"Fine, but I still look like a mess."

"A hot mess."

The car stops, and Victoria immediately goes to the window, trying to look outside.

I grab her hand and pull her back to me. "No peeking."

She pouts. "Well then, show me where we are."

The driver opens the door, and I get out before I hold out my hand to help her out.

Her eyes immediately dart around. "Um...you brought me to a neighborhood? I thought we were going on a usual date, like dinner and movie or something."

I tighten my grip on her hand. "What fun would that be?"

"The normal amount of fun," she teases as I lead her up the stairs to the house.

"Please tell me we aren't meeting your long-lost parents or something. I'm not ready for that."

I laugh. "Nope. I met them years ago. They were horrible people. Not quite as horrible as my foster parents, but still pretty bad."

"I'm sorry," she says, stopping, her brows furrowed in a look of genuine concern.

I stroke her cheek. "Don't be. I'm not. Family has never been important to me."

She frowns and fidgets with the hem of her dress. "Then, why do you want to get married if family isn't important to you?"

I sigh. She's going to ruin every surprise I have planned for her today. "Just come inside with me, and then we can talk."

She wants to fight. I can tell from the fierce stare I'm getting, but she relents and follows me up the stairs to the front door. I reach into my pocket and pull out the key.

She inquisitively looks at me, but I don't answer her unspoken question yet. I put the key in the door, unlock it, and push the door open.

I hold the door open for her, and she walks inside the large house.

"Wow, this house is beautiful," Victoria says, looking at the quaint home.

I take her hand and lead her to the back of the house, out the French doors, and out onto the large patio. Twinkle lights hang overhead, already on, and large trees and flowers cover most of the yard.

"It's so peaceful out here," she says, standing on the patio, looking out over the large backyard, which has a pool where I plan on fucking her later.

I get down on one knee and pull out the box that I snatched back up after Victoria found it in my pants pocket.

She grins this time, unlike the last time when I took her completely by shock. I wouldn't change it for anything though. I loved hearing her say yes with my dick inside her.

"Victoria, I love you. I don't have any family, and I never thought I needed one. Not until you and Logan. Logan has always been a brother to me, but for some reason, I could never make you my sister. That's because I'm meant to be your husband, not brother. I already think of Sailor as my niece. And Amber as a sister. I want us all to be together to figure out whatever our problems are—together.

"This house is ours if we want it. It's big enough for us all to share when we are in town. I think, after Amber recovers, it would be good to get her out here to live with Logan and us when we are here. This house is so peaceful and beautiful.

"But, if that's not what you want, then I will find another solution. Because your family is my family now, and I will do anything for them.

"Now, I've already asked you this once, albeit not in the most romantic way."

I open the box, revealing the large diamond. "Marry me."

"Yes," she says behind her laughter. "It's crazy, but I'll marry you."

I put the ring on her finger before grabbing her in my arms and twirling her around.

"You have to promise me some things though if I marry you."

I laugh, putting her down but not out of my arms. "Of course you have demands in order for you to marry me." I sigh. "Let's hear them."

She thinks for a minute with a goofy smile on her face that I love. I love that she has demands. I love that she doesn't just say yes without having her own needs met.

"One, we get this house, no matter if my family wants to live here with us part-time or full-time or whatever. I love it."

"Done."

"Two, you have to promise me that you will respect my decision if I decide not to have kids. I don't know what I want right now. I love Sailor, but I already have enough people to take care of in my family. And I love my career. I'm not ready to give it up yet."

"Done."

"Three"—she twists her fingers deep into my hair—"you will never stop fighting with me."

I frown. "You want me to fight and argue with you? Seriously?"

"Yes, fighting with me makes both of us better. It ensures that we will never get bored. It will push us if we have to compete over the same clients in our careers."

"Or we could work together?"

She laughs. "How well has that been working for us so far?"

"Good point."

"Promise me?"

"We will have a lifetime of fighting and arguing about everything."

"Good."

"Are you done?"

She smirks. "You think I have only three demands?"

"I think I want to kiss you, so you'd better hurry up."

"Four..." She takes her time, thinking really hard, while my patience for not being able to kiss my fiancée grows strong. "Four is, you have to take me down to the pool and fuck me."

I grab her ass and lift her up. I begin running down the stairs toward the pool. "Thank God we think so much alike."

"Shut up, and kiss me."

Her hands grab my neck as she forces my face forward to kiss her. Her tongue pushes deep inside my mouth as I push back equally with my own tongue. We are perfect equals who will challenge each other in life. I want exactly what she said she wanted.

I try to pay attention to where I'm walking. But I can't focus on anything but her lips, her tongue, her body. I need all of it. Fast, slow. Hard, gentle. I need her in every way possible.

I take another step and don't feel anything beneath my foot. I try to lean back to keep from falling, but I can't stop us once we've started moving. We fall into the water, still clothed and still grasping on to each other, desperate for a kiss.

We come up for air at the same time. I expect her to be pissed or to be full of giggles over what just happened. Instead, we continue kissing right where we left off. Deep, passionate, *I will never let you go* type kisses.

I grab the hem of her dress and pull it up over her head until it is off her body.

"Damn, you look hot," I say, biting my lip, as I stare at her in the pool with the twinkle lights shining down on her.

"And you look far too clothed."

I take my jacket off and throw it onto the side of the pool. She helps me remove my shirt, and then I push my pants and boxers off, not caring if they make their way out of the pool or not.

"Better?" I ask.

"Much," she says, undoing her bra and pushing her panties off before she dives under the water.

Damn it. I forgot how much of a good swimmer she is.

I dive under after her, chasing her across the pool. She stays under the water when I finally catch her. She used to swim, so I'm sure she can hold her breath for hours. I can't.

I kiss her hard, convincing her to come up for air to get another kiss. She does. When we get to the surface, I grab her and push her against the wall of the pool, kissing her hard as my cock pulses at her entrance.

"I want every day to be like this," she whispers against my lips.

My cock thrusts inside her, stretching her wide. "It will. Always."

I fuck her hard against the edge of the pool. And she fucks me right back. As much hate as we had toward each other, I wouldn't change anything because it created this perfect kind of love where we are truly equals who fight for what we want in this relationship.

"THANK God you brought extra sets of clothes," Victoria says, naked, as she climbs out of the pool to scoop up our clothes.

I frown. "I disagree. I think it would have been better if I hadn't bothered with clothes. I much prefer the view when you're naked."

She laughs and scoops up our wet clothes. My phone falls out of the jacket pocket and bounces on the concrete.

"Sorry," she says, wincing.

I laugh. "The water probably destroyed it anyway."

"I'll try to fix it," she says, running into the house with my clothes and phone, which I'm sure is unfixable. I stay in the pool, planning on doing a couple of laps and then going inside to try to convince Victoria to have sex in one of the rooms in the house before I take her to a late dinner.

I do a couple of laps, loving that this could be my new life. Married to Victoria. Waking up to sex, then a couple of laps in the pool, and then off to my dream job. *How could my life get any better?*

On my third lap, I feel something hard hit my head. I stop swimming and look up to see Victoria still dripping wet but with a new dress on, which is getting wetter by the second. But that isn't what matters. I look at Victoria's face, and I know something is wrong.

"What's wrong?"

She holds out my phone.

"I told you it wasn't fixable."

She shakes her head, looking at it. "It works just fine."

I raise an eyebrow, not believing that the phone works.

"Your assistant, Ruby, called."

"Okay," I say, not understanding why Ruby called or why it would make Victoria upset.

"You got me fired. All those times I thought I had done something wrong. I hadn't gotten enough clients. I hadn't worked hard enough. I'd worked too hard. I'd demanded too much money."

I shake my head. "No, let me explain."

"Every time I was desperate to do a job I loved to take care of my family, you took it away from me. Every. Single. Time."

Victoria's face is bright red, her nostrils are flared, and she is trying to hold back the tears in her eyes.

"Victoria, it wasn't like that."

She throws her hands up. "How was it then? Tell me because I don't understand it. Were you that threatened by me? Is that why you did it? You hated me that much? Has this all been just one big game to you? Or were you pretending to love me to gain some forgiveness?"

The tears fall freely now, mixing with the anger steaming off her cheeks.

"Victoria, I'm sorry. I—"

"You're sorry that you are actually in love with Lily and just pretending with me?"

"No!" I swim to the edge and jump out of the pool, running toward her. "I love you, Victoria. That's always been the truth. Lily is nothing to me."

"Then, what?"

I take a deep breath. "I had to win at all costs. That was always who I was. When I heard there was a new woman in the game who was starting to beat me out for some clients, I felt threatened. I couldn't allow you to win. So, I got you fired."

"But it was me! I know we used to hate each other as kids, but really? You would do this to me? To Logan?"

I wince. "I didn't know it was you."

"How could you not?"

"I always thought of you as Tori, not Victoria. I never connected the dots until—"

"Until I said to call me Victoria, not Tori?"

I nod. "I was going to tell you."

She laughs harshly. "Sure you were." She throws the phone at me and then begins running inside.

"Victoria, wait! Let me explain more. I was an ass. I would do anything to win. I didn't care about anyone. That was before I knew you and loved you. I'm sorry."

I chase Victoria through the house and then outside. I don't care that I'm naked. I can't just let her go.

I catch up to Victoria just as she is about to climb into the limo.

"Please, just stay. Let's talk. Tell me how I can make this better."

"You can't."

"I'll do anything."

She shakes her head. "No, you won't. You're selfish and cruel and savage. You won't do anything for me if it means having to give something up for yourself."

I don't have words. I can't come up with anything to say that will make her stay. Nothing that will make this any better. I can't fix this. I don't know if I'll ever be able to fix this from the look on Victoria's face. So, I let her go. I watch her climb into the limo and close the door. I watch the driver drive her away while I stand in the driveway, naked.

"YOU LOOK LIKE DEATH," Lily says to me when I walk into her office a week after Victoria ran out on me.

"I've been sick for a week. What do you expect me to look like?"

"Happy, cheerful, sexy, ready to work."

I groan. "I don't think I can be any of those things ever again."

She laughs. "Oh, stop being so dramatic, Carter. You have a cold. You'll survive."

"No, I won't."

She rolls her eyes. "I'll have to have my makeup team work on you, too, to make sure you look good for our appearance tonight."

I wince from just thinking about it. "Lily, you know, I've been thinking."

"Shh. You're sick," Lily says, sitting next to me at the table, stroking my hair. "You don't need to worry about any of the plans. Victoria got everything covered before she had to leave."

"What do you mean, she left? She quit?" I ask, annoyed that she isn't even going to show up to work. I thought this was my best chance at seeing her since my best friend had decided to take sides after all—choosing Victoria's, not mine. So, I haven't been able to get into his apartment all week.

"She said she had family things that she had to deal with and, unfortunately, couldn't continue. Don't worry; she came up with an excellent plan for going forward, and I paid her well for her idea."

I frown. I don't like this at all.

I sit up, straighter, swiping Lily's hand off my head. "What exactly is her plan?"

Lily grins. "I'm not going to tell you."

My face turns bright red. "Why not? Shouldn't I know the plan that I'm supposed to execute with you?"

"No, all you and Victoria did was fight. If I tell you her plan, then you will try to change it, and it's perfect as it is."

I narrow my eyes as I stare into Lily's eyes, trying to figure out what the plan is, but I see no hint in her eyes other than seeing that she is happy.

"Don't worry; I'll pay you well, too," she says, petting me again.

I grab her wrist, needing her to stop touching me.

She reluctantly pulls it away, getting the hint. I stand up and walk toward the door.

"Where are you going?" Lily asks.

"To get ready for tonight. Apparently, I'm only a hot body that needs to look good for our TV appearance tonight."

She smiles. "Try to sleep. It will help with the circles under your eyes."

I nod, giving her a fake smile before I leave.

I don't have a plan. Not yet, but I do know Victoria. I know that she needed this job, so she convinced Lily to pay her a large amount of money for whatever her plan was. I also know that, after I hurt her, she will retaliate. So, whatever the plan is, it isn't going to be in my favor.

But I also know that I still have a chance with Victoria if I can form my own plan. She thinks I'm selfish, cruel, and savage. She's probably right. But it doesn't mean that I don't love her and that I won't do anything I can to keep her. She's giving me another chance by retaliating and getting her revenge. She's showing just how selfish, cruel, and savage she can be. I'll let her. I deserve whatever revenge is coming my way. It will equal the score. And then maybe we can get back to the love part after we get all of our hate out.

15 VICTORIA

I haven't seen Carter in a week. But I'm going to tonight.

I squeeze my hands into fists and then release them.

I try to replay Sailor's voice in my head. *You look great.* I repeat those words over and over. *I look great, and tonight, I'm going to make Carter suffer.*

He's going to hate me by the end of tonight and also want me more than he's wanted any other woman. He's going to feel pain when he realizes that I'm not here for *him*. I'm here to make him pay for all the years of pain he has caused me.

I walk backstage of the television show that Carter and Lily are going on. I walk right up to both of them, trying to squash any nerves about still having any feelings toward Carter. I can't have any feelings. He hurt me; now, I'll hurt him. That's all we will ever be to each other.

"Hello, Lily. Are you ready to go tonight?" I ask.

Lily throws her arms around me. "Victoria, it's good to see you! I wasn't sure if you would make it."

I grin brightly at her. "I wouldn't have missed it."

"I'm very sorry to see you go. You really are the best."

"Thank you, but you won't need my services anymore after tonight. Your crisis will be over, and you will be able to focus on running an effective campaign."

Lily smiles. "You're right, but if I need someone to handle a crisis in the future, I'm calling you."

"Hopefully, you won't need to."

I glance over at Carter, who is intently watching me but doesn't say anything. I don't say anything to him either. I just stand there, letting him wish that he had treated me like I deserved. Because I'm going to make sure he'll miss my body.

His eyes travel over my body, like I knew they would, soaking in his last glimpse of me. He takes in my legs, which look curvy in my dark jeans and high heels. He takes in my white spaghetti strap top, which has plenty of cleavage and shows off my arms. And then he settles on my face. My hair is curled in loose waves, and my makeup makes it look like I'm going out tonight to pick up a guy. And I might just do that. I could use a night to forget about everything.

"You're on in five," one of the assistants says to the couple.

"Good luck," I say to Lily. Then, I give Carter one last glare before I walk over to the monitor to watch Carter's life end.

They are announced, and I watch them walk out, hand in hand. All smiles for each other.

I feel the stabbing in my heart. *Damn it.* I'm not the one who is supposed to feel pain. He is.

They take a seat in the chairs, and the host begins asking them easy questions at first. They both make jokes and laugh.

And then the host says the words that I planted. The words that I'm here to watch. "I hear that the two of you have some big news to share."

Lily holds tighter on to Carter's arm, leaning in like she is really in love. She probably is—or at least, what she thinks is love. "We do have some exciting news."

"Care to share?" the host asks excitedly.

Lily holds out her left hand, proudly displaying the engagement ring that Carter used to propose to me a week ago. "We're engaged!"

I carefully watch Carter's expression. He's surprised. He raises an eyebrow for a split second when he sees it, and his eyes are a little wider than usual as he stares at the ring on Lily's finger instead of mine. But he quickly recovers from the surprise. What he doesn't recover from is the pain. I know he was expecting me to do something, but I don't think he was expecting that. He looks away from Lily and over to the backstage area where I'm standing, off camera. I look away from the screen to look at him with a smirk. He deserves this. He deserves the pain. He deserves to suffer, being her fiancé. If I get my way, until death do they part.

"Tell us how you proposed," the host asks Carter, forcing his attention back to the interview.

"Oh, it was so romantic! We were in a limo, and...well, things got steamy," Lily says, fake blushing. "But, Carter, you should really tell the story."

Carter takes a deep breath. "I had rented a limo for the night because I wanted everything to be perfect. And it was. We started kissing. Then, one thing led to another, and our clothes were off. She was digging through my pants, looking for protection, when she found the ring. I proposed. But she was more worried about being with me than being very clear with her answer.

"The limo driver kept driving to our destination—a home that I bought for us to start our life together as a family. And I proposed again on the deck of the house, under twinkle lights and the stars. She said yes."

"Oh my God, that is a romantic and steamy story," the host says.

Carter smiles, but it's fake. He hated retelling that story and replacing me with Lily. It hurt. My job here is done.

I walk toward the exit, feeling the weight of what I just did hit me harder and harder with every step. I just hurt a man whom, despite everything, I'm desperately in love with. A man who, minus a few flaws, is perfect for me in every way. I just ruined my chance at happiness with him.

I throw the door open and step outside, wrapping my arms around myself, trying to comfort myself, as I walk the two blocks to the nearest bar. I stop outside the bar and turn around, hoping that, just like in the movies, Carter will be there, running after me, about to give me some fantastic speech that will make me feel like we can be together. But he's not there. No one is.

I'm all alone.

I need to get used to it. This is my life now.

16 CARTER

The interview ends, but my relationship with Lily is just beginning thanks to Victoria.

She hurt me.

It felt like she ripped out my heart and then tore it into tiny little pieces. I couldn't breathe. I couldn't think about anything other than the fact that she gave her engagement ring to Lily. It was a cold move forcing me into a fake engagement with Lily.

And I deserved every ounce of the pain she caused me. That much I know. Up until a few days ago, I have spent my whole life hurting Victoria. When we were kids I did it because it was fun and I was deflecting from my own pain, but as we got older I realized it was because I cared about her, but I was never good enough for her. But I couldn't let anyone else have her.

I couldn't let her beat me because that would only reinforce that I'm not good enough for her.

But now, neither of us win. Because we can't be together.

I look over at Lily who is showing off her ring to everyone that will look at it backstage.

I do have a choice. I can tell the truth. I can let everyone know that Lily's and I's relationship is a farce. I can ruin my career along with Lily's and probably Victoria's. I can be selfish in order to have a shot with Victoria now.

Or I can do my penance. I can continue to pretend to have a relationship with Lily. Follow the plan that Victoria set in place and then try for a relationship with Victoria afterward.

I'm not sure I like my odds of either option working out. I'm a fixer. I fix things, but I have no idea how to fix my relationship with Victoria.

I duck out of the back door while Lily holds everyone's attention. Apparently, no one cares about the guy in all of this. I don't know what choice I'm going to make, I just know I need to talk to Victoria. If I can talk to her and see where she is at, then maybe I will know which choice I should make.

I run down the street hoping that she is still nearby. She would have wanted to stay and watch the interview. I know she would want to see the pain she caused burned into my mind. But I'm not sure where she would go afterward.

Alone. She would want to be alone. I look into the bars as I walk and stop dead in my tracks when I see her sitting at the counter of an almost empty bar. I grab onto the handle of the door as I watch her talking with the bartender.

I want to throw the door open and run over to her and carry her out. I want her to be mine. I want her to want me. I want her to forgive me for all the horrible things I've done. But I know looking at her now that I can't. She's not mine.

The only way she will ever be mine is to let her go. Show her that I've changed. That I would put her first above my own needs. And the only way to do that is to do what she wants. I have to pretend to be with Lily.

I just have no idea how to earn her forgiveness for all the pain I've caused her.

I take a step back and think about my options. I don't have many.

I duck into the next restaurant and ask the hostess for pen and paper. She hands me a napkin and her pen uninterested in what I'm doing.

I scribble down a note to Victoria and then give the hostess a twenty to deliver the note to Victoria. I stand outside as the hostess enters, but disappear before Victoria has a chance to come after me.

I can't talk to her today. I can't talk to her tomorrow. I can't talk to her next week. It's going to take a long time to undo the damage that I've done. But I'm willing to wait. However long it takes. A year. More.

I want her to wait for me. I want her to think only of me. But that's not fair. She shouldn't wait. She should live her life while I do everything I can to make it up to her. Because she deserves to be happy. Even if it means without me.

IT'S BEEN SIX WEEKS, twelve hours, and fifty-two seconds since the last time I saw Victoria. And every single one of them has been a living hell. I hate my new life. I hate pretending to care about a woman that I don't. I hate being paraded out to interview after interview. To event after event like a show pony.

I hate running my company from a distance, not really able to take on new clients because it interferes with the work I'm doing with Lily.

But most of all I hate not hearing from Victoria.

I walk into the bar where Logan works with Lily draped all over my arm. The new shiny ring that I bought her to replace Victoria's ring sparkling brightly on her finger. I couldn't really change the style of the ring after she showed it on national television, but I couldn't spend a year with Lily watching her wear the exact ring that I had used to propose to Victoria with. It hurt too much.

One year. That's how long I promised Lily I would keep up this farce. Long enough for her to win, and then we would come up with a reason that I leave her. A drug problem. I cheat on her. Something. I just have to survive one year and then I'll be free.

I spot Logan behind the bar and walk over to it with Lily clawing at my arm the whole way. Our bodies don't sync together like Victoria's and I's do, which makes it almost impossible to walk together naturally. We make it to the bar and I pull out a stool and take a seat not bothering to help Lily with her stool.

She huffs beside me as she has to pull her own barstool out and take a seat without the help of her charming fiancée.

Logan smiles as he walks over to us and leans on the bar.

"Hey, Carter! It's good to see you in person man. I'm not used to having to turn on my TV in order to see my best friend."

I exhale. "Sorry about that. I'll try to stop by more now that things have settled down a bit."

"Can I get you something to drink?"

"Beer," I say.

"Oh good of you to look at me," Lily says when Logan finally gives her attention. "I'll have a white wine."

He gives me an *it sucks to be you* look and then turns to get us our drinks.

"You don't have to be such a bitch to everyone you know. Logan and I are best friends, be nice."

She smirks. "You and Logan are no longer best friends. I own your ass for the next year and I don't want you hanging with a slum like him. It's not good for our image as a couple. So you better say your goodbyes now."

Her phone buzzes in her purse and she pulls it out and answers in her annoying high-pitched voice before giving me an *I'll be right back* look and gets up to take the call away from me.

I sigh. I don't know how I was ever able to stand her when we dated in high school. Probably because we just had lots and lots of sex and very little talking. Probably because she was just a distraction from my best friend's sister that I could never admit that I had feelings for.

Logan returns with my beer and Lily's wine. He sets them down on the bar.

"Where did the evil witch go?"

"Phone call," I say drinking down half the beer.

Logan laughs and pulls out two shot glasses and fills them both with whiskey. "I think you could use one of these." He slides me one of the shots and takes the other in his hand. We clink them together and down the shots.

"So what did you really come here for, because it wasn't to see me," Logan says.

I frown. "I did want to see my best friend, but..."

"But you want to know how Victoria is doing?"

I nod. "But I shouldn't know. I won't be able to keep doing what I'm doing if I know too much about Victoria."

Logan laughs. "What are you doing? Because it seems like you are making the biggest mistake you've ever made."

"I'm paying for all of the mistakes I've made with Victoria."

"You're going to be paying for a long time, you made a lot of mistakes when it came to Victoria."

"I know. I'm just hoping that I can pay for them within the year. And I have to keep working for Lily. It's the only way that I and, more importantly, Victoria keeps getting paid for the job that she did fixing Lily's mistakes."

I glance to the lobby where Lily is pacing on her phone. She will be back soon and who knows when I'll get a chance to talk to Logan again face to face.

"How is she? I don't need to know all of the details. I just need to know that she has more than enough money to take care of the family. And that she is happy."

Logan rubs the back of his neck and I can see in his eyes that he wants to tell me something, but is not sure if I want to hear it.

"She's happy."

I stare at my glass of beer, watching the bubbles fizzle as I try to be good. She's happy. I don't need to know more.

"What do you want to tell me?" I ask, not looking up at him because I hate myself for asking about her.

"It's not mine to tell. If you want to know more about Victoria, you're going to have to ask her yourself."

"Damn it, Logan! Just tell me. Tell me she's dating someone else." I grip the glass too tightly and watch as it crushes in my hand. Little pieces of glass stick to my hand along with the beer.

Logan shakes his head at me before he walks over and grabs a wet rag, tossing it to me to clean up the mess.

"Victoria isn't going to want you if you are a jealous mess. You were the one that decided this was for the best. You decided that the only way to get her back was to put in the work. Then do it.

"And in the meantime, Victoria is going to live her life. She deserves to be happy. She takes care of all of us. She may be the youngest, but she somehow was always the one that was strong enough to deal with all of our crap. We wouldn't be here without her.

"So do the work man, and when you are done, you'll have Victoria's forgiveness."

"And her heart?" I ask, swallowing hard.

Logan shrugs. "You'll either have it or you won't. But either way, Victoria will be happy."

"I need a napkin and a pen."

Logan frowns as he moves down the bar and grabs me a napkin and a pen from his pocket and places them on the bar in front of me.

I start scribbling on it.

"What are you doing?"

"I'm starting at the beginning and writing an apology for every time I've ever hurt her."

I stop writing and Logan snatches the napkin out of my hand and starts reading.

"I'm sorry for stealing your only barbie from you when we were little. It was mean. I was six and didn't know better, but it still isn't okay. I watched you cry and I didn't give it back. I'm sorry," Logan reads. He glances at me. "You really are starting at the beginning."

I nod.

He flips the napkin over and I try to snatch it back before he reads the other side.

"I know you are too old for barbies now, although I'll send one for Sailor to play with. But for you, I need you to do something for me. I miss kissing you, desperately. Your lips are what I dream of every night. Don't let your luscious, fuckable lips go to waste. Kiss a stranger, or a lover. Kiss someone for me."

Logan stares down at me when he finishes, completely silent. "You really love her, don't you?"

I nod. "I think I've always loved her. I just didn't understand how to love someone. I'm still not sure I do. My family taught me how to treat people like shit. And the only way I got out of the situation was by having a ruthless career that took down anyone and everyone in my path. Even Victoria."

"Why a napkin?" Logan asks, offering me no comfort. He doesn't say that I already know how to love, which only makes me realize that taking this time is my only chance at figuring out exactly how to love.

"Because it's what I wrote on and gave her the night Lily announced our engagement on television. The night Victoria decided to get her revenge. I could write on paper, but writing on napkins lets her know that I'm thinking about her always. Even when I shouldn't. Even when I'm just having a drink or grabbing a bite to eat. I'm not just sitting down to write a long note in order to try to win her back when it's most convenient for me. I'm always thinking of her." Always, forever, I'll never stop.

17 VICTORIA

I hold the envelope in my hand as I walk out onto the balcony.

I lean over the edge of the railing and take a deep breath as I stare at the envelope addressed from Carter in my hand. I turn it over and over again deciding if this will be the one that I finally just toss into the pool instead of opening and reading. Every time I receive one, which is at least once a week, sometimes more, I do this. I tell myself I'd be better off just tossing them out and forgetting about Carter, but I can never actually do it.

As much as I want to be over him, I'm not. I bought the house that he proposed to me. I will never stop thinking about him. Never stop loving him. But I need to get over him.

I look down at Amber and Sailor playing in the pool together. They are happy. Happier than I've ever seen them.

If I'm thankful for one thing about Carter it was his idea to buy a house that we can all live in. That's what I was trying to do in San Fransisco, but it was too close to our mother. Too close to our pasts that we needed to escape. And it didn't include Logan.

Now all of us live together. I started a PR company and have been teaching Amber and Logan how to work with me.

And our mother is out of our lives for good after what she did to Amber.

I take a seat in the lawn chair, still holding onto the envelope. I lift it to my nose and take a deep breath, smelling the hints of his cologne that always seem to rub off onto the envelope reminding me of everything I'm giving up, by giving up Carter.

I FEEL his lips on mine and my body immediately wakes up. I open my eyes and stretch, loving waking up to him in San Fransisco.

"I could get used to this," I say wrapping my arms around his neck and pulling him into another kiss.

"I brought you breakfast," he says.

I bite my lip. "What if I want you for breakfast?"

He grins and pushes my arms above my head. "I figured you would say that."

"What are you going to do about it?" I tease.

He reaches to the nightstand where I see he's made eggs, toast, and bacon. Suddenly, my stomach growls at the sight of food.

Carter grabs something next to the plate that I don't realize is a tie until he ties my arms above my head and then to the headboard.

"Carter, I don't think I can handle being tied up," I say, my voice nervous.

He grins. "I know. You like control too much. But sometimes, this is what you need."

He grabs the hem of my tank top and lifts it up, but not all the way over my head. Instead, he lifts it just high enough until it is covering my head.

"Carter, I can't see."

His lips come down on mine and he kisses me gently.

"I know," he says again.

His lips trail down my chest sending chills all over my body. He's kissed me like this before, but I've never felt such intensity. My arms squirm over my head and my breathing picks up. I love it and hate it at the same time. I don't want him to stop, but I really want him to untie me and uncover my eyes.

"Just focus on your breathing Victoria. You can do this."

I take a deep breath in and out and then I feel his lips back on me again. And I forget about breathing. I forget about anything but him.

He pushes my legs apart as his cock rests between my legs. His lips and tongue continue to kiss me and I can't breathe. I need air. He needs to remember that I need to breathe.

My arms pull hard at the tie, but I can't get my arms free. My body squirms beneath his, trying to remind him to let me breathe.

His lips finally leave mine, and I take in a gasp.

"Do you trust me Victoria?" he asks in my ear, his breath hot against my skin. "Because if you trust me, then you can relax. You can know that I will take care of you and I'm not going to do anything to cause you pain. You can relax and let me fuck you."

He kisses my neck. "Do you trust me?"

"Yes," I breathe, even though I'm not sure I do. But I want to. Desperately. And maybe this is what I need in order to trust him.

One word and he owns my body. He kisses every inch of my body, making me squirm and feel electricity I've never felt before, even though he's kissed my entire body before. Somehow the blindfold and being unable to move my arms makes it that much more intense.

He pushes his cock hard at my entrance, begging me to let him in while he kisses my lips. It feels like he's asking me to open my heart as well. I'm not sure if I'm ready. Not after everything we've been through.

But as his cock pushes inside me, I know that I've let him far into my heart. I love him. I want him. I trust him.

Three things I've never thought I'd feel about Carter.

A TEAR ROLLS down my cheek thinking back to that morning. The sex was amazing, but he was equally as amazing afterward. He fed me breakfast bite by bite. He took care of me. And for once it felt good to be the one taken care of, instead of the one that has to take care of everyone else.

But it was all a lie. He didn't really care about me. He just wanted me to sleep with him. And he sure as hell didn't love me. He isn't capable of love.

I stare down at the envelope that I'm sure contains another napkin with another apology. His apologies are good. Seemingly heartfelt even. But they aren't enough. Not now after everything that has happened.

My life has changed, but I'm still the same person. I live my life taking care of my family. And even if I can find a way to forgive him, I won't forgive him for getting me fired and hurting my family. My family comes first. I can't forgive him for hurting them.

My heart wants to know that he's been thinking of me, but instead of opening the envelope, I don't.

I stand up and walk to the edge of the railing. I drop the envelope over the edge and let it fall slowly down to the pool beneath. It hits the water and I know there is no going back. It's soaking wet, even if I tried to recover it, there is no guarantee that I'd be able to read his words.

It feels right. It feels like after all these months, almost eight to be exact, that I'm finally over him. But the pain still remains.

He's ruined my life in so many ways. There is no way I will trust a man, not after him.

But I'm not done ruining his.

I pull my cell phone out of my pocket and I dial Lily's number like I often do every few weeks. I can check in on Carter and earn the paychecks that Lily still sends me by tweaking things to ensure that she stays on top of her game.

But this time, it's not just to benefit her, although it will. It's to benefit me as well. Because I need to see him truly pay for what he's done to me and my family. He's never going to stop paying for what he did.

18 CARTER

I'm tired.

So incredibly tired.

Being separated from Victoria has driven me mad. I can't keep doing this. Every day that goes by is like another needle getting shot into my body. And after almost eight months of getting stabbed over and over again, I just can't take it anymore.

I've been sending her almost daily napkins with apologies. I thought sending them would make me feel better, but they don't. They make me feel worse as I realize just how many things I've done to hurt her. I deserve to be in a lot more pain than I am in.

I thought she would respond. I thought that she would send me a text message. Send me a letter back. Even pass a message along through Logan.

But she hasn't. Not one single word. I can't handle not hearing from her. So even though I have four months left, I need to see her. Now.

"You're wearing that?" Lily asks, eyeing me out of the corner of her eye from where she sits getting her hair and makeup done for another show tonight. This one is on Phoebe's show again.

I look down at my jeans and buttoned down shirt, the same thing I always wear when we go on television. "Yes."

She sighs. "You need to wear something more dressy. This is the last month before the election and I need you to look your best. Go put a suit on. The grey one with the turquoise tie."

I don't argue with her. I've found that it isn't worth it. I just do what she says, whether I agree with it or not. At this point, I hope she loses the election, that way I don't have to stay with her longer than another month.

I walk down the hallway to the small dressing room, where I find the suit that she wants me to wear, already hanging on the rack. I put it on, but something doesn't feel right. It doesn't make sense why she would want me so dressed up unless something special was happening tonight.

I get an uneasy feeling in my stomach. Lily likes to spring things on me during the interview, that way I can't protest what she is saying. I just have to go along with it as true.

Lily is happier than usual. She's far too excited about our interview. Something's up. I just hope I can figure it out before she tells some other ridiculous lie about our relationship.

LILY SLIPS her hand into mine. I fight the urge to pull my hand out of hers. I still haven't figured out what she's planning for the interview, but honestly, I'm not sure I care. Whatever it is, I'll smile and go along with it. I only have a few months left and then I'm gone anyway. There is nothing she can do to hurt me anymore.

We are announced and then we walk out, hand in hand, to the couch where we will be interviewed.

I smile and pretend I'm the happiest man in the world, even though I'm the most miserable one. I've gotten pretty good at faking it though. That, or no one really wants to look past what I display on the surface.

We take a seat, still holding hands. Phoebe starts asking us questions and I let Lily do most of the talking as usual. I'm just here as arm candy. I'm just here to make Lily look better.

"So you two have more big news to announce? Is it wedding plans?" Phoebe asks excitedly.

"We haven't set an exact wedding date yet. I've always wanted a summer wedding so maybe June," Lily says, looking at me with a toothy smile.

I nod. Thank God she's not announcing that we are getting married next week. That would be a hard no for me. There is no way I'm marrying Lily.

"But we do have some exciting news to share," Lily says, rubbing her stomach.

No! I scream in my head. She is not going to pull this crap on me. I can't keep a happy face, I glare at her a little, trying to put a stop to this before it starts.

Lily grips my hand tighter to try and get me to stop.

"We're expecting!" Lily shouts.

"Oh my god! How exciting!" Phoebe says.

The crowd cheers and my scowl deepens.

Phoebe doesn't miss my change in expression. When the crowd stops she turns to me.

"Carter, you look less than excited about this news. Care to share your feelings about this development?"

The crowd falls silent.

I take a deep breath. "Don't get me wrong. I'm more than excited to be a father. I just thought we were going to wait a little while longer before we shared the news. It's still very early in her pregnancy and a lot could go wrong. I just wanted to share this special time with her in private."

"Aw, how sweet. Well, don't worry. I'm sure her pregnancy will go perfectly and you two will have plenty of intimate time together."

I don't listen to the rest of the interview. I'm too frustrated to pay attention. I don't know how she came up with this hair-brained idea anyway. There is no way she can pull off a pregnancy. And what's going to happen when she is supposed to have given birth and there is no baby?

I look over behind the stage and I see her. Just for a split second. Victoria. She's here. This was her idea. She's trying to hurt me. Still.

She can continue to hurt me the rest of our lives if that's what she wants, but I would prefer for her to hurt me while being mine. Or at the very least talking to me again so that I can see that she is happy without me.

The second that the interview is over, I jump up off the couch and run, needing to talk to her again. I just need to hear that she is through with me, if that's what this is meant to be. I'm tired of playing games. If she still hates me, I need to hear it from her own lips.

When I get backstage though, I don't see her anywhere. As usual, she disappeared before I have a chance to talk to her. She ran. Again.

I run my hand through my hair and take a deep breath. I'm going to find her. This ends now.

"It was Victoria's idea, but I'm guessing you have already figured that out," Lily says from behind me.

I turn around glaring at her. "I'm done, Lily."

Her lips curl up into a sly smile. "No, you aren't. We are just getting started."

"No, I quit."

"You can't."

"I just did."

She shakes her head and places her hand on my chest. I grab it and remove it.

"You're mine, remember? If you want me to keep paying you and Victoria, you will do exactly as I say. I'll ruin your careers if you leave."

I smirk. "I have a feeling Victoria negotiated her own contract that doesn't include me behaving."

Lily narrows her eyes and her smile falls. I know I'm right about Victoria.

"You'll never work as a fixer again."

"I don't plan on fixing anyone's problems other than Victoria's ever again."

"It's too late. If you leave now, everyone will just think you're running out on this baby."

"No, because there is no baby Lily. You'll tell them you miscarried and the pain was too much for our relationship. We couldn't stay together. You might actually get some sympathy votes."

I turn and walk away not caring if she follows the miscarriage plan or not. I don't care if every person on the planet thinks I walked out on a baby that doesn't even exist. And if the baby does exist, it's definitely not mine. The only person I care about is Victoria.

"She doesn't love you," Lily says, trying to get one last punch in before I go. "That's why she came up with this plan. To send a message that she hates you. That she wants you out of her life. She wants you with me."

I hesitate for just a second. Lily's right. I'm sure that Victoria hates me. But we've hated each other before, and somehow also loved each other. The hate can still be there, I just hope the love isn't gone.

I walk out of the building and straight to the bar that I found her in last time, eight months ago.

I look into the window and find her sitting in a booth, her back to me.

I smile and take a deep breath. She may hate me, but she wanted me to find her. She wanted me to fight for her. So here I am.

I walk into the bar and take a seat across from her at the booth. The table is high, and she leans on her folded arms that rest on the table. She looks different when she looks at me. Her eyes glow brightly. I can't read her emotions, whether that's a happy or sad look. Of anger or joy. I can't make sense of her expression.

"I missed you, Victoria."

She looks down at her hands. "I missed you, too."

My heart beats wildly at that. I still have a chance. But this is probably the last chance that I will ever get.

"Can I get you something to drink?" I ask, hoping that if I get her a drink, then maybe she will stay long enough for me to convince her that she still loves me.

She shakes her head.

I run my hand through my hair trying to figure out where to start, but there is no good place to start. So I start with the truth.

I place the engagement ring that I gave her months earlier onto the table in front of us. I watch her eyes look at it and I swear I see the desperation that she is fighting back. She wants to take back the ring, but something is holding her back.

"I'm sorry. Truly. If I could take it back, I would. I would take back every drop of pain I ever caused you. Every heartache. Every fear. Every anxiety. I would take it all away, but I can't."

I watch her suck in a breath as she continues fighting her real feelings.

"You should just go, Carter. There is nothing you can say that will make this any better. Just go."

"I can't. I can't just go. Not without you—or at least, not without knowing I did everything I could to make it better."

I shake my head. "You got me fired. At least six times. How do you recover from that?"

"With love. Lots and lots of love. Because this is what our life would be like together. Maybe not at this extreme level, but we like fighting; you said so yourself. You like fighting and arguing. I do, too. And I like making it up to you. I've heard makeup sex is pretty good, too."

She scowls at me.

"Because you are my whole life. I quit my job today. I passed my company along to my number two, although I warned him that he would struggle to get a job as long as you were working. I'm giving up everything that I thought I ever wanted to have a chance at a life with you. I'll stay home and cook and clean for you while you go out and live your dreams. I'll take care of your family. I'll take care of you. I'll help you fix your life, like you fixed mine."

She doesn't breathe.

"I hope you've gotten all of my apologies, but I have two apologies left that I need to say in person. One, I need to apologize for making you think I was going to ask you to prom in high school and then asking Lily instead. I ended your relationship with Mark before it started and then prevented you from having a chance at another relationship by starting that nasty rumor. I'm so sorry. If I had listened to my heart, I would have taken you to prom instead of Lily. But I was scared. Lily was easy, she wasn't real love. But I knew that I could really love you.

"And two, I need to apologize for what I put your family through by getting you fired. They relied on you, and I hurt them. I've already apologized to them, but I will continue to apologize to them over and over again until I make it up to them."

She bites her lip and I know I'm starting to break through her walls.

"How am I doing?"

"Pretty good," she says in almost a whisper.

I can't hold back any longer, I grab her hands and hold her as close to me as possible, while I lean over the table and kiss her. I expect her to pull away. Slap me maybe. Instead, she kisses me back. It's a desperate kiss full of hope and need. Our lips crash hard together and our tongues dance together like they've never been apart.

It feels right kissing her.

Slowly we stop, but we don't stop holding hands.

"I'm so sorry, Victoria. Please, let me spend the rest of my life attempting to make it up to you."

"I can't marry you."

My heart stops.

"I'm pregnant," she says and for the first time, I see the difference in her that I couldn't figure out before. Her breasts are larger, her face fuller, and I can finally see a bit of her belly protruding out as I glance over the table.

I wanted her to move on with her life while I was gone. I wanted her to be happy. She did that. And now, she's having another man's baby.

Anguish doesn't even begin to touch what I'm feeling. Sadness. Desperation. Depression. Disappointment. Fear. Guilt. Frustration. None of the words fully cover what I'm feeling.

Hurt. I'm beyond hurt.

"Congratulations," I finally say, because it's what I should say. I should be happy for her. I want to ask who the father is, but I can't get the words to leave my mouth. It is also clear now why she gave Lily the idea to pretend she was pregnant. Because she, herself, was pregnant.

I want to scream that this can't be happening. She can't have another man's baby. She should be having mine.

I grab the ring that is still lying on the table untouched and hold it out to her. "I want you Victoria. All of you. I want your family. Your baby. I want to spend the rest of my life loving you. I want to spend it taking care of you and your family. I would love to do it as your husband. But I'll take it as your friend. Or if you won't let me back into my life then just know that I will always be looking out for you. Even if it has to be from afar."

She stares down at the ring. "You hurt me, Carter. You're the only person who has truly been able to hurt me."

I watch the tears starting in her eyes. "I thought that by becoming heartless, like I thought you were, would make me feel better. I thought it would make me be able to protect my heart more and, in turn, my family. But sitting here now looking at you, my heart still hates you and loves you in equal parts."

"I'll take the hate, as long as I can take the love part too."

She wipes a tear off her cheek. "Can you forgive me?"

I raise an eyebrow and smile. "You don't have anything for me to forgive you for. I deserved everything that you dolled out to me in regards to Lily."

She shakes her head. "I'm not talking about Lily. I wasn't going to tell you the truth about the baby."

She rests her hand on her stomach that looks larger every time she moves. She must be pretty far along, which means she met the father quickly after we broke up.

"I don't deserve to know about the baby. You lived your life while I was picking up the pieces to mend mine."

She bites her lip and then the words fall out of her mouth. "The baby is yours."

I freeze. "What?"

"The baby is yours."

I jump out of the booth and over to her side climbing into the booth next to her. I get a better look at her stomach and realize that she is about to pop any day now.

"Can you forgive me? I wasn't going to tell you about the baby even though it's yours. I wasn't sure I could take the chance that you wouldn't hurt this baby too. But after I thought more about it, I knew you would never intentionally hurt this baby. I was hiding the baby from you to get back at you. I had turned heartless and wanted you to feel the pain that I felt."

I laugh. "I don't care. I'm just so happy that the baby is mine and not some other asshole's." I put my hand on her stomach, feeling the baby kick inside her. *Magical* is all I think as I feel the baby inside her.

"God, Victoria, I know I've made plenty of mistakes in the past, but know that I'm going to love this baby with everything I have."

"It's a boy," she says grinning.

"I'm going to love and protect our son with everything that I have."

She nods. "I know."

I hold out the ring to her, not sure where we go from here, except that I love her and I need to be a part of her life.

She takes the ring hesitantly in her hand, then places it on the ring finger of her right hand. "Maybe someday I'll move it to its proper place on my left hand, but for now I just want to be happy. I want to work hard. I want to take care of this new baby. And I want you to be a part of that."

I grin and kiss her long and slow.

"I know that you have mixed emotions toward me, but how do you feel about me right here in this moment? Do you still hate me or love me?"

"Why?" I ask.

"Because there is a restroom behind you that I would love to fuck you in."

She grins. "Love. Definitely love."

EPILOGUE

VICTORIA

I hear Charlie crying as I clasp my bracelet onto my wrist. We were supposed to leave five minutes ago for our dinner date, but it seems that Charlie really doesn't want us to go.

I walk out of my bedroom and head down the hallway toward Charlie's room. I guess our dinner date will have to wait a little longer. I make it almost to his room when Carter grabs my hand and pulls me into the hallway closet as he shuts the door behind us. He puts his hand over my mouth and makes a *shh* sound.

I raise an eyebrow at him and wait for him to remove his hand from my lips.

"What are you doing?" I ask.

"We aren't here remember. We are on our date. We haven't had a date since Charlie was born six months ago and we aren't going to get trapped here again. What is the benefit of living with your entire family if you don't take advantage of the free babysitting?"

"But Charlie—"

"Is fine."

I listen and I hear Amber and Sailor comforting Charlie down the hallway.

"See?"

I nod.

"You look sexy, by the way," Carter says, looking me up and down in a skin-tight red dress.

I bite my lip. "I thought you would like it."

"I'd like to see you out of it more."

He grabs the back of my neck and pulls me into a deep kiss. My arms fall around his neck as I breathe in his cologne. He smells good, almost as good as he tastes.

He pushes me hard against the closet wall and I let out a squeal.

His hand covers my mouth again. "You have to be quiet Victoria. I'm going to fuck you and you wouldn't want anyone to hear you."

"We can't," I whisper. "They are all just down the hallway."

"Then you better be very, very quiet."

He slides his hands up my thighs pushing my dress up until he reaches his goal. He hooks one finger under my panties and pulls them down, hard. He kisses me to keep me quiet as his fingers move to the slit between my legs.

"Carter," I moan.

"Shh," he says as he unzips his pants and pushes his cock against my stomach.

"Wait," I say.

He stops. "What? I'll make sure we don't miss our reservations, but I need you baby. Now."

I bite my lip. "I know."

"Then why are we waiting?"

He kisses my neck and I forget what I wanted to tell him.

I moan and he grins.

"God, I can't get enough of that sound."

He pushes his cock inside me hard and fast, while I wrap my legs around his waist and ride him hard. Sex with Carter is never normal. We rarely fuck in a bed and he always likes to keep things interesting. I sometimes pick a fight with him, just so we can have savage, rough sex that only he can give me. But right now, it's not about that. Because after seeing how Carter is with Charlie, I couldn't hate him.

"You want to come, don't you baby?"

I nod.

"Good, don't scream. Or I'm going to take you to our bedroom and really have my way with you and we will never make it to dinner."

I bite my lip as hard as I can as Carter fucks me into my orgasm. I try to keep my mouth quiet, but my whole body is screaming. My body tightens around his and my hands claw at his neck.

My orgasm finally stops and Carter grabs my left hand that is clawing at his neck far too hard.

"Jesus, Victoria. You don't understand how to be gentle, do you?"

I bite my lip. "Sorry."

He grins and then looks more closely at my left hand. His eyes widen when he finally realizes what I wanted to tell him.

"Does this mean what I think it means?" he asks, staring at my engagement ring that I finally put on my left hand.

I nod. "I want to marry you and have more babies with you and live happily ever after with you Carter."

He kisses me hard on the lips and I couldn't be happier. I never thought that I could be this happy. None of us did. Our lives started out so crappy. But somehow, we came back together and became a family, all under one roof taking care of each other.

"I'll marry you under one condition," he says.

I smirk. "Oh? I don't think you are in any position to be making demands."

"I think that's exactly where I am." He kisses me again and he knows I would give him anything.

"I'll marry you if you promise to never stop hating me as much as you love me. I'm not sure I could ever give up our rough, *love to hate you* sex sessions."

I grin. "I think I can give you that," I say, half lying. There is no way I can hate Carter, but pretending that I hate him is easy. I've had years of practice hating him. I'll spend eternity loving and hating him.

The End

Thank you for reading Savage Love!

Continue on to read Not Sorry...

NOT SORRY

---

1 SEAN

I don't know what the hell I'm doing here. I promised I would never come back to Chicago. It's too damn cold here. Still, I find myself stepping off a plane at O'Hare International Airport in Chicago. Why?

Because I'm an idiot.

And, when Jamie Parks calls me, saying she needs help, I come running. I would do anything for that girl, and she knows it, including marrying her, if she would only say yes. But I know that's not in the cards for us. It's been over a year since the last time I saw her. I'm just hoping she'll let me take her on a date after I help her save her real estate company.

I wheel my carry-on bag through the airport and out to Arrivals where Jamie said she would pick me up, but I don't see Jamie waiting for me anywhere. I sigh. Jamie always used to run late.

I pull my phone out of my pocket and get started on answering emails and returning daily phone calls to check in with my company. I pace back and forth as I talk, trying to stay warm, which is impossible due to the snow and cold wind that are whipping around the side of the airport and hitting me straight in the face over and over again.

Fuck this.

I head back into the airport to wait for Jamie. I text her that I'm just inside Arrivals and then continue doing work until she gets here.

I hang up on my latest call and glance at the time. She's over forty minutes late. This is getting ridiculous. I should have just taken a cab to her office.

The doors slide open, letting in another burst of cold air that I'm getting more than annoyed with, but there isn't anywhere else for me to wait. I glance at the woman standing in the doorway, hoping it's Jamie, but I immediately realize that it isn't.

Still, I continue to stare at the woman in the doorway, transfixed with how much of a giant mess she is. She's wearing dark snow boots that look white from the snow that is covering them. Her legs are shivering because, for some crazy reason, she decided not to wear pants or tights or those yoga pant things women usually wear. And she is wearing the smallest yet puffiest pink coat I've ever seen. In her hand, she is carrying a cup of coffee from what I assume is a local coffee shop because I don't recognize the brand on the side of the cup.

She nervously glances around the room and then smiles when she sees me. She walks over to me, and I think she is going to ask for directions or how an airport works because she looks completely out of place here. Hopefully, she is traveling someplace warm, which would explain her bare legs. I will admit, those legs do look hot—long and lean, just like I like. I guess it would be a waste of good legs if she covered them.

"Are you Sean?" the woman asks.

My eyes widen a bit in shock, partially from the fact that she knows my name and partially when I see that she is wearing makeup on only about half of her face. I laugh a little at the sight. I can't help it. But then the door opens, and another breeze of cold air pushes through us. Her long, frizzy dark hair blows in her face, and my nose breathes in her sweet smell. *Apples and cherries maybe?*

This woman is clearly having an off day. I hope it's an off day because I can't imagine anyone going through life every day like this. But, underneath all of the mess, something has me intrigued.

"Yes, although no one calls me that."

"Oh, I'm sorry. Jamie didn't tell me that you went by a nickname."

I shake my head, chuckling a little bit. "I don't go by a nickname."

"Oh." She frowns, unsure of what I mean.

"I go by Mr. Burrows."

She bites her lip. "I'm sorry, Mr. Burrows. I'm just so happy I found you. You have no idea about the morning I've had."

I snicker as I look her up and down and cock my head to one side. "I have a pretty good idea."

She blushes. "Anyway, I'm Olive. I'll be driving you to the Parks Real Estate office."

I frown. Jamie couldn't even bother to come pick me up.

"It's so nice to meet you, Mr. Burrows," Olive says as she leans forward.

I have no idea what she is doing. I assume she has to tell me something privately, so I lean forward a little, too, and the next thing I know, her lips graze my cheek before brushing against my lips.

I smile when her soft lips touch mine. I assume she is passing along a greeting from Jamie, and her lips are very nice. I will never turn down a kiss.

But, the next moment, I feel hot coffee all over my body, and I look up to see a blushing Olive with a cup of coffee in her hand that I'm sure is empty now.

"Oh my God. I'm so, so sorry. I didn't mean to spill coffee on you. I bought it because I figured, with your early morning flight, you would need some coffee to get through today. And I'm sorry. I didn't mean to kiss you. Um...I'm sorry. I'm not used to the two-cheek-kiss thing you do in Europe. I'm sorry."

I look down at my light-blue shirt and black slacks that are now covered in coffee. It's just not as visible on my pants as it is my shirt. I packed lightly. Everything I brought with me is inside a small carry-on. I doubt that I'm going to be here very long. Jamie just said she needed some help. I'm sure I can have her company headed in the right direction in no time.

"It's fine. I'll just need you to point me in the direction of a dry cleaner later."

"When you get to the office, you can change, and I'll have this dry-cleaned for you by the end of the day."

I nod. "Lead the way."

I follow Olive outside and am thankful that she parked against the curb even though I'm sure it is breaking the rules. You aren't supposed to park your car against the curb.

A security officer is standing outside of Olive's Mercedes.

"Is this your car, miss? It's a no parking zone," the security officer says.

"I'm so sorry. I didn't know. I'll move it right now," Olive says, climbing into the driver's seat.

The officer gives her a stern look but then nods. I toss my carry-on into the backseat and then climb in the front seat, next to Olive. She immediately pulls out and begins driving.

I glance around the interior of her car. It's nice, really nice. "Your car is nice. Jamie must pay you well for you to afford something this nice."

Olive blushes. "It's not my car. It's Jamie's. She gave it to me to come pick you up since I don't own a car."

I look around now, more amazed with Jamie. She's doing well for herself if she can afford this.

"So, what do you do for Jamie?"

"I'm her assistant," Olive answers.

I nod. It makes sense, although I'm not sure Olive is doing the best job she could as an assistant. Maybe that's what Jamie needs me to do. Prune the employees who aren't doing so well to help her continue to grow.

Olive surprises me with how she manages Chicago traffic for someone who doesn't own a car. She drives efficiently and safely but quickly gets us to the office.

"Thanks for picking me up, Olive," I say as I climb out of the car.

"Of course, Sean—I'm sorry. I mean—"

"Don't worry about it. I don't mind if you call me Sean."

She smiles and then leads me into the office building. Then, we ride up in the elevator to the floor that Parks Real Estate occupies.

We climb out, and to my surprise, it seems like the whole team has gathered to welcome me to the building. There are about fifty people gathered with all their eyes focused on me and Olive. I glance over at Olive, who also seems surprised at the gathering.

Olive begins speaking before I have a chance to, "This is Sean—uh, Mr. Sturrows."

She bites her lip when she realizes she said the wrong last name and begins to open her mouth to, I assume, correct herself, but I cut her off.

"I'm Sean Burrows. I'm excited to work with all of you for as long as you and Jamie will have me. I've heard wonderful things about all of you. As for my stained shirt, I've heard that's what happens when you work in real estate and when you have an assistant like Olive pick you up," I joke.

The room chuckles and laughs, obviously used to Olive doing things like spilling coffee on a regular basis, but when I glance over at Olive, I immediately regret my joke. I expected her to look embarrassed or maybe a little upset with my joke. But she doesn't look embarrassed. She looks downright angry.

"I'm so happy you could make it," Jamie says, softly kissing me on the cheek.

"I'm happy to be here. I would do anything for you."

She smiles, and I have a chance to study Jamie. She looks different.

Her cheeks look the slightest bit fuller. In fact, her whole body looks slightly fuller. Not in a bad way, but in a perfect way. Her skin seems to be glowing, and her long blonde hair is shinier than I've ever seen it.

I realize immediately why she brought me here, and it's not because she wanted another date or a one-night hook-up or anything to do with me other than she trusts me.

"You're pregnant," I whisper in her ear.

Jamie blushes, and I know it's true.

"Have Olive take your clothes to the dry cleaners and get changed. We have a lot to discuss."

Jamie heads to her office, and I can't help but stare at her gorgeous ass as she walks.

"Come on, Romeo. I'll show you to the restroom, so you can get changed, and I can get your clothes to the dry cleaners. Although no one believes it, I do have more important things to do with my day," Olive says, walking toward the restroom.

I follow her. "Is it that obvious that I like Jamie?"

She shakes her head. "You are unbelievable. How about an *I'm sorry?*"

"Why would I say sorry?"

"Because you said something hurtful at my expense."

"It was a joke. It wasn't hurtful. It was truthful."

"You should apologize instead of worrying if it's obvious that you like Jamie. It's obvious that everyone likes Jamie, so it's not that unusual. No one but me notices because everyone else is already too busy pining over Jamie."

"So, who's the baby daddy?" I ask.

Olive stops and looks at me seriously. "She told you she was pregnant?"

"No, I just guessed. You confirmed."

"I didn't confirm anything."

I smile. "Yes, you did."

"Whatever. Just get changed, so I can take your clothes." She

186

pauses at the restroom for me to go inside. "Although you probably want to take them yourself since I will just ruin them."

I begin unbuttoning my shirt and watch as her eyes drift to my chest and then abs. I remove the shirt and hand it to her. "Just take the shirt. It's a favorite of mine. I'll just buy new pants if I need them."

Olive sucks in a breath and then walks away. I watch her ass sway in her dress. I watch her toned, tan legs move, and then I see that she is still wearing her snow-covered boots. She's adorable and a tiny bit sexy. And a giant mess.

I could have her in my bed as many times as I want while I'm here. Or I could fire her because, if she is this incompetent in how she dresses, she can't be much more competent as an assistant. It's a tough decision—think with my dick or my business sense.

Jamie walks over to me as I pull a shirt out of my suitcase and begin to put it on.

"That wasn't very nice—what you said about Olive," she says.

I roll my eyes. "I was being truthful, and you know it. I don't want to talk about Olive right now. If I do, it will be to suggest firing her. There are a million assistants out there who are better than Olive."

She raises an eyebrow. "Wow. For once, you don't want to fuck my assistant. I thought Olive was just your type."

I laugh. "A complete mess isn't my type."

"Olive is anything but a mess. In fact, she might be the most put-together person in this office."

"So, that's why you pay her so well then?"

"I have my reasons for not paying her as well as I should."

"Yeah. Greed?"

She shakes her head. "Well, I'm glad that you don't want to sleep with Olive."

"Why?"

"Because, as you have already guessed, I brought you here to run the company for me for a few months—a year at most."

"A year? What the hell, Jamie? I can't stay here for a year! I have my own fucking company to worry about."

"Which is doing just fine. And, if I recall, last time we were together, you said the company could run itself."

I frown.

"Anyway, the doctor said I needed to be on bed rest, starting, like, now. I shouldn't even have come into work today. I just wanted you to get settled and to let you know that Olive is the woman you should go to for advice. She's the smartest person at the company. She's more than just an assistant. She is the only person I trust."

"So then, why isn't *she* running the company?"

She sighs. "You'll understand soon enough. You aren't going to fire Olive. Olive is my assistant, and I expect her to still be here when I get back. Plus, she'll be reporting to me about everything that is going on. So, you'd better not fuck up."

"And what if I do fuck up? It's not like it matters anymore. I came here to try to get you back, but you have clearly moved on. What motivation do I have to do the right thing?"

She smiles and moves her lips close to my ear. "Because I know you, Sean Burrows. I know you still love me and will do anything I ask. And I know you've always wanted to own your own real estate company. That's your next venture. I'll make you a fifty-fifty partner after this year."

"It would be easier to just start my own company than do this for a year."

Jamie shrugs and spots Olive out of the corner of her eye. "Maybe. But maybe you wouldn't find something better, something you'd never experienced before."

"And what's that?"

She glances at Olive, and I do, too.

"Real love."

I laugh.

Jamie is crazy. She didn't bring me here to run the company for her, although she definitely needs the help. She didn't bring me here to entice me with an offer to own half of the company. She brought me here to play matchmaker.

She thinks Olive is the woman for me. She couldn't be further from the truth. Olive is a nice girl with what I'm sure is a nice body underneath the bulky clothing. But she is also a complete mess. She apologizes every five seconds and has zero confidence in herself. She's still an assistant. I want a strong woman, like Jamie, who can equal me in bed and in the business world. Not Olive.

"I think you're crazy, Jamie, but you do have one thing right. I love you and will do anything for you."

"So, you'll run the company for the next year in exchange for owning half of it?"

"Yes, but me asking Olive out on a date is not part of the deal. She's an unconfident mess."

Jamie laughs. "Olive is the strongest, most confident woman I know. Who else would have the confidence to wear half of a face of makeup, boots, and no pants in winter? I know I wouldn't."

I laugh. "I guess that's one way to look at it."

2 OLIVE

I hate him.

Sean.

He's an asshole.

I don't know what he's doing here, but he's been in Jamie's office for almost an hour now while I've been sitting outside, at my cubicle, waiting. All I was told was to pick him up from the airport. Jamie didn't tell me anything else. And, even though we are best friends and she tells me everything—including that she found out she was pregnant from her boyfriend of a total of two months—she is often forgetful. I don't think she would remember anything if it wasn't for me.

But, still, I can't stop thinking about how handsome he is. I can't stop thinking about his dark brown eyes, the five o'clock shadow that covers his strong jaw, or how his muscles bulge beneath his clothing.

The door to her office finally opens, and Sean steps out. He walks past me without even glancing at me or anyone else in the office, and he leaves just as quickly as he got here.

"Olive, can you come in here a moment?" Jamie calls out from her office.

I stand up and walk into her office with a large grin on my face, carrying her dry cleaning that she asked me to pick up on my way into the office today.

I've been Jamie's assistant for far too long. Today is the day I have been waiting five years for. Today is the day I'll finally get promoted. There is a management position open, and I know that she wants me in it. That way, when she takes a couple of months off to be with her baby, I can step in and run things for her. She just needs to make it official.

This is the moment when my life changes. This is the moment when I stop being an assistant. I can stop getting coffee or baking cookies. Although I have a feeling, no matter what position I hold in the company, I'll have to keep making cookies. But at least I'll get paid well. At least well enough to afford more than a studio that holds nothing more than a bed and a small couch and something that resembles a kitchen that wouldn't even fit in one of those tiny houses that you see on TV. They should start videoing my life if they want to know what it's like to live tiny.

"You're an angel, Olive," Jamie says standing as I hand over her dry cleaning. "I couldn't very well work today in sweatpants."

I smile as I look down at Jamie's attire to see that she is indeed in sweatpants. I know she has two closets worth of clothes in her apartment, so she should have had something else to wear. Unless she didn't sleep at her apartment last night.

Jamie takes a seat behind her desk and motions for me to do the same.

I take a seat and wait for her to speak, trying to be as polite as I can even though, inside, I'm bursting to say, *Yes, I'll take it!*

Whatever job she is going to offer and whatever level of money that comes with it will be better than what I get paid. I know everyone else in the company makes at least three times as much as I do, and that's being conservative. The best in the company make ten or more times than I do.

"So, I bet you are wondering why I called you in here this morning."

I nod even though I know exactly why she called me in this morning instead of just emailing me a long list of things she needs me to take care of, like she usually does every morning.

"As you know, some things are about to change with how the company is run around here."

I nod again, smiling brightly, as my suspicions seem to be confirmed.

"And, as you know, I'm pregnant. But, at my last checkup, my doctor said I needed to start taking it easy and be on bed rest until the baby is born."

I nod as I look down at her still-flat stomach. There is no way this woman is five months pregnant. I still can't believe it.

"But, anyway, I want to take at least six months off when the baby is born. I want to just be a mom, which means I need to leave someone I trust in charge of the company to ensure it will continue to head in the right direction."

My eyes widen, and my jaw drops a little bit at what she is suggesting. "You think I am capable of doing that?"

Jamie laughs. "Oh, no. I'm sorry. That's not what I meant at all. That would be a huge jump for you, and you are not ready for that at all. But I don't trust my realtors to lead the company either. We both know, if I let that happen, they would just use the leverage to start their own company. No one is loyal like you are to this company."

I smile, but my smile is weak because I have no idea where she is going with this.

"So, anyway, I hired Sean to be me when I'm gone. He's the best, the absolute best. And I just need you to report to me about how things are going while I'm gone and he is in charge. If things aren't going well, I'll end my maternity leave and come back, but if you tell me things are going well, then I will leave him in charge. Can you do that?"

"Of course. Does this new job come with a promotion?"

She laughs again. "I'm so happy you are my assistant, Olive. You always know just what to say to brighten my day. Of course it's not a promotion, just a favor between two friends."

I nod, but I can't keep smiling. I'm not getting promoted. My heart sinks.

I don't understand. Jamie and I have been friends for years. I've been completely loyal to her and the company, but I still haven't earned a promotion. I don't understand, but I'm not going to question her. I trust her completely, and anyway, I owe her.

"Is that all you need?" I ask.

"Yep. I'm still planning on going to your boyfriend's concert tonight. I need one last night out before I'm confined to my bed for these next few months."

I try to smile, but it's impossible to be excited about spending time with my friend tonight. I nod and then leave Jamie's office to try to go about the rest of my day like usual.

I walk back to my cubicle.

"Hey, Olive. Where is the coffee?" Lewis, a realtor in the company, asks as he walks by my desk.

"I'm sorry. I had to go pick up Sean and dry cleaning on my way into the office today. I'll make it soon."

Lewis frowns but walks away, grumbling, "It can't be that hard to make coffee, can it? What are we paying an assistant for anyway if she can't even make coffee?"

I sigh and try to remember that he doesn't mean it. He just hasn't had his morning coffee today, so he's grumpy.

"Olive, where are the cookies for today's open house?" Audrey, another realtor, asks.

"I'm sorry. I was never told you were doing an open house today. I thought it was scheduled for this Saturday."

"It was, but my client moved it late last night. I really need the cookies."

"I'm sorry. I think there are some frozen ones in the fridge that you can warm up and use. They'll taste just as good. I promise." I try to smile to reassure Audrey.

"You really should start making cookies every day. That way, we'll always have cookies. You know clients want us to move things at the last minute all the time."

"I'm sorry. I'll do that in the future. I can go grab you some fresh ones if you want. There is an awesome bakery just around the corner."

Audrey laughs. "I'm sure they are great, but they aren't as good as your cookies are. Your cookies sell houses."

I smile even though, inside, I feel like dying. I like baking cookies. It's a huge stress reliever. But, when I baked a batch of cookies for Jamie's birthday about a year ago, I never thought it would turn into everyone relying on them on a weekly or now daily basis.

I sigh and then get to work. At least, tonight, I'll get to have a little fun, watching Owen, my boyfriend, play his guitar.

"WHEN DOES your ass of a boyfriend go on?" Keri, my friend who used to work at Parks Real Estate with me, asks.

I sigh as I glance at my watch that now reads after eleven p.m. It's going to be another long night with little sleep. "I thought he was already supposed to be on."

I take a sip of the white wine I ordered. It's only my second glass. Though, after the day I had, I am tempted to drink something stronger.

"We are waiting ten more minutes, and then we are leaving," Keri says, sipping on a margarita.

"Oh, relax, and have some fun. Tonight will be the last night I go out in months," Jamie says, sipping on her water.

I frown. "I can't do that to Owen. I promised I would come to his show today."

Keri shakes her head and finishes off her margarita. "You are too good to that boy. You have to be up in less than eight hours. You need to go home and get some sleep."

"Maybe, but I would feel horrible if I missed his show." I take another sip of my wine.

Keri raises an eyebrow. "You wouldn't feel horrible if you broke up with him."

Wine spews out of my mouth. "Why would I break up with him? I love him."

Now, it's Jamie's turn to raise an eyebrow. "Because he treats you like dirt, and you are so much better than him."

"He does not! Just last weekend, he took me to that amazing hotel—"

"And you spent most of your night cleaning up his puke," Jamie says, also ganging up on me.

"He just drank a little too much! It can happen to the best of us."

"It was your birthday, Olive! He was supposed to be taking care of you! Instead, you probably spent the whole night apologizing for letting him drink that much."

I blush. She's right. I did.

"I don't want to talk about Owen anymore." I ask Keri, "How are your classes going?"

She has gone back to school to get an English degree. A degree that I don't have the heart to tell her won't make her more money than what she was making when she was a real estate agent.

"I quit."

My jaw drops open. "What? Really? That's great! There is a new management position open that I think you would be perfect for."

Keri starts laughing until she is snorting.

"What's so funny?"

"I didn't quit. I just wanted to get your honest feelings about if I should be going to school or not, and I knew you wouldn't give me an honest answer unless I told you I'd quit."

"Oh my God! I'm so sorry, Keri! I didn't mean...I mean, you should—"

"Stop apologizing, Olive."

"I'm sorry."

Keri raises an eyebrow at me.

"I'm sorry. I mean—"

Keri shakes her head. "Anything new going on at work?" she asks, looking from me to Jamie.

"I hired someone to be me while I'm gone these next few months," Jamie says.

Keri eyes me but doesn't say anything even though I know she thinks I should be the person for the job.

Jamie turns to me. "What did you think of Sean? You think he'll make a good me while I'm gone?"

I blush. "I'm not the best person to judge Sean. We didn't get off to the greatest of starts."

Keri leans back in her chair, glancing up as Owen and his band finally take the stage. "And why not?"

"Because I didn't make the best first impression with Sean."

"How bad of a first impression?" Keri asks as she studies me with her eyes.

"The kind where I spilled coffee on him, accidentally kissed him on the lips, and introduced him to the team by the wrong name."

Jamie laughs. "You did not! I didn't realize. He usually tells me everything."

I blush a brighter shade of pink.

Keri grins. "Plus, you probably apologized about a million times."

I frown but have to nod.

Owen starts playing with his band, and we all fall silent as we watch him.

An hour later, Keri says, "I need to go home, or I'm never going to get out of bed on time in the morning."

I nod. "Good night."

Keri glances from me to the stage. "Just don't stay all night." She hugs me and then starts walking out of the club. She stops and hollers over her shoulder, "And don't stay up all night, making those asshole real estate agents cookies for their showings tomorrow! You need your sleep."

"I won't!" I yell back.

I'll just get up a couple of minutes early and throw some cookies in the oven while I'm getting ready.

I turn my attention back to Owen and his band onstage. At least I have Owen. He might not be perfect, but I love him, and he loves me back. That's enough.

Jamie lays her head on my shoulder. "I'm exhausted. I'm not going to last much longer."

I laugh. "I'll get you into a cab then."

I take Jamie to a cab, and then I go back to my seat to finish watching Owen play. I love watching him play, but I really wish he would book more weekend gigs and less during the week.

I rest my head in hands as I watch him continue to play. I know they still have three or four more songs before they finish their set. I can make it through. I close my eyes. I'll just listen and rest my eyes...

"Olive!" Owen shouts, jolting me awake.

I jump awake.

"I don't know why you even bother coming if you are just going to fall asleep," Owen says.

"I'm sorry. I've had a really long day. Let's just go back to my apartment and go to sleep," I say.

He sighs. "My apartment is so much nicer though. Your apartment is tiny."

"But my apartment is closer to my work, and I haven't seen my cat all day. You don't have to be anywhere in the morning."

He shakes his head. "I'm going to my apartment. You coming?"

I think back to this morning—how late I was going into work because he'd turned my alarm off again, how long of a subway ride it was to get into work.

"I'm sorry. I can't tonight. I'll stay over tomorrow night," I say.

Owen frowns and then leaves without so much as a good-bye kiss.

I love Owen. He loves me, I keep repeating to myself.

We've both just had a bad day today. Tomorrow will be better.

But then I remember that I have to deal with Sean tomorrow, and I realize that tomorrow is going to be just as bad.

3 SEAN

It's eight o'clock sharp when I make my way into Parks Real Estate Office. It's not early by anyone's standards, but considering I own a company that operates mainly in the evenings, it's early for me. I expect to see an office full of life as I walk through the office. Instead, I find a mostly empty office.

What the hell? Does no one come to work on time?

I keep walking toward Jamie's office. I need to take some time to make it mine if I'm going to be working here for a year in Jamie's place. I can only handle so many motivational quotes and hippie incense.

"Good morning, Sean," a sweet voice says as I walk to my new office.

I stop to greet the person when I realize it's Olive. I cock my head to the side as I look at her sitting behind her desk. She looks slightly more put together today than she did yesterday. Her long hair is a little more tamed but still frizzy. She's wearing dark dress pants with dress boots that are much more appropriate for the weather and the office, but somehow, it disappoints me. I quite enjoyed looking at her bare legs yesterday. She looks put together, except when I study her further. Her eyes have the tiniest of bags underneath them. Her lips are stifling the need to yawn. She's exhausted.

"Coming into work early isn't going to win you any favors if you are exhausted and worthless to the team, especially when it's clear that no one comes in this early," I say.

"I'm sorry. I mean..." She shakes off her apology. "I always come in this early. I try to beat Jamie in, so I can make sure the coffee is ready and everything is ready for her. I'm always the first to show up and one of the last to leave. That's who I am. I'm sorry if I seem a bit tired. I had a bit of a long night last night. Tomorrow, I'll be better."

I narrow my eyes at her and resist the urge to laugh at her ridiculous apology. I continue into my office without another word to her.

I begin moving the incense, candles, and pictures of Jamie and her boyfriend off the desk and put them on the floor to make room for my laptop on the desk. I fire it up and open my email. Over a hundred unread messages pop up with more coming in each second as I stare at the computer. Some are from my business, and some are from Jamie's business. Either way, it looks like I'm going to be spending most of my day answering emails.

I really need to find a manager who can be me when I'm not here. I know Jamie doesn't believe in managers, but she doesn't get to complain about how I run the company if she isn't here.

I decide to start with looking through the applicants for the management position that I sent out yesterday. I said that all applications had to be in by noon today, so I expect most everyone who is interested in applying has already applied. Although I'm sure I'll get a few stragglers today. Those who wait until today to send in their applications will get a mark against them. I need people who know what they want and are prepared for anything. Not someone who waits until the last minute.

I pull up the emails that are in reference to the position and am in shock when I see only five applications. Out of more than a hundred employees who work here, only five have applied so far. Hopefully, it's the best five employees.

Did I not make it clear that the position would come with a huge raise?

Everyone should be fighting for the position, not unconcerned about it. Jamie really must have convinced these people that it's better to be happy and have work-life balance than make money because this is not how normal people respond to the opportunity to make a lot more money.

I open the first email. It's from Sandie. She has only one year of experience and is fresh out of college. Not what I'm looking for.

I open the second email from Melissa. Three years' experience. Slightly better but still not what I want.

The third email is from Floyd. Seven years' experience. He claims he brings in more commission than anyone else at the company. And he's male, so he won't distract me from what I need to be focused on. He sounds perfect.

I open the last two emails, and while I know I'll interview all of them, my gut tells me that Floyd is my guy.

The first is more of the same. From Clay, who has limited experience.

The last email almost knocks me on my ass. It's from Olive.

Maybe there is another Olive in the company? One who isn't an incompetent assistant?

But, as I read the email, I know this is the Olive sitting right outside my office. The Olive who spilled coffee on me and apologized for kissing me. That was a first. Most women don't apologize for kissing me. And that was the one thing she did right. If she would just kiss me every time she fucked up instead of apologizing, I would like her a lot more.

I begin reading the email from her.

To Sean Burrows,

I am writing to inform you that I would like to apply for the management position. As an assistant, I know I have limited qualifications, but I am loyal and have been an assistant here for almost five years.

I apologize for the initial meeting where I was late in picking you up from the airport, spilled coffee on you, and introduced you incorrectly, among other things. I know I did not make a great first impression, but I need this job. No one should still be an assistant when entering their thirties.

I have attached my résumé. I'm sorry for taking up so much of your valuable time.

Thank you for your consideration,

Olive Porter

P.S. I'm sorry for kissing you on the lips. I really was trying to kiss you on the cheek. I was told you were European, so I was trying to make you comfortable. I was clearly wrong about both.

I chuckle, reading her email. I don't know why she thinks she should be our manager or why I would even consider her. She has no experience, and on her résumé, she doesn't even list if she has her real estate license. She has no qualifications for the job. But I have to hear her try to explain herself to me. Maybe it will cheer me up from the fact that Jamie will never be mine, but I'm stuck in this frigid, cold place anyway.

I stand up and walk over to my office door before opening it. Olive is seated at her desk, typing away on her computer.

"Olive, I'd like to see you in my office."

She narrows her eyes and frowns but then slowly turns her frown into a fake smile before getting up from her desk. "Of course."

I hold the door open for her as she walks into my office and takes a seat across from me. I take my time in walking back to my seat behind my desk, letting the anxiety that I know she must be feeling creep up higher and higher until I'm sure it's seeping out of every pore in her body.

"Do you know why I called you into my office?"

"No idea," Olive answers honestly.

It's strange not to hear a sir or Mr. Burrows. That's how I'm always treated—formally and with respect. Olive doesn't bother with sir or misters though. At least, she doesn't today.

"I wanted to talk to you about your application."

Her eyes widen. "Is this an interview?"

I smirk at her thinking I would give her an interview so easily. "No, this is more like a preinterview."

"Oh."

"Tell me why you think you have the qualifications to even apply for this position?"

She takes a deep breath, and then for the first time, I see the tiniest spark in her eyes.

"Because I have more experience than anyone other than Jamie in this company. I know my title says assistant, but I do a lot more than a typical assistant would. I am Jamie's right-hand woman. And I know that, if she had to choose a manager, she would choose me. I deserve this position. I've worked my ass off for five years. I've earned a promotion. I don't have my real estate license because it's expensive to take the test, and there was no need to get it if I was never going to get promoted, but I could pass the test in my sleep. I know everything there is to know about real estate, and if I don't get this job, then I quit." She bites her lip when she says the last word, like she didn't mean to reveal to me that she planned on quitting if she didn't get the job.

But her biting her lip has drawn my attention back to her lips instead of staying focused on the task at hand. It would be nice to have that lip on my mouth again.

"You should quit."

Her eyes widen so much, I'm afraid they are going to pop out of her head. "What?"

"If you quit, then I can fuck you, and I really want to fuck you. If you stay, well, then I can't."

God, what am I saying? This is definitely harassment.

I've been forward with women before, but this might be taking it a bit too far. It's just been too long since I've had a woman in my bed.

"I have a boyfriend."

I smirk. "I doubt that."

She frowns. "His name is Owen, and he's a musician. And I quit, but not so that I can fuck you. I quit. Good luck running this company on your own without me. You're going to need it."

I watch as she stands up and begins to walk out of my office. This really isn't going how I planned it.

"Wait," I say, standing up.

To my surprise, she pauses. I don't know why I'm going to say what I'm going to say next. I suspect it's because I'm thinking with my dick instead of my brain. I should just let her walk out of here, but Jamie would be upset with me. And, for the first time today, I've seen something in Olive that I think could be developed into a more confident woman with just a little help. And I know just what she needs to do that. She could become my pet project, and just maybe, I can show Jamie that I'm not such a bad guy. That, if things don't work out between her and her baby daddy, then she should give me a second chance.

"I'll give you a real interview, just like everyone else."

"And you'll stop talking about fucking me and being an asshole in general to me?"

I take a step forward until I'm invading her personal space. "I'll stop talking about fucking you, and I'll try to behave more like your boss instead of an asshole."

"Good. I'll see you for my interview..."

"Tomorrow," I answer.

"Tomorrow. If you need anything taken care of today, let me know. It was nice speaking with you, Sean," she says.

She extends her hand, but she's not paying attention to how close we are, and she grazes across my dick that is hardening more each second.

"I'm so sorry," she says, retracting her hand.

I laugh. She almost made it out of here without apologizing.

"I'll see you tomorrow, Miss Porter."

She turns and walks out of my office without looking back.

I smile to myself as I walk back to my desk chair and picture what it would be like to bend her over my desk and fuck her here. How pink would her cheeks get? Has she ever been fucked properly by a man? Or is she secretly one of those quiet, insecure girls who becomes a fierce tiger in bed?

I promised I wouldn't mention fucking her again, but I didn't promise not to *think* about fucking her.

And that's how I get through the shit-ton of emails I have—by envisioning her naked ass up in the air as I bend her over the desk.

4 OLIVE

I sit nervously at my desk as I watch Floyd enter Sean's office. Floyd is the last person to interview before it's my turn, which means I only have fifteen, maybe twenty minutes tops, until it's my turn to interview. Most of the interviews have taken less time than even that. If I've learned anything from watching Sean interview, it's that he is quick and efficient, most likely because he's already made up his mind of who's going to get the job. If I had to guess who Sean is going to pick, it's going to be Floyd. The other women who applied don't really have the skills for the job or the boobs to make hiring someone with a lack of experience worthwhile.

Floyd is my only real competition. And who am I kidding? I'm no competition for Floyd. The fact that I know more about this company than anyone else other than Jamie doesn't mean I'm qualified for the job. I'm nothing but an assistant. An assistant who's never been promoted and who doesn't have any real responsibilities—at least, not on paper. There's no way that Sean's going to hire me, no freaking way.

I already spent most of my evening looking at the classifieds, trying to find a job that would be a step up and provide me with a lot more opportunities for growth. But, so far, nothing. At least nothing that doesn't require a college degree that I don't have. It means that I will continue being an assistant.

Besides, with all my talk about quitting, I would have a hard time doing that to Jamie. Despite the fact that she's never promoted me, we are good friends, and I know that she's counting on me to make sure that Sean doesn't fuck up her business. I'll stay for the year and maybe take some college classes or something on the side. I'll learn all that I can, and then I'll be better prepared to find a new job when Jamie comes back.

I look down at the blue blouse that I bought to go with the black skirt. I just bought the outfit last night, so I could look my best for this interview for a job that I know I have no chance of getting. I sigh as I undo the top two buttons on my blouse. I know I have no experience and that I have no shot at getting the job. Well, that's not true. My only shot is to look sexy as hell and to convince Sean to give me the promotion because he wants to keep looking at me every day, not because he thinks I'm the most qualified. My only shot is to make him think that he has a chance at sleeping with me even though he has no shot.

I try to focus on answering emails while I wait for my turn to interview. But I can't focus, just like I haven't been able to focus all morning. I shouldn't feel anxious. There's nothing to be worried about. After the interview is over, I'm going to be no better off but also no worse off. Sean already doesn't think well of me, but Jamie will never fire me.

My heart stops when I see the door to Sean's office open. I watch as Floyd exits with a large smile on his face. I glance down at my computer to see the time. Ten minutes. He was in there for ten minutes. That's five minutes less than everyone else's previous interviews. So, if I can keep Sean talking for ten minutes, maybe I'll have a chance. Should be easy, right?

I nod at Floyd as he passes, but he just gives me a smirk and then walks off, like he knows he has the job in the bag. I close my laptop and then take a minute to straighten out my skirt and blouse one last time. I decide to really go for it and unbutton one last button, making sure that my lace bra pokes through just enough beneath the blue blouse.

Then, I stand up. I walk over to his office and knock quietly. "Mr. Burrows, are you ready for me?" I ask, my voice a bit shaky.

"Come in, Olive," Sean says matter-of-factly with no emotion in his voice.

I try to shake off my nerves as I step inside, and I take a seat in the chair across from his desk. The office has changed a lot since Jamie occupied it. Gone are all the girlie candles and paintings, replaced with art that is dark, black, and manly. He doesn't have any picture frames on his desk. Nothing personal at all.

I open my mouth to ask how his day is going, but he speaks first, "What skill sets do you have that you think makes you right for the job?" Sean doesn't look up from his computer.

I blink several times, confused because he's not even really giving me the time of day. But it does make it easier for me to answer him. When he's not looking directly at me, it somehow makes it less intimidating.

"I'm loyal. I think that the most important trait when it comes to being a manager is someone who puts the company first. Someone who cares so deeply about the company that they are willing to give up a part of themselves. They are willing to make sacrifices in order to do more for the team. In real estate, I think it can sometimes get extremely competitive, and I think there needs to be a fair amount of competition in order for individual realtors to do a good job. But we also work for one company, and I think the manager of that company should be one who can inspire and support the team as well as help foster a healthy level of competition."

"And what weaknesses do you have, and how do you plan on overcoming them in this job?" Sean asks, still not looking up from his computer. He clicks on something with his mouse, not paying attention to me.

"You. You're my biggest weakness. Every time your hot-ass body comes in the office, I lose my mind. I can't think about anything else other than you. I struggle to get my work done because all I can do is think about you and how big your cock must be beneath your slacks. And how do I plan to overcome it? By getting you to fuck me a lot," I say because I realize it doesn't really matter what I say. He's not paying any attention to me.

I wait for his next pointless question, but he doesn't ask a question right away, like he did previously. Instead, he slowly closes the laptop sitting in front of him and looks up at me. His eyes travel from mine to my breasts. I glance down and find that I'm exposing a little more of my cleavage than I was planning on.

"What are you doing?" he asks as his eyes travel back up to mine, not bothering to hide the lust that is there after getting a taste of my body.

I fold my arms across my chest. "You aren't taking this interview seriously, so why should I?"

"Maybe because you're the one being interviewed," he says as he leans back in his chair. He cocks his head to the side as he looks at me with an expression I can't read.

"I'll just let myself out and get back to work. Do you want me to let Floyd know that he got the job?" I ask as I stand up.

"Sit down, Olive," Sean commands, like I'm a dog.

"No. I'm tired of being humiliated. I'm sorry if you expect me to quit now, but I'm not. I'm good at this job, and I would have been good at the manager job as well if you had given me a chance. But I promised Jamie that I would stay here as her assistant and keep an eye on you while she was gone. And I'm a woman of my word. So, I'll stay here and report back to her until she returns. Then, I'll find a new job."

I start walking to the door when Sean jumps up, and just as I begin to open it, he slams it shut. I jump back, startled.

"Sit back down, Olive."

Whatever confidence I had a moment ago vanishes when he

growls at me that way. The look he is giving me is more than enough to make my panties wet. And I don't even like this man. But the way he's looking at me now is enough to make me forget about all of that.

We cautiously sit back down as we stare intensely at each other.

"What makes you think I'm giving the job to Floyd?"

"Aren't you?" I ask.

"I was, but then you came in here and did that."

My eyes widen. "I don't understand. I just said some ridiculous crap about finding you attractive, and you're going to give me the job because of that?"

He shakes his head. "No. I'm not giving you the job."

"Oh."

"But I am giving you a chance to learn to become a manager. I'll put you through a training program of sorts, and if you pass, then you'll get the job."

"What kind of training program?"

Sean leans forward on his desk as a slow grin spreads on his face. "The kind that's going to test your limits. The kind that will prove to me who the real you is—that confident woman you were just a few minutes ago or the shy, pathetic woman I met the other day. Either way, you're probably going to hate me after this is all over. And there's no way I think you're going to follow through with the program to the end in order to get the job." Sean pauses as he leans back, smiling. "But then again, I've been wrong before."

My mouth drops open in complete shock. I have no idea what Sean is talking about. All I know is that he's giving me a chance to be manager if I complete whatever silly training he has planned. And I'll do anything to make this work.

"Well, I already hate you, so what difference does it make?"

"Is that a yes?" he asks.

"Sorry. Yes, that's a yes."

He shakes his head. "I don't want to hear *sorry* drop from your lips again. That's your first lesson. No more saying *I'm sorry* or apologizing of any sort. Managers don't apologize for the decisions they make. They stand behind them. And, if I hear anything like it again, you will be punished. Do you understand?"

I bite my lip as he says the word *punished*. Because all I can think about are naughty things involving spankings and whips. But I know that's not what he means. It's just my dirty mind playing tricks on me.

"Understood."

"Good. Now, our first real lesson will begin at dinner tonight."

I scrunch my face. "Dinner?"

"Yes, dinner. We both have to eat, and I don't have time to train you during normal work hours. I have enough on my plate with running my own business and keeping Jamie's afloat while she's gone. I need a manager to get on board as fast as possible to help me out when I need to travel for my own business."

I nod. "I understand that, and I'm willing to come in after hours or do whatever it takes to get this job. It's just that I was unaware that training was going to start tonight, and...well..."

"For goodness' sake, spit it out, Olive!"

"It's my and Owen's one-year anniversary tonight. We were going to go out to dinner."

"The training times and places are nonnegotiable. I don't want to hear your excuses or reasons for not being able to attend them. Either meet me for dinner tonight or consider yourself out of the running for the job, and I'll just give it to Floyd. It will make both our lives easier. You can go out with Owen or whatever after we finish our training. I don't care if you starve and wait and eat until after we're done, most likely nine thirty or ten, but I will be eating."

I frown, trying to think about what I should do. I think about what Keri would say. That I should go out with Sean. Do something for me for once. Give myself a shot at taking my career to the next level. Owen and I can always go out tomorrow night to celebrate our anniversary.

"What time and where do you want me to meet you for dinner?" I ask.

Just the tiniest bit of a grin forms on his face. "Seven. And we can leave from here. I'm sure you have more than enough work to get caught up on 'til then since I know you got nothing done this morning," he says with a smirk.

I frown and storm out of his office before he can say anything more to me. I have to cancel my date with Owen, but I have a chance at a job that could change everything for me. Absolutely everything.

As I walk back to my desk, I see the men in the office staring at my chest, and I quickly button up my blouse. I have a chance at the job I want, but somehow, I'm worried that it's going to feel more like a date than training. I shake my head.

Jamie would be proud of me for what just happened. She always says I need to use everything I have to go after what I want. Not just my head, but my body, too. It turns out that maybe she was right. That my body and dirty mouth might actually come in handy. They might actually get me the promotion. I just hope I'm not biting off more than I can chew when it comes to Sean.

5 SEAN

What the hell am I doing?

That's the question that keeps running through my head as I try to answer the dozens of emails that fill my inbox. I've hardly gotten anything done this afternoon since Olive's interview.

I had no intention of turning Olive into a manager. I don't even know if it's possible to turn her into a competent manager. She's a complete mess. She has zero confidence in herself, which makes me have zero confidence in her ability to manage people. And, to make matters worse, she doesn't even have her realtor's license.

But the way she acted when she entered my office changed everything. She had me entranced from the second she spoke. She brought me further under her spell when I looked up and saw how provocatively she was dressed. I usually hate women who dress so provocatively to try to get ahead in the world, but it's a proven fact that it works. And I had no idea that Olive had it in her to pull such a dirty trick like that. But, evidently, there's a hint of a strong, fierce woman beneath her weak exterior. Maybe, just maybe, I can find a way to keep that strong, fierce woman on the surface.

But there's another reason I asked her to dinner tonight. Because

I want her all to myself. After seeing her in my office, I want her more than I've ever wanted anything. Even money.

I glance at my watch. I still have thirty minutes until I told her to be ready to go to dinner. But I can't wait any longer, and I'm not getting any useful work done anyway. I close my laptop and roll my sleeves down before I walk over and grab my coat off the coat rack in the corner of the room. Then, I walk out of Jamie's office and find Olive sitting at her desk.

She immediately spots me, like she has been staring at my door, waiting for me to come out, but when I catch her gaze, and she realizes she has been caught, she begins clicking furiously on her mouse while burying her head behind the computer screen, trying to act like she has been working this whole time. But I know that she hasn't gotten any more work done than I have.

I know that I affect her. As much as she tries to deny it and pretend like she has a boyfriend, I know that she wants me as badly as I want her. And, despite how wrong it might be to fuck my assistant, who has led me to believe she could be a manager, I don't care. I've done much worse in the past.

"I hope you got all your work done, Olive, because I finished early, and I'm ready to go to dinner now."

She nods and then fidgets with her computer a second more before closing it. I examine every inch of her body as she closes her laptop. I notice that her shirt is buttoned much higher than it was in my office, much to my disappointment. Although I'm happy that the rest of the men in this office didn't get the same show that I did.

I shake my head. *Where did that come from?* I can't be jealous of other men looking at Olive.

I watch as Olive puts her computer into a backpack. I sigh but don't say anything. She then walks over and grabs the same bright, puffy pink coat that she wore to pick me up from the airport. I grab it out of her hand and then walk over and drop it in the trash.

"Hey! That was my coat! What are you doing? I can't go outside without a coat. It's freezing."

"You can wear mine," I say, shrugging mine off and handing it to her.

She frowns as she takes my coat from me. "What's wrong with my coat?"

"If you have to ask, you'll never understand what's wrong with your coat."

"You owe me a new coat."

"Fine. I'll have my assistant send a new coat to your place in the morning."

"Aren't I your assistant? So, doesn't that mean I will be buying myself a coat?" she asks.

I sigh. "You aren't my only assistant, Olive."

She frowns. "But I like my puffy coat. I don't need a new coat."

I frown. "If you want the manager job, you're going to have to start dressing like a manager, and that means, no puffy coats."

"Fine," she says, rolling her eyes.

I start walking toward the elevator, resisting the urge to grab her hand because I know it would be inappropriate. But I do manage to place my hand on the small of her back as I lead her into the elevator. I do get close enough to smell the pretty apples and cherry scent oozing off her frizzy hair. I need to remember to get her a salon appointment. I know that alone would do wonders for her confidence even though I do like her untamed hair a bit.

"Should I get an Uber?" Olive asks as we ride down in the elevator.

"No."

"No?" Olive asks, cocking her head to the side to look at me.

"I leased a car since I'm going to be here for months."

"Oh."

The doors open, and I can't handle it anymore. I grab her hand and pull her hard out of the elevator. "Come on," I say impatiently, giving her a reason for why I am holding her hand that has nothing to do with how badly I need to touch her.

I lead her down the hallway and out to the parking garage where my Audi S4 is parked. I reach into my pocket and pull out my keys to unlock the car. I walk her to the passenger side and open the door without thinking.

Olive looks up at me, wide-eyed, as I help her into my car. I try to look annoyed, like the reason for me helping her is because I don't think she is capable of quickly getting into the car by herself. Her wide-eyed expression quickly turns into an annoyed frown.

I smirk as I run around to the driver's side. She really doesn't think that I'm into her at all. And I'm going to keep it that way. If she thinks I want her, then I'm giving up some of the control to her. And I hate doing that. I'd rather her come to me. I want her begging, willing to do anything, because she needs me so badly. And, until she gets to that point, I'll keep my hands off of her.

I drive quickly out of the parking spot. The tires squeak against the pavement as I turn too fast around the corner of the parking garage. Olive sucks in a breath and grabs hold of the door handle. Her eyes stay open wide as I whip out onto the street. But she doesn't ask me to slow down. She doesn't say anything. It's like, in the last couple of hours since her interview, she has reverted back to the unconfident, quiet woman she was before.

I smirk. We will see how long she can last without getting that confident, sassy mouth back. I press my foot down harder on the gas. We speed up, flying past cars at a speed that I know is far past her comfort level.

She still doesn't say anything though. Instead, her grasp on the door handle gets tighter. She squeezes her eyes shut as I speed up faster to zip around another car, barely squeezing in front of the car as I switch lanes.

I frown, determined to break her. I slow down, pausing at a stop-light, allowing her to catch her breath for just a second. Her eyes slowly open, and her grip on the door handle loosens.

"Have you been to Alinea before?" I ask.

Olive looks at me with wide eyes, but I can't keep my eyes focused on hers. Instead, I move them to her chest that is rising and falling hard as she breathes heavily, giving me a great view of her breasts as they poke in and out of the blouse she is wearing.

"No. Is that where we are going? That place is really expensive," Olive says.

I grin. "Good thing I make a lot of money then," I say as the light turns green.

I whip around the corner, and she tries to grab hold of the door handle again, but I caught her off guard, so she can't. I can feel the panic oozing off her body as I drive.

Still, I keep driving faster. Not because I love it—although I do like driving fast, like any other warm-blooded male does—but because I need her to tell me to stop. I never drive this fast, preferring instead to drive safe and planned, like everything else in my life, but I'm more than willing to change all of my plans when it comes to Olive.

"Stop!" Olive screams as I accelerate again, getting far too close for her comfort to the car in front of us.

I slam on the brakes, immediately slowing us down to a more reasonable speed.

I glance over at her panicked expression on her face.

"What are you doing? Trying to get us killed?"

I frown. "No. Just trying to get you to actually speak up for yourself with some confidence."

She glares at me. "You did this on purpose to try to get me to yell at you? You could have killed us!"

"You should have told me to stop."

She runs her hand through her hair, her hand shaking a little as it combs through her long strands. "I was trying to be nice. This is your car. I don't like telling people how to drive or what to do."

My frown deepens, and my grip on the steering wheel tightens. "Then, why did you apply for the manager job? All it is, is telling people what to do."

She opens her mouth and then quickly closes it again. "I meant, in my personal life."

I shake my head as I pull over in front of the restaurant. "You don't get a personal life. If you are going to keep working for me, everything is about business."

The valet opens her door, and I open my own. I step out before walking around to her side of the car to wait for her. I flip the valet the keys and resist the urge to hold my arm out to her. I take a step forward, but Olive is no longer by my side.

"You coming?" I ask.

Olive scurries forward and then whispers in my ear, "I think we should go somewhere else. This place is really nice, and I'm not really dressed that nicely."

I look up and down her body that is covered in my coat as she wraps it even tighter around her body.

"I'm wearing slacks and a button-down shirt. Do you think I'm dressed nicely enough for this restaurant?"

She pauses a second, studying my clothing. "Yes. You look great. I mean, hot. I mean..."

I grin when she says I look hot. "And why do you think I'm dressed nicely enough to eat at this restaurant?"

She studies me a minute and then shrugs.

I sigh. "Because of the way I carry myself. I don't give anyone the option to even think that I don't belong in here. I'm going to eat here because it is one of the best restaurants in the city. I like splurging on the finer things in life. And I'm freezing my butt off. You can join me or not."

I turn and walk inside, hoping to God that she follows me because, more than anything, I want to torture this woman all through dinner. And then I want to torture her in my bed.

6 OLIVE

I survived the death trap that was the car ride over here, only to learn it was a test. A stupid test. And it all could have ended if I had just said stop.

That's how Sean is going to play it. He's going to throw test after test at me and hope that I give up and quit. This is all just a fun game to him.

A game he isn't going to win.

Now that I know his game, he no longer has the upper hand. I'm prepared for anything now.

I'm just not prepared for the stares as I walk into the most expensive restaurant that I have ever walked into. I'm wearing the dressiest clothes I own, but it still doesn't feel like enough to be inside this restaurant.

"Can I take your coat?" a man asks as soon as I enter the restaurant.

I nod even though I don't want to give up my coat. I want to keep wearing it because it hides the fact that my outfit isn't enough. It's far too cheap, and it shows the second that Sean's coat is gone.

Sean continues walking once inside, like he owns the place. Maybe he does.

I follow but immediately feel everyone's eyes go from Sean to me as we walk through the restaurant. When they look at him, they are in awe. When they look at me though, they are wondering why I'm with a guy like him. Even in slacks, he looks like he belongs while I look like...an assistant.

I sigh.

We finally make it to our table, a small circular one near the window that looks out at the city. We take a seat across from each other. I smile, trying to act like walking through the restaurant and getting stared at didn't bother me.

Sean smirks, and I know that he knows how uncomfortable I was while walking in here.

The waiter comes over and looks at Sean. "Mr. Burrows, so nice to see you again. Would you like your usual?"

Sean nods.

The waiter then looks at me, a bit surprised. "And what can I get you? Or do you need a few moments with the menu? I can start you off with something to drink."

I know I need to make a decision quickly. That is what Sean wants. A decisive woman who is willing to stand up for herself.

I glance at the wine menu in front of me. "I'll have your house pinot grigio and..." I glance down at the menu and find the cheapest thing I can find. "The Caesar salad."

The waiter raises an eyebrow and then looks at Sean, like he is going to approve or deny what I just ordered. Sean and him exchange some kind of secret conversation that I'm not privy to.

"Very good, sir," the waiter says.

"What was that about?" I ask after the waiter has left.

"You come to the best restaurant in town, and that is what you order? A salad and cheap wine?"

I frown and then lean back as waiters begin pouring us water, and a napkin is placed in my lap.

"You know what my salary is. I can't afford anything more."

He chuckles. "You think I would let you pay?"

I feel the anger growing fast inside me. "Excuse me? Let me pay? I'm more than capable of paying for my own dinner, thank you." I throw my napkin down on the table, not caring that I am making a scene. "You know what? This job isn't worth it."

Sean stands and grabs my hand. "Stay. I'm just trying to push your buttons. It seems it's the only way to get that fierce, sassy mouth to tell me how you really feel."

I frown. "You can push me without insulting me."

He nods and slowly sits back down while I still stand, towering over him.

"I would love for you to have dinner with me. I'll try my best to behave."

He grins, and everything inside me calms. One stupid grin, and I believe everything he says. I slowly sit back down.

An appetizer platter larger than anything I have ever seen and a bottle of wine are brought out. My eyes grow large as I watch Sean taste the wine and then nod in approval. I can't believe the amount of food that has been placed in front of us, and this is just the appetizer. The waiter pours me the red wine as well and then leaves us in peace.

"I don't like red wine," I say, looking at the full glass in front of me.

"You'll like this one."

I frown. "I doubt it."

"Just try it," he says, sighing.

I take a sip and immediately say, "I don't like it."

But it's a lie. I've never tasted anything so smooth, sweet, and delicious as this glass of wine.

He raises an eyebrow.

"Fine. It's delicious. Why do you have to be right all the time?"

He smirks. "I like being right. So, you'd better get used to it."

"So, Mr. Right, what do you recommend I try from this appetizer platter since there is no way I'll be able to eat it all along with whatever you ordered me for dinner?"

He laughs and then says, "Try the squash blossoms. But I would try to make room for a bite of everything."

I sigh and take a bite of one of the squash blossoms. I close my eyes as the food swirls around my taste buds before I finally swallow. When I look up, I see Sean smiling at me.

"What?" I ask.

He shakes his head. "Do you know that you moan when you eat?"

"I do not."

He laughs. "You just did."

"Well, that is because this food is delicious."

I take another bite and try not to moan, but I can't help it. The food is the most delicious thing I have ever eaten. I keep my eyes open this time while I eat, staring intently into Sean's eyes. He swallows hard, like he is struggling with something as he watches me eat, but I can't imagine a man like Sean struggling with anything.

I take a sip of the wine, and I watch his gaze shift from my mouth to my throat as the liquid goes down. It's almost like...I'm turning him on. But that can't be. He doesn't find me attractive. I've messed up too many times for him to find me the least bit attractive. And it would be entirely inappropriate for anything to happen between us. He's my boss.

But the way he is looking at me tells me something different. It tells me he wants me. And the way my heart is beating in return tells me something that I thought was impossible to feel. That I want him, too. Strictly in a sexual way. After all, from what I can tell with his clothes on, his body is all muscle. I'd love to see what is beneath his clothes.

I have a boyfriend though, whom I love deeply. I'm not going to throw a year away just so I can see what my boss looks like naked. I have to stop whatever is going on between us. Now.

"So, should we talk business since that is why I am here? What would you like to discuss?" I ask.

Sean smirks. "We don't need to talk business. It would be a waste until I'm confident you have the skill set to be a leader. I don't really think understanding how the company works is your problem. I'll pay for you to take the realtor's test, and I'm sure you'll pass with no problem. Once you have the leadership skills, then we can talk business. That is the easy part to teach."

I take another bite of food. "Then, why am I here? I thought you brought me here to train me."

"I did."

I blink rapidly. "I'm confused."

"Eat, and then I'll give you your first lesson," Sean commands.

And so, we do. We eat mostly in silence, just enjoying our food. We don't have to say much to each other because the food more than makes up for entertainment. It is the most delicious meal I have ever eaten. But, as our dinner comes to an end, I grow more and more anxious, trying to figure out what his plan is.

The waiter brings Sean the check, and I try my best not to snoop and find out how much this extravagant meal cost. But Sean doesn't even glance at the number. He just throws his credit card down on the bill, like it's nothing. I need to spend some time researching him later to understand what he does when he's not driving me crazy. Then, maybe we can be on a level playing field.

"So, what is this training you have planned?" I ask.

Sean shakes his head. "You're impatient, aren't you, Olive?"

I frown. "No. Just curious."

The waiter returns with the bill.

Sean signs the receipt and then gets up. "Follow me," he says.

I stand and follow him, but we don't go far. Just to the bar. Sean takes a seat in the booth, and I take a seat opposite him, more confused than ever.

"Relax, Olive. You are going to have to learn to trust me if you are going to work for me."

"I work for Jamie. She was the one who hired me. You're just a temp."

Sean sighs as he runs his hand through his hair. He glances over at the bar. I assume he's found a hot woman to take home for tonight.

"Lesson number one: Confidence. That is the number one thing you need to be a leader. Get that guy over there to buy you a drink."

"What?"

"If you can get that guy to buy you a drink, then you can convince someone to buy a house or an employee to change how they work."

"I have a boyfriend though."

Sean laughs. "I'm not asking you to date the guy. Just get him to buy you a drink. If you can do that in a place like this, then I must have really underestimated you."

I narrow my eyes. He doesn't think I can do this.

"Fine." I get up and look at the man Sean is looking at.

He's dressed in a suit, sitting at the bar by himself. He's about my age, but far more successful, it seems. He's good-looking. Not as good-looking as Sean, but he's still way out of my league.

He doesn't know that though. All the man knows is that I ate at this restaurant, same as him. And, as long as he doesn't know much about fashion, then he won't know that my whole outfit cost less than thirty dollars and that I got it from a thrift store.

I start walking toward him, trying to be as confident as I can, when I hear Sean say, "I would unbutton that top button or two if I were you. That's what got me."

I feel my body fuming. But then I remember everything else Sean has done today. Every time was to get a reaction out of me. Every time was to build that fire up inside me. Well, it worked. I'm fired up, but I'm just not sure I can handle any more of Sean's *training*.

I have to find a way to prove to him that I can be a strong, confident woman who is perfect for the job. I'm not sure how to convince him, but I'll start with getting this guy to buy me a drink without unbuttoning my shirt.

I slide onto one of the high-top chairs next to him. Even though there are dozens open, I've chosen the one right next to him.

The man looks over at me.

"I'm Olive," I say with a large smile on my face.

"I'm Dave. And, as much as I would love to sit next to you while we both enjoy a drink, my wife is going to be here any second and would love to sit next to me. So, if you don't mind scooting down a couple of seats, that would be great."

I nod and bite my lip as I make my way back over to where Sean is sitting.

He laughs. "Failed already?"

"He's married and meeting his wife here. I don't think that was really a fair fight."

He shrugs. "It wouldn't stop most married men."

I frown while he laughs at me again.

"Okay, fine, fine. You can try again." Sean glances around the bar and then spots the next target. He nods toward the guy who must have just sat down at the bar. "Get him to buy you a drink."

I smile. "Done," I say, getting back up and walking over to the man seated at the bar.

Of all of the men Sean could have picked, he picked the one I know I will be able to get to buy me a drink. I'm almost to him when a blonde woman takes a seat next to him.

I frown. She isn't going to get him because the man she is flirting with is already taken. By *me*.

The woman grabs hold of his neck and begins kissing him. He doesn't fight her off. He kisses her back.

I freeze.

I never thought I would be in this situation, but here I am.

It doesn't take me long to decide what to do. I finish walking toward him and tap him on the shoulder. Slowly, Owen, my boyfriend, soon-to-be ex, turns around and looks at me with wide eyes.

"Olive. Hi, baby! Uh...this isn't what it looks like," Owen says.

I slap him hard across the cheek. "We are through, Owen."

I turn back and walk toward Sean, angrier than I have ever been. Owen wasn't perfect; I knew that. But I loved him, and he loved me —or so I thought. Now, that's gone.

I look over at Sean, who now has a large grin on his face. I know I'm about to do something else I never thought I would do. I'm going to fuck my boss.

7 SEAN

Olive slapped the guy. My eyes are so wide that they are practically popping out of my head as I stare at her. I can't believe that she is the same woman who wouldn't even tell me to slow down when I was driving at reckless speeds. This woman has two very different sides to her personality. I just can't figure out which one is the real her.

She hasn't even slapped me yet, and she hates me. So, whatever this guy did must have been really bad. Or she thought that it would impress me since she couldn't get the guy to buy her a drink.

Olive stares at me as she walks back to our table.

"What was that?" I ask.

"Can we go?" Olive asks.

I raise an eyebrow. "Is that a question or statement?"

She sighs. "I don't have time for your tests or training or whatever this is right now. I want to go. Now."

I nod and get up from the booth, but she doesn't immediately storm out. Instead, she freezes. I put my hand on the small of her back because, honestly, it looks like she needs me to guide her out of the restaurant and keep her standing.

When we finally get to the front of the restaurant, the hostess goes and gets my coat. I take it from her and help Olive into it. She puts it on, but it's almost like she's a zombie. Her eyes are blank, and she's just going through the motions. She's not really here with me.

I guide her outside where the valet, thankfully, already has my car waiting. The valet opens the door, and I help her into the car before going around to the driver's side. But I don't immediately start driving off. I need answers. Now.

"What happened back there?" I ask.

"Did you see what happened with the guy at the bar?" Olive asks.

I nod.

Of course I watched her at the bar. I'd set up this test for her, hoping that seeing her hit on another man would make me stop wanting to fuck her. But it backfired on me. Seeing her attempt to pick up another man drove me even wilder with need. My whole body grew furious at the sight of her anywhere near another man. Because I want her for myself. I don't want to share.

"Well, the guy sucking face with the blonde was Owen, my boyfriend."

My eyes widen. The boyfriend was real. I truly thought it was something she'd made up.

"Well, ex-boyfriend now anyway." She looks up at me, cocking her head to one side as she studies me. "I guess you aren't going to tell me that you're sorry."

"Would it help?"

"No, it wouldn't."

"Then, why would I waste words by saying something that'd never make you feel any better?"

She nods in agreement. "I guess I didn't pass your test since I didn't get a guy to buy me a drink."

"I would say you passed the first lesson with flying colors."

She raises an eyebrow at me.

"You slapped a guy in the nicest restaurant in all of Chicago. I would say you showed that you have more than enough balls to be a leader. Now, you just have to learn to be that person on a regular basis."

She laughs. "So...your place or mine?" she asks.

I choke on nothing. *Did she just say that?*

Of all the ways I saw tonight ending, this wasn't it. Sure, I hoped in my own twisted way, but I didn't think it would actually happen.

She bites her lip, trying to keep her grin at bay. She's not blushing or showing any signs that she's embarrassed by what she said. She meant every damn word.

"Are you sure you want me to fuck you? He won't take you back after this, if that's a concern of yours. I'm not sure you're ready for the severe consequences of saying yes," I say, reminding her of the boyfriend—or ex-boyfriend.

"I'm not taking him back after this. And why are you asking me if I'm sure anyway? I thought you would say something about how managers always make a decision, and once that decision is made, they don't go back on that decision. Managers just deal with the consequences, so be sure of your decision before saying anything."

I smirk. "That does sound like me. But that was a lesson I was saving for later."

She takes a deep breath and then exhales slowly while she thinks for a moment and then another.

She's going to say no. She's going to come to her senses and realize that fucking me is not going to solve any of her problems. It's just going to create new ones. New problems that involve a complicated relationship where she fucked her boss and would have to come into the office tomorrow and every day after, wondering if the reason she got promoted, was getting special attention, was yelled at, or fired was because she'd fucked me.

And, as much as I know that the sensible thing to do is for her to say no, I'm begging her to say yes. Not to mention, my own experience. I know better than to fuck an employee. Jamie might have been the worst mistake of my life. I ended up losing the only woman I ever cared about.

"Your place or mine?" Olive asks again, more slowly this time. I grin. "Mine."

"HOLY CRAP!" Olive says when I open the door to my condo.

I smirk as I hold the door open for her. "Are you going to go inside?" I ask.

Olive tears her eyes away from my condo and looks up at me. "Please tell me this isn't your condo. Tell me that you have some rich friend you're staying with or that this is your parents' place."

I chuckle and rub the back of my neck, feeling weird for the first time ever about how nice of a place I have. I've never cared what a woman thought, and I for sure have never felt ashamed to have a place this nice, but the way that Olive is looking at me right now makes me feel like maybe I should be ashamed.

"It's not mine."

"Thank God," Olive says, exhaling.

She finally steps inside my condo while I walk in behind her, enjoying the view as I stare at her tight ass in the tight black skirt she's wearing.

"Technically, it's not mine."

Olive flips her head around and looks at me. "What?"

I smile, loving throwing her off her game. "Technically, it's not mine because I'm just leasing it for the year. I'll decide after that if I want to buy the property or not."

Olive's mouth drops open, and then she slowly looks around my condo—up at the ceiling that's two stories tall and around the large room that contains everything, except my bedroom and bathroom. Her eyes go over the kitchen that is full of stainless steel and granite, then across the dark hardwood floor to my living room where all the furniture is pointed at the floor-to-ceiling windows that look out over the city, and then over to the dining room that can easily seat twelve beneath a large chandelier.

"Where's your TV?" she asks.

I walk up behind her and inch as close as I dare without touching her. Close enough that I can smell her and feel every emotion oozing off her body. Nervousness. Anger. Excitement. Need for sex.

"Why would I need a TV for entertainment when I can have this?" I reach out my hand and gently caress her neck, turning her toward me before I press my lips against hers.

Her whole body shivers at my touch, which only makes me want to kiss her more. Deeper. So, I do, and when I finally pull away, all I see are her gorgeous, big eyes staring at me.

I smile weakly. I know she's not ready to throw her whole life away, which is what she would be doing if she fucked me. I'm not boyfriend material, and Olive is the kind of girl who needs a boyfriend. She's not ready. Not yet. Not without some liquid courage at least, and even that I'm sure won't be strong enough to convince her that she wants me to fuck her tonight.

I know women like her. They want commitment, a relationship. They want to be wined and dined first before they fuck. It's best I stay clear of women like Olive because I would destroy them.

"Can I get you something to drink?" I ask as I start heading for the bar my kitchen.

Olive doesn't say anything. She just follows me as her eyes continue to look around my condo. When I get to the bar, I pull out a bottle of wine similar to the one that she drank at dinner. I uncork the bottle and then pour us each a glass since I doubt she's going to tell me her drinking preference when she can barely speak at the moment. I slide the glass over to her where she's leaning against the counter, still staring up at the ceiling that feels small to me compared to my place in Las Vegas, although it's comparable to my place in New York.

"What do you do to make all this money?" are the words she finally says when she opens her mouth. Not, *How dare you kiss me,* or something along those lines. She just continues her thoughts, as if the kiss never happened.

I narrow my eyes as I take a sip of my wine, trying to understand this woman. I slowly set the glass back down. "You're not ready to know what I do yet."

She pouts. "What's that supposed to mean? How could I not be ready to find out what another person does for a living?" She pauses a second and then says, "Unless it's because you do something illegal. Are you in the mob? Do you kill people for a living?" Olive says, taking a step back.

"You'll find out soon enough."

Her eyes widen, and her soft pink lips fall apart. "You expect me to fuck you without even knowing what you do for a living?"

I sigh. "I don't think you're really going to let me fuck you."

"Then, why am I here?"

I lean forward, inching closer to her, while trying to convince myself to stay back. That this isn't actually happening and to not get too excited. "Because you're scared. Scared because the only guy you ever loved cheated on you, broke your heart, and you're trying to find some answers to make yourself feel better. You think sex with me is that answer, but you'll never really go through with it—at least, not until you drink a bottle or two of wine first. But, if you do that, I'm not going to fuck you anyway. I don't have sex with women who are that out of it."

"Well, I'm sorry, but you're wrong because the only thing I'm certain about tonight is that you're going to fuck me," she says. She glances down at her wine. "And I'm sorry you're wasting your expensive wine on me because I don't want any of it. I want you to fuck me, make me forget about my ass of a boyfriend, whom I spent an entire year with."

I grin.

"What?" she asks slowly as she looks at me.

"I told you what would happen if you said sorry in front of me. I told you that you'd be punished. And I'm a man of my word."

8 OLIVE

Punish me.

Those words keep running through my head as a look on Sean's face gets more and more serious. I've been trying with everything in my power to remind myself not to say *I'm sorry* since the moment he told me that he would punish me if I did. But all it took was a little bit of distraction, and now, I'm right back into slipping into my old habits. And I'm terrified to find out what kind of punishment he has in mind. I always assumed that the punishment would be sexual in nature. From the look on his face now, I know that it is.

"You're not seriously going to punish me because I apologized for not drinking what I know is a very expensive wine, are you?" I ask.

Please, God, let him be joking.

I want him to fuck me. I want to feel what it's like to be with a man with experience, who knows exactly what he's doing with my body, but I'm not sure I'm ready for any sort of pain first. I've never done anything the least bit adventurous when it comes to sex, but I know I don't like pain. I didn't even like getting my ears pierced.

"I'm going to punish you, Olive, because it's the only way for you to learn your lesson. But you're lucky this time because I think you're going to enjoy it, too."

I open my mouth to speak, trying to come up with something to say to keep him from punishing me. But, before I get a chance to say anything more, his lips claim mine. This kiss is different than the first. This time, he devours me without any hesitation. Last time was a test. This time, he doesn't ask for permission to kiss me. He demands it. And, through his kiss, I forget about any promises of punishment because any level of pain would be worth this kind of pleasure.

He suddenly breaks the kiss, and I gasp like I need him as much as I need air. He grabs hold of my hand and starts pulling me down the hallway on his left.

"I want to show you the reason I'm leasing this place. I like the openness of the main room for guests and parties." He pulls me further down a long hallway to a door at the end. He stops while he grabs hold of the door and looks at me with a mischievous grin. He turns the knob and pushes the door open. "But this is why I love this condo."

I gasp when I see the dark room. It looks like a dungeon and is so different than the bright openness of the rest of his condo.

"What is that?" I ask even though I clearly know what it is. His bedroom and torture chamber.

He chuckles. "My bedroom. What did you think it was?"

I warily look at him, and he laughs again. He puts a finger under my chin, lifting my gaze to his, before he tenderly kisses me on the lips.

"Relax, Olive. It's just a man's bedroom. I don't have whips hanging on the walls. I don't have handcuffs hiding in drawers. Just a dark, manly room where I can retreat to when I need a break from the world."

I exhale deeply, not realizing that I was holding my breath the whole time.

"Oh, and I also like it because it's soundproof."

And, just like that, he takes my breath away again.

"Now, for that punishment. Since this might be the only time I get to punish you in any sort of sexual manner, I'm going to take full advantage."

"Just no whips or bondage," I whisper loud enough for him to hear.

He laughs. He walks over and softly kisses me on the lips again. "You weren't listening. I already told you, I don't have any whips or bondage in this bedroom. I've used it in the past, and I will again if that's what you really want, but I prefer to use other means to punish and control."

I cock my head to the side as I look up at him, confused. "Control?"

He nods. "That is going to be your punishment. For your lesson tonight, you're gonna learn what it's like to not have any control and therefore learn that you never want to give it up again."

It doesn't sound like that bad of a punishment since it's not like I would know what to do in the bedroom with a man like Sean anyway.

"Why does everything have to be a lesson with you? Why can't we just get back at Owen for breaking my heart, and that's it?"

"Because what fun would that be? And, besides, our time together is limited. I need to take advantage of every second we are together to teach you everything I know."

He doesn't have to say that he thinks our time is numbered because, after tonight, I might give up and quit. He thinks I can't handle working for a man who fucked me and then wanted nothing to do with me. But he doesn't know me at all. He doesn't know how loyal and determined I can be to do something when I've set my mind to it.

"Do we have an arrangement then? Will you give up control and do whatever I say? Let me fuck you however I want?"

I stare into Sean's eyes as my heart races in my chest. I've had sex with a total of three men in my life. None of them were amazing in bed. All were pretty selfish, more worried about their own pleasure than mine. And I have a feeling that's what Sean's about, too. But I know he'll have a different intensity than the rest, and that intensity will at least make me forget about Owen and what he did to me. I want to know what it's like to be fucked by a real man. And, if I have to give up some control to get it, so be it. I can always back out in a moment anyway. All I have to do is say no, and he'll stop. I know that much about Sean. This is him just trying to prepare me for whatever test he has up his sleeve now.

"Yes."

As soon as I say the word *yes*, the door slams shut, making me jump. I'm trapped. Saying no isn't going to get me out of this. I'm not even sure I would have the strength to say no anyway.

"I think I'm going to enjoy this a little too much," Sean says as he walks toward me.

I don't move. I can't move. There's too much excitement and fear running through my veins for me to be able to think clearly enough to do something as simple as move.

He walks forward until his lips are hovering over mine. He looks me in the eyes one more time, challenging me to stop this, giving me one last chance before I completely relinquish all my control to him. It's just a second, but it feels like forever while I wait for him to kiss me.

He doesn't wait for words this time. He just kisses me. I can't breathe, and I'm not sure I want to ever again because all I want to feel is his tongue on mine, pushing further into my mouth, claiming every inch of my mouth as his.

I never thought a kiss could tell me so much, but his kisses tell me everything he's feeling. How his lips press firmly against mine and how his tongue pushes inside me—it shows me how much he wants to fuck me. His hands holding firm on my neck and my ass show me how much control he has over me.

He lets go of me, breaking the kiss, and then says, "Breathe, Olive."

I do, but I don't take a deep enough breath before his lips cover mine again, making me forget all about the fact that I'm not getting enough oxygen. He pushes the kiss right to my limit, knowing full well that I won't breathe again until his lips leave mine—not because I can't, but because I'm completely under his spell.

His lips leave mine, and then again, he says, "Breathe."

I do but only because he said so. It's no longer an automatic response for me. I'm too consumed by his kisses to even do something as simple as breathing.

He laughs. "This is going to be far too enjoyable for me, Olive."

He takes a step back and then another, leaving me feeling empty and alone even though he's only a few feet from me. He takes a seat in a chair in the corner. I walk forward, assuming he wants me in his lap, kissing him further.

"Stop."

I do—not because I want to, but because I can't help but give in to him when he says words in his sexy voice. I can't think straight enough to come up with a coherent argument for me to keep moving.

"Undress for me."

That seems to break the spell. Because, as much as I want to have sex with him, the thought of having to undress in front of him while he inspects every inch of my body terrifies me. He's built like a Greek god. I can see that without him ever removing an ounce of clothing. While I'm skinny, I'm an assistant who spends far more time at work than I do in a gym. I like cooking and baking and eating far too much to slowly undress in front of him.

"Why don't you remove my clothes? It will be far more enjoyable for you to rip them off my body," I say. I'm hoping that, if he has his hands on me, he won't be able to get a good look at my body and imperfections.

Sean frowns. "You gave up control, remember? Now, strip slowly for me, or you won't get what you want. And, trust me, you want what I'm going to give you, Olive. Because I guarantee you, no man has made you come like I'm going to. But, first, you have to pay the price."

I don't know how he does it, but his voice makes me change my mind. It makes me want what he promises. So, I move my hands to the buttons on my shirt, and I pop open the first one and then another and another until the shirt hangs open on my body. When I'm finished, I look up at Sean, who is waiting patiently for me to take off my shirt.

"Take off your shirt."

I meet his gaze as I slowly slip off my shirt. I let the shirt fall to the floor and show the first level of imperfections that grace my body —the large birthmark on half of my stomach and the large scar on the other half where my gallbladder was removed. He sees the weight that I'm still carrying from Christmas when I ate a few too many chocolates and drank a little too much wine to deal with my family.

It's just the first layer. Soon, when I remove my bra, he will see that I wear a push-up bra to make my boobs look bigger. When I remove the skirt, he'll see the cellulite and stretch marks that cover my ass, something that I know a man like him has never seen on the models I'm sure he usually dates.

When I look at his eyes going over what little of my body is exposed, I don't see him finding my imperfections. His eyes tell me how much he doesn't care about them and how much he still wants to fuck me. I wait for some smirk or comment. For him to tell me that he's changed his mind.

Instead, he says, "I want more."

I grab my skirt and slowly shimmy it down my body until it falls around my ankles while I continue to stare into his eyes.

"Step closer. I want to get a closer look at you."

I suck in a breath and then take a step forward. I quickly feel myself losing my balance because my skirt is still around my ankles. I fall flat on my face on the floor. I wait for the laughter or teasing, but instead, I feel his arms around me as he lifts me up and then softly places me on the bed.

I open my eyes and see Sean looking at me with such lust and need that I forget that I just looked like an idiot in front of him. I forget that I'm half-naked and exposed in front of him.

"Fuck waiting and punishing you. I need you now."

A second later, he has my bra off and one of my nipples in his mouth. I moan loudly as his tongue swirls around my nipple.

He sucks hard. "You like that, baby?"

"Yes," I say, half-breathing, half-moaning.

His lips move to my other breast, giving it the same attention he just gave the other. "Fuck, your tits are perfect, Olive."

"Don't stop!" I scream.

He continues to torture my breasts, bringing me ever-so close to coming from just what he is doing to my boobs.

He grins against my breast and then says, "But, if I don't stop, then how am I going to do this?" He grabs my panties and sharply pulls them down. He grabs my legs and opens them wide before burying his face in my pussy.

I've never had a man go down on me before. Sure, I've had boyfriends who have tried to get me excited with their hands, but it was nothing like what Sean is doing now. His face is buried between my legs, his tongue expertly moving in and out of my folds, inside my pussy, and then up over my clit. It's a feeling I've never felt before, and I wasn't expecting it.

I'm seconds away from coming as his tongue licks over my clit, and suddenly, his fingers bury deep inside my pussy. I scream, and he knows I'm close to coming. Just as I'm about to come, he stops. He sits up and pulls his shirt off over his body.

Yummy.

His body is beautiful. It's all abs and muscles and tan, not like my fair skin that never gets to see the light of day here in Chicago.

He walks over to the nightstand and pulls out a condom before slipping out of his jeans and underwear. As he walks back toward the bed, I turn my head away, too embarrassed to even look at him.

He laughs. "You can look, Olive."

I do even though I know my cheeks are now bright red with embarrassment. I eat him up with my eyes.

But the way he carries his body and walks toward me before climbing up on top of the bed makes me realize how much I want to be like him. It's a crazy thought that I want to be like a man I hate. But I can learn a lot from Sean. I'd love to be able to walk into a room and carry my head high, no matter what stupid things I end up doing.

"Like what you see?" he asks with a smirk.

"Yes. You like what you see?" I say bravely, shocked at myself for being so bold.

His eyes travel down my body and then back up to my eyes. "I already have your body forever etched into my memory. I love it so much."

I bite my lip, and then he shocks me by tossing me the condom and rolling over onto his back.

"Fuck me, Olive."

I can't tell if he is giving me the control or if he's keeping the control by demanding that I fuck him instead of him fucking me. Now, I'm suddenly nervous again. He clearly has much more experience than I do.

I swallow hard as I rip the condom wrapper open and take the condom out. And then I look at Sean's eyes as he dares me to prove to him that I'm not some naive, scared woman. It's just another test. It's just, this time, the test is sex.

I grab his dick harder than I should but enough to show him that I'm taking back control. And then I roll the condom down on top of it before I throw my leg over him, straddling him as my hands claw at his chest. I lower my lips to his and kiss him hard, like he did to me, before I fuck him.

I wince a little as his dick slides inside me. I'm not used to someone his size—or used to sex much anyway. I haven't had sex in over a month. Owen simply didn't have the time. Now, I know why. Owen was seeing another woman on the side. He was fucking. Just her and not me.

"Use it," Sean says with a grin.

He knows what I'm thinking, that I'm thinking about Owen. He knew I would the second I started having sex with another man who wasn't Owen. So, I do. I thrust up and down on top of Sean's dick, using my hatred for Owen, taking it out on sex with Sean. And, as good as it feels, I need Sean to help me get there again. I can't move like he does.

"What do you want, Olive? Tell me," Sean says.

"I want your tongue on my nipples again."

He sits up, and his lips cover my nipple. His tongue teases me again as it dances between my breasts while his eyes find mine. He makes me moan louder, bringing me closer but not quite there. Sean raises an eyebrow at me, challenging me to keep telling him what I want, to take control. I'm thankful to have some control again, but I know that, as I long as I keep fucking him like this, I'll never get what I want.

"Fuck me, and make me come," I say.

He grins as he grabs my hips and starts moving me up and down and in a circular motion, much faster and harder than I could on my own. His mouth stays on my tit, and I groan loud, like I've never groaned before. So loud that I'm sure the whole building heard me. He doesn't tell me to come or to quiet my screams. He just gives me one more dirty look and thrusts harder, making me scream and orgasm all over his hard dick.

It takes me a second to calm my breathing, but when I do, he says, "That was for you. This one is for me...and maybe you."

Before I have time to think, he pulls out of me and flips me over face-first onto the bed. His dick enters hard from behind me. I struggle for air as he fucks me hard against the bed. He smacks my ass hard twice. Hard enough that it brings tears to my eyes, but not so hard that I want him to stop. And then he comes hard and fast while screaming out my name before collapsing onto my back. We stay like that, stuck together, both recovering from one of the best fucks of my life.

Sean slowly gets up and says, "Want to take a shower with me? I'm sure we can find something fun to do in the shower." He winks at me.

I roll onto my back, smiling, trying to give myself a few more seconds to recuperate before I say yes to my first time getting fucked in a shower.

But then Sean's eyes grow wide as he stares at me, and I'm afraid, now that the sex goggles are gone, he sees something in me that he doesn't like.

"What?"

Sean frowns and seriously looks at me. "Olive, please tell me you weren't a virgin."

I bite my lip to try to keep from laughing because he will be far too fun to play with in this moment. I look down at the two spots of blood staining his white sheets. "It was my first time..." I say.

"Oh my God, Olive! I can't believe you tricked me like that. I would never have fucked you if I knew you were a virgin. I don't do virgins. Far too clingy, and I'm not good with all the emotions and crap..." Sean keeps rambling, but I don't hear him because I'm dying laughing at him freaking out.

"It's not funny, Olive. You need to tell a man before you let him fuck you for the first time."

I start laughing so hard that I snort. "You didn't let me finish," I say between laughs.

Sean narrows his eyes. "Of course I let you finish. You came twice if I recall. It's not my fault you don't know what an orgasm is yet."

I laugh even harder. I finally get up from the bed and shake off the laughs as I put my hand on his hard chest. "It was the first time that a man made me orgasm while having sex. Not my first time having sex. I must just be starting my period or something."

I walk past him and into the bathroom, enjoying having the upper hand for once. My jaw falls open again though when I see that the size of his bathroom is larger than my entire apartment. And the shower is big enough to comfortably hold half a dozen people at least.

I feel Sean behind me.

"You know, it's not nice to test people."

I grin as I turn and face him. "I'm just learning from the best," I say with a wink.

"I'm going to have to punish you for that."

I grin even wider. "Good. Because I think I like your punishments."

9 SEAN

I'm running away. I don't ever run away from anything, but I'm running away from Olive.

I didn't expect one night with her to affect me so much, but it did. She is so different from any woman I've ever dated before.

I enjoyed fucking her more than I'd thought I would. I know that she is inexperienced, and inexperienced women aren't usually my type, but, man, did I love breaking her, showing her what sex could be like with a real man.

But she can't get attached. I don't date women, and I sure as hell don't fuck the same woman more than once. Because that leads them to thinking that I'm willing to date them, and I'm not. The only woman I've ever considered dating again is Jamie. She's the only person I've ever really cared about. I'm not going to let another woman cause me any pain if they don't even compare to Jamie. I'm not going to put myself in that kind of pain ever again.

I've never met a woman who can compare to Jamie, but Olive and Jamie are so different that it would be hard to compare the two anyway. Jamie is confident, determined. She knows exactly what she wants and how to get it. Olive is a sweet, clumsy mass with very little confidence. But I'm also discovering how beautiful she really is, how strong, how sassy she is when she wants to be. And there's just something about Olive that I can't quite understand. She has this quality, and I don't know if I love her or hate her. She just gets under my skin in a way that no woman, even Jamie, ever has before.

I look out the window as the private jet takes off from Chicago. I never pay for private jets. They are a waste of my money since I usually just fall asleep on the plane the second that it takes off anyway. I'd rather spend my money on other things—cars, condos, expensive wine and food. But, today, I just need a plane with no one else on it. One that will take me wherever I want, mainly away from Chicago and Olive.

I need to put some space between me and her now because nothing else is going to happen between us. We had our one night of fun, and now, it's back to business. And I need Olive to know that because, if she fucks up one time, she's gone. I'm not giving her any special treatment just because I like fucking her.

The copilot comes back toward me after we've taken off. "Mr. Burrows, it's a ten-hour flight to San Paolo. Are you sure you're only going to need three hours after we arrive before wanting to return, sir?"

"Yes."

"Okay, sir. We will have the plane ready to turn around three hours after we land," the copilot says, closely studying me before heading back to the cockpit.

He knows better than to question why we're flying all this way to a place that I don't even have any business ties to. He doesn't understand, that's the point. This weekend isn't about business or women. This weekend is about getting away and making me forget about Olive even if that means wasting money and spending most of my time in the air, drinking and sleeping.

I lean my chair back and close my eyes, trying to sleep—something that I didn't get any of last night because I spent all my time fucking Olive or watching her as she slept, trying my best to understand her. But, the more I tried to understand her, the more intrigued I became with her.

I try to sleep and think of something else, anything other than Olive, but my brain automatically goes to her. It's eight o'clock. She's probably just waking up and finding the note I left her. She's probably mad, cursing my name because I left her all alone after I fucked her. I hate that I'm hurting her, but it's better to hurt her now than a year from now, like Owen did.

And, for once, I need to look out for myself. That's what I've learned after all these years. No one else is going to look out for me, so I have to. And I always put me first. And, right now, what I need is to just be gone.

10 OLIVE

Sean's gone.

I know it without opening my eyes. He thought he was being sneaky this morning when he snuck out of bed, threw on clothes, and then typed a message onto my phone. He thought I was sound asleep. That he had fucked me so hard last night that I wouldn't even be able to function until hours later.

But he doesn't know me at all.

I grin. Well, he knows me a little bit. He knows the sound I make when he enters me. He knows the look on my face when I come. He knows every imperfection on my body. He knows exactly how to fuck me. He just doesn't know me.

He doesn't know that I'm used to waking up early. That I hardly ever get any sleep.

But, when he left early this morning, I acted like I was asleep. I didn't let him know that I was awake. I'm not going to become a clingy girl who needs him to basically propose to me the morning after. I got what I needed out of him. Sex. And, now, it's time to forget about Owen.

Honestly, right now, I appreciate that there will be some distance between us. The distance will help with the awkwardness when I see him at work on Monday.

I stretch and yawn as I roll over to grab my phone and read the message he left for me.

"Ow," I moan as I move. *Damn, I'm sore.*

I click on the message and read it.

I got a call. I need to handle some emergencies that came up at work. Help yourself to any food you can find in the condo. Your training will continue Monday.

—Sean

I sigh. He lied to me. He didn't get a call this morning. He just jumped out of bed like it was on fire, and he couldn't get out of here fast enough.

I read through the message several more times, searching for any kind of clue as to what Sean does for a living or how he feels about me. But I find nothing, no matter how many times I read it.

He gives no clue to what he does for a living, and it's pretty obvious how he feels about me. He fucked me, and now, he's done with me. I'm going to be lucky if I even still have a job on Monday. Because I have a feeling that, if I fuck up at work, then I'm done. He doesn't need the hassle. Plus, if I'm gone, then he can hire a new assistant he can fuck.

He said I could help myself to his food, but I have a better idea.

I get out of bed, shivering immediately from the cold air. I wrap my arms around my body and begin searching the floor for my clothes, but I can't find them. I sigh. *Shit.* I'm going to have to wear some of his clothes out of here.

I walk toward the bathroom and then stop when I see a white robe hanging in the doorway that wasn't there before. I hesitantly pull the robe off the hanger like it's going to bite me or something and then put it on.

"Oh my God!" I moan as I wrap the soft robe around my body. It's the softest, most comfortable thing I have ever worn. I walk into the bathroom and find my clothes nicely folded up on the counter.

Did Sean do that?

He must have because no one else came into the room to collect them, just like he must have put out the robe for me, knowing I would be cold the second I stepped out of the bedroom. I blink, thinking I've imagined this. That the same guy who flipped me over and fucked me against the bed just for him last night would do something so considerate as folding my clothes and putting out a robe blows my mind.

I don't understand Sean any more than he understands me.

I grin. But I know how Sean looks naked, I know how his tongue can do things to me I never thought were possible, and I know how hard his dick is when it drives inside me. And that is all I care to know about Sean. Everything else doesn't matter. I already know that he is a jerk in every way that matters. He just happens to be better than any man I've ever fucked combined in bed.

I DECIDE to just wear the robe while I go in search of breakfast, but as I walk down the hallway to the main open room, I stop at a door that I don't remember seeing when Sean led me to his bedroom last night. Curious, I open the door, but I'm let down when I see just a large desk sitting in the center of the room, looking out the large floor-to-ceiling windows, instead of a sex dungeon or some other crazy thing that I imagine Sean having.

I start walking toward the kitchen, my stomach leading the way, when my curiosity gets the better of me. I walk back to his office and sit down at his desk. I glance up in the corners of the room, looking for a camera or some sort of security system that is watching me, but I find none.

It doesn't mean they aren't there, I think.

I sit for a minute, trying to decide if my curiosity is worth the punishment that Sean is going to give me if he finds out that I searched through his office.

It's worth it.

I start opening drawers, searching through papers and files, looking for anything that will let me know what Sean does for a living when he's not running Jamie's company. Because, as much as I wish that I didn't care at all about figuring out Sean, I do care. At least, I care enough to find out what dark, dirty thing he does to make the millions that he has

∗

I DON'T KNOW what Sean does for a living, and I'm afraid I might never know. My curiosity is going to kill me if I don't find out though. I spent three hours searching through his condo for any clue, but I found none. Not one damn thing that pointed me in any sort of direction.

My phone doesn't get reception while riding the L train, so I couldn't even spend my ride home looking him up. Instead, my mind came up with all sorts of crazy things. *He's in the mob. He sells drugs. He's a porn star.*

Everything that I came up with just made me more and more concerned that, whatever Sean does, it isn't good. I need to text Jamie. She knows what Sean does. Surely, she wouldn't let him run the company if he was into illegal stuff. Would she?

I climb up the seven flights of stairs to my apartment since the elevator is still broken—and most likely, always will be. I unlock the door and step inside, still thinking about Sean.

"Where have you been? I've been going crazy here!" Keri says as I walk into my one-room loft.

After seeing Sean's place, I feel even more like I live in a closet. My kitchen has a fridge that barely fits a bottle of wine, a microwave that also functions as an oven, one burner plate, and three cabinets for storage. The rest of the room consists of a small TV balanced on top of a trunk filled with my clothes, and sitting across from it is my daybed that also functions as my couch. The door to the bathroom is next to my bed where I have a toilet and a shower that I can barely turn around in. The only nice part about my apartment is the balcony that I can barely fit a chair on, but if I sit out there and squint really hard while tilting my head to one side, then I can see Lake Michigan from between the buildings.

"What are you doing here?" I ask.

Keri shakes her head. "No. You answer me first. I was this close to calling the police to report you missing!" she says, moving her index finger and thumb close together.

"I was with Sean," I say, as I put my purse down.

"Who?" Keri asks.

I blush just a little. "My boss."

Now, Keri's eyes grow big. "Why didn't you answer any of my messages then? It's not like he took you to Antarctica or someplace that doesn't have any reception!" Keri yells at me.

I pull my phone out of my purse and blush, more embarrassed that I didn't even notice that I had any messages from anyone other than Sean.

"Oh my God!" Keri says slowly as she realizes what happened. "You let him fuck you, didn't you?" She throws up her hands. "I can't believe you. I give up on you, Olive. I've really tried to get you to see your own self-worth and to stop dating these horrible guys who do nothing but hurt you, but you have to help yourself, too!"

"Sean didn't hurt me. Owen did, but Sean didn't! I knew what I was getting into with Sean."

"How could he not? He fucked you and then left you, didn't he? They all do."

I frown. "But, unlike Owen, he was up-front and told me he was going to leave me. I knew what I was getting into with Sean. I don't even like him! I just needed some mind-blowing sex! I just needed something to make me forget about what Owen did."

Keri shakes her head. "It might not hurt now. But I know you, Olive. What happens when you want this guy to take you out to dinner or hold your hand during a romantic movie, and he says no? Then, how are you going to feel?"

My frown deepens. She really is never going to understand how I feel. That, for once in my life, I made the right decision for myself and not the wrong one.

I dig my phone out of my purse and search *Sean Burrows* on my phone and wait for his image to show up, and then I push the phone in her face. "Do you really think I thought a guy like this was going to be into anything more than a one-time fuck? And do you really think I would pass up an opportunity to fuck a guy like Sean?"

"Holy shit!" Keri says, grabbing the phone from me. "You really fucked him?" she asks, not able to tear her eyes away from the image that really doesn't even do him justice.

I grin. "Yes."

"Oh my God! Tell me everything! Was he as amazing in bed as I imagine him to be?"

"Better."

"No way!" Keri says, typing something on my phone.

"What are you doing?" I ask.

"Sending the picture to my phone," Keri says with a smile.

I roll my eyes and grab my phone back before walking over and taking a seat on my daybed. I grab one of the pillows and squeeze it in my lap while Keri sits down next to me.

"As much as I want to hear more about Sean, I have to ask you about Owen. What happened? He called me last night, frantic that you had gone crazy and said you broke up with him. That's why I came over last night."

That's when I notice that my bed isn't made, and it's clear that Keri spent the night sleeping in my bed.

"He kissed another girl in a bar on our anniversary. So, I broke up with him. He's a douche bag, just like you always said he was."

Keri looks down, not meeting my eyes.

"What are you not telling me?" I ask.

Keri slowly looks up at me. "It's just...are you sure he was cheating on you?"

I jump up in disbelief at what Keri is suggesting. "You can't be serious! You've hated Owen since the day I first started dating him! Of course he was cheating on me! I saw it with my own eyes! He was making out with another girl!"

Keri gets up. "I know, I know. But you didn't hear him on the phone last night, Olive. He was...heartbroken."

"So what? I hope he was heartbroken. How do you think I felt when I found him with his lips locked on another girl?"

Keri sighs. "I know, Olive. It must have felt horrible. But...but what if you were wrong?"

"How could I have been wrong? I saw him kissing another girl!"

She nods. "But was it a quick kiss or a full make-out session?"

"Why does it matter? He was kissing another girl!"

"What if the girl he was with was his sister?"

I laugh. "That's sick if it was his sister. They were making out!"

She shakes her head. "Were they? You just said a second ago that you couldn't remember if they were making out or if it was just one quick kiss."

My head is pounding as I think about Owen as I pace around the room. "They were definitely making out."

Keri grabs my arms, forcing me to stop pacing around the room and look at her. "I seriously doubt that. Because I know for a fact that it was his sister who was with him last night. And, since I didn't get any weird vibes from them when they came over here together, I seriously doubt they were making out. It was more than likely just some friendly quick kiss between siblings."

I shake my head. "I know what I saw. He was cheating on me with that bitch."

Keri sighs. "No, he wasn't."

I shake her hands off me. "And how would you know?"

"Because he came over here, and I talked to him. I talked to his sister. She's really a nice person. And, while Owen hasn't always treated you the best, after talking to him last night, I do really think that he loves you and will try to do better in taking care of you."

I shake my head. "That's not possible. He doesn't love me. He's treated me like dirt all these months we have been together," I say as strongly as I can, but my voice breaks.

"Olive...he was going to propose last night. That's why his sister is in town. She brought him their grandmother's ring. He was going to propose to you last night. And how he was going to do it was good, Olive. He went all out with fireworks, a carriage ride, the whole bit."

"But..." I can't speak as my legs give out beneath me.

Keri catches me, and we both slink down to the floor.

I stare at Keri as one tear escapes from my eye. "Are you sure? You're sure he didn't cheat on me?"

Keri nods.

"You're sure he was going to propose?"

She nods again.

"You really think he loves me?"

She exhales. "Yes."

"Fuck."

Keri laughs. "Oh, honey! This is a good thing. Owen is finally stepping up and showing that he really cares about you. You could finally be getting everything you want. You're going to get married to a man who loves you. A man who can support you and take care of you. You don't have to be alone anymore. You don't have to live in this shithole anymore."

I know her words are meant to comfort me, but they are doing the exact opposite. Twenty-four hours ago, I wanted nothing more than for Owen to propose. I would have said yes. I would have done anything for him. But that was before Sean. Before I realized that I like rough, dirty sex that leaves me wanting more. I don't like boring sex with Owen, who doesn't even know how everything works. I want a man who knows my body just as well as he knows my soul.

"It doesn't matter now. I slept with Sean. Owen won't want to marry me now."

Keri frowns. "I wouldn't say that. He doesn't even have to know if you don't want him to."

I look at Keri, feeling a little empty. "I'm not going to lie to him. But, honestly, I'm not sure that I want Owen anymore."

Keri's eyes widen again as she gently strokes my back. "What? Are you sure? I don't think this Sean guy is going to be dating material. He might be hot, but I doubt he will want anything serious."

I shake my head. "It's not because of Sean. I'm just not afraid to be alone anymore. I don't need a man to be happy."

Keri doesn't move or say anything. She just stares at me.

I start clicking my tongue as I call for my cat, "Here, Milo." I search for my kitty under the bed where he usually likes to hang out. But I don't find him there. "Where's Milo?" I ask Keri.

She frowns and bites her lip.

"What happened to him?" I ask, jumping up.

"Relax. Owen took him. He said he bought the cat. That he was his, and he needed the comfort in a time like this."

"And you just let him take him?" I scream at Keri as I run toward my door to grab my purse and some sort of jacket. I froze on the L train on the way over here, and I'm not going to do it again. I open the door just as a delivery person knocks.

"Are you Olive?" the man asks.

I nod. "Yes."

He hands me a package, and I step back inside for a second to open it. I pull out the coat. It's gorgeous. It's Gucci. It's expensive. I slip it on as a note falls to the floor. I pick it up and read it.

A coat fit for a boss. Prove to me that you are one.

—Sean

I smile at the note. He got me an expensive coat. A beautiful coat that costs three times what my rent is.

"How did you afford that coat?" Keri asks.

I frown as I look at her. "Sean."

Keri blinks several times but doesn't say anything.

I grab my phone and begin typing a message to Jamie. Now, more than anything, I need to know what Sean does. I have to know how I hate a man that I also kind of love. He's taken care of me more in the last few hours, not even being near me, than Owen did the whole year we were dating.

I press Send and then walk out the door with Keri running behind me.

"Where are you going?" she asks.

"To get my cat back and to make sure that Owen knows we are still broken up."

11 SEAN

Fuck, I'm hungover.

And tired.

No, exhausted.

I could sleep for another week straight and still not get enough sleep. I thought I'd feel better after spending the last forty-eight hours doing nothing but sleeping and drinking. But I was wrong. All it did was make me feel worse. I feel no more rested than I was when I left, and I haven't gotten the images of Olive out of my head any more than I could before I left.

So, that's why I'm taking some drastic measures. I can't get Olive out of my head, and I'm not sure if abandoning her in my apartment and not calling her is going to be enough to really make her hate me. I'm going to tell Olive the truth about what I do for a living. That's the only solution I've come up with. If I tell her what I do for a living, then she'll hate me. And, if she hates me, she won't want to fuck me again. Problem solved. I might even get lucky, and she might quit.

Then, I can focus on what I really came here to do. Run a successful real estate company and to see if I still have a shot with

Jamie. And, if I don't have a chance with her, then I need to learn to get over her.

I step foot inside the office and expect it to be bustling with people, as it usually is on a weekday. I've learned from my week here and from speaking with Jamie on the phone that Monday through Friday are the busiest office days while the weekends are the busiest days for the realtors to be doing open houses and showing houses to clients. And my role as the boss is to get people straightened out during the week so that they can do their best at selling the most houses over the weekend.

But I don't expect what I see when I enter the office. I was expecting the office to be a bit chaotic on Monday morning after a busy weekend and since I wasn't here over the weekend to ensure that everything was running smoothly. But what I see when I walk into the office is complete chaos. People are running around every-where with no clue as to what they're doing. Papers are flying and strewed all over desks in complete and utter disorganization. But that's not what worries me. Disorganization, I can easily fix. What scares me is the look on everyone's faces as they run around the office. Something's not right.

"What's going on?" I ask Jennifer, one of the realtors, as she walks by.

She stops and looks up at me with fear in her eyes. "It's Monday?" she half-asks and half-says, but I know it's not the truth.

I sigh and continue walking to my office. I need answers, and I know the only woman who is going to give me any sort of honest answer as to what the hell is going on is Olive. And, as much as I'd rather hide in my office all day and wait to talk to her until later, it doesn't seem that I'm going to get to wait.

I walk straight to her desk, but she's not there. I glance at my watch. It's a quarter till nine. Olive is always here by this time. Usually, she's already been here at least an hour or more. I glance around the office to see if I can find her. But I don't see her anywhere, and I don't know where to start looking.

Floyd walks over. "Where is Olive?" he asks.

"I was wondering that myself."

Floyd's face turns to panic. "Shit."

"What?" I say a little too sternly.

Floyd's eyes dart from Olive's desk to my eyes. "It's just that there's only been one other time when Olive was sick with the flu and didn't come in to work. Happened about two years ago, and it was the worst week. Nobody sold any properties that week. It's like she's a good-luck charm or something. Or she put a curse on this place, and we can only sell properties as long as she is here."

"What makes you think Olive is sick?" I ask.

"Do you see her anywhere?" Floyd says, annoyed.

He runs out to do God knows what while I stand, frozen, staring at the chaos. I'm beginning to think that the reason for the chaos might be because Olive isn't here.

I haven't had enough time this week to really see what Olive contributes to the team, but it seems she might contribute more than I ever gave her credit for. But whatever it is that she contributes, even if it's as simple as just providing stability and normalcy for the rest of the employees, I'm going to figure it out.

But, in the meantime, there's one thing I know for sure. Olive isn't sick. She's avoiding me. She's too embarrassed to come into work after she let her boss bang her.

I stop the next person who walks by even though I don't know her name. "Can you tell me Olive's address?"

The woman shrugs. "No, but I'm sure Jamie has it somewhere."

I pull out my phone as I walk into my office. I try Olive's number first, but I get no answer. She is definitely avoiding me. I frown. It's like everything I've taught her has already gone out the window. I'm fine with Olive quitting or thinking this isn't the position for her. I'm not fine with her hiding. She doesn't get to take the easy way out. I need her to fight for what she wants. So, I text Jamie and head back out to find Olive. And I hope that, in the meantime, the company doesn't come to a crashing halt.

I PULL up in front of her apartment building, but I can't believe that this is where she lives. Jamie must have made a mistake when she sent me her address. I try calling Jamie and Olive, but neither of them answers. So, it leaves me no choice but to go inside and see for myself that this isn't her place.

The apartment building doesn't have a valet or parking garage that I can find, so I have to circle the box three times before I find any sort of street parking that's close. Although, after seeing the neighborhood that she loves, I really wish I had taken a cab and left my car back in the parking garage at the office.

I jump out of my car and run inside the building, determined to make this as quick as possible so that nothing happens to my car. I head over to the elevator and see the large sign that says it is out of order.

Really? How can an elevator be out of order in an apartment building this tall?

I dash over to the stairs and run up, quickly taking them two at a time, struggling for breath. I might be in shape. I run and lift, but I'm not used to climbing stairs like this. When I finally make it to her floor, I'm sweating and out of breath. This is ridiculous. I've done all this, and I still don't think she lives here.

I walk over to the door that is supposedly hers and knock, and I don't hear any movement inside. I knock one more time before I decide to give up. But, just as I'm about to leave, the door opens, and Olive stares at me, wide-eyed, in the doorway.

"What...how...what are you doing here?" Olive asks, crossing her arms.

I grin, thankful that I finally found the right place. "Aren't you going to invite me in?"

"No."

"Fine. Then, I have no choice but to believe that the reason you called in sick today is because of me. That you're too embarrassed to see me again after we fucked."

Olive frowns but opens the door wider, and I slip inside. I stare around the small place that she calls an apartment. But that's obviously not what it is. It's a closet or storage room. It's definitely too small to be an apartment. I look around for a place to sit, but there is none. Because every inch of space in her apartment is filled with cookies, brownies, cakes, or muffins. I glance over at what is supposed to be her kitchen and have no idea how she's made this many bakery items in such a small kitchen that I'm not even sure functions any better than one of those Easy-Bake ovens that kids use.

If this is all she can afford, she's definitely not getting paid enough. Especially now that I know that, for some reason, the company practically falls apart without her there. But I'm not going to tell her that—at least, not yet. Not until I know that she has the confidence to actually earn the respect and that they think of her as a boss and not just a good-luck charm.

"Yeah, looks like you're sick to me," I say.

Olive glares at me. "I am sick."

I look around at all the bakery items. "Then, why are you baking if you're sick? Shouldn't you be in bed? And aren't you going to have to throw out everything now that they are contaminated with your sickness?"

An alarm goes off, and Olive walks over to the tiny oven. She pulls out a small pan of brownies and places it on the only space left on the counter. Then, she throws the dish towel at me. "Baking makes me happy. It relaxes me."

"Relaxing won't help you get over whatever sickness you have."

"Migraines. I get migraines, especially when I'm stressed."

"So, you're telling me that I gave you a migraine?" I say, smiling.

She takes the tray of cookies off what I can't tell is either a couch or bed and sits down, plopping the tray on her lap. She takes one of the cookies off the tray and starts eating it. "No, I don't have a migraine because of you. I don't care that you left me alone this weekend and didn't call me. I'm not too embarrassed to go to work because I fucked my boss."

I raise an eyebrow, waiting for her to continue because I just don't believe her.

She sighs. "I'm anxious and stressed because Owen won't give me my cat, Milo, back."

I narrow my eyes at her. She's never talked about a cat before, but then she does seem like the type to own a cat. Although I have no idea how two creatures could survive in such a small place.

"Have you learned nothing from me? If it's your cat, you don't have to ask permission. Just take the cat back," I say.

"I tried, but it's not as simple as that. Owen paid for the cat. I have no legal right to Milo, and he's trying to blackmail me, so I'll take him back. Because it turns out, he didn't really cheat on me. It was just a quick kiss between him and his sister. It turns out, he was going to propose."

My eyes widen when she says *propose* because Owen definitely doesn't seem like the type, and it pisses me off that anyone would think they had a claim to a woman I just fucked.

"And you don't want to marry him anymore because of me?"

She looks up from her tray of cookies as her eyes grow darker. "No, not because of you, you idiot. I don't want to marry him because I've realized that I don't really love him. I'm not ready to marry anyone yet. I want to be by myself for a while and figure out what I want without a guy. I just want my cat back."

I stare at her a second longer, trying to tell if she is telling the truth or not. "Then, let's go get him."

12 OLIVE

My heart is pounding right along with my head as Sean drives us toward Owen's apartment. Sean is talking, trying to pep me up to talk to Owen, but he doesn't understand that it isn't going to work. I've already tried talking tough to Owen. I have no legal right to the cat. And I doubt that Owen will even open the door. It's before noon. He's probably still asleep. And I was stupid enough to date a guy for a year without asking for a key to his place.

Maybe Sean will know how to break into his place, or maybe he knows the owner of the apartment complex, and he'll let us into Owen's place. I grab my head that is pounding worse than it ever has before. I shouldn't get my hopes up. I'm not getting back my cat or anything else I left at his place.

"Olive, are you listening to me?" Sean asks.

"Huh?" I say, looking at him, as he pulls the car in front of Owen's apartment building.

Sean searches my eyes for a second as the valet opens my door. "You got this, Olive. Just treat him like you would me."

I nod and get out of the car, but my legs feel unsteady the second I get out. I start walking toward the door, but between my head pounding and my legs being weak and wobbly, I know there is no way I'm going to make it without falling and embarrassing myself even more in front of Sean.

I feel myself going down when Sean catches me.

"Thank you," I say weakly.

"You should go training with me sometime. Build up some strength in your legs."

"It's not—"

Sean grabs my chin and kisses me, stopping me from thinking. I don't know how he does it, but when he kisses me, it's like he transfers some of his confidence into me. The kiss isn't meant to be loving or sexual. It's a confidence boost.

When Sean pulls away, he stares at me with a serious expression. I was expecting his sexy grin or a smirk to be smeared on his face because he knows full well that his kiss affected me. But it's not there.

I narrow my eyes as I study him and try to understand what he is feeling, but I can't. I don't know him well enough, and it's clear that he doesn't let anyone in.

So, I turn my attention away from Sean and start walking into the apartment building with his hand on the small of my back, ensuring that I'm not going to fall again. But I don't want his hand on me. I don't want his help. I want to do this on my own. So, I walk faster until Sean is no longer keeping up with me. I automatically go to the stairs instead of the elevator.

"You know this place has an actual functioning elevator, like a normal apartment should?" Sean says.

I pause at the entrance to the stairwell and turn to look at Sean. He's standing with his hands in the pockets of his gray suit pants. He looks so perfect, beautiful. He looks like a successful adult who knows what he wants in his life. Meanwhile, I'm wearing pajama pants, a sweatshirt, and the coat Sean got me. I'm a mess while he is perfectly put together.

"You have a problem with my apartment? Then, pay me more. It's the best I can afford."

One of Sean's eyebrows rises.

"I'm taking the stairs. I like the stairs. I don't like elevators," I say.

Then, I realize that I might have made a mistake because Sean's face lights up at that. He thinks he knows some deep, dark secret about me, but he doesn't. I don't like elevators. I like the burn and the time to think that climbing the stairs offers better than the silence and awkwardness that an elevator provides. That's it.

I start running up the stairs, but I don't hear Sean behind me. I finally make it to Owen's floor, and I'm completely out of breath, but it feels good. I walk out of the stairwell and down the hallway toward Owen's apartment when I see Sean leaning against the wall with a smirk on his face. I stop, completely out of breath, in front of him.

Sean leans down to my ear and says, "I like elevators better. Why waste energy on anything you don't need to? I'd rather reserve my energy for other more enjoyable things."

A shiver runs up and down my spine. I walk past Sean, ignoring his smirk and comment. I walk up to Owen's apartment door and knock loudly. I ignore what Sean is doing to my heart. I can't do this if I'm thinking about Sean.

I don't give Owen much time to come to the door before I start knocking loudly again, and this time, when I start, I can't stop. I knock on the door the same way that others might punch a pillow. It's a way to get my frustration and anger out. But, instead of making me feel weaker, the pounding on the door makes me feel stronger than ever.

I feel myself punching air as the door swings open, and Owen stands in the doorway, looking at me.

"I want my cat and stuff back," I say before Owen has a chance to say anything.

I look him up and down while I wait for him to speak to me. I no longer feel embarrassed by how I look because Owen looks worse. It's clear he just woke up, and while I have the excuse of being sick with a migraine, Owen just looks hungover and pathetic.

Owen rubs his head, like my voice was too loud for him. "What are you doing here, Olive? We already had this conversation."

"We are going to have it again and again until I get what I need, Owen."

"What you need? What about what I need, Olive? You can't just break up with a man over a misunderstanding, Olive. That's not fair!"

I laugh. "Fair? You want to talk fair? How about how, in our entire year together, you never once treated me well? We did everything your way, never mine. How fair is that? I'm not sorry that I broke up with you, Owen. I don't have to have a fair reason or any reason to break up with you. I broke up with you. Find someone else to fuck or not. I don't care. But, most importantly, give me back my cat!"

My face is red, and I'm completely out of breath. But my body is steady. I don't feel dizzy anymore. I don't feel like I'm about to faint or fall over. I feel strong.

I search Owen's eyes, but I know that he is so much of a dick that he isn't ever going to give in to me. And I know, if I involve the police, I'm going to lose. I only see one option left at getting my cat back. So, I take it.

I run as hard as I can, trying to fit between the tiny gap that Owen has left between his body and the opening to his apartment. I run and think that I've made it inside when I feel his hands come around me, pushing me back. His hands go around my neck as he pushes me back out of his apartment, and his eyes are dark with rage. I've never seen Owen so pissed off before. Not even when he was drunk and thrown out of a bar.

"You don't get to do this to me, bitch. I propose, and you marry me. I didn't throw the last year away on you to have you say no. Do you understand me?" Owen asks, his hands still firmly around my neck.

He isn't really trying to choke me, more just to contain me.

I kick him hard in the balls, and his hands immediately let go of my neck. I feel Sean walk up behind me. I look up at Sean and see an even darker rage in his eyes as he peers down at Owen.

"You're lucky that Olive got to you before I could. If you ever touch her again, I will tear your body into pieces before burying each body part on a different continent to make sure you are never found or thought of ever again," Sean says, his voice full of fury.

I look up at him, but his eyes don't soften.

"Let's get your stuff, Olive, and then get out of here," Sean says, guiding me away from where Owen is crumpled on the floor.

I step back inside Owen's apartment, and my heart is pounding so fast that I can't even think.

"Olive, where is your stuff?" Sean asks.

"Bedroom. The cat is probably also under the bed."

Sean grabs my hand and leads me that way as Owen stumbles back into the apartment. Sean pulls me into the bedroom and then locks the door behind us. He stops and strokes my face as I look up at him.

"Are you okay?" I ask, looking at the anger still in his eyes, afraid he is going to go kill Owen if we don't get out of here soon.

He laughs gently. "I should be asking you that."

I smile weakly. "I'm fine because of you."

He shakes his head. "No. You're more than fine because of you."

His lips gently find mine again, like he's afraid to roughly touch me because he might break me.

"You can kiss me harder than that. I won't break," I say.

He takes a deep breath. "I know. You're stronger than I ever thought possible. And you've learned something."

I cock my head to one side. "What?"

"You said you weren't sorry."

I grin widely. "Well, I'm not, and he needed to know that. We should get my stuff and get out of here."

I turn and head toward the closet to grab the couple of items that

I have stored there when Sean grabs my hand and pulls me back to him.

"No, I think we have more important things to do first."

His lips crash down on mine, and his tongue pushes into my mouth. My whole body comes alive again when he kisses me. It's a strange feeling that I thought I would never feel again. I thought we were done after the last time. Evidently, Sean has changed his mind. And I'm more than happy to go along with his new plan until he pushes me back onto Owen's bed.

"No! We can't," I whisper as my eyes grow large.

Sean removes his suit jacket and then slowly undoes the buttons on his shirt. "I want you, Olive. Watching you put Owen in his place was a major turn-on."

Sean removes his shirt, and all I can think about is how I want to feel his hard body on mine again.

"What better way to get back at Owen than by fucking in his bed?" Sean asks, his eyes full of hunger and need.

It doesn't take any convincing for me to decide that I want him to fuck me on Owen's bed.

"Is that what you want, Olive? For me to fuck you?"

I nod as Sean undoes the buttons on my coat and pushes it off.

"You want me to touch you like he never did?"

I nod as Sean undoes the button and zipper on his pants.

"You want me to make you scream like Owen never could?"

"Yes," I breathe.

Sean takes his cock out of his pants and holds it in his hand. He pulls a condom out of his back pocket and slips it on while he stares at me the whole time.

Sean grabs my pajama pants and pulls them down hard, and I squeal just a little bit. And then I bite my lip when I realize I was far too loud for what we are about to do.

"Don't bite your lip. I want to hear every dirty moan."

He grabs my legs and spreads them wide. He buries his face between them. His tongue makes me forget about how angry I was just a second ago. I try to keep my senses about me to remain quiet because, even now, I don't want to get hurt. I don't want to become a monster, and that's what I'll feel like if I scream and make what we're doing in Owen's bed apparent.

But that's not an option.

Sean's tongue is moving faster than I ever remember him moving it before. He slides a finger into my pussy and then another and another, stretching me wide, while his other hand slips under my top until it finds my nipple, flicking across it.

The sensation is too much for me to contain, so I scream, "Fuck, more!"

But Sean stops as soon as I say *more*. "You don't get to come without me inside you. He needs to know exactly what I can do to you."

Sean pushes his cock inside me, and I grab his face, meeting his lips to try to keep my moaning at bay. But Sean only kisses me once on the lips, and then his lips move to my neck. His lips kiss up and down my neck and then nibble on my ear as he continues to affect me.

"I want to hear you scream my name."

He thrusts harder, fucking me harder and harder into the bed. I've never been fucked this hard or this fast before in my life, but it makes me want to have sex like this again and again. Harder, faster, like animals.

"Scream my name, Olive," Sean says again.

He fucks me harder and faster, to a level that I didn't know existed, until I can barely breathe or think. Until all I can do is scream.

"Sean!" I scream as I come, clawing my nails into his back.

He continues to fuck me hard and fast, each thrust harder, until he thrusts one last time, coming inside me with a force I've never felt before.

Just as I'm about to take a breath, I hear a loud pop, and then the bed collapses to the floor. I scream again as Sean's arms protectively wrap around me as we fall to the floor.

I look up at Sean, and we both laugh at the bed that is now in a collapsed mess on the floor.

"Milo!" I say, looking around for my cat, hoping to God that he wasn't under the bed in his usual hiding place.

Sean rolls off me and begins cleaning himself up while I pull my pants up. I run, searching around the room for my cat. I open the closet door and find him trapped inside, lying in the corner of the closet. I smile as I pick him up and cuddle him in my arms. He meows and nuzzles his head up against my face, happy to see me.

I look back at Sean as he pulls his pants back up. I just had him, but I want him again. Now. I take a deep breath, hoping that feeling will pass, but it only intensifies as I look at him. My headache is gone, and I feel alive for the first time since he last fucked me. He's turned me into a sex-craving lunatic.

But it's not just the sex that I want. I want him. I want the guy who, even while he was trying to keep his distance, still took care of me. If he can do that while pretending not to care, I want to know what it's like for him to truly care about somebody.

Damn it, what has he done to me?

13 SEAN

What the fuck have I done?

I keep can't keep having sex with Olive. I'll ruin her. Because I can never love her. Not when my heart is already taken. And she needs someone to love her.

But I can't seem to stay away from her. The first time was for fun and was harmless, but this time was a relapse, one that I can never repeat again, no matter the fact that I so desperately want to.

"Do you have everything?" I ask Olive, who is firmly clutching her cat with a large smile on her face.

"Just one second," she says as she searches through the closet and finds a couple of items of clothing. She finds a small bag in the closet and puts all the items into it. Then, she picks up her coat, putting it on as she stares at the broken bed. "I feel kind of bad about the bed," she says, looking at it and then back at me.

I pick up my jacket and put it on. Then, I dig into my wallet. I pull out several hundreds and throw them onto the bed. "There. Now, he can buy a new one," I say.

She stares at the hundred-dollar bills, and I know she wants to ask about my job again, but she doesn't. Instead, she just puts the bag with her things over her shoulder and then picks up her cat again. She deliberately walks toward the door and opens it. Owen stands in the doorway, glaring at her.

I know that she didn't hear Owen screaming and pounding on the door when I was fucking her. She was too much in her own world, oblivious to anything else other than me. And that's how I wanted it.

Owen pushes past Olive and into the bedroom. His eyes grow wide as he sees the state of his bed. "What the fuck did you do to my bed?" Owen shouts at Olive.

"We fucked. He made me come and scream like you never could." Olive cocks her head to one side with a sly smile on her face. "But then I'm sure you heard that part."

Owen takes a step toward Olive, and I can't stand the thought of him going near her again, so I step in front of him, stopping him from moving any closer to her.

"Don't you dare touch her," I say.

"I should call the police. This is breaking and entering. And, now, you can add damaged property to that list of laws you broke," Owen says.

I take a step toward him so that he can feel how much stronger I am when I stand over him. "Call the police. I dare you. It will be your word against ours. And I'll tell the police how much of a piece of shit you are to put your hands on a woman like that."

Owen steps back, but he doesn't say anything. He doesn't argue with me, but I'm still not sure he gets it.

"Leave Olive the hell alone. Don't call her. Don't try to contact her. Do you understand?"

Owen's eyes dart from Olive's and then back to mine before he nods slowly.

I walk to Olive, putting my hand on the small of her back and guiding her to the front door of the apartment. I stop for just a second and turn to Owen who has started following us.

"There should be more than enough cash on your bed to cover the damages," I say with a smirk before Olive and I leave.

"You have to promise me something, Olive," I say as we walk down the hallway.

"What's that?" she asks, snuggling with her kitty, only half-listening to me.

I stop her and force her to look up at me so that she can see how serious and important this is. She gives me her full attention when she sees the intensity in my eyes.

"You have to promise me that you will stay far away from him. Guys like Owen turn into crazy exes who do crazy things, and I just want you to be safe. So, promise me, you'll stay away, and if you do have to talk to him again, bring me."

She laughs. "What happened to me being independent and strong and standing up for myself?" she asks.

"I already know that you can do that. You being safe is more important. I just need you to be safe," I say, stroking her cheek.

"Okay, I promise," she says, staring at me with eyes that show me how much she wants me.

"Take the elevator with me," I say.

She cocks her head to one side and looks at me with narrowed eyes. "What? Why?"

"Just trust me."

She bites her lip and then sighs, "Okay."

I smile and grab her hand as we run down the hallway, toward the elevator. I know before we even reach the elevator how much of a mistake this is. I'm going to regret it as soon as it happens, but I don't care. Right now, all I can do is think with my dick instead of my head.

I press the elevator button, and then we wait while Olive holds on to her cat, studying me like I'm going crazy.

The elevator door opens a second later, and I make my intentions very clear. I push Olive into the elevator. I take the cat out of her arms and place him on the ground along with the bag that she has been carrying over her shoulder. I kiss her like I'm desperate for her, like this is the last time I'll ever be able to kiss her again. Because it just might be. Each time I kiss her or fuck her, it should be the last time, so that's how I consider it—like it's the last time.

My hand slips inside her pajama pants and panties until I find her spot between her folds that will make her forget about the fact that we're riding down in an elevator and that anyone could step on at any moment and see my hand down her pants.

I lean back and click the button for the ground floor. Then, I whisper into her ear as my fingers rub over her clit, "You have until we get to the ground floor to come. But don't worry, baby; I'll make you come long before we get there."

I watch as she sucks in a breath. Her cheeks flush pink, and she closes her eyes, trying to keep in the sudden sensation I'm causing inside her.

But she can still get words out. "But what if someone gets on the elevator before we can get to the ground?"

I bite her earlobe, making her let go of the tiny bit of control she was holding on to. "Then, you'd better come fast."

I slip a finger into her pussy while I keep rubbing against her clit. I kiss down her neck, loving the moans. I love how I can control her, make her think anything, make her do anything that I want. I can even make her stop breathing. I've never been with a woman whom I've had such control over—at least when it comes to sex. I just wish I had the same control over the rest of her, too.

I bring her close to coming over and over, but I don't let her come until we're almost to the ground floor, just one floor above.

"Come, baby," I say.

She comes, screaming my name again, while grabbing my hair, clawing at my body, as she completely loses control.

I slip my hand out of her panties just as the door is opening, and then I put my fingers in my mouth, sucking her juices off them.

Olive's eyes grow wide. She looks from me to the elevator door opening where I'm sure there's someone standing. I firmly kiss her on the lips and then pick up the bag from the floor before scooping up her cat and placing it in her arms.

Then, I grab her hand and lead her out of the elevator, not even paying attention to the people who are staring at us with disgust on their faces. I don't care what they think. I got to make Olive come again. I got to hear her sexy voice as she screamed. I got to feel her body one last time.

I watch Olive breathing quickly while we wait for the valet to bring my car around. She is still breathing hard and fast five minutes later when we both climb into the car. Her cat immediately curls up into a circle in her lap, feeling perfectly comfortable in my car.

I start driving, already knowing exactly where we're going, but I know that Olive is going to ask me soon where we are going.

"Where are we going?" she asks just a second later when she realizes I'm not heading in the direction of her apartment.

"Vegas."

"We can't go to Vegas! We have to work...the company. I don't have any clothes or things packed. I'm wearing pajamas, for Christ's sake!"

I grin. "Are you finished?"

She frowns. "No, I'm not finished. My life isn't like yours. I just can't up and decide to leave. I have people who rely on me. I need to work for money, unlike some people."

I pull out my phone, pressing one of my assistant's numbers. When she answers, I say, "I need you to go to Olive's apartment and gather her things to go to Vegas for a few days. And then I need you to go to my condo and do the same thing. Make sure the jet is ready to go in an hour."

I hang up the phone without waiting for her to respond because I already know that it's going to be done. That's her job to make sure that she gets done whatever I tell her to.

"There. Does that make you happy?"

"No, it doesn't make me happy. How will your assistant know what to bring me?"

"Because it's her job to know things like that. You will have everything you need and everything your cat needs to go to Vegas for a couple of days."

"Why are we going to Vegas? What's so important that we need to go there? Because I can already see, you're slipping on your rule about having sex only one time."

I frown. "Don't worry; I won't slip up again—at least, not until you know everything important there is to know about me."

She raises an eyebrow. "And what is that?"

I look at her. "I'm going to show you what I do for a living."

That will solve the problem. When she knows what I do for a living, she'll hate me again.

"And I'm going to give you your final lesson before I make my decision about if you're right for the manager job."

If she doesn't decide to leave first.

14 OLIVE

I try not to care about the fact that Sean is basically kidnapping me or that I don't get a say in my life with him any more than I did with Owen. I should learn my lesson and take back control. Let Sean know that he doesn't get to control me. Let him know that no one controls my life but me.

But there is a difference between giving up control to Sean versus Owen. The difference is, I kind of like it when Sean takes control, whereas I hated it when Owen did. When Sean takes control, I know that he has my best interests at heart while Owen couldn't have cared less. Plus, Sean helped me get rid of Owen and get my cat back. I should go along with him to thank him.

But the real reason I'm going along with his crazy plan is because he told me that I'd get to find out what he does for a living. I know curiosity can lead me down dangerous paths. I just hope that my curiosity doesn't get me into too much trouble this time.

Sean pulls up in front of a building near an airport. I didn't really believe him when he told his assistant to get the jet ready. I thought maybe he just meant to get us a flight to Vegas. I didn't believe that

Sean actually owned a jet. I'm still not convinced yet that he does. Maybe we're just catching a ride on someone else's small plane.

But an employee comes running out of the building. He opens my door and helps me out of the car.

"Mr. Burrows, your plane should be ready to depart in about twenty minutes. The crew is already here, going through all the usual safety checks and preparing the plane. Your assistant just arrived with your luggage. So, if you'll follow me, I'll take you to your luggage to ensure you have everything before you board," the man says to Sean, both men ignoring me.

I hold on to my cat as I follow the men into the building and then into another room where there are at least half a dozen suitcases on the floor. My eyes widen at the sight of so many suitcases, but none of them are mine. Maybe the three bright pink ones are supposed to be mine, but I don't own any suitcases like that.

"I'll give you a few moments to make sure you have everything you need before the flight," the man who still hasn't introduced himself to me says before leaving.

"You can change if you want, or you can stay in pajamas and change later on the plane. It really doesn't matter. Whatever makes you most comfortable," Sean says.

"I'm not sure your assistant went to the right apartment. These aren't my suitcases."

Sean rolls his eyes and then bends down. He opens the first suitcase, and it mostly contains my clothes. "She probably just used some new bags because yours weren't suitable."

I frown as I walk over and start digging through the suitcase to find a pair of jeans and a shirt to wear. "My suitcases were perfectly fine," I say angrily even though I know that's not the truth.

I own one duffel bag that has a decent-sized hole in it, and that's it. Nothing that even comes close to being called luggage by Sean's standards. But I don't want Sean to know that I have no money for things like suitcases.

I find some pants and shirts that aren't mine. "Some of these clothes aren't mine."

Sean shrugs. "My assistant might have picked up some additional clothes for you to wear."

I frown. "And why would she have done that? I thought this was going to be a short trip. Why do we need so many clothes?"

"I'm sure she just wanted to make sure you had plenty of options. Your regular clothes are fine."

I stand up and walk to the door to go find a restroom to change in. I'm not changing in front of him right now with him bossing me around and thinking my things aren't good enough.

"Watch my cat while I change," I say as I leave, hoping that my cat is just still breathing when I return.

I change quickly, feeling much more normal when I'm wearing actual clothes instead of pajamas. Back in the room, I put my pajamas into the suitcase while Sean stares at me. It takes me a second to notice, but he's cuddling my cat in his arms, gently stroking her head absentmindedly, while he stares at me. I walk over to him, giving him a small smile as I take the cat out of his arms.

"Well, I'm glad that at least Milo likes you."

Sean smiles.

"Are you ready to board the plane?" the employee from earlier asks as he pokes his head into the room.

"Yes," Sean says, looking over at me.

I nod slowly. Sean walks over and puts his hand on the small of my back, like I have found that he often does. He guides me out of the room and then out of the building to where I see a jet waiting for us.

I look from it and back to Sean. "Do you really own this plane?" I ask about the huge jet sitting in front of us.

Sean shrugs. "Yes, it's really mine. It's not a big deal. Really."

Owning a jet is a big deal, I think.

Sean leads me up the stairs and onto the plane. When we get on, I realize just how much of a big deal it really is. The plane is bigger than my apartment. I stop in the doorway, unable to move, not sure if I can handle going on a trip with someone who has a vastly different amount of wealth than me.

"What is it?" Sean asks.

"It's just so big."

Sean laughs. "I'm glad that size impresses you."

We both laugh as I walk further onto the plane. There are several regular chairs toward the front, followed by a small dining area, and then a door labeled *Bedroom* at the back. I turn back and look at Sean.

"No," he says before taking a seat in one of the chairs at the front.

I narrow my eyes at him as I take a seat next to him. I buckle my seat belt, just like he does. I put Milo down on the ground, letting him explore his new surroundings before we take off.

"What do you mean, no?"

"I mean, no. I can already tell what you're thinking. What your body is saying. You don't hide your feelings when it comes to what you want."

"And what do I want?" I whisper.

Sean grins. "You want me to take you to the back room, tie you up, and do something crazier than you've ever done before. Fuck you on this plane and make you feel things that only I can make you feel. That's what you want, but the answer is no."

I frown, hating his answer, but then maybe, once we're up in the air, I'll be able to convince him.

"No," Sean says again.

"What this time?" I ask.

"No. You aren't going to convince me. I don't care if you strip naked in front of me. I'm not going to fuck you on this plane."

I pout. *What good is it to be fucking your boss if you don't even get to fuck him on his private jet?*

Sean shakes his head. "I'll fuck you on the way back if you still want me to then."

I smile and sink back into the chair as the captain boards the plane, explaining all the safety features and how long it'll take to get to Vegas. Then, he enters the cockpit, leaving us alone in the back.

Vegas. We're going to Vegas.

I'm excited to be going to a city that I've never been to before. Even though Vegas isn't on the top of my list of places to visit, I'll take it. And I get to find out what Sean does for a living. Since we're going to Vegas, I have some pretty good guesses at what Sean does. He owns a casino, strip club, or hotel chain. It has to be something like that.

Our plane takes off, and I close my eyes, trying to rest since I won't be able to get Sean to fuck me on the plane. But then I look over at Sean, who is studying me with a worried expression on his face. I don't know what he has to worry about. He's a businessman who deals with what I'm sure is some level of shady business, just like every other millionaire on this earth. Whatever it is, it isn't going to make me change how I feel about him, and that's what scares me. I care about him a lot more than I should.

15 SEAN

Olive slept the entire plane ride while I was a complete wreck. It's a feeling I rarely feel, and I don't plan on feeling it ever again. She slept calm and peacefully, not even realizing what her future holds. I know exactly what my future holds, and although I know it is for the best for both of us, I hate that I'll have to let her go so soon.

I was really a mess through the whole plane ride. I don't think Olive knew that, or if she did, she didn't let on. She just slept like an angel while I tried to ingrain her memory forever into my head. She probably thought it was helping us both to resist temptation if she slept, but all it did was make my desire for her worse. Ever since she gave me that look when she saw the bedroom on the plane, I've been going crazy, trying to keep my hands off her.

I'll admit that I've used the bedroom numerous times before. In fact, it's the main reason that I bought the plane. But I've never wanted to take a woman over my shoulder, carry her to the back of the plane, and fuck her. But fucking her wouldn't solve anything. I would just want to fuck her again and again and again and again. Because fucking her once didn't satisfy me. Fucking her twice didn't satiate me. Fucking her three times will just make me want her more.

Thank God the stress of what I'm about to do will distract me from how much I want to fuck her. But I can't help but notice how beautiful and curious Olive is, riding in the car from the airport to my place. Her eyes are glued on all the shiny lights, buildings, and people as we turn onto the Vegas strip.

"Have you ever been to Vegas before?" I ask even though I already know the answer from how excited she is to see everything. It's clear she's never been here before.

"I've barely ever left the state of Illinois. The only other major trip I've taken was an eighth-grade field trip to Washington DC. I saved all my babysitting money for a year in order to go on the trip."

I suck in a breath. It makes it so much harder, and it is going to be so much more shocking to her when she finds out what I do. She is so innocent and pure. So different than what my life is.

Even though I know I should be distancing myself from her, I can't help but ask her, "If you could travel anywhere in the world, where would it be?"

"Everywhere," she says with a smile on her face.

It kind of shocks me that the girl that has barely ever left Chicago wants to travel everywhere, yet she hasn't. She hasn't traveled anywhere, not really, not on her own. It makes me more curious than ever as to why she's stayed with Jamie when it's clear that Jamie doesn't pay her what she's worth.

Yes, there are some leadership skills that Olive lacks, mainly the need for brutal honesty and forcefulness, but with a little nourishment, she's already shown that she can grow, and it's clear that she has the skills to be anything she wants.

So, again, I ask a question that I shouldn't want to know the answer to, "Why do you keep working for Jamie? It's clear you're destined for much greater things. Jamie doesn't even pay you what you're worth."

Olive's eyes drop as she thinks back to a memory that I'm afraid is much darker than I'm ready to hear. "Because she saved me, and I owe her."

I blink as I try to remember Jamie ever telling me about saving Olive, but I can't remember anything.

"Whatever she did for you isn't enough for you to stay in a job where you aren't growing."

"But it is," is all she says before turning her eyes back out into the bright lights.

She's clearly not going to tell me exactly what Jamie did to save her. That's okay. She doesn't have to tell me. I'll find out from Jamie. She tells me everything, and I know she'll tell me this as well.

We ride in silence while the lights get brighter and then finally softer as we turn from the excitement of the strip to the business area of town where I work and live. My driver pulls up in front of the tall building, and Olive's eyes immediately go up and down the huge skyscraper.

"Do you live or work here?" she asks.

"Both."

She looks back at the building, studying it, trying to figure out how I could do both.

"Most of the floors are offices or places where the business is run, except for the top floor. That is where my personal condo is. I like being close to my work."

The driver opens Olive's door, and she stares back at Milo, who is sound asleep between us.

"Leave him. I'll have my staff take him up and get him settled into my condo. I need to show you what I do first before we head up to my condo."

Olive nods, but I can finally see the hint of anxiety in her eyes. She is just as nervous to find out what I do as I am to tell her.

I climb out of the car and walk over to her side, linking my fingers with hers to hold her hand. It feels so good, holding her hand like this, most likely for the last time.

I lead her into the building and over to the elevator that opens automatically when I press the button. We walk inside, both anxious as we enter an elevator again. Both thinking about the last time we were in an elevator together, wishing that we could go back to that place, but we can't.

But I can bring one quick moment back. I kiss her one last time. Our lips connect as we ride up the three floors, and that's all it takes for our breathing to become even again, our hearts to stop beating so rapidly, and our world to be okay again. One kiss, and everything's okay again.

But, a second later, the elevator doors open, and I don't hesitate because I know, if I hesitate, I won't go through with it. I take her hand, and I pull her out of the elevator and into my world.

I look around as I see everyone walking around, staying busy and trying to make things happen. Today is a great time to take Olive here because she gets to see exactly what goes on here.

But I'm not here to ensure that everyone is working hard like they should be. I'm here to see how Olive reacts.

Her eyes grow large as she takes everything in. The amount of people in the room, the cameras, and then finally the naked people. I expect her quick, immediate response to be painful for me, but it's not how she reacts. She takes her time studying everything, taking it in and trying to understand.

"You make porn for a living?" she asks, slowly scanning the room, trying to make sense of it.

"Yes. I'm in the adult entertainment industry. I make porn movies, and I sell sex toys. My job is to sell sex."

She swallows and nods, like it all makes sense. "I figured you owned a strip club or something like this," she says.

I grab her chin and tilt her head toward me. "This isn't like owning a strip club. Stripping is nothing compared to this. I hire people to have sex in front of a camera in order for me to make millions."

She sucks in a breath as she looks at me. Then, she finally nods, but she's not running away yet. Maybe she's in shock.

I take her hand again and pull her toward the camera. Many people nod and smile and acknowledge me as we walk by. Most of my employees like me because I'm a fair boss, and they know exactly what I expect of them. I show up at work often, trying to be as involved as I can be. I try to make the working conditions the best they can be.

"Watch," I say as the director starts shooting another scene.

The scene the two actors are in is pretty tame compared to some of the things I've seen and produced.

They are supposed to be in a classroom. The woman is a teacher, and the man is supposed to be her student. The woman eventually seduces her student, and then they fuck on her desk. It's a good scene to ease Olive into this world. The actors truly enjoy what they do, and they want to be here. But that's not the same for everybody. I've seen too many actors come and do this just to make a quick buck and not because they love it, and it ends up destroying them.

I watch Olive's face as she watches them have sex in front of her. She blinks a lot as she watches. Her face occasionally flushes a slight shade of pink. But she doesn't turn away in disgust. She doesn't say that I'm degrading women or anything that I was expecting.

When the scene is over, I grab her hand and pull her out of there and into the side room that we use for interviews and meetings. I shut the door and flip on the lights so that I can see her. I need to know how she feels. Now.

"What do you think?" I ask.

"I think...I think...I don't know what to think. I don't like it. I don't understand it."

My heart sinks.

"But I don't hate it."

I can live with that, I think.

"And what do you think of me?" I ask, needing to know if she hates me.

She narrows her eyes at me. "I think I like you more than I should, more than what's good for me."

I grin even though I shouldn't. I get to keep Olive in my life for a little bit longer. She doesn't hate me...yet.

I grab her and spin us around while kissing her hard on the lips. When I put her down, I say, "I can't wait to fuck you in the bed on my plane."

She bashfully bites her lip, and then her eyes catch something in the corner of the room. She stops grinning. She stops paying any attention to me as she walks slowly over to the corner. I slowly turn around, but I already know what's in the corner of the room.

Everything I thought I had with her, the little time I thought I had left with her, is now gone.

I look at Olive looking at the DVDs of me on the front, shirtless, with words like, *Sean and Stacey in* College Facials. I knew that she wouldn't be happy when she found out that I not only produced porn, but I also starred in them. What's worse is, the other person on the covers of most of them—Jamie.

"Olive, I can explain..."

But I know I can't. There's nothing to explain. There's nothing to be sorry for. This is my life. This is what I do, and if she can't accept me, then I don't want her in my life.

Olive slowly turns around, and I see the tears rolling down her cheeks. "I need some air," she says, pushing past me and out of the room.

This is why I wanted to show her the real me—so she could run away. But, now that she has, I know that isn't what I wanted at all.

16 OLIVE

I wrap my arms around myself because the cool night air hits me hard when I walk outside into the night. But I can finally breathe, alone in the dark. Except I'm not alone. I'm in a busy city full of people walking by who don't bother to stop and ask if I'm okay when they see the tears burning down my cheeks. I should be thinking about Sean, about who he is and what he does, but all I can think about is that I should've brought a damn jacket.

I pace up and down the sidewalk, trying to warm my body and figure out why I had the reaction that I just had. I shouldn't be upset that Sean owns and runs an adult entertainment company. I shouldn't be upset that he did or still stars in porn. I shouldn't be upset that he had sex with Jamie at least a dozen times on film for the world to see. I shouldn't be upset because he is not mine.

I don't have any claim to him, and I definitely don't have any claim to his past. For all I know, he's had sex with women in between our times together. But, still, the tears fall because it hurts to know how intimately involved Sean and Jamie were. They make sense together, unlike me and Sean. Jamie has always been strong, powerful, driven. She knows what she wants, and she goes after it, just like Sean. I don't understand why I feel so strongly about them.

No, that's not true. I know exactly why it makes me so upset.

One, because I care about Sean far more than I hate him.

Two, I know I'm the real reason that Jamie and Sean are no longer together.

It all comes back to me.

The endless nights of listening to Jamie talk about her baby, honey, sweetheart. It took me a while to connect the dots because she hardly ever used his real name when talking about him when they were together.

I try to push the thought out of my head, but I can't. I broke them up. I just didn't realize it at the time.

They were perfect for each other, and I ruined it. And, now, I'm making it worse by fucking Sean. Jamie will never be able to forgive me, and I can't handle being in any more of her debt.

How do I tell Sean the truth? How do I give him up? How can I fix this now that Jamie is pregnant with another man's baby?

I can't.

That's the only thing I know for sure. There is no way to fix this. What's done is done. I just have to figure out how to move on from this.

I take a deep breath and wipe my tears off on the back of my hand. I fluff my hair before I turn around and walk back inside the building. I don't take the elevator. I take the stairs, needing time to think as I climb each step.

I step out onto the floor where there's a whole crew of people shooting the film, not paying any attention to me. I scan the crowd, looking for Sean but don't immediately see him. I wander around on the floor, continuing to look for him while taking everything in.

"He's not here," a woman's voice says.

I turn around and realize that the woman is talking to me. She's beautiful with long, long blonde hair, and when I see the robe wrapped around her body, I realize instantly that she's the woman from the film.

"Who?" I ask.

"Sean. He's not here. That's who you are looking for. You're his new girlfriend."

"I'm not sure I would say that. More like his new plaything for a little while."

The woman laughs. "If you are just his plaything, then why did he bring you here? He hardly ever brings women here unless he's serious about them. It's one of his tests. And you're failing horribly."

I frown. "I know. But I didn't freak out because of what he does. It's more complicated than that."

She nods. "It always is."

"Where is he?"

The woman glances up, and I know immediately that he retreated to his condo.

"Thank you," I say. I run to the elevator and press the button for the top floor.

"You're going to need the code to access his floor," the woman says from behind me.

I feel in my pockets, but I don't have my cell phone to text him. It's with my personal belongings that I left in the car for Sean's staff to take up to the condo. I have no way to reach him. *Shit.*

The elevator doors open, but I don't know what to do because I can't reach him even if I step on. The woman steps on and starts entering a code into the panel. I step in behind her and try not to think about the reason she knows the code to access Sean's floor.

"Don't hurt him," she says as she steps off the elevator.

I frown. *Why does she think that I would hurt him?*

The doors close, and they don't open again until I reach the top floor.

When the doors open, I expect another obstacle in my way, preventing me from getting to Sean, but that's not the case. When the doors open, they open straight to his condo. And it's the most massive condo I think I've ever been inside of. His condo in Chicago isn't even half of the size of this place.

But I try not to focus on how massive and beautiful and expensive his place is. I try to focus on the man sitting on the couch with Milo in his lap and a drink on the end table as he stares out the window in silence.

I know that he knows I'm here because Milo's head pokes up, looking at me, and there's no way he didn't hear the elevator. But, still, I cautiously walk over and take a seat on the other end of the couch, tucking my feet under me. I prepare for a fight of some sort or a breakup to happen even though we were never really together. But he doesn't say anything to me. He just blankly looks at me, unfeeling.

"I don't know what to say," I say.

Sean takes a drink of his amber liquor and then says, "Tell me that you hate me."

He says what he wants me to say. I know that he brought me here to end whatever was going on between us. But it's not what he wants. He wants to be with me—or at least, he wants to fuck me again. I'm not sure if he really wants me. He probably wants to be with Jamie.

"I don't hate you. I wish I did. It would make everything easier," I whisper.

He nods.

I want to apologize. I want to find a way to fix things, but I can't. I know that's not what he wants anyway.

He just wants me to accept him for who he is. And I do, and I don't care what he does for a living. But it still doesn't mean that we can be together. I just don't know what it means yet.

I feel entirely exhausted and drained even though I slept for hours on the plane. I feel so tired. I'm tired because I didn't get much sleep the night before due to my migraine. I'm tired from dealing with Owen. I'm tired of trying to figure Sean out.

"What's my final test?" I ask, hoping that shows him that I still approve of him enough to be here.

He raises an eyebrow, surprised at my question. "You need to hire five actors tomorrow for a new film. The script is on the kitchen counter for you to read through."

"I'll read it before I go to sleep, which I need to do soon," I say, waiting to hear what he's going to say. I try not to think about the script that is basically just a sex scene that I'm somehow supposed to audition actors for. Instead, I think about the sleeping part. *Am I going to sleep in his bed? Am I going to sleep alone?* I don't have an answer.

"Like I said, the script is on the counter. You won't need to be ready until one tomorrow afternoon. That's when the auditions start. And you can take any of the rooms in this condo."

I suck in a breath because he's not making the decision of where I sleep tonight. I am. I can sleep in his bed if I want, or I can sleep on my own in any of the other beds.

I get up off the couch and walk over to the kitchen where I pick up the script. Then, I head down the long hallway. I pass door after door, each bedroom all more than acceptable rooms to sleep in. But I don't stop until I find the door on the end. When I open it, it looks just like his retreat in his Chicago condo.

I hesitate for a second, knowing that this is just going to make things even more complicated, but I don't care. I want to sleep with Sean tonight even if there's no chance we'll have a tomorrow. So, I walk into his bedroom, and then I wait.

17 SEAN

That was the first time that I slept in a bed without fucking a woman first. I probably could have. Olive probably even wanted me to with the way she was lying in my bed, sound asleep, when I came in. She'd climbed into my bed completely naked, and by the time I came in, the covers were halfway down her body, exposing her perfect breasts, begging me to touch them. But I was good—mainly because I didn't want to wake her up. She looked so peaceful, sleeping in my bed.

But, now, it's the next day, and I honestly have no idea where we stand. I thought that bringing her here would make everything clearer. I thought she would return to hating me like she did before, and that would be that. That, no matter how much I wanted to fuck her, she would say no every time, and I'd eventually give up and move on to another woman. But that's not what happened. Everything became more complicated.

My dick still wants her. Man, does he want her. I want her lips, her ass, her pussy. I want to push my dick inside every bit of her. *But do I want more than just to fuck her? Does she want more? I'm not sure. What would that even look like? How would we manage a rela-*

tionship while working together? And I'm still not sure she's okay with the fact that I sell sex for a living even if it's not my body I'm selling anymore.

And there is still a past between her and Jamie that I don't understand. I tried to get Jamie to tell me this morning when I called her. But she wouldn't tell me. That could be another complication. And, since Jamie won't tell me, I'll have to work on Olive telling me.

But, for now, I get to push that all aside and just enjoy the afternoon. Because, right now, it's time for Olive's final test. I've already decided that she's going to be my manager for me when I'm gone. She's the only person I trust, and she's already proven herself more than capable of handling any situation. I still want to do the test today because it's going to be a hell of a lot of fun to watch her be uncomfortable all afternoon while trying to pretend like she's not.

I hand Olive the stack of headshots of the actors. She takes them from me and places them on the table next to the script and her notebook that she has some things scribbled on. I'm guessing she has written interview questions and things like, *Remain calm*, and, *Don't stare at the guys' dicks too much.*

"This is your final test, so make sure you really prove to me that you're capable of leading and taking control of any situation," I say.

Olive rolls her eyes at me. "Don't act like you haven't already decided who's going to be the manager. I know I already have the job. And, if I don't, I'm suing you for sexual harassment," she says with a smile.

I grin as I look at her. Then, I lean down, so my lips hover just over her ear, and I whisper, "Cocky. I like it, but just remember how much I enjoy punishing you when you mess up, and remember that we're in a building full of all sorts of sex toys that you told me earlier you were afraid of. I could use far too many things in this building to punish you, and it would be far too enjoyable for me to make you so uncomfortable that you won't be able to walk straight for a week."

I take a seat in the chair at the table next to her as her eyes follow me. I see the hint of fear but also lust in her eyes at that thought.

I grin, happy to have made this challenge even harder for her. "Are you ready, Olive?" I ask.

She nods.

"We're ready for the first round of actors!" I shout out the door of the audition room.

One of my assistants opens the door and lets the first five actors in. I watch as Olive calmly folds her hands together and lays them on the table, watching the actors walk into the room.

"Can you please tell me your name, a little about yourself, and what your last project was?" Olive says politely to them.

I don't pay attention to the actors, just Olive. She listens with a bright smile on her face as each actor introduces themselves. She pulls out each headshot and résumé from the stack as they speak.

"I'll now have you act out the first scene," Olive says without an ounce of hesitation or fear in her voice.

I keep my eyes on her as actors get in position. But I can see them out of the corner of my eye, stripping most of their clothes off in order to prepare for the scene. The scene is much darker than what she saw yesterday. It's a gangbang. Four men, one woman. And I don't know how far she's gonna want them to take the scene for her to decide who the best people for this job are. There is not really a right or wrong answer, although I usually have them take it far enough that I can decide how well they work together, enough for them to get into the scene and make me believe them.

Honestly, I don't care if she picks all the wrong people for this next project. I just want to watch her grow uncomfortable and twist in her chair because I know watching her will drive me wild. I hear them start the scene with some seductive conversation. But Olive doesn't change her expression. She just calmly sits there, like she's watching an audition for a musical. The scene progresses, and I know that she is staring at guys holding their dicks as they prepare to fuck the actress.

But, still, Olive remains calm. Her eyes don't show any fear or anxiety. Her breathing is calm and relaxed, but there is one tiny thing that gives her away. Her heart. I brush my hand against her leg, and I can feel her pulse beating rapidly through her body.

I grin. She might be pretending to be calm, but this is driving her wild inside.

She stops the scene a minute later, and I glance over to see where she stopped it—the exact moment after each of the men have had a chance to interact with the girl. It's where I would have stopped them as well.

"Thank you all for coming. We will get back to you within the next couple of hours," Olive says, standing out of her chair and extending her hand. As she does, her chair falls backward, making a loud clash.

One of the men whom she's holding out her hand to, who is still standing completely naked and covered in sweat—among other things—says with a grin, "I don't think you want to shake my hand right now."

She retracts her hand. "You're probably right," she says, wincing. "It was nice to meet you all," she says, sitting back down after picking up her chair.

I can't help but laugh at her just a little.

She playfully punches me in the arm. "Stop laughing. You have to admit, I handled that pretty well, and I don't think I'm ever going to come across a situation like this ever again in my life."

I keep laughing because I can't help it until she gives me a serious look. I stop it as the next few actors come into the room.

The process repeats over and over again, but every time, I look to see if it still affects her. And, every time, her heart still races in her chest, and her blood still pumps quickly throughout her body, letting me know that, despite her cool exterior, the auditions are driving her wild.

The last actors finally leave, and then I ask, "So, who would you pick?"

She digs through the headshots and places the third group out on the table.

"This group. But, if I'm allowed to exchange some actors from different groups, then I'd replace this guy with this guy from the first group," she says, pointing to the various headshots.

I nod, entirely agreeing with her.

"Did I pass? Do I get the job?" she asks, crossing her arms and leaning back in the chair.

I scrunch my lips together, pretending to think about it for a couple of minutes, watching her frown, which in turn makes me laugh. "Yes, the job is yours. You're the only one I trust to be me when I'm gone."

She jumps up and throws her arms around me. She firmly kisses me on the lips, surprising us both.

"What was that for?" I ask when she slowly pulls away.

"Sorry. I guess watching people have sex all afternoon has made me a bit horny," she says, blushing for the first time all afternoon.

I laugh and then kiss her again, more than happy to remedy the situation.

My phone buzzes in my pocket for about the dozenth time this afternoon. I reluctantly pull it out and see text message after text message from Frank and the other employees back at Jamie's real estate company.

I sigh. "I think we'd better get back sooner rather than later. It seems the company is falling apart without us there."

Olive frowns.

"Don't worry; this time, we can actually fuck on the plane."

Her eyes light up at that thought. Then, she reaches over into her purse that is sitting on the floor next to her and pulls out a DVD with me and two women on the front, half-naked.

"And maybe we can watch this?" she says with a goofy grin on her face.

I laugh. And I nod.

I can't believe she did that. I think it's her way of showing me that she accepts me, no matter what I've done or what I still do for a living. And I don't know if I've ever wanted a woman more.

18 OLIVE

We barely make it back onto Sean's private jet before our lips lock, our hands clinging to each other without a thought of letting go.

"Mr. Burrows, you need to take a seat for us to take off," a man, who I assume is our captain, says.

Sean moves us further onto the plane.

"We'll be in a seat in the back," Sean says between kisses.

He starts pulling me down through the aisle of the plane. His hands travel over my body while his lips stay glued to mine.

I'm not sure if the captain is going to allow us to sit in the back. I'm sure he knows that we won't be sitting in the bedroom. But he doesn't say anything to us. I guess, when you own your own jet, it doesn't really matter if you follow all the rules.

And, right now, I want to break all the rules. Every. Single. One.

I want to feel things I have never felt before. Do things I have never done before.

I want to know what it is really like to be loved by a man who truly loves me. I'm just not sure if Sean is the man I will get to experience real love with. But I do know that I get to experience the best sex of my life with him.

Sean pulls me into the bedroom and slams the door shut behind us.

"I want it dirty. Show me how dirty and rough you can be, just like in the videos you make," I say.

Sean stops kissing me long enough to cock his head to one side with a look I haven't seen before. "I don't think you understand how dirty it can really get."

I grin. "I think I've seen plenty dirty so far. But I want more."

Sean kisses me hard. "Tell me what you want, Olive."

I bite my lip as I think about what I want. "Tie me up, spank me, talk dirty to me. I want everything."

Sean's eyes intensify.

"Show me how to fuck like a porn star," I say.

He grabs my arm and forces it behind my back, and then he pulls the other one behind my back as well. "You like it rough, you'll get it rough, baby," Sean says.

He ties my hands together behind my back with rope that I have no idea where he got it from.

"I knew you would want it rough, so I brought some things with me," Sean whispers into my ear, answering my unspoken question.

He spins me around to face him and then rips my shirt open, exposing my lace bra that I found packed in my suitcase, which one of Sean's staff must have bought for me. It's more expensive than anything I own, and it makes my breasts look amazing. From Sean's gaze, I think he agrees.

But then he rips the thin material holding my bra in place. "My dirty girl thinks she needs to wear lace to impress me, but I'd rather just have you naked."

I suck in a breath as his tongue travels down my body and then over my breasts, teasing me in a way that only he can.

"I need you," I say. But I don't know what I need. All I know is that I need more. I'm consumed by need for him, and I'm not sure that I will ever get enough.

He rips my pants off my body and then throws me on the bed.

I've never been so turned on as I am right now. The excitement of not knowing how far he is going to take it, how dirty it is going to get, is driving me mad with need.

I feel his palm hit against my bare ass, and I scream from the shock. Then, I realize that we are on a plane that, albeit is huge, is not huge enough to hide my screams.

Sean grins. "You can scream, baby. This room is just as sound-proof as any of my bedrooms."

His hand hits my ass again, and I scream again. The pain is more than I expected, especially since I can't move. My hands are tied behind my back, my face is smushed into the bed, and my ass is up in the air.

He hits me again, and I cry out, but as much as I don't want to admit it, being controlled like this turns me on even more.

"You like it like this. Dirty, filthy," Sean says.

I pant. "Yes."

I feel the sting on my ass again.

Then, he says, "I want to fuck your ass. I want you to feel what it's really like to feel dirty. I want to claim every last bit of you."

I suck in a breath. Liking and hating that thought at the same time.

I feel his cock already pushing at my ass, begging to enter.

I feel him tug on my hair, pulling my head up as he kisses down my neck.

"Tell me you want me to fuck your ass."

He kisses my neck as his hand finds my pussy. His fingers rub over me until his hands are soaked with my wetness. His fingers move the wetness from my pussy to my ass. He gently slides his finger in my ass, and I moan as he stretches me.

"I want you to fuck me in the ass," I say, barely able to get the words out because it feels so good.

He slaps my ass again just as his cock replaces his fingers.

I forgot how large he was until he pushed inside my ass.

He slaps me again as he thrusts inside me.

I scream, "Fuck, Sean."

He kisses my lips. "That's my dirty girl."

I nod, loving being his dirty girl. If only I were really his. If this is how he fucks me now, I would love to know what it would be like for him to fuck me when and if he actually made me his.

But thoughts like that easily leave my mind when he fucks me harder. Pounding into me until I can't take it any longer.

I come as he fills my ass with his own cum.

He cuts the rope off my wrists and then wraps his arms around me as he sweetly kisses my neck.

I suck in a breath, letting the emotions I feel run through me.

"I lo—" I begin but then stop myself.

"Hmm?" Sean says, barely awake.

I shake my head as I continue to breathe heavily. "I think I like being your dirty girl."

He softly kisses me on the lips and pulls me tighter to him. I know, within seconds, we are both going to be sound asleep.

But I can't help but think that I could love him. I might even already be in love with him.

I just need to stop loving him. He's my boss, and he's made it perfectly clear that he is in love with Jamie, not me.

This was a last fling, and I just got carried away. I don't love him.

19 SEAN

I could hear it in Olive's voice. She has something else she wants to tell me, but she's hiding it from me. So, while she thinks I'm sleeping, I'm doing anything but. Instead, I'm reliving every last second, trying to figure out what she could be hiding and wondering if it's the same thing that I'm hiding.

Olive's eyes flutter open, and then a slow grin creeps up her face.

"I love naked naps with you," she says, her cheeks bright and flushed with warmth from her nap.

I stroke a piece of hair out of the way of her face as I continue to hold her in my arms.

She smiles brighter and stretches her arms above her head before snuggling her head against my chest again. "How much longer is left in our flight? I need to know when I should start getting dressed again, so it doesn't look like we just fucked the whole flight."

"Half an hour," I say.

"Oh. I should get up then and start looking presentable," she says, moving out of my arms to go get dressed.

I grab her arm and pull her back into bed.

She giggles. "Fine. I guess we can fuck one last time. But we have to make it quick." She moves to kiss me but stops short when she sees the look in my eyes. "What is it?" she asks.

I take a deep breath as I tuck her messy brown hair behind her ear again. "I think I might just fall in love with you if given the chance."

She sucks in a breath and then stops breathing altogether.

"Say something," I say, needing to know how she feels.

But she doesn't. She doesn't even breathe.

"Olive, say something. Anything."

She doesn't.

I grab her cheeks, pulling her face toward mine, and kiss her, sweeping my tongue into her mouth.

When I pull away, she finally breathes again, coming to after I kissed her.

"Say something."

"I..." She grins.

I cock my head as I wait, second after second, for her to finish her sentence. My heart beats fast as I wait the unbearable seconds.

"I think I already love you."

My lips crash down on hers as my hands cling to her body. Now, I need to fuck her again.

She laughs. "Wait...I love you, and it's clear you love me even if you won't fully admit it yet. But what does that mean? How will this work? We work together. You're still in love with..." But she doesn't finish her sentence.

I grab her chin and look her square in the eye. "I'm in love with you."

Her eyes flitter back and forth between mine, trying to find the truth. But I'm not hiding anything. I'm telling her the truth.

When she's satisfied, she says, "And what about at work? The realtors aren't going to be happy with us dating and my promotion."

I nod. "They don't have to know that we are dating."

She narrows her eyes. "How? I can't keep a secret from the company for more than a couple of hours. I'm sure they have already figured out that I broke up with Owen, and they probably already know that I'm here with you, that we are together. We can't hide it from them."

"They have probably figured out that you broke up with Owen. But, as far as they know, you and I still hate each other. And I'll just say, I brought you here for training, which is the truth."

She nods, but I don't think I've convinced her.

"We will go to work and pretend to hate each other, as always. Then, at night, we will be free to do as we please. I can take you on fancy dates. Do more unthinkable things to your body."

Her breathing slows again.

"It will be fun, sneaking around the office, trying not to get caught," I whisper into her ear.

She bites her lip, and I know I have her.

"Now, come here, and let me fuck you before we land."

She squeals as I grab her.

Olive is mine.

"WHAT THE HELL IS GOING ON?" I ask Floyd as I get back to the office.

Olive walks into the office past me and straight to her desk, practically ignoring me.

She's good, I think.

"We lost the Margo account. They were our biggest client. We helped them find properties for their businesses and homes all over the world," Floyd says.

"How in the world did that happen?" I ask, not understanding how, in less than twenty-four hours, everything has fallen apart so horribly.

Floyd looks down. "We missed a few deadlines and weren't able to find them what they were looking for. They were already on thin ice before when we couldn't negotiate a lower price for a restaurant they opened last month."

I run my hand through my hair, not ready to deal with this now.

"You're fired," I tell Floyd.

"What? You can't do that! I'm the best realtor you have," Floyd says.

I shake my head. "No. You used to be the best realtor until you lost the most important account we had. Honestly, the only account that mattered since they made up almost sixty percent of our profit each year."

Floyd still stands there, stunned.

But I don't have time to deal with him. I brush past him and head straight toward my office, walking past Olive's desk.

"Olive, I need to see you. Now," I say with an angry voice.

I feel everyone's eyes on us as Olive stands up and follows me into my office. I glance behind Olive to see the employees looking on with fear instead of suspicion over Olive and me.

This is going to be too easy.

Olive shuts the door. "We lost the Margo account? We have to fix this! If Jamie finds out, it's going to destroy her. She's worked too hard for this company to lose everything in a few days," she says.

I nod. "I'm going to go speak with the CEO of Margo Enterprises in person and see if I can get things straightened out. I need you to keep everything running smoothly here for the rest of our accounts. We can't afford to lose anyone else."

I start gathering my things to leave. "What are you doing? Get to work!" I shout, letting my anger get the best of me.

Olive folds her arms across her chest and raises an eyebrow at me.

"I'm sorry. Olive, can you please get to work and help me straighten everything out? I don't want to ruin Jamie's company any more than you do."

She grins.

I cock my head to one side. "What?"

"I just never thought I'd hear you say *I'm sorry.*"

I roll my eyes. "I guess there is a first time for everything."

"I'll help you...under one condition."

"What's that?"

"You kiss me first. And promise to come to my apartment after work tonight."

I grin. "I'll do everything I can to get to your bed as quickly as I can."

Her eyes light up.

I walk over to her, take her in my arms, and kiss her with everything I have. I forget about how much I'm screwing up by letting down one of my closest friends by basically ruining her company. I just kiss Olive until we hear a knock at the door.

I quickly let go of Olive and walk to the door while Olive stands, frozen.

"Yes?" I snap as I open the door.

"Here are my keys to the properties I was selling. I hope the whole company goes down in flames," Floyd says, throwing his keys at me.

He turns and leaves. Olive pushes past me and walks out after him.

She's mad at me. I can tell.

For firing Floyd? For yelling at her?

I'm not sure. I run my hand through my hair again and then rub my neck. I don't have time to figure it out now. I have a company to save.

I flash her a we-will-talk-later-and-we-are-still-on-for-fucking-at-your-place-tonight look as I walk by her desk, but she doesn't even glance up at me. Working with Olive is going to be harder than I thought.

20 OLIVE

Sean never made it to my apartment last night. He stayed at Margo's hotel, speaking with her employees most of the night, working out a new contract with them.

But he did call to apologize. Twice.

And I'm beginning to love hearing him apologize.

I can't wait to get into work today. Because it means that I will get to see Sean again. And, hopefully, now that the Margo account has been settled, we can get back into a normal swing of work, which will involve lots of sneaking around in his office to have sex.

So, I jump out of bed thirty minutes before my alarm even goes off, far too excited to get into work today. I jump in and out of the shower even faster. I throw on some clothes, but when it comes to doing my hair and makeup, I take a little more time then usual.

I want Sean to find me irresistible. I want him to not be able to think straight because all he can think about is me.

Milo brushes up against me while I finish applying my makeup. I pet him, giving him the attention he wants.

My phone buzzes, and I see the message is from Sean. I smile as I open the text message, and immediately, my heart sinks.

Sean: I have to go to NYC for a week. Margo wants me to personally find her new property there to assure her that we can honor our new contract.

I frown. I don't get to see him today. I don't get to kiss him.

Is he running away from me?

I immediately push the thought out of my head. He's not running away at the thought of a serious relationship with me. He's not hiding. He's just working, doing what's right.

Still, it doesn't keep me from feeling horrible. I wish I could see him again before he goes.

It's a silly thought. I just saw him yesterday. There is no need to be so needy.

I take a deep breath trying to keep from letting the thought of him not being at work today make me fall apart. It's probably better actually that he won't be at work today. It will help keep people from getting suspicious about our relationship and it will allow me to start being respected as a leader without him here.

I text back.

Me: I'm going to miss you. Good luck!

He doesn't respond immediately. I try to distract myself by finishing getting ready, but that is no longer a distraction for me. I no longer care about what I look like when I get into work or getting in early.

I sulk while I finish getting ready. I do my best to take my time now that I don't have Sean to look forward to. But I quickly run out of things to do at home. I might as well get into work early. It will at least distract me.

I head downstairs. I decide to call an Uber when I see more than a foot of snow covering the ground. Sean and I never discussed what my new salary would be, but it has to be enough for me to at least afford an occasional Uber ride to work instead of taking the subway every morning.

I wait in the lobby until the Uber pulls up, and then I step out into the cold air, happy that I have the new coat that Sean bought for me to keep me warm and remind me of him on a day like today.

"You didn't think I would leave without saying good-bye first, did you?" I hear Sean's voice cut through the cool air.

I grin and turn around to see Sean walking toward me.

I run over to him, throwing myself in his arms like I haven't seen him in months instead of only hours. He catches me and wraps his arms around me like he is just as desperate for me as I am for him.

He firmly kisses me over and over, turning the kiss into a longer make-out session.

I slowly pull away. "You are full of surprises," I say.

Sean smiles and then walks me over to one of two cars parked along the street.

"Your chariot, fully stocked with coffee and chocolate chip cookies to get you through your day," Sean says.

"You got me a ride into work today?" I ask.

He nods.

I light up. "Oh, crap. I need to cancel my Uber then." I pull out my phone and quickly cancel it.

"You're going to do great today," Sean says, sweetly kissing me on the lips.

"Thank you," I say, blushing, still amazed that he is here and that he did all of this for me.

"This is Joe Hubbert. He'll be giving you a ride every day while I'm away," Sean says.

I smile and shake Joe's hand before turning back to Sean.

"And what about when you return?" I ask.

Sean kisses me again. "Since you'll be waking up in the same bed as me, I can give you a ride to work."

I bite my lip, trying to contain my excitement at that thought.

He groans as I kiss him again. "I really need to go."

I grab his neck and kiss him again. "Are you sure?"

He groans again. "No. But, if I'm going to make my flight, I have to go."

"You're flying commercial?"

He nods. "I'm reserving my private jet for flights with you. Otherwise, what is the point?" he says, winking.

"All right, get out of here. I'll keep you updated about how the realtors are doing."

He kisses me one last time. "I just want to hear how you are doing."

I nod. "Same."

He smiles and helps me into the car before shutting my door. Joe starts driving me toward work and away from Sean. Sean waits a second to watch me leave and then jumps in his car behind me before speeding off toward the airport.

THAT'S the last I saw of him in over a week.

He calls to talk to me every day, usually multiple times a day, but it's still hard to have a real relationship with him when he's gone. It's why I have been looking forward to him coming back at the end of the week.

But, when Friday comes around, he calls to tell me it would be at least another week.

The thoughts of him running away from me immediately creep back into my head. Until he tells me he loves me and sends me a large bouquet of flowers to my desk at work. He didn't sign it with his name, just *Your love*.

But it is enough to get me through another week.

But, when the second week passes, I almost expect him to call again, saying that he isn't coming home for another week. But, to my relief, he says he is coming home tonight. I just have to make it through one more day at work, and then I'll get to see him.

Work has actually been great the last couple of weeks. I have loved being in my new role as manager. I passed my realtor's license test. I have made dozens of cookies for clients this week. My week has been great. The only downside has been not seeing Sean.

But, when I get into work on Friday morning, I'm afraid my luck has changed. Because sitting in the office when I first get in is Jamie. She's crying, sitting at what used to be her desk.

"Oh, thank God you are the first one here, like always, Olive," Jamie cries out.

I walk into Jamie's office and close the door behind me in case anyone else comes in.

"What's going on, Jamie? I thought you were supposed to be on bed rest?" I ask as I walk over to her and tightly hug her.

Jamie continues to cry as I hold her in my arms.

"Nicolas broke up with me," Jamie finally gets out through sobs.

"Oh, sweetie! I'm so sorry," I say, holding her tighter.

I don't know what to say to make it any better for her. She only dated Nicolas two months before she found out she was pregnant. I'm not sure what she expected. But I know telling her that now isn't helpful.

"Are you okay to be out of bed?" I ask.

Jamie nods. "The doctor said I was fine as long as I take things easy. I was just too stressed at work. But, right now, I need some sort of distraction."

I hold on to her. "Why don't I take you to brunch? Food always makes you feel better, and then you can tell me everything that happened."

Jamie nods. "That sounds good. Sean is supposed to be back soon, and he can handle things here for us."

I smile. I'm not sure what Sean has told her about me and him. But it hurts me that Sean still talks to her so often, knowing their history. Knowing that they used to work together. Sleep together.

I stand up. "Let me just check in with everyone here first, and then we can go."

Jamie nods.

But, when I stand up, I feel off. I feel dizzy, sick, like I'm about to puke.

I close my eyes and sit back down on the ground to try to make the nausea and dizziness go away, assuming that I just stood up too fast. But it doesn't immediately go away.

"Olive, are you okay?" Jamie asks.

I nod and stand up again, but the feeling intensifies.

"Sorry, no, I'm not okay. I feel sick. Maybe I'm coming down with the flu. I'm sorry, Jamie, but I'm not sure if I can go to brunch with you after all."

Jamie studies me a moment and then says, "You're pregnant." She doesn't ask it. She says it.

I laugh. "You're crazy. I'm not pregnant. I'm just sick. The flu has been going around here lately."

Jamie shakes her head. "I could be wrong. It could be just because I'm pregnant that I expect everyone else to be, too. But humor me, and let's go get you a pregnancy test."

I frown, not understanding at all what is leading her to think I'm pregnant. I look down at the outfit I chose, and then I realize why. I chose a tight-fitting sweater that makes my pooch of a belly stick out just enough for Jamie to think that. I look bigger than Jamie does. Her belly still looks completely flat to me. She works out a lot, which I guess explains it.

"Please...at the very least, it will distract me," Jamie says.

"And what if I'm really sick with the flu? You think hanging out with me while you're pregnant is a good idea?"

She huffs. "You're right. How about you run to the drugstore next door and then come back here and take the test? If it's negative, then I'll keep my distance, but if it's positive..." Jamie lets her sentence trail off.

I sigh. "Fine," I say, realizing that Jamie isn't going to let this go.

I open the door and go grab my coat. Then, I head outside to walk the half a block to the drugstore to get a pregnancy test that I know is going to be negative.

I enter the drugstore a couple minutes later and easily find the pregnancy tests. There are about a dozen different brands though, and I have no idea which to choose. So, I just grab the cheapest brand, and then I walk over to the cold-and-flu section and pick up some meds because that is the more likely reason for me feeling so bad. I debate on picking up soup, but I can order delivery later. I'd rather have that than the cans of soup the drugstore carries.

I pay for the items and then walk back to the office through the freezing cold. *I can't believe I went outside and dealt with the cold just for a freakin' pregnancy test.*

When I get back to the office, more employees have arrived. I nod and greet them as I walk through the office building, trying my best to hide the contents of my bag. I don't want any rumors started about me, especially since I know I'm not pregnant.

I make it back to the office and slam Jamie's door shut.

"Did you get the pregnancy test?" Jamie asks.

"Shh. I don't want the whole office to know. And, yes."

"Well, what are you waiting for? Go take it."

I sigh and take the box out of the bag. I quickly read the instructions, not really paying that close attention, as I pull one of the tests out of the box and slip it into my purse. I then put the box back in the bag and hide the bag in the corner of the room in case anyone comes into Jamie's office while I'm gone.

"I'll be right back," I say.

"Good luck!" Jamie shouts at me as I leave.

I sigh. I don't need luck. I'm not pregnant.

I walk to the restroom on the third floor that no one from the real estate office ever uses just in case. The restrooms on this floor are single stalls, so when I enter, I lock the door and don't have to worry about anyone coming in.

I open the test and pee on the stick, and then I wait. I have to wait three minutes for the results. I set a timer on my phone.

I feel my heart begin to race as the seconds tick by. I wasn't nervous before, but I'm nervous now. This is ridiculous. I'm only taking this test because Jamie thinks she has a pregnancy sixth sense now that she is pregnant. I'm not pregnant.

Sean and I use condoms every time we have sex. Plus, it would be far too soon to know if I was pregnant.

The timer finally goes off, and then I remember. Owen. I could be pregnant with Owen's baby.

I stare at the test, unable to flip it over and read it.

"This is ridiculous! I'm not pregnant."

I walk over to the sink where the test rests and flip it over.

I WALK BACK into the office to go tell Jamie the news when I freeze.

I watch as Sean hugs Jamie. It's clear that Jamie is telling Sean about how Nicolas broke up with her. Sean wraps his arm around her and tightly holds her as they walk into her office together. I watch Sean close the door but not before he gives her a look that I've only seen once before—when he told me he loved me. It's the same look he's giving her now.

He still loves Jamie.

The door shuts, but he slams it too hard, and it bounces open just slightly.

I don't know what to do.

Should I just walk in like I didn't know that Sean returned?

Should I just leave and not speak to either of them?

Should I just wait until one of them comes out of the office?

I still haven't decided. But, still, I walk toward the office and hesitate just outside the door.

I hear Sean's voice. "I'm so sorry, Jamie. I want to take care of you. I'll do anything for you and the baby. You know that."

I can't hear this. It will destroy me.

I turn to walk away when Jamie spots me through the small crack in the door.

"Olive!" she says brightly.

I open the door and step into the office. Sean doesn't immediately run over and hug me, like I expected. In fact, he stands, frozen, cold. Like he barely even knows me. Not like a man who is in love with me and has fucked me half a dozen times or more.

"Sean got back early, so we can go to brunch now, if you're feeling up to it," Jamie says.

Sean looks to me. "Are you sick?"

"No, I'm fine. I'd love to go to brunch with you, Jamie."

Jamie's face lights up when she realizes what it means.

"Oh my God! I was right then?" Jamie squeals.

I try to smile, but it's hard to smile. I nod slowly.

Jamie runs over and tightly hugs me. "I'm so excited for you!" she squeals.

I glance over at Sean, who is suspiciously staring at me.

Jamie finally releases her hold on me.

"What are we excited about?" Sean asks, looking from me to Jamie, trying to get one of us to give him an answer.

"Oh, nothing. I'm just excited to go to lunch with a good friend. Nothing you need to worry about," Jamie says, trying to protect my secret.

But I can't hold it in any longer. He needs to know the truth. Now.

I plaster a fake smile on my face. "I'm pregnant."

21 SEAN

Pregnant.

Olive can't be pregnant. We haven't been having sex long enough for her to know if she is pregnant or not.

But then, all at once, it hits me. Owen. She's pregnant with Owen's baby.

I can see the fear in her eyes as she pretends to be excited with Jamie about being pregnant.

"I'm so excited for you and Owen. I know he isn't the perfect guy, but you two will make great-looking babies! And we get to experience this together! It's amazing!" Jamie continues on and on.

I can see the moment that Olive just can't take hearing Jamie any longer.

"I think I'm going to be sick. Can I take a rain check until a bit later, Jamie?" Olive asks.

"Oh, honey! Of course. I'll send you all my morning-sickness tricks," Jamie says.

That's all it takes for Olive to run out of the room.

"I'm going to go check on Olive," I tell Jamie.

"That's sweet, but you should just get her some Sprite and crackers for when she gets back," Jamie says.

I ignore her and chase Olive down the hallway to the restroom. She goes inside, and I follow her. I lock the door behind us.

"What are you doing? This is the woman's restroom," Olive says.

"And you aren't really sick. So, what are you doing in here?"

Her eyes slowly look up to mine. "I'm running away."

I walk toward her, needing to put my arms around her, but she takes a step back.

"I'm sorry that I ignored you back there, but I wasn't sure if you wanted Jamie to know about us," I say.

She folds her arms across her chest. "I'm not mad that you acted cold toward me back in Jamie's office. I understand. I really do. I just think we need to stop whatever this is. It doesn't make sense anymore."

I feel like she just slapped me.

"Why? Because you're pregnant?" I ask.

She nods. "I'm pregnant, and you already know it's not yours."

I rub my neck, trying to find the words to defuse the situation. "Yes, I know the baby isn't mine. But that doesn't matter. We can still date. Still see where this goes. And, no matter what happens, I will always be here for you and your baby."

"Like you are going to be there for Jamie?" she says solemnly.

"Yes," I say slowly, not understanding.

"I think you should just be there for Jamie and not for me. I have plenty of things to worry about without having to worry about where you and I stand."

"What are you talking about? I don't want Jamie. I want you."

She shakes her head. "You still love Jamie."

I frown but don't have any words to fix this. I can tell her that I don't love Jamie, but it is clear that she wouldn't believe me.

"I don't want to give you up," I say.

I see the tears starting, but Olive shakes them away.

"I broke you and Jamie up," she says almost defiantly.

"What are you talking about?"

"About five years ago, I was homeless. I was living on the street. Occasionally, I would get to sleep in a homeless shelter, but I mostly slept on benches in parks, tucked in the doorways of shops, or under highways.

"One night, I fell asleep on the doorstep of Jamie's small office. She only had two employees at that time. She had to wake me up to get into her office that day. She was running late, as always, so she asked me if I would get her a coffee. She offered to pay me ten bucks if did it, so I did.

"And then, the next morning, I got her coffee again. Eventually, she started paying me to be her assistant. She got me off the street and into the apartment that I live in now. She saved me.

"And so, a year ago, she told me about you. Except she never used your name. She always referred to you as her baby, honey, sweetheart, et cetera. She was so in love—or so she said. She thought you were going to propose soon. She was living the fairy-tale life.

"But, over the next couple of years, I got to know Jamie. I knew that, even though you had dated on and off for years, she wasn't ready to settle down. She had a company to run, and all she talked about was, once you proposed, she would sell the company and be a stay-at-home mom. But she wasn't ready for that. And, from everything I'd heard about you, you weren't ready for that. So..."

"So, you broke us up," I finish for her.

She nods.

"You showed her that message," I say.

She nods. "You left your phone at her apartment. So, I just let her see what an ass you were."

"She broke up with me because she thought I was cheating on her. But I wasn't."

The tears fall now. "I didn't realize it until later—when your mother texted that she loved you back. I hadn't realized it was your mother, but by then, Jamie had already broken up with you, and I thought it was for the best. I thought I was saving her from a life of unhappiness. I didn't want her to give up everything she had worked so hard for. She needed a man who fit into her life.

"I was one of her closest friends, yet the guy she had been seeing for over a year never even made an attempt to meet me. He never came to her work. She spent most of her time traveling to see him. I didn't think it was the healthiest relationship."

She takes a deep breath.

"But, now that I see you two together, I realize how mistaken I was. You two are perfect for each other."

Her tears flow freely while I'm in a state of shock.

"I'm so sorry, Sean," Olive says before she pushes past me, leaving me feeling completely empty.

My heart is broken. And I have no idea how to put it back together.

22 OLIVE

I quit.

I'd been calling in sick all week long, and tonight, I finally quit. Jamie invited me over to her house to get some maternity clothes that she said were too small for her, although I can't imagine them ever fitting me. And I told her that I was quitting.

She was sad but understood. I told her I was moving in with Owen, but I'm not sure she bought that. Honestly, I haven't even talked to Owen yet. I've been completely avoiding it like the plague.

Jamie wanted me to stay and talk about it, but I couldn't. I couldn't handle the thought that Sean could come over to her place at any moment or text or call her. Jamie was clearly back to her happy and bubbly self, so I'm guessing that she and Sean are back together.

I take a brownie from the tray I made earlier today and take a seat on my bed to eat it. Other than talking to Jamie, the only thing I've accomplished all week is baking and then eating everything that I baked. At this rate, I'll gain a hundred pounds in a month.

That can't be good for the baby. I should start making some

avocado brownies or something, so at least, I will be getting something other than sugar into me.

I sigh.

I'm pregnant, I think, looking down at my stomach.

It's something I've always said I wanted but not this way with a man I hate. Although I've always wanted to be a mother, thinking about the fact that it is actually happening right now scares me to death.

Because, right now, if you asked me if I wanted a baby, the answer would be no. And that is a horrible thought.

I need to do something. Plan my life. Maybe then I'll feel better. If I have a plan for my life. A job. I need to find a new job ASAP if I don't want to end up back on the street.

It's too big to figure out right now. I don't know what I'm going to do. I have my real estate license. Maybe I could find a job with a new company or start my own. I have skills now. I'll find something to do.

There is something I need to do that I've been putting off all week. I need to tell Owen. He deserves to know. As much as I never want to see him again, I no longer have that choice.

I finish my brownie. Then, I get out of bed and get an Uber to Owen's apartment.

I'VE PACED in front of Owen's door a dozen times now. I've lifted my hand several times to knock, but I've come short every single time.

Sean was wrong. He used to tell me that he thought I was brave and strong. But I don't have a brave or strong bone in my body right now.

I stand in front of Owen's door again. I raise my hand, and then the door suddenly opens.

"What the hell are you doing, Olive? I'm about to call the police," Owen says.

"I'm sor—" But I stop myself before I apologize because I'm not sorry. Not at all. "Can I come in?"

Owen raises an eyebrow. "Why would I let you in after you destroyed my property last time?"

I fold my arms across my chest. "We need to talk. So, either let me in or go to a coffee shop or something with me so that we can talk."

"I have nothing else to say to you," Owen says, trying to shut the door in my face.

"I'm pregnant!" I shout at the last minute.

The door slowly creeps back open, and Owen stares at me with narrow eyes. "And how is this my problem?"

I close my eyes, trying to remain calm and be the bigger person. "Because I thought you might want to know that it's yours."

He laughs like it is the most ridiculous thing he has ever heard. "How do I know it's mine? You've been with who knows how many men since me, and you were probably cheating with who knows how many men. It could be anyone's."

My mouth drops a little at the shock of what he said. Of all the ways I imagined this conversation going, I didn't imagine it going like this.

"The baby is yours."

He laughs again. "I don't believe you." He starts to close the door again and says, "Don't come back here again unless you are bringing brownies. That was the only thing you were ever good at anyway."

He slams the door shut in my face while I'm frozen at the door.

I'm on my own. Owen doesn't care. And I don't know if that makes me incredibly happy or incredibly sad. I'm happy that I don't ever have to see Owen again, but I'm incredibly sad that my child will grow up without a father. I know the feeling.

But I do have to thank Owen for one thing. He just gave me an incredible idea and the motivation to make it happen.

23 SEAN

"What is going on?" Jamie asks. "You're falling completely apart on me. Do I need to come into work to help you out for a bit?"

"No. You need to stay right here on this couch, relaxing, like the doctor told you to," I say as I rub her feet on my lap.

"I don't know if I can. I thought I was leaving my company in the hands of the best two people in the world, but one quit on me, and the other one is falling apart," Jamie teases.

"What do you mean, one quit?"

"Olive quit. I've been expecting it for some time. Real estate and management have never been right for her. It's one of the reasons I never gave her a raise. I was hoping it would motivate her enough to find something else."

"That's not fair. Olive would have made a great manager," I say.

"I know that she would have. She just wouldn't have been happy. She needs to find something that truly makes her happy on her own."

"Olive never left before because she felt like she owed you. She was trying to be loyal to you."

Jamie bites her lip as she thinks for a moment. "You might be right. But it all worked out in the end. I think the thought of having a baby finally pushed her to find something that truly makes her happy."

I nod. I wasn't sure that Olive would leave. I thought she might stay and ask to open an office to run somewhere else. But she's gone. And I can't decide if it makes my life easier or harder.

"You're tickling me," Jamie says, laughing, pulling her feet out of my lap.

"Sorry," I say, looking at her again.

"Stop looking at me like that. You are freaking me out," Jamie says.

"Have you ever thought about us getting together again?"

Jamie frowns and sits up on the couch with her feet on the floor. "Why would I think about that?"

"Olive told me about what happened when we broke up. That it was all just a big misunderstanding. I didn't really cheat on you."

Jamie bites her lip. "I knew you didn't cheat on me."

"You mean, Olive told you?"

"No, I mean, I knew when she showed me that message that it was from your mom."

"I don't understand. Then, why did you break up with me?"

"Because I wanted the white picket fence, the house, the baby. And you didn't."

I frown. "I did, too. I always told you that I wanted to settle down, start a family, and have a normal life."

Jamie sighs. "Yes, you always told me that, but it isn't what you wanted."

I shake my head. "It is what I wanted. It's still what I want."

Jamie laughs. "I know you, Sean Burrows, better than you know yourself. You don't want a suburban house, and you don't want kids. I'm not even sure if you want a wife. You want adventure. You want someone who challenges you. You don't want to settle down."

"You're wrong."

Jamie sighs. "Then, tell me what you really want." She folds her hands in her lap and gives me her full attention, like that is going to make me change my mind about how I feel.

I open my mouth, but then I close it because I don't know.

"Tell me you want to fuck a hot blonde. Tell me you want a threesome. Tell me you want to travel the world and meet every woman you can in every city."

"I can't."

She rolls her eyes. "I'm right about this, Sean."

Her phone buzzes, and she picks it up to read the text message she got.

"Is that from Olive?" I ask.

Jamie starts typing into her phone, responding to the message. "No."

I frown and sink back into the couch, wanting to hear any news about what Olive is doing now. *How is the baby doing? Did she take Owen back?*

A slow smile creeps up on Jamie's face. "I can't believe I didn't see it before."

"See what?" I ask.

"That something is going on between you and Olive."

I stand up from the couch. "There was something going on."

She stands up, studying me, and then she points a finger at me. "Oh my God! You love her."

"Yes."

"Then, what are you doing here? Go get her."

I shake my head. "It's more complicated than that."

"How so?"

"For one, she's pregnant with another man's baby."

"So?"

"Didn't you just give me some speech about how you and I couldn't be together because you wanted babies, and I didn't?"

"Yes, but Olive is different."

"How?"

"She wants the same things you do."

I run my hand through my hair. "You are frustrating, Jamie."

Jamie smiles. "I know. Now, get your ass out of my house, and go tell her that you love her."

"Five seconds ago, you told me that I should go have a threesome and that I might not even want to get married. Why would you want me to go tell Olive that I love her?"

"Because you do love her."

I feel the steam coming out of my nostrils as I listen to Jamie.

"Do you love Olive?"

"Yes."

"Then, that is all that matters. If you love her, then nothing else matters."

I pace back and forth in her room. *Jamie is crazy.*

"Do you still love me?" Jamie asks.

I stop pacing and look at her. "I love you, of course."

"But not like you love Olive," Jamie finishes for me.

I nod.

She grins. "I knew it. Go! Get out of my house!"

I grab my coat and start walking toward the door. Jamie is right. I don't know what is going on with Olive. What she is doing or if she is trying to work things out with Owen, but the problem is, I still love her, and I will do anything to stay with her.

"Where is Olive? Is she still at her apartment?" I ask Jamie.

Jamie bites her lip.

"What is it?"

"She moved out."

"What's her new address?"

Jamie thinks for a moment. "I can't tell you."

I raise an eyebrow at her. "Why the hell not?"

"Because it would be a betrayal of my friendship with her. And it's more romantic this way. It will mean more to Olive if you took the time to find her."

"Jamie, just tell me."

"No," she says with a giant smile on her face.

I sigh. "You are the most frustrating woman in the world."

I walk to the door.

"Where are you going?" Jamie asks.

"To find Olive and win her back without your help."

I hear a cheer from Jamie as I leave.

She's right. I love Olive. I want Olive. I have no idea what our future together would look like, but I have to try to find her. Wherever she is. And I know that as much as Jamie wants to help me she won't disrespect Olive's wishes. She won't tell me where Olive is.

I immediately open my phone and call one of my assistants.

"Hello Mr. Burrows," my assistant says.

"I need your help to find Olive. Call airlines. Call any relatives or friends of Olive's that you can find. Do anything and everything you can to find her? Do you understand?"

"Of course Mr. Burrows. I'll get right on it," she says.

"No, get everyone on it. Now."

I end the call and then jump into my car and race to Olive's apartment. Even though Jamie said that Olive moved I have to see for myself.

It takes me twenty minutes to get to her apartment and the entire time all I can think is please be there. Or please let a neighbor know where she is.

I pull my car over on the first available spot I can find and jump out to run inside her apartment building. I notice the no parking zone sign as soon jump out of my car but I don't care. I need to see her as soon as possible. I'll worry about my car later.

I run up the stairs and to her apartment. I knock holding my breath that she is going to come to the door. I hear footsteps and my heart races faster. The door opens and woman that is double Olive's age is standing in the doorway looking at me with annoyance.

"Yes?" she says.

I frown. "Is Olive here?" I ask hoping this woman is Olive's mother or something, but I know without asking that she isn't. She looks nothing like Olive.

"There is no Olive here," she says starting to close the door.

I grab the door. "She lived here before you. Do you know where she went?"

She glares at me. "Why the fuck would I know?"

She slams the door shut this time before I have a chance to stop her.

I run my hand through my hair. This is getting me nowhere but I have to keep trying.

I run to the next door and knock furiously, hoping that a neighbor knows where she is. I don't get an answer so I move to the next door. It opens almost immediately.

"Do you know where your old neighbor Olive moved to?" I ask.

The man frowns. "No idea."

I run to the next door and I get the same answer. I'm not going to find any answers here.

I run down the stairs while I pull out my phone to call my assistant back, hoping that in the last twenty minutes she has found something, anything for me to go on.

"Hello Mr. Burrows," she says politely when she answers.

"Do you have anything yet?" I snap.

"No sir. I'm sorry. We will keep looking."

I end the call and run back to my car. But it is no longer there. Towed most likely.

I don't have time to deal with finding it though. I call an Uber and when it arrives I tell him to go to the airport. I should get my private jet ready but I have no idea where to have it go. So it seems silly to spend all of the money and time flying form place to place endlessly until I find her.

But maybe if I just go to the airport she'll still be there. Maybe she hasn't left yet.

But after searching the airport for half an hour I know she isn't here. I try calling her but she doesn't answer her phone.

I stand in front of the ticket booth trying to figure it out. Where would a woman who has never traveled before go? Where would she go?

I have no idea.

I find myself in the ticket line inching closer to the front as I try to figure it out. When I get to the front the lady asks, "How can I help you?"

I rub my neck. "I'm not sure."

She laughs.

"I'm sorry. I should just go."

"Or you could buy a ticket to anywhere. Sometimes going somewhere is better than going nowhere."

I nod. "Where do you think I should go?"

She thinks for a second. "Well Florida is nice this time or year. Same with California. We have cheap flights to Las Vegas and Houston going on right now. I always like NYC."

"Wait...What did you just say?"

"I always like NYC."

"No, before that."

"We have cheap flights right now to Houston and Vegas."

I smile. Vegas.

My phone buzzes and I see that it is from my assistant. I answer. "Yes."

"She's here. In Vegas," she says.

I smile. "I know. I'll be right there."

I end the call.

"I'm going to Vegas."

24 OLIVE

One Week Earlier

I HAVE three thousand dollars in my savings account. That's it. That's everything I have to survive on before I run out of money and end up back on the streets again.

I don't have a specific plan, other than I need to get the hell out of Chicago. And I'm going to find some way to make money along the way, hopefully with something that involves the only thing I've ever really loved doing. Baking.

I sold everything that I could from my apartment, and everything I own is in a single suitcase. I'm doing this on my own. I didn't even bring Milo with me. Keri is watching him until I get settled somewhere.

I walk up to the airport counter, having no clue where I'm going.

"Hi. May I help you?" the woman says from behind the counter.

"Um...yes. I would like one ticket, please."

"To where?"

"Anywhere but here."

She laughs. "That doesn't really narrow it down for me."

"How about the cheapest flight to a decent-sized city?"

The woman types into her computer. "How about Las Vegas? We have a flight that leaves in an hour."

I nod without thinking.

Las Vegas is the last place I want to go. But then it might give me a chance to run into Sean again. And, as much as I have tried to get over him this past week, the thought of a chance encounter gets me more than a little excited.

PRESENT

I'VE SPENT a week in Las Vegas, and I haven't had my chance encounter with Sean. Not that I was really expecting to run into him in a city with thousands of people, but I was hoping. It also helps that I walk by his office building every morning on my way to the small building that I got a loan to turn into a bakery.

But, every morning, when I walk by his building, I think about going inside. I think about trying to talk to him.

But I don't. Not because I'm scared, but because I don't want to destroy his life or make it more complicated.

So, instead, I just walk by. It's the best and worst part of my day. I love walking by his building. I get to think about Sean. I get to feel my heart beating rapidly in my chest again, and I get to know that there is a chance every day that the love of my life could come back into my life.

But then, every day I walk past it, I know that chance is over.

It's torture really.

I shouldn't have bought a place in Las Vegas where I'm going to have to deal with thoughts of him every single day. But I couldn't help it. It felt like destiny when I walked down the strip the first night I was in Las Vegas and found this tiny little space that was available at the far end of the strip.

In my wildest dreams, I didn't think I could get a loan for the space, but I did. Now, the only thing between me and owning my own successful bakery is a lot of hard work and a little bit of luck.

I suck in a breath as I walk past the last section of his building, like he is going to be waiting just around the corner for me. But, as I walk past the building, I know it's another day where I won't see him.

I should change my walk from where the bus drops me off over a block so that I won't have to walk past his building, but I just can't force my legs to walk a different route. Maybe after I've been here a while, I will be able to walk in this city without thinking about Sean.

I stop by my bakery shop to make sure the construction inside is going well. There isn't much that needs to happen to the space to make my bakery a reality, but a few things are needed, like a basic counter, restroom, and new flooring, before I can start operating out of it. When I am confident that everything is going well, I glance at my watch and realize it's time for my doctor's appointment.

I feel unsure about my appointment. Maybe because, once a doctor tells me I'm pregnant, then it is going to feel more real. Or maybe it's because I'm going to the appointment alone.

Keri and Jamie offered to go to my first appointment with me. But I turned them both down. It didn't seem right to go with them. This is about my journey, and I'm going to be doing this alone. So, I might as well get used to it.

I take an Uber to the doctor's office, and then I walk into the building alone. I check in and then take a seat, trying to get excited about the possibility of seeing my baby on an ultrasound.

I pull out my phone, planning on getting a head start on reading about what to expect while I'm pregnant since I have no idea what to do.

"I'm sorry," I hear a low voice next to me as someone bumps into me while taking a seat next to me.

I frown. I can't believe someone sat next to me when there are half a dozen empty seats in the waiting room.

I look up to try to figure out a reason to move when I see Sean sitting next to me with a hint of a grin.

"I'm sorry," he says again.

"For what?" I ask.

"For not telling you this sooner. I love you, Olive. I realize that I never actually said those words to you before. That's probably why it was so easy for you to believe that I could be in love with a woman other than you. But I can't. I only love you, Olive. Crazy, goofy, gorgeous you."

I feel a tear roll down my cheek.

"I'm sorry that I let you walk out of my office without running after you.

"I'm sorry that I didn't call you every night since then.

"I'm sorry I almost let you go to a doctor's appointment by yourself.

"I'm sorry that I never believed in us. I do now. And, if you're willing to give me a second chance, I would love to spend however long you'd be mine making it up to you."

I smile. "I'm not sorry."

He frowns in disappointment.

"I'm not sorry that you were an ass to me when we first met.

"I'm not sorry that I hated you initially.

"I'm not sorry that I fucked you too many times to count.

"I'm not sorry that I quit my job.

"I'm not sorry about any of it because it got me to this point."

He nods.

"Olive," I hear the nurse shout.

I stand up and start walking toward her with a smile on my face, but I don't feel Sean walking behind me.

I glance over my shoulder and see Sean is still sitting in the chair in the waiting room, looking disappointed.

"You're going to have something else to be sorry about if you don't get your ass up and come with me to my appointment."

Sean laughs as he gets up and follows me into one of the exam rooms.

"Lie back on the table. The doctor will be in and will want to do an ultrasound first. Then, he will go from there," the nurse says before she leaves.

Sean looks at me as I climb up onto the table. "You still love me?"

I laugh. "Yes, you goof, I still love you. I thought that was clear."

He shakes his head and then kisses me hard on the lips as his hands travel down my body to my hips. Sean slowly stops kissing and looks down at my stomach and then up into my eyes. "I'll love this baby like it's my own. Don't worry about that," he says reassuringly.

I smile. He's right. I know he will. And I'll love this baby, too. I'm just still getting used to the idea.

We hear a knock on the door, followed by the doctor entering.

"Let's take a good look at how your baby is doing," the doctor says.

I nod and lie back as the doctor gets the ultrasound equipment together. I lift my shirt up, and he places the instrument on my stomach. I take a deep breath as I stare at the screen, waiting for the first image of my baby. But my eyes quickly go to the doctor, who is humming a little to himself, taking his sweet time with finding my baby.

Another minute passes, and the doctor still doesn't say anything. I glance over at Sean, who grabs hold of my hand and looks awfully nervous himself.

"Is something wrong?" Sean asks because I can't get any words out.

"Please sit up for a moment," the doctor says.

I sit up without bothering to wipe the goop off my stomach first. I don't care. I just need answers.

"When did you take a pregnancy test?" the doctor asks.

I think for a moment. "About two weeks ago."

"How many tests did you take then?"

"Just the one." I dig into my purse, pull out my phone with the picture I took of the positive pregnancy test, and show the doctor.

The doctor laughs and visibly relaxes. "I was worried that you'd had a miscarriage, and that is always hard news to break to someone because pregnancy tests these days are almost always accurate. But looking at this picture shows that isn't true."

"What do you mean?" I ask, not understanding.

"I'm so sorry, Olive, but you aren't pregnant. You just read the test wrong."

My eyes shoot wide open, and a grin creeps over my face. "I'm not pregnant?" I say, not believing it.

"I'm sorry again, but you're not pregnant. I'll give you two a few moments alone," the doctor says, getting up.

I turn to Sean. "I'm not pregnant."

"Are you okay with that?" he asks hesitantly, not sure what to say.

I laugh. "I'm more than okay with it."

He laughs and scoops me up in his arms, spinning me around. "I can't believe you read the test wrong. Let me see."

I show him the image on my phone.

He laughs. "Two pink lines mean you're pregnant. One line means you're not."

I blush. "I read the instructions quickly."

Sean shakes his head. "I love you even though you're always going to keep me on my toes."

I smile. "You'd better."

"So, what now? What do you want, Olive?"

I think for a moment. "I want you to use that butt plug like you did in Anal Adventures 3."

Sean laughs. "So, you watched some of my porn movies?"

I bite my lip. "I needed something to get me through these last couple of weeks."

Sean kisses me. "I'll give you anything you want. Babies, houses, jets, and of course, all the sex you could ever want."

"What if I just want the sex and put a hold on all the rest? Would you regret going out with me if it meant that you might be giving up the mansion and two-point-five kids?" I ask, not sure how he is going to respond.

"As long as I have you, that's all that matters."

He kisses me again, and I lose myself in the kiss. I want him. Now. But we are in an exam room. We have to make it to one of our apartments first.

"We need to stop," I say.

"Why?"

"Because you can't fuck me in a doctor's office," I whisper, like the room is bugged and someone can hear us.

But Sean grins, and I forget about everything else.

"I think you want me to fuck you right here, right now," Sean says.

I bite my lip and try to shake my head, but I end up nodding.

The next thing I know, Sean has me bent over the exam room, and his cock is pushing inside my pussy while I try my best to be as quiet as I can. But, of course, I can't stay quiet. I scream Sean's name, and three seconds later, there is a knock on the door, followed by one of the nurses poking her head in, probably to make sure I'm okay.

"Oh my God! You can't do that in here!" she shouts at us.

Sean slips out of me, and I quickly pull my pants back up.

"Get out!" she screams.

Sean grabs my hand, and we run out of the room and don't stop until we are outside.

I suck in a breath. "I think I'm going to have to change doctors," I say, laughing.

Sean laughs, too, before pulling me toward him and softly kissing me on the lips.

"I'm sorry we got caught. But you were such a dirty girl that I couldn't resist."

I bite my lip. "I'm not."

EPILOGUE

SEAN

One Year Later

"HEY BABY, WHAT'S THE EMERGENCY?" I ask, as I enter her new bakery shop. It's her second bakery and it's opening in three days, hence the emergency text message I got this morning.

I look at Olive covered in flour standing in her kitchen. I know she's stressed and needs help, but I can't help but get turned on when I see her living her dream and being so successful at it. I know she has her doubts, which are always good to have when starting something new but she has no reason to worry. Her last bakery has done better than either of us ever imagined. This second location is going to do just as well and after this, the sky is the limit.

She grins when she sees me, like just my presence here takes away all of the stress.

She stops pouring the batter into the cupcake tins and walks over and kisses me on the lips.

"I'm so glad you are here," she says.

I grab her neck and kiss her again. She melts into my arms as I kiss her and take away her anxiety. I wish I could just spend the rest of today kissing her, but I know that I shouldn't. She needs to work.

"How can I help?" I finally ask, tearing my lips away from hers.

Her eyes grow wide and the expression on her face is one of guilt.

"What is it?" I ask cautiously.

"I need you to help me bake some things for tomorrow. I'm catering for a large wedding and I need help."

I frown. "What happened to the other bakers?"

She bites her lip. "They called in sick."

I narrow my eyes as I study hers. "You let them all have the same day off again, didn't you?"

She kisses me softly on the lips to keep me from scolding her.

"They deserved it. They've been working hard," she says.

"And what about you?"

She grins. "I have you to help." She throws me an apron.

I sigh but put it on. "I'll help but I can't promise I'll be any better than the last time. You'd be better off just baking everything yourself."

Her face lights up as she looks at me. "But then I wouldn't get to see you looking so hot in your apron."

She pinches my ass before returning to baking.

I groan. "Fine. I'll help you, but only if I get to fuck you in nothing but your apron later."

She bites her lip again. "Deal."

She gives me a task and I try to focus on it instead of on her ass, but she makes it impossible. She rubs up against me every chance she gets. She smears flour on my face at least half a dozen times. She sways her hips even more than usual when she walks. Little whimpers and sounds leave her lips while she is working.

I break, faster than I would like. Olive drives me insane with need on a normal day much less when she is trying to drive me mad.

I grab her and push her against the wall, pushing her hands high above her head.

"What are you doing?" I ask as I stare intently into her eyes.

She breathes heavily. "Getting you to fuck me."

I raise an eyebrow. "Well, that's easy. All you have to do is ask."

She grins. "I want you to fuck me here."

I see the naughtiest look in her eyes when she says it.

I don't think about the fact of how unhygienic it is to fuck in her bakery's kitchen. I'll have a cleaning crew come in later.

"Tell me what you want Olive," I say because I know her. She has a plan in her head.

She takes a deep breath. "I want you to fuck me on the counter."

I grab her and give her what she wants. I lift her up, wrapping her legs around me as I kiss her. She claws at my back as I sit her on the counter before grabbing her jeans and pulling them off at the same time that she undoes her apron and pulls it off. I grab the hem of her shirt and yank it off of her head.

Olive pushes her body back onto the table and that's when I get a full look at the lingerie she is wearing. She planned this. There was no emergency. The emergency was that she needed to get fucked.

I glance around the room until I spot it. The video camera that she set up.

I laugh and shake my head. "So which porno is this that we are reenacting?" I ask. She's been trying to get me to come out of retirement and make a porn movie with her. Just a private one.

She blushes. "The one where you fuck me in my bakery."

I shake my head but then I climb on top of her anyway. I would do anything for her. Even recreate a cheesy porn movie with her if that is what she wants.

I kiss down her neck and then unclasp her bra.

She arches her back and moans loudly as I do, exaggerating everything for the camera. I'm going to make it the best sex of her life then.

I move my lips down her body until I reach her red lace panties. I bite the band of her panties with my teeth and pull them down slowly as Olive stares at me, waiting for the moment that my tongue moves inside her.

I hesitate, letting her anticipation build as I hover over her. Then I lick her pussy and she screams.

But it's not her usual scream. This scream is terrifying.

I stop immediately, sitting up and pulling her to me to find out what is wrong. I see the blood and panic.

It's a lot of blood. Too much blood oozing down her arm.

"What happened?" I ask, as I grab the nearest clean dish towel and grab her hand to apply pressure to her wound that is most definitely going to need stitches.

She winces when I wrap the towel around her hand.

"I was trying to grab onto something because what you were doing felt so good... I think I grabbed a knife."

"I know we will laugh about this later but right now I need to get you to the emergency room. I think you need stitches."

She nods and I help her get dressed and then into my car so that I can rush her to the emergency room. As soon as we are both in the car, I step on the gas to get her to the emergency room.

"Slow down Sean," she says.

"No. I need to get you help," I say speeding up instead of slowing down.

"Sean. Stop," she says more firmly and I sigh but slow down a little.

I look at her to make sure that the bleeding hasn't gotten worse. I know it's only a cut on her hand but it's deep and I don't know what I would do without her. I don't think I could survive without her.

"Why are you looking at me like that?" she asks.

I shake my head. "I'll tell you after we are finished."

We make it to the hospital and after waiting twenty minutes in the waiting room, far longer than I was happy with, Olive was finally brought back to a room where they stitched up her hand.

"So how did this happen?" the doctor asks Olive when he finishes stitching her up.

She looks at me and blushes but says, "Baking accident."

He nods. "Well, you should be all better now. Hopefully we

won't see you back for any more baking accidents," he says empha-sizing the last words and looking at me like he knows what really happened even though he couldn't know.

He finally leaves us alone in the room and I kiss Olive's forehead. "I'm so glad you are okay. I was worried about you."

She laughs. "You need to stop freaking out every time something like this happens. I'm a klutz. Stuff like this happens to me all the time. If you are going to be with me you need to be used to going to the emergency room."

"I'll never get used to you being in pain or almost dying."

She shakes her head. "You're over exaggerating. I didn't almost die."

"I know. It was still hard to watch you go through that much pain."

"What did you want to tell me earlier in the car?" she asks.

I look at her in the eye and know that this is the wrong place and the wrong way to do this but I don't have a choice. I have to tell her how I feel.

"That I want to marry you," I say.

Her eyes widen a little but she doesn't seem that shocked that I would ask. We've been dating for a year. We love each other. It's the next natural step.

But she doesn't say anything. She doesn't show excitement or say that she wants to marry me too.

"What do you think? Will you marry me? Or do you want to wait to answer until I do it right? Get a ring and find some romantic place?"

"Why do you want to marry me?" she asks.

I frown. "Because I love you and I want to spend the rest of my life with you."

She nods. "I love you and want to spend the rest of my life with you too but it doesn't mean that we should get married."

"Shouldn't it?" I ask.

She smiles. "I don't need to get married to know that you love me and will do anything for me for the rest of your life. One look today from you when my hand was cut was all it took to know that I'm yours forever."

"And I'm yours forever." I study her closely. "Will you marry me?" I ask again.

Her face lights up. "Yes. I'll marry you, but only because I want an excuse to go on a long honeymoon where you can fuck me in a dozen countries."

I grin. "God, I love you," I say kissing her.

Olive is mine. I'm going to make it official by marrying her. And then take her on a year long honeymoon. I know she can find the right bakers to handle her bakeries while we are gone. After all, I was the one that taught her everything I know. She's going to kill this running a business thing. She already is. She's everything I never knew I wanted in a woman and more. And she's all fucking mine. Forever.

THE END

Thank you so much for reading Not Sorry!

Continue on to read Finding Perfect...

FINDING PERFECT

1 MILA

Life sucks.

Like really, really sucks. Trust me, I know. I've dealt with my fair share of tragedies. I've had my heart broken, dragged through the mud, and then stomped on. I've woken up hungry and slept under a bridge on the streets. I know what abuse feels like. I've seen, first-hand, how bad addiction can be. Death is a cold friend, instead of a stranger. Loss is all I've ever known.

That's why I have a plan for everything. I stick to a schedule for my day and my life. I know what I'm doing every minute of every day. I know what my next steps in life are. And that keeps me in control.

Chaos is when the worst happens. Tragedy lives in the craziness. I thrive in normal.

In ordinary.

In the expected.

I plan for every mistake, every tragedy, every misstep. That way I'm always prepared. I can handle anything because I've already thought of it first. I know how to bounce back and get my life on track in a second.

So why is today so hard?

Why am I not bouncing back?

Because five years ago today was the worst day of my life. I made the worst mistake, and I've been paying for it every day since.

I'm spiraling. I can feel the anxiety climbing into my chest and tightening until my lungs burn with each breath. My stomach is twisting in knots, and my head is pounding with an unshakable ache.

I need to plan. I need to find a solution and start implementing it.

But for once in my life, I don't want to think about my responsibilities. I want to feel free, if only for a few moments.

I roll the window down of my Subaru, the classic car all Denverites drive. It's cheap and gets the job done. I drive through the mountains, hoping the fresh air filled with aspen and pine trees will soothe my soul. The wind whips through the car too fast to have the window down, but I don't care. I need to feel the wind. It's the only thing keeping me from going into a full blown panic attack.

A man on a motorcycle rides my ass on the single lane road. I'm driving fast, but apparently not fast enough for the dipshit behind me.

The tiny smile I forced onto my lips earlier vanishes. I zoom around a curve faster than I should, and I feel out of control.

I *hate* it.

But Mr. Dangerous isn't driving fast enough. Driving around curves without guardrails isn't enough. He's driving so fast; one mistake could cause his motorcycle and my car to tumble down the side of the mountain. He's risking actual death.

I look for a space to pull off so he can go around me, but there are none. We are in the freaking mountains, on curvy road after curvy road. I'm driving ten miles over the speed limit as it is. I'm not going to let him bully me into driving faster.

I hear the rev of his engine, and the blast of heavy metal music from his motorcycle.

Can he be any more obnoxious?

I don't understand motorcycles. I don't understand the need to make life any more dangerous than it already is. The asshole isn't even wearing a helmet.

I shake my head and try to focus on the road in front of me, instead of the man behind me making me equal parts pissed and anxious. But I drive faster. Too fast. I can't help it. I barely stay in my lane around the next curve.

And I see the bicycler too late.

I slam on the brakes, praying I don't hit the cyclist. I can't slow down enough, and another car is coming toward me in the other lane. I have no choice but to pass the cyclist who is hugging the line of my lane.

I squeeze my eyes closed. *Stupid, I know.* But I can't watch my car scrape the man off the road.

I open my eyes and glance in my rearview mirror. The man is still on the bike as Mr. Dangerous passes him on his motorcycle. I didn't hit the car driving the opposite direction either.

I exhale and try to loosen my death grip on the steering wheel. But I won't be relaxing anytime soon. I see a gravel road leading off the main road, and I take it. I need to get away from the anxiety-inducing motorcycle behind me.

My heart slows as I drive over the bouncy road. I don't know where the road goes, nor do I care. I just need away.

The road winds up a mountain and stops in a parking lot of a trailhead. I pull the car into one of the last remaining stalls and exhale. A loose hair that had fallen onto my face blows up as I exhale.

And then I hear the motorcycle. I glance in my rearview mirror as the dumbass double parks his motorcycle behind mine.

I'm not confrontational. Not unless I need to be to survive. But I'm livid.

I jump out of my car and march over to him.

"What the hell are you doing? You could have gotten us killed earlier! And you can't park behind me. That's illegal."

He raises an eyebrow with a wicked grin on his face as he stares at me like I'm a child. He folds his arms over his chest, revealing his rippling biceps covered in tattoos.

Figures.

"Sorry, sweetheart. If you don't know how to handle a car in the mountains, then you should stick to the main highways. They might be more your speed."

My cheeks puff out as I hold my breath and anger in. I'm sure my face is bright red by now, and my eyes are popping out of their sockets.

"I'm not your *sweetheart.*"

His head cocks lazily to one side as his smile brightens. "You are definitely somebody's sweetheart."

"I'm nobody's anything."

He nods. "Good."

He removes his shirt, and I stare speechlessly at his long legs in running shorts. Damn, his body looks better than any superhero's I've ever seen. He could play Thor easily. His muscles are bigger, his tattoos darker, and his hair is long, like a Greek god.

He smirks and walks closer to me like he knows exactly the effect he has on me.

I can't fucking speak. That never happens. I always have the words for every situation. I can be a smartass when I want. My voice is my best quality.

It's sexy and raspy, and everything men want.

His eyes rake over my body. I'm wearing my scrubs. I just got off my shift, and the loose scrubs do nothing to attract a man. I look like a box instead of a voluptuous woman. Although, even the tightest dress in the universe wouldn't help my cause much. I just don't eat enough to have curves. My scrubs make me look like a dark green blob. Not sexy. The blood stains and mashed potatoes from a patient last night aren't helping either.

He winks at me though, and I think he sees something he likes.

No. He's probably just the type of man who flirts with every woman. He's not interested in me.

He turns a second later and starts jogging toward the trailhead.

"Wait!" I shout, getting my voice back, although the raspiness of my voice makes it sound like my voice just cracked.

The stranger doesn't pause. He keeps jogging but turns his head in my direction flashing me another panty-melting smile. He's too damn good-looking. Some men are handsome in a safe way. The kind who don't threaten everything you've worked for. The kind who smile at you and appreciate you for how beautiful you are.

This man is the kind who glances your way, and you are already signing away your heart, your bank account, and your self-worth for a chance with him.

I usually stay far, far away from men like him. And in about two seconds, I will drive full speed in the opposite direction and never think about him again. But for one moment, I let myself drink him up.

"Your motorcycle is blocking my car!" I shout.

He shrugs. "So? I'm running; you're hiking. I'll be back to move my motorcycle long before you get done with your hike." His eyes tell me he's challenging me. He doesn't think I came up here to hike based on how I'm dressed, but he's daring me to say differently.

I don't.

I don't say anything.

And the sexy stranger disappears onto the trail at full speed.

I stare at the trail and then down at my scrubs and white tennis shoes. I'm not prepared to go for a hike. These shoes have no grip and will turn brown in about five minutes from the dirt on the trail. I didn't even bring a bottle of water with me.

Hiking is not what I need right now. But I don't really have a choice. *Unless I want to back over his motorcycle...*

I grin, liking that idea far too much.

I sigh. I don't have the balls or insurance to destroy his bike like that. I'll hike for an hour, and if Mr. Wrong-for-me-in-all-the-ways isn't back by then, I'll reconsider my running over his motorcycle plan.

THIS IS EXACTLY what I don't need, and exactly what I do need.

I'm not a hiker. I don't have time to take out of my day to drive into the mountains and spend hours hiking. Most of the exercise I get is pulling patients in and out of a hospital bed. Occasionally, I'll make time to head down to the gym after classes finish, but that's rare.

The fresh air and wildflowers covering each side of the trail make the hike worth it. I've never seen such bright shades of purple, yellow, and pink. I've never filled my lungs with the scent of pine. Never had my muscles burn as I climb my way up the mountain.

For the most part, I focus on nothing. Just putting one foot in front of the other.

Despite the pretty scenery, my thoughts always go back to planning my life. I'm going to get a job offer from the current hospital I'm doing clinicals at. I've done a great job so far. I only have a semester left of school before I graduate. I've been putting in my time. I'll get the emergency room job I applied for. I just have to make what little money I have left from my savings last for a couple more months.

I will survive. I always do. I just need to tweak my plan a little.

This year was supposed to be about finding a man. A husband, even. I'm graduating from college. I'm ready to be in a serious relationship. But I might have to postpone that for another year or two. I don't have any time to date. Not when I'm working all the time.

A husband might be a lot of help. Especially if he's rich. Even if he wasn't, two incomes are better than one. My siblings don't offer much support. A wealthy hubby would be perfect right about now.

No, it's not in the plan.

My lungs burn as the oxygen up here is thin. My legs ache and throb. I glance up, and the top doesn't look much further. I can make it. I've made it this far. Just a little further.

Lies.

I climb over the ridge, but it's a false summit. I've heard about these. My life has given me plenty of experience. Just when I think I've gained some traction, everything I've gained gets wiped out, and I have to start all over again.

I'm determined now, though. I won't stop until I've reached the top of this mountain. I don't know how long the trail is, or how high it goes. But nothing will stop me now.

Forcing my legs to keep climbing holds my entire attention now. I can't think about my family problems. I can't think about the jackass who almost ran me over. All I think about is putting one foot in front of the other. Over and over. Until finally, I reach the top.

Breathtakingly, beautiful.

I've never seen anything like it. Gone are the wildflowers, replaced with expansive views. I see the top of dozens of mountains around me. And a small lake sits on top of the mountain. The water's turquoise color is shimmering against the backdrop of the slope in front of me. A small snow patch scatters against the flawless grey rocks.

I smile, really smile, at what I just did. I don't have a clue how high I'm up. 10,000 feet? 12,000? Did I just climb a "14er"? I don't know. But I feel like I'm on top of the world. This was my Everest. And I beat it.

I sit down on a rock on the edge of the water, wishing I had a water bottle and snack to enjoy along with the view. Several other hikers are relaxing around the lake, enjoying the fruits of their efforts. But I don't see the man who caused me to be hiking in the first place.

Good, I might get to run over his bike after all.

After resting my legs for a while, I decide it's time to head back down. Should be much easier and faster than my way up.

I'm so wrong. The rocks that were so enjoyable to hike up are now death traps. My shoes have no traction as I climb down their slick surfaces. The streams of water I walked over before now race with enough water to soak my feet as I step through them, drenching my shoes and socks. And the slick dirt causes my feet to slide with each step, making each movement exhausting.

My thighs tremble. I used too much energy climbing, and have almost nothing left to climb down. I consider just rolling down the mountain, but with my luck, I'd probably roll off the path and plunge to my death.

And don't even get me started on my knees. I've never been in so much pain in my life. Each step stabs into my knees, making me grit my teeth with each step.

I thought I understood the beauty of why people spend their free time hiking. Now I think it's just because they like torturing themselves with pain and fear.

I try to make my legs move faster. The faster I run, the faster I will be off this treacherous cliff.

Faster is good. My momentum is carrying me down. I can do this.

One more step and then another and then...

"Fuck."

I'm not one to curse. I've probably sworn less than a dozen times in the last year. But the sharp pain I feel in my ankle, knee, and hip as I hit the ground is enough to warrant it. My ankle is hurt the worst; my hands grip it as I writhe in pain.

"You should be careful. The rocks are slippery," a boy, who looks to be about seven, says as he jumps over me wearing flip-flops.

I frown. I'm sure his parents are with him, but right now I want to throw the kid off the cliff for his snide remarks.

He disappears, and I do in fact see his father chase after him a second later. He doesn't stop to see if I need help. This trail isn't heavily trafficked, so apparently, I'm on my own at the top of Everest. I'll probably die up here. Does it snow up here in the summertime? Will frostbite get me? Will a bear or mountain lion be my end? Or will I die slowly from starvation?

Dammit! Why the hell did I decide to climb this mountain?!

Oh yea, because of a cocky, arrogant smile with dimples, tattoos, and muscles. If I survive this, I'm getting my eyes carved out. I don't need them. They get in my way and cause me to make bad decisions.

"You okay, sweetheart?" a deep voice asks.

I keep my eyes closed shut because I know the source of the voice. It would be my luck he is the one to find me and offer to help me.

"Perfectly fine. Just enjoying a nice relaxing nap in the middle of the trail."

He chuckles and touches my leg.

I jump. My eyes fly open at the jolt shooting through my leg. I don't know if it's because of my injury or the electricity of his touch.

"That hurts," I pout, as he examines my right knee after pushing my ripped scrubs up.

He ignores me and places my leg down before picking up my left ankle.

I wince and bite my lip to keep from cursing him as he touches me.

"It doesn't look broken. Probably just a sprain."

I know his words are meant to be encouraging, but I don't like hearing 'just' anything. Whatever it is, it hurts. Sprain or broken makes no difference.

"Thanks, doctor, but I got it from here. I know all about RICE."

"Rice?" he asks, cocking his head to look at me like I'm crazy.

I roll my eyes. "Rest, ice, compression, elevation. I know how to take care of a sprain. I'm a nurse." *Well, not technically. But I will be a nurse in a few short months.*

He nods, looking at my scrubs again like he's just now realizing why I'm wearing such a thing on a hike.

He holds out his hand to me, but I'm too stubborn to take it. I don't need his help.

He looks amused as I try to push myself off the dirt. It takes a couple tries to get my shaky legs under me, but I'm finally able to get up.

"Need any help?" he asks, smiling at me like I'm the funniest thing in the world.

"No."

I take a step, and my ankle gives out. Luckily, there is a tree nearby I can grab to keep from falling again.

"Seems like you could use some help." His hands grab my hips trying to steady me. And I swear I feel his erection on my ass. "I could always kiss it and see if that helps."

I swat his hand away as I turn glaring. "I don't need help from a man who almost got me killed and just wants to hit on me."

I start stomping down the mountain ignoring the pain of each step, and the man slowly walking behind me. It takes everything in me not to turn around and check him out again. Sweat drips down his chest from his run, but when he approached me earlier, he barely seemed out of breath.

I will not look at him.

I will not ogle him.

I will not think about him.

I will not ask him for help.

Ten steps later, tears are filling my eyes. I can tolerate pain just fine. I have a high pain tolerance. But knowing it's going to take thousands of more steps to get down the mountain is melting my morale.

I stop, unable to continue on my own.

The man behind me stops as well. If he ran down, he'd probably already be down by now.

I sigh and turn slowly to him. "I guess you are my only option."

"Oh? I didn't think you wanted my help."

"I don't." I exhale into a frown. "But I want to live more than I don't want your help."

He smiles smugly but doesn't move to help me. In fact, he crosses his arms like he's not going to touch me now, even if I asked.

"What are you doing? I need your help. You've been following me this whole time because you intend to help me. So help."

He shakes his head.

"What?"

I'm so impatient with this man.

"I think you owe me something first."

My mouth gapes. He can't be serious. His eyes say he is dead serious. I see the lust there.

"I'm not going to blow you or fuc..." He raises an eyebrow as he realizes I hate using foul language. "Or have sex with you. I'm not that desperate."

He steps toward me, filling my personal space with his strong presence. It consumes all my thoughts, my smells, and my space.

"I think you are that desperate," he breathes onto my neck.

I freeze. *I'm not. I'm not. I'm not.*

But I am. He's not my type. Not at all. I like men who are good for me. Good-looking but not too good-looking so they think they can do better than me. Smart, caring, cautious, sturdy.

This man is none of those things. He's dangerous, threatening, and mysterious. He lives by a different moral code.

My lip trembles, considering what I should say or do. *Should I kiss him?* He might carry me down if I did. Make him think I'd have sex with him later, only to disappear before he has a chance.

He laughs, seeing the conflict in my eyes.

"But I'm not asking you to be that desperate. When I fuck you, it will be with your full permission and willingness. Not because I saved you."

"You are so not saving me. Let's not be dramatic. You are helping me walk down a mountain, not saving me from a burning building."

I snap my mouth shut when he stares at me. Damn me and my snarky mouth.

"What do you want then?"

"An apology."

I frown. "I don't owe you an apology."

He shrugs and starts walking down the trail past me.

Dammit!

"Fine!" I shout as I watch the only help I might get walk away from me.

He pauses and turns. I hate apologizing. Especially to his smug ass when I have nothing to apologize for. But he's right; I'm desperate for the help.

"I'm sorry..."

"Ace Knight."

I roll my eyes at his last name. I'm sure it's not his real name. He's no knight in shining armor.

"I'm sorry, my knight in shining armor, for saying I don't need your help when I clearly do. Will you please help me down the mountain?"

"No," he says deadpan.

Shit. Now what? Does he expect me to suck his dick? Because I so won't...okay, I totally would. That's why this man is dangerous for me, and I need to stay far, far away.

He grins. "Kidding."

He approaches me. "Climb on."

"No."

"Get the fuck on my back, sweetheart. I can carry you down in twenty minutes, or you can hobble along with me by your side and take five times as long."

He's got a point. I climb onto his glistening, muscular, tattooed back. My thighs wrap around his waist as he carefully grabs my legs to help keep me up. He feels thick, hard, and strong between my legs. I can only imagine what another part of his body would feel like between my legs.

Not going to happen, I remind myself.

"Hold on, sweetheart."

"My name is not sweetheart."

"Then what is it?"

I scrunch my nose. I don't want to tell him. If I do, he could find me after this.

He bounces us roughly as he jumps over a stream, and I groan as his back rubs against me turning me on more than I want him to know.

"Sorry, sugar tits."

356

"My name is most definitely not sugar tits."

I can feel his grin even though I can't see it.

"Sweet cheeks?"

"No."

"Hot stuff?"

"No."

"Fuckable mouth?"

"No."

"Pussycakes?"

"No."

"Cocksucker?"

Ugh, this is getting ridiculous. I know he's just trying to goad me to get me to tell him what my name is, but I'm tired of the curse words. They make me flinch every time he says them.

"Mila Burns. My name is Mila Burns."

Shit. I didn't mean to tell him my full name, but it just slipped out.

"Mila Burns," he repeats cautiously, his voice slightly higher than it was before. "So what are you doing out here, Mila Burns?"

I keep my mouth locked tight. If I don't speak, then I can't say anything stupid. I can't agree to go on a date. I won't drool all over his back. I won't say anything rude. Mouth tightly shut is good.

He laughs, shaking his head. Then, pulls out his phone and presses a button before loud heavy metal music starts blaring, just like when he was on the motorcycle.

Obnoxious prick.

I sigh, resting my head on his shoulder as he jogs down the hill singing along to the music, while I do everything to not fall in love with him. Because he's wrong for me.

So, so, so wrong.

He's all the things I'm not. He would be a complication. He probably spends all his free time smoking joints and getting more tattoos. Not what I need right now.

I don't know how the time flies so fast, but we are down the mountain in record time. He should compete professionally at something he's that good.

"Thanks," I mumble as he gently lets me down next to my car.

"Do you need me to drive you to a hospital?"

"No."

"How about dinner?"

Nope, nope, nope. He doesn't get to hit on me. I can't handle it.

I don't respond. I don't look at him. I pretend this is all a dream. I slip into my car, not paying attention to what he's doing, and back out before I even get my seatbelt on.

And then I speed down the gravel road. I only look in the rearview mirror when I'm far enough away I know I won't turn around and go back and say yes no matter how charming he is.

Shit.

His motorcycle is in tatters. *I ran over his fucking motorcycle! How did I not notice when the metal started crunching as I backed out?*

I expect him to chase after me. Demand to see my insurance or exchange numbers so I will pay for the damage I caused.

Instead, he's standing there with a broad grin and determined eyes. I'm afraid I may have started a war.

2 MILA

"No Ren, I can't babysit this weekend," I say into my cell phone, as I stare at my watch. I have exactly one minute left of my break, and I don't have time to argue with my sister.

"Why not? I thought you said you had Saturday off?"

I sigh and close my eyes trying to keep my heart rate calm. I should start practicing yoga or meditation or something with the amount of stress I deal with.

"I have Saturday off, but I work a twenty-four-hour shift on Friday. I will spend my Saturday sleeping. There is no way I can babysit."

"Fine, fine. I get it. The kids just haven't seen you in forever. You should stop by Sunday at the very least to have dinner with us."

I roll my eyes. What my sister really wants is to check up on me and make sure I haven't lost my mind again. She tried to get me to come over on the anniversary, but I couldn't. I love my sister, but she has everything I want. A wealthy husband who loves her. Two children: a boy and a girl. Her own private practice as a pediatrician. Her life is perfect.

I can't handle seeing her when I feel like my life is falling apart.

It's not really, but every year, on the anniversary of when my life as I knew it ended, I feel how easily I could lose everything again. But I won't let it. I'm in control. I can make my life anything I want.

"Okay, I'll stop by on Sunday," I relent. "But only for dinner! I'm not going to play board games or any of the family time afterward."

"Great! I'll see you on Sunday!" Ren says, ignoring my conditions.

I pocket my phone in the front of my blue scrub pants and then head toward the nurse's station as my twenty-minute break ends. I didn't even have time to pee; Ren took up all my time talking on the phone. But I need to sit down and rest my ankle. It's better now that I've iced it, taken some pain medications, and wrapped it.

"Any new patients?" I ask Felicity, my clinical supervisor. She's been manning the desk while I've been on break.

She frowns. I think she permanently has a frown on her face, or she hates me. I bite my lip. Felicity is grumpy, that's just the way her face is. I shouldn't take it personally. I've been doing a great job. It's just too bad Felicity is the one who will determine whether I pass or fail.

Felicity rolls her eyes like she can't believe I asked the question.

I ignore her and force a smile on my face. She can be grumpy all she wants, I'm happy. I'm positive. I'm in line for getting a job offer here. Just keep working hard, and this will all be worth it.

Felicity huffs as I sit down in the chair next to her.

"What?" I ask.

She nods her head in the direction of the waiting room.

"You shouldn't have your boyfriend showing up at work. Get rid of him," she says.

"I don't have a boyfriend..."

She eyes me again. "Oh, sorry, lover, hookup, one night stand, whatever he is, he needs to be gone. I can't have him hogging my waiting room."

"I don't have a boyfriend or any kind of guy friend."

Felicity ignores me, typing on the computer.

I bite my lip again as I try to think who could be in the waiting room. I won't know until I walk over to see. So I force myself up even though I just want a moment to sit. I'm toward the end of a twenty-four-hour shift, and I just want to relax and rest.

Instead, I'm storming to the waiting room, sure whoever is there isn't for me.

"Henry," I say when I open the door and see my brother pacing like he's waiting to find out if I made it through surgery or something.

"What are you doing here?" I ask as I make a mental note of telling Felicity later he's my brother, not my boyfriend.

He frowns. *Why does everyone do that? Do I have one of those faces that need to be frowned at?*

"You know why I'm here. I left you a message yesterday on your cell phone."

I shake my head as I grab his arm and lead him out of the waiting room. If he's going to scold me, I'd rather him not do it in front of dozens of patients' families I may have to talk to later.

"I didn't get any message."

He runs his hand through his hair in disbelief. "You are such a child. You can't even be bothered to check your voicemail and call your brother back."

I steer Henry away from the nurses' station, down a hallway I hope is empty.

"Why are you here, Henry?" I ask, already tired of his scolding.

"I want to make sure you are okay. Today's the anniversary of—"

I give him a dirty look.

"Well, you know what it's the anniversary of. And you get a little crazy. I want to make sure you don't do anything stupid this year."

"The anniversary was yesterday. Not today. And I didn't do anything crazy." *Unless you count climbing a mountain for the first time, rolling my ankle, and having to get carried down by a hot stranger, before running over said stranger's motorcycle. Nope, definitely not crazy.*

"Whatever. It's still around that time, and I'm not leaving until I'm sure you are fine."

I put my hand on my hips, staring my brother down. "No, you mean until you ensure I won't do anything that will put the Burns back in the papers again and ruin your business." I didn't do anything that bad last year. I just got drunk, and I didn't have any money for an Uber home, so I slept under an underpass. The cop that found me wasn't happy with my decision, even though I thought it was the right one.

He shrugs. "I'm here to make sure you don't fuck up again."

I shake my head. Everyone in my life has a perfect life, except me. Even though my mistake was years ago, it still haunts me. I still have the guilt and nightmares, even if I can't remember the details of that day. My family will never forgive me for what I did. No matter how much I've changed. No matter how much I try to be exactly like them. Maybe when I have a husband and kids, they will feel differently, but until then, they think of me as the screwup who they have to fix every year.

I hear the sirens, and I know we have another patient coming in.

"I have to go," I say, running down the hallway to meet the ambulance. My pager goes off, and Felicity starts giving me the info. Two male patients. Both critical. Not sure what happened, but they need all teams on hand.

"Mila! I'll be waiting until the end of your shift to talk to you," Henry says.

I keep racing down the hallway, ignoring my brother, who thinks I need a babysitter. I don't. But he won't leave until I prove to him I'm okay. Last year was just a fluke. It wasn't my fault. This year, I'm better.

I run to emergency bay one and start collecting all the supplies we could need to take care of the incoming patients. Two other nurses enter as well. When I turn around a man is being pushed in on a gurney. We transfer him quickly to the bed.

"What happened?" I ask the nearest paramedic.

"Not sure exactly. It was a car accident. He was riding in the passenger seat. His heart stopped once during transport, and he's struggling to breathe. Blood pressure is low. He's been unconscious almost the entire time and is now. Bleeding from a wound in his chest and leg." He doesn't have to say more about the car accident. I can see in his eyes he suspects a drunk driver.

I start cutting off his clothes, while the rest of the staff begins jumping on their jobs. IVs, tending to wounds, checking blood pressure, oxygen. We work in unison, a perfect dance, moving and speaking with each other in synced rhythm with each other. We all know exactly what needs to happen to keep this man alive.

The fabric I cut from his clothes is expensive. It takes a lot of energy to cut the suit from his body due to the thickness. He wears a Rolex on his wrist, which I remove as well. And then I grab gauze to press to the lesion on his head. It doesn't appear horrendous, compared with the wound on his chest. Another nurse is addressing that gash.

I flick his hair up so I can continue covering his laceration. Despite his condition, I can't help but think how beautiful he is.

Gorgeous man. His body is fit. His hair is thick and brown. His eyes are blue and sparkling.

His eyes!

Are open.

"Sir, can you hear me? You are at the hospital. We are going to take good care of you."

He doesn't speak, but his eyes tell me he understands what I'm saying.

"Relax. Do you remember what happened?"

"No," he says carefully.

I smile, happy to hear his voice.

"The paramedics said you were in a car accident. We are assessing your injuries now and determining if you need surgery or not."

He smiles back at me. Patients in this much pain usually don't smile back at me.

"How much pain are you in on a scale of 1-10?"

"0."

I frown and look down at Felicity who administered his IV. The drugs shouldn't have taken effect that quickly. She looks back at me just as concerned. He's probably in shock.

"0? Are you sure? You don't feel any pain in your head or chest or leg?"

"No."

Concern covers my face. He may be worse off than I thought. I look at the doctor who shares the same worry.

"I'm not in any pain because I'm staring at a beautiful angel who I would have never met had I not gotten injured. So the pain I feel is masked by how lucky I feel to have found you."

I blush and shake my head. I've been hit on plenty as a nursing student. But never so blatantly by a man in such a serious condition before.

The doctor in the room laughs. "I think you are going to be just fine if you can joke at a time like this."

"I'm not joking. Before I leave, I will have your number. And we will start an epic love story."

I blush more and laugh nervously. If he asks, I will give him my number in a heartbeat. He seems like exactly the kind of man I'm looking for.

"Okay, Romeo. Just relax and focus on getting better, then we can talk about dating," I say.

COLE TRAVER'S THE ONE.

Blue eyes, prince charming, and I saved his life.

He's exactly what I'm looking for. I haven't been able to stop thinking about him all day. He's the last one on my rounds to check on. I have one more patient first.

And then I get to have my fairy tale come true. I get to go out with a man who is charm itself. It will be better than the fairy tales. They could make a movie out of our love story. "Love in the Emergency Room" they could call it.

I scrunch my nose. Obviously, the movie people would think of a better name than that. But our story will be epic. I can't wait to shove it in my brother's face later. And tell Ren about it on Sunday. She's going to freak when I tell her I fell in love so quickly. Okay, maybe it's not love yet, but it will be. I can tell from his tailored suit, dreamy eyes, and smile, he's the one for me.

I knock on the door and then enter, hardly waiting for a response from the patient before entering.

"I'm Mila; I'm here to give you more pain medication and check to see how you're feeling," I say, as I head to the computer to look up the patient's information.

"I know who you are, Mila."

No. Fucking. Way.

I was too much in my own fairyland to even get a good look at the patient when I entered. Usually, I would have looked up my patient on the computer before entering their room to ensure I was prepared. I didn't this time. I'm too blissful and wrapped up in my prince charming in the next room to worry about this one.

I narrow my eyes as I look at him. Ace Knight. This can't be happening.

"Are you stalking me now?"

He chuckles and then lifts the cast on his arm. It's then that I see the gash on his head. The broken leg and the IVs coming out of his body. Whatever happened was serious.

"No, they typically don't give you a say in which hospital you go to when you're unconscious."

I flip my head back to my computer ignoring him. I need to get this done as quickly as possible. I scan the computer looking for my orders from the physician. Check his vitals and administer his next dose of antibiotics and painkillers. Easy enough.

"I need to check your blood pressure and oxygen levels."

I grab the blood pressure cuff and tighten it around his bulging bicep. His arm is so big the cuff barely fits, after a few rough jerks from me to get it to fasten.

"Jesus, woman! I didn't do anything to you," he says at my aggressiveness.

I narrow my eyes. "You called me *sweetheart*." He called me a lot worse, but I won't be repeating those words.

He grins, and it only pisses me off more.

"You ran over my motorcycle. I think we're even."

I glare. "We are most definitely not even."

"You're right. You owe me twenty grand to fix my bike."

Shit. Are motorcycles really that expensive? That's more than my car costs. I can't afford that.

"Your blood pressure is fine." I put the blood oxygen monitor on his finger, and it reads above ninety. Great, he's breathing just fine, while I'm sure if I tested my oxygen levels right now, it'd be below fifty, and my blood pressure would be sky high.

I don't bother listening to his heart. I don't want to be that close to him. Instead, I fetch his medications and walk over to his IV to administer them.

"So what do you think, sugartits? Am I going to live?"

I push in the antibiotics, but toss the painkiller in the trash without administering it. I shouldn't do it, but I'm pissed. I'm tired of dealing with his crap.

He grins. He won't be grinning in an hour when he's writhing in pain. I'll be off my shift by then, so it will be some other nurse's responsibility to give him pain medicine. He won't be in agony for more than an hour.

I purposefully drag my hand over his IV, tugging on it.

He growls. It's a deep, menacing, sexy sound that comes from deep in his belly.

"Oops."

"You aren't much of a *sweetheart,* are you? I'll have to think of another name to call you."

"You won't be calling me anything. I won't see you again after my shift is over." I'm too angry to suppress the raspiness in my voice. I'm used to talking in a high pitched, bubbly voice to hide my natural sultry sound. But now, it slips out.

Knight cocks his head, and his eyes darken into tight slits. If he thought I was a prize before, now he thinks he's hit the jackpot. I'm the ultimate possession he wants to claim.

He's never going to have me. He's the absolute wrong man for me. And I'm the wrong woman for him. Knight is looking for a woman to have fun. A one night stand. Or a string of nights. Nothing serious. It's clear from his tattooed covered body and tattered clothes that he doesn't take life seriously. I would just be his next conquest.

I've been down that road before. It leaves me in tears. My heart, broken. And my family telling me, "I told you so." I'm done with bad boys. I want a good man with a steady job, and his priorities straight. It may be a bit boring, but it's what will keep me safe.

"I think I will see a lot of you. You owe me for my bike."

I glare at him. "No, I don't owe you anything. I probably saved your life."

He cocks an eyebrow like he doesn't follow. "How do you figure that?"

"You were in a car accident, right?"

He doesn't answer, but his silence tells me I guessed right. I could check his chart, but I've seen enough patients to know the exact cause. And a man in his twenties is usually brought in for only a few reasons: brawl, being an idiot showoff, overdose, or car accident. His severe wounds lead me to guess car accident. Drunk driver or reckless driving most likely.

"If you had been riding your motorcycle, especially without a helmet, you probably would have been killed."

Knight pauses, drinking in every word falling from my lips like

I'm playing an orchestra just for him. I need to focus on not sounding like a harlot around him. I don't know what it is, but my sultry voice comes out near him.

He leans forward, and I find myself doing the same until we are inches apart. Eye to eye, nose to nose, mouth to mouth. I lean in further, thinking he's going to kiss me. And despite how angry I am, I'm desperate to taste his lips.

"You owe me, sweetheart."

Stunned. That's how I feel.

He chuckles like he knows just how much control he has over me.

My body may respond to his like any other warm-blooded woman's would react to a sexy man. It doesn't mean I'm going to act on my feelings. I have self-control.

And I have the perfect man waiting for me in the next room.

I won't let Ace think he has any hold on me. Men like him won't ever let me go if he thinks he has any power over my body.

I tug on his IV again, this time not being sneaky at all about it. It's clear it's not an accident.

"Stop calling me sweetheart or I'll—"

I don't finish.

His rough hand finds the nape of my neck, and he closes the distance between our lips. I gasp, my mouth opens as he swallows me.

I hate him, I think.

I hate him. I hate him. I hate him. I repeat the mantra in my head. Trying to convince myself to not fall into his trap.

Too late.

I've fallen. I'm lost in his kiss. The kiss is as rough as I expected a kiss from him would be, but also softer. Sweeter. Gentler.

The way his thumb presses at the base of my jaw is less controlling than I expected the gesture to feel. It's tender like he knows how his touch is radiating down my neck and into my core, persuading me to keep kissing him instead of pulling away like my head is telling me.

"You're fired."

I blink several times, not registering the words I just heard.

The kiss ends. I don't know if Knight or I was the one to end it, but it ends. And I've never felt sadder to face an end.

I lean back, my eyes focused on Knight's. His dark brown eyes aren't on mine though. They are behind me.

How could he think about anything but me at this moment?

His eyes slowly drift back to mine, and that's when I see it. The sadness. It matches mine. I don't understand why he's sad or where it's coming from. But it's there. Same as mine.

"Mila? Did you hear me?" Felicity asks.

Felicity!

I turn toward the shrill woman.

"I'm sorry. No, I didn't hear you."

"I said, you're fired. Go to your desk. I'll have security meet you to take your badge and change your computer logins."

"Wait? Fired? I'm not an employee here." *Stupid.* It doesn't matter if I'm an employee here or not. I'm no longer finishing my clinical rotation here. I might not even be graduating this winter at all.

She smiles like she has been waiting for years for a reason to fire me and the moment has finally come, even though she's only dealt with me for four weeks. "It's against the rules to kiss patients. I'm failing you. You'll be lucky if another hospital takes you after the report I write."

She walks over to the bed. "I'm so sorry, Mr. Knight. That was highly inappropriate for her to behave that way. I assure you the rest of our staff will behave with the utmost professionalism toward you the rest of your stay. We will ensure you get the best care while you are here. And as I said, she will be let go for her indiscretion."

Knight glances my way. But his eyes barely focus on me before he glances at Felicity. His eyes focus in on her cleavage.

Asshole, I think as I walk out of the room, my lips still tingling from his kiss.

I feel tears welling, my heart clenching. This can't be happening. I did everything I was supposed to do. I planned. I'm a few months away from graduating. From being forgiven by my family. I did everything I was supposed to.

And now...

Now, I'm going to end up with nothing. Living on my sister's couch. I'll be a nanny for the rest of my life. Trapped and unable to leave the sanctuary of my family.

I will never be on my own. Never live up to my potential.

I'll never graduate college now. I know that. I know, without even talking to the administrators, I'll be expelled. *Who kisses a patient and then gets to become a nurse still? No one.*

I watch as a tear falls and lands on the linoleum floor. I did everything right, and I still fucked up.

I look up and see Henry staring at me. The disappointment plain on his face. He doesn't know what happened. He doesn't have to. He knows me too well. It's why he's here.

I always fuck up. I ruin everyone's lives. But this time, I just ruined mine.

I won't ask my brother for money. I won't live on my sister's couch. I'll live on the streets under an underpass before I ask for their help again. Not after everything I've put them through.

I walk past the door of Cole Traver's room. I consider bursting through the door and telling him to save me. He probably could. He has enough money to more than take care of someone like me.

I'm tired of being saved. It's underrated. Being rescued doesn't make anything better. It just puts me in their debt and makes it that much harder the next time I fail again.

"I could have loved you. We could have had an epic love story," I whisper under my breath, staring at the tiny crack of light peering around the edge of the solid door.

I sniffle, trying to keep the tears away.

"What happened now, Mila?" Henry asks. His voice isn't angry.

But he doesn't try to hide the disappointment. That's all I am: one big disappointment.

"I was born, and then tragedy attached itself to me. I'm tragic, a dark storm cloud, a thorn that when pulled free from the skin finds another place to jab into and cause pain."

Henry rolls his eyes. "Stop being so dramatic, kiddo."

I wince at the nickname. That's all I am to him. A kid. A burden he can never get free of.

It ends today.

"I need to be alone." When I'm alone, I can't hurt anyone but myself. No matter how much I fuck up, I'm the only one I'll break.

3 KNIGHT

"What are you doing here?" I ask as I stand in the doorway of my office.

My best friend, Cole, sits in the chair with his feet up on my desk.

He raises an eyebrow. "I could ask you the same question."

I roll my eyes and shut the door behind me, before walking over to the mini bar and pouring two fingers of bourbon.

"I'm working."

Cole eyes the glass in my hand. "It looks like you are drinking your problems away. Didn't the doctor tell you not to mix pain medications with alcohol?"

I sip the liquor down in one shot.

Cole smirks. "I guess not."

"What do you want, Traver?"

I pour more amber liquid into my glass.

"What happened?" Cole says, removing his black loafers from my desk and sitting up straight in my oversized leather chair. I know what he's asking. The police finished their investigation and determined it was an accident. No one's fault. But it's hard to understand how someone could lose control of a car on a sunny day, with little traffic, and no texting, alcohol, or distractions.

I shrug and slowly sip the liquor.

"I lost control of the car. The road was slippery. Another car slammed into us," I say, trying not to relive the night. It happened weeks ago, but it still feels like it was yesterday. At least my body healed quickly. The only signs I was in a car accident are the scars on my body and pain whenever I move.

"You fucking lost control? That's the story you are going with?" Cole stands up, and I know he's going to punch me for what happened. I deserve it. He could have died. As it is, he's never going to walk right again. He'll always have a slight limp. Scars will mar his body. Nightmares will invade his sleep. *Because of me.*

I take another drink of the liquor, wishing it would take away the pain. And I'm not talking about the physical pain I'm in. Although that would be nice too; my ribs burn every time I fucking breathe. But that's not why I drink. I drink to get rid of the undeniable pain embedded in my heart.

"You were fucking drinking? Weren't you? Barely under the legal limit, huh?"

I don't answer. He wouldn't believe me anyway.

Cole drops his head. He's not going to punch me, even though I wish he would.

He walks over to the bar, pours himself a drink, and returns to my chair to perch his feet on my desk. He doesn't look at me as he nurses it. We both sip our drinks in complete silence. It's not normal, even for high powered men like us to be drinking this much alcohol on a Monday morning, but then our lives have never been normal. Most people don't become millionaires before their twenty-fifth birthdays either.

"You owe me," Cole says, breaking the silence as he studies the picture of Abri and me on my desk. He takes a seat again. "Although, I did meet this attractive nurse. Young, hot, long brown hair. Sharp eyes, perky boobs, and her voice. My god, I could listen to her all day."

His lips curl up a little in a smile as he pictures the woman in his head. A woman I know all too well.

"I thought she would come back to my room, but she didn't. Probably got off shift early. I'm sure she'd be interested in giving me a checkup." He chuckles to himself at his crude joke.

"Mila Burns?" I ask.

Cole stops laughing. "She was your nurse too?"

I nod.

His eyes light up. "We haven't competed for a woman in a long time. Not since high school. This could be fun."

"You already lost. I kissed her." *And got her fired. Most likely, ended her college career.* But I don't tell him that.

He smiles like I just said the greatest thing in the world. "I don't believe you."

I walk over to the expansive window and look out at the city below. So many people are walking, going through their regular, ordinary days. Hoping they make enough money to make it through the next day. I would give anything to be them.

"It doesn't matter if you believe me, it's true."

Cole studies me closely. "Are you saying she's off limits then?"

"No, I don't care. Fuck her. I got what I wanted from her."

He shakes his head, muttering under his breath.

"But I do want to pay you back," I say.

"There is nothing you can do to pay me back."

"I could sell you my company."

He sighs. "I don't have enough money to buy your company even if I wanted to, which I don't. How is that paying me back?"

I down the rest of my drink. Not because I need encouragement to say my next words, but because I need the alcohol just to breathe.

"The favor is I'm selling it to you for twenty dollars."

Cole laughs hysterically. Like it's the most absurd, ridiculous thing he's ever heard. It probably is.

"You're not serious."

"I am."

"I don't want your boring company. I'm into much more risky endeavors."

"Liar."

Cole takes his feet off my desk for the second time since I've entered the office. He looks at me like I'm insane and he's considering having me admitted. He studies me, but I don't give anything away. I don't have any emotions to feel.

Cole curses under his breath. He knows me too well. He knows what I'm doing.

"I'm not helping you hide your money from Abri."

"That's not what I'm doing."

"You fucking asshole. It's exactly what you are doing. You'd rather sell your company and get nothing, then let her have a penny of it."

I shrug. He's not wrong. My bitch of an ex-wife doesn't deserve any of my money. *Well, almost ex-wife.*

"Abri would take both of our asses to court if I bought your company for so little and cut her out."

"She won't."

"She will. And it will be deserved. She deserves to have half of the company. Or half of the money when you sell it."

"Fine, I'll give her ten bucks when I sell it to you."

Cole shakes his head. "What happened to you, man? You were so in love. Abri was your partner in crime. She gave up everything for your company. For you."

I don't answer.

"Fine, I get it. You were way too young when you got married. You grew apart. Love didn't last. Just sign the divorce papers and give her half of everything she helped you build, then go your separate ways. Move on."

I've tried moving on. But he has no idea what I've been through. No idea how badly I need to cut her out of my life permanently.

Giving her half of my money won't stop her. Giving her all of my money won't slow her down.

If I told him the truth, he wouldn't believe me. If he did, he'd try to talk me out of my plan. It's my burden to bare.

Cole studies me. He's my best friend. He's been with me through everything. My highest and lowest. He's like a brother. He would do anything for me. And the look in his eyes tells me as much.

He stands up and walks to me until he's inches in front of me.

"I'll buy your company for twenty dollars. If that's what you really want. I'll help you make sure Abri doesn't get anything from you."

I sigh in relief.

"But you have to do something first."

I narrow my eyes, not liking the tone of his voice. I don't like making deals.

"Prove to me you've moved on. Prove to me you will get past Abri. That you will date again. Prove to me that selling your company isn't just about Abri, that it's about starting over."

Mila pops into my head. Beautiful, sexy, flawless Mila. Her voice so sultry I could listen to her ramble about nothing for hours. Such a stark contrast to her sweet, innocent personality.

Damn her lips. Her red, fuckable lips. All I've thought about since she spoke when she got out of her car is her lips. How it would feel to have her wet, plump lips wrapped around my cock. Her innocent eyes, big with desire. I expected innocence when she spoke when she couldn't even swear. She wouldn't let herself curse. But then, she spoke, and I was captivated. She was all I thought about as I ran up the mountain. The last image I had as the headlights came crashing toward us and there was nothing I could do to stop the impact.

The car crash almost killed us. It should have been the single worst moment in my life. For most people, it would be.

Not mine.

Abri changed my life. For better and worse.

But Mila, she's like a comet headed straight for me. We've been on a collision course for years now. It would be easy for me to step aside. Avoid the impact, but I can't force my legs to move. Even though I know how this ends.

I know we won't ever be together.

I know if we were, we'd end up like Abri and me, devastated and alone. I won't put another person through what Abri and I have been through.

But Mila is the solution to getting free.

"Do we have a deal?" Cole asks, extending his hand.

Mila can help me convince Cole I've moved on. She can help me get rid of Abri once and for all. Then we can both start a new life, alone.

But that damn kiss. I can't get the kiss out of my head. Just thinking about it makes my cock ache. A feeling I haven't had in years.

Mila is going to hate me for that one. I got her fired. I ended her college career. Never has one kiss been so destructive. But it was necessary. Or at least I thought it was. It didn't end in exactly the way I thought it would.

Mila will come around though. She doesn't have a choice now that's she broke, and possibly homeless.

I brush passed Cole's hand and take a seat at my desk.

"Deal."

4 MILA

Sweat is disgusting. It's sticky and wet, and there is no hiding it. I don't care how much deodorant I wear; I can still smell the sweat dripping off my forehead, armpits, and ass. *Why does my ass sweat so much?*

Because my life is on the line right now, that's why. The sweat gives me a gross distraction. The smell infiltrates my nostrils, and every time I move, I feel the slimy liquid. My clothes cling to my skin like they are attached with glue.

Focus. I've spent the last couple of weeks reading everything I could about how I can continue with school. How to convince people you are innocent and deserving. Be confident, but not too confident. That means don't let them know you're sweating. Look them in the eyes when you talk. Smile, but not too brightly. Be firm in your words, don't use um, or like, or uh. But don't get defensive when you speak. Dress professionally, but show enough skin that you don't look like a young teenager instead of an adult. Admit your faults, but highlight your strengths.

I got this.

"Miss Burns, we have heard Felicity's account of what

happened. We have a written statement from the patient in question. Can you tell us in your own words what happened?" Mr. Warren, the dean of the college, says, staring at me with serious eyes.

This is it. This is my chance to finally explain.

I open my mouth, and the dryness prevents me from speaking. It's like a desert in my mouth. Dry, and no words form.

"Miss Burns?"

"I'm sorry, um..." *Shit, don't use um.* "It was a misunderstanding. The patient, Mr. Knight, I had met previously on a hike. He helped me with a minor leg injury. When I went to take care of him, he thought I wanted more. He was on a lot of pain medication and was delirious. He kissed me before I could tell him it wasn't appropriate."

"Did you report to your supervisor that you knew the patient and it would be inappropriate for you to take care of him?"

"Well...um...no, but as I said, I didn't know him. I met him for like five minutes on a hike." And he carried you down on his glistening back. But unlike the sweat pooling in the armpits of my white, I'm-so-innocent blouse, his sweat was sexy. I wanted to lick it off his pristine body.

"Mr. Knight kissed you?"

I nod.

"I've kissed many people, Miss Burns. They were always aware when I was about to kiss them. They gave me permission before I kissed them. They could stop the kiss at any time and could prevent it from happening in the first place. Why did you let Mr. Knight kiss you? Was it because you wanted it to happen?"

"What? No! I didn't want him to kiss me. I wasn't expecting it. We were arguing before he decided to kiss me. I had no idea what he was about to do." I sound defensive.

"What were you arguing about?"

"Um..." *Why did I say we were arguing?* "Just about how he treated me when he helped me on the hike."

Silence. The ten people in the room all stare at me, waiting for me to continue. I stare down at my hands which I have carefully folded on the wood table in front of me. It's supposed to show how confident I am. Confidence equals innocent.

"Mr. Knight called me some words I would rather not repeat here."

"Is that all that happened?"

I suck in a breathe. *No, but I'm not going to tell you.* But the words spill out of me. For some reason, the look on his face prevents me from holding anything back. "And I might have accidentally hit his motorcycle when I was backing my car out of the parking lot."

"I see." He writes something down on his notepad.

I scan the room, and everyone is either writing notes or scowling at me like a five-year-old who spilled milk on her mother's favorite shoes.

This is hopeless.

"Thank you for meeting with us, Miss Burns. We will discuss your case and have a ruling for you by the end of the day. But I think I can safely say I don't think you are fit to be a nurse. I think you should seriously consider a new career. One where you aren't dealing with vulnerable patients."

He looks at me like he thinks I might rape a patient in their sleep.

"Yes, sir," I say because there's nothing left to say. I stand, listening to the high pitched scrape of my chair against the fake wood floors.

I wince and then scurry out of the room. My legs can't move me fast enough. I find the bathroom down the hall, vomit in the nearest stall, and then wash my face. I can't believe that just happened. I can't believe I'm a semester away from graduating, and I'm going to let it all slip away.

I walk back out of the bathroom.

"Miss Burns," I hear the dean's voice.

I turn and stare at him with big eyes.

"I wanted to let you know our ruling. You'll get a formal letter with our decision in the mail, but we decided to suspend you."

"Suspend? What does that mean?"

"It means you will not be allowed on campus for any reason for the semester. You will not be allowed to take any classes or live in the dorms. Your scholarship will be revoked. And in the spring you can reapply. We will reconsider your case then, although as I said, I might recommend you finish your degree in business or something more cutthroat. It would match your personality better."

Tears sting my eyes. "I can reapply in the spring?"

He nods. "Know the only reason we didn't expel you completely without a chance to reconsider is because of Mr. Knight's testimony."

I frown. *This wasn't a murder case. Testimony? I know he wrote a statement, but did he do more than that?* Whatever Mr. Knight said I'm sure it didn't help my case. He's the reason I'm in this mess in the first place.

"Thank you, Mr. Warren. I'll consider reapplying in the spring."

I walk away before the tears fall. I've been embarrassed enough. I head back to the dorm room I share with Lana. I don't look anyone in the eye. I know the other students see my tears, but it doesn't matter. I don't look around at the campus. At the tall buildings I love. I don't think about any of it. I focus on my goal. Getting to my dorm room.

Lana is lying on her bed with a textbook resting on her lap while she paints her nails.

"How'd it go?" she asks.

I crouch down and reach under my bed until I find the bottle of contraband. This alone could have gotten me kicked out of the dorm rooms. I unscrew the bottle of tequila and take a long swig.

"That bad, huh?"

I don't respond. I don't even feel the burn as it sets my throat on fire. I just keep gulping.

Lana gets up and slowly takes the bottle from me, before she wraps her arms around me.

I sob into her bony shoulder.

"Shh, it's going to be okay."

"No, it's not. I have to move out. I have nowhere to go. No

money. I think I have a twenty dollar bill in my pocket. I can't even afford a tank of gas, let alone food or a place to stay."

"Stay here. How will they know?"

A knock on the door. *Ugh.*

I walk to the door and throw it open as the RA stands there frowning at me. "I'm here to ensure you move out today. I will need your keys."

I glance back at Lana in an I-told-you-so sort of way.

"Thanks, Aurora, for being so sensitive in Mila's time of need."

"It's not my fault she kissed a patient and got expelled."

"Suspended. I can come back in the spring. It's just for a semester."

"Well, you can't be here now."

"I know. I'm going to need some time to pack."

She folds her arms across her chest like she's going to stand in my doorway and watch me pack the entire time.

"Leave," Lana says walking to the door.

"I'm supposed to collect her key."

Lana rolls her eyes. "I'll make sure she drops it off by noon. In the meantime, this is still my dorm room, and I can still kick you out whenever I want."

Aurora sighs, but leaves.

"Bitch," we both mutter after she leaves.

Lana smiles. "Swearing again, are we?"

I nod. "Only when people deserve it."

She hugs me again. "It's good to see the old you back."

I frown. I hate the old me. The old me is what gets me into trouble. Although, the new me also seems to get me in trouble. But the old me has to come back if I'm going to survive.

"Are you going to go live with your sister?"

"No."

"Where are you going to go then?"

I shrug. "I'll live in my car until I find a job and figure something out. It will be fine. I'll wait tables, bartend, babysit Ren's kids some.

I'll make enough to survive, and then I'll come back next semester. It's not a big deal."

Lana knows I'm lying. It is a big deal. And I'm not even sure if I can come back yet. But she doesn't call me out on the lie.

She digs into her pocket and pulls about a ten and a five dollar bill. "It's not much, but take it."

I shake my head. "I can't."

"I'm not asking."

"No, I'll be fine. I'm not taking your money, Lana." She's broke, same as me. She doesn't have family helping her. And she deserves the money more than I do. She isn't the one with a constant stream of fuck-ups.

Damn, the cuss words just keep coming back. I haven't even thought a curse word in years. Now they are staining my every thought and spilling out of me far too fast.

She sighs and puts the money back in her pocket.

"You can help me pack though."

"I'd rather just give you the money," she moans.

I chuckle and toss her my backpack to start filling up. I have a backpack and a duffel bag with a broken zipper. That's all I have to pack my possessions in. Good thing I don't have many possessions because there is no way I can even afford boxes right now to pack.

It takes us all of ten minutes to pack up everything I own. Some of my textbooks don't fit so I'll have to carry them, but otherwise, everything fits in the two bags.

Lana hugs me one last time. "Call me every day."

I nod. "I'll keep in touch. You can't get rid of me this easily."

"I'll make sure our bitchy face RA gets your key."

"Thanks," I say putting my backpack on, draping my duffel bag over my shoulder, and picking up the textbooks I plan on selling. I won't get much, but twenty dollars might mean the difference between eating or starving.

I glance one more time at the dorm room that had become my sanctuary. I had a full scholarship that covered everything. My classes, books, dorm room. All I had to cover was food. Something an occasional bartending job could cover. I took extra classes so I could graduate early. Now it's all gone.

I will not cry. *Not again,* I repeat to myself as I walk out of the dorm and into the sun. The sun always shines in Colorado. Over three hundred days of sunshine a year. I usually love that about Colorado, but not today.

"Can't I get some rain? Some clouds? Anything but your cheeriness?" I mumble under my breath, but of course, the sun still shines, making me feel like I'm the only person in the world dealing with a shitty day.

My arms grow tired as I walk across campus to my car. At least I only have to make one trip. That's a positive. Although, I have no idea what I'm going to do when I get to my car. Start applying to jobs I guess.

No, I need a new plan, that's all. When I have a plan, my life is good.

I will apply to the bar on the 16th street mall that just opened. It's in a touristy part of town, and I would make great tips. I will sleep in my car until I get my first paycheck. Or I'll ask for an advance. Then, I'll find a roommate who has a cheap room to rent out. A closet-sized room is about all I'll be able to afford. I heard there are some cheap apartments near north Denver. I'll—

"Umf," I grunt as I run into a brick wall.

My books tumble to the ground, and my duffle bag falls off my shoulder, clothes tumbling out of the bag.

"Shit," I say when a scarf gets caught in the wind and starts blowing away.

"I got it," a man says.

I look up as he catches the scarf. I didn't run into a brick wall. I ran into Cole, the perfect specimen of a man from the hospital. He looks like he's healed well in the weeks since I last saw him. His face is still bruised, and he will always have a scar on his forehead, but it will fade over time. He seems to be walking well, although I see a tiny limp as he brings the scarf back to me. Most people wouldn't notice the limp, and it shouldn't have a significant impact on him unless he were an athlete or something before the accident. Very possible considering how built he is.

He grins, and I melt.

"I didn't think I was going to get to see my favorite nurse again."

Swallow, breathe, stop drooling.

He chuckles at my speechlessness. "Didn't mean to make you speechless. I think your voice might be my favorite thing about you."

"I'm sorry for running into you."

He shakes his head. "Entirely, my fault."

We both bend down and start picking up the rest of my clothes before they blow away. Cole holds up my red lace thong, the only sexy item of clothing I own.

He raises an eyebrow before I snatch it out of his hand. I know I'm blushing and won't be able to look him in the eye again.

He puts a finger under my chin, so I have to look up at him.

"Don't do that. You have nothing to be embarrassed about. I've had dreams about you in similar underwear. Now my dreams are about to get a whole heck of a lot dirtier."

I blush more.

"Um...thanks." *Great word choice,* I think to myself. *God, can I embarrass myself any more?*

Cole stacks my books up. "Let me help carry these to your car."

"Thanks," I mumble because I don't trust my voice to say anything more.

"Can I ask where you are going? A last-minute trip before school starts again? Or are you ditching classes?"

I should keep my mouth shut. But the alcohol has now loosened my tongue, and I'm beyond exacerbated at this point. "I got expelled. Well, not expelled, suspended. They're kicking me out, and I will probably spend the rest of my life alternating between sleeping on my sister's or brother's couch and sleeping in my car, while I wait tables and get hit on by drunk guys who like to grab my ass and listen to my voice and think that because I can't help but speak sultrily it gives them permission to fuck me."

Cole's eyes go big, but he doesn't speak. He probably thinks I'm insane after witnessing my mini-meltdown. He's probably trying to figure out how to get away from me as fast as possible.

We make it to my car, and I pop the trunk, not even caring to move the McDonalds wrappers in the back. I put my bags in, and Cole places the books next to the bags.

He opens his mouth, and I know words come out, but I can't hear them over the engine of a motorcycle speeding into the parking lot. My gaze focuses on the motorcycle.

No fucking way.

Knight parks the motorcycle in a no parking zone and then spots me.

Shit. This is not happening. He can't see me like this. I'll kill him.

I turn to the still bumbling Cole. He can save me from Knight. Knight won't come over if he thinks Cole is my boyfriend.

I move up on my tiptoes, barely grab Cole's cheeks, and kiss him. Our eyes both take a second to close as I've taken us both by surprise, but it happens. I push my tongue into his mouth, needing to take this kiss with me when I go. It might be a while until I get to kiss a man like this. *Unless I decide to whore myself out to survive.*

Cole wraps his arms around me caressing my face as he does. His tongue is gentle in my mouth, exploring but not as frantic as my tongue. He moans softly, showing me he enjoys the kiss, but nothing more.

No sparks fly.

No electricity lights.

No emotions form.

Nothing. The kiss is nice, but nice isn't enough. Not when the fucker who got me fired's kiss did all of that and more. I've been getting myself off every night to the memory of that kiss. A kiss that should be my worst nightmare has become my fantasy.

We both pull away and smile at each other like we've just been having a friendly conversation. *Nice.* Cole Tracker is the hottest man I've ever kissed, and all I felt was nice. He's tall, dark, and handsome. He's wearing an expensive suit. It's clear his life is together. I should fall for a man like him, but instead, I want the bad boy who is barreling toward us.

Cole doesn't turn around, but I can see in his eyes he feels the danger approaching. "This is going to hurt," he mumbles so quietly I'm not sure I hear him correctly.

I see the blood before I realize what happened. I expect them to get into a brawl. I expect Cole to whip around and punch Knight in the face like he deserves. I grab my phone ready to call in reinforcements to break them up if I need to.

Nothing happens though. Cole laughs as blood drips from his nose. His eye is already swollen and turning different colors with every second that passes. Red, purple, and blue.

Knight glares at me and then walks back to his motorcycle. He looks good. His tattoos hides the scars on his arms; I only find a faint one on his cheek. His hair is cut shorter, but still longer than most men's. And his eyes see through to my soul. The engine roars, and he's gone as quickly as he came.

"What just happened?" I ask, my mouth gaping. "Do you know him?"

"You don't want to know."

I stare in the direction of Knight's exit. I really do want to know, but I don't push Cole. Instead, I watch as the dust settles back on the asphalt by the curb.

"I might have a job for you," Cole says.

I stare at him, dumbfounded.

"What?" I have no idea what he just said.

He strokes my cheek. It's not a loving gesture, more like a goodbye.

When he finishes, I'm left with nothing. No chills, no goosebumps, no reaction. Knight had a stronger reaction to me, and he didn't even touch me or speak to me.

Cole reaches into his back pocket and pulls out a business card. He hands it to me.

"What's this?"

"A way for you to do more than just survive."

I blink, not believing my luck might have changed. That Cole might not be able to get my panties wet, but he is obviously successful. He might be able to get me a job. Which, right now, I need more than a boyfriend.

"What's the job?" I ask.

He smirks. "Meet me at the address tonight at eight. And wear your nicest outfit. I'll make sure you have a job by tonight."

He turns to leave.

"Thanks!" I say, suddenly getting my voice back.

He nods solemnly. "And stop kissing strange boys, it keeps getting you in trouble."

I blush and smile at his words. He has no idea how much kissing men has gotten me in trouble. He said boys though, not men. I watch Cole walk away, while Knight's body flickers in my head. Neither of which I would call a boy. They might be closer to my age than I realized at first appearance, but they are successful. They have built a life. They know how to charm me. Only a man could do that.

5 KNIGHT

I sit down next to my asshole of a friend. I don't know why I'm even here except for a chance to pummel his face again for what he did.

"No ice? You didn't even bring me a drink?"

I roll my eyes. "You don't need me to bring you anything. You have women to do that for you."

Cole shrugs and then eyes one of the waiters who smiles at him. She comes over immediately.

"Can you get me ice for my face? And two double Maker's Marks, neat."

"Blanton's for me."

Cole rolls his eyes as if he thinks he ordered the better bourbon. He didn't.

Neither of us talks as we sit in the corner of the bar in our usual booth. Cole watches the ass of our waiter as she prances away, while I spend my time glaring at him. But we both know better than to speak until we have alcohol in us.

The waiter returns quickly. Chrissy is her name, I think. She usually waits on us when we are here. Although, I'm too much of a dick to remember her name or anyone else's in this club.

She sets our drinks down and then makes a show of pressing the ice pack to Cole's face, showing him her boobs in the process.

"Thank you, Chrissy," I say, needing to get this conversation over with. I have better things I need to be doing.

She smiles. "I'm surprised you know my name."

"I don't. It was a lucky guess."

She huffs but leaves us alone after a glance from Cole encouraging her to go, with a promise he'll make it worth her while later.

"What the fuck was that about?"

"I was flirting with the waitress. What's so wrong with that? I enjoy mixing business with pleasure." Cole winces as he presses the ice to his eye.

"I'm not talking about Chrissy. I don't care what you do with her. I'm talking about Mila."

"Mila? I'm not sure I know who you are talking about."

"The woman whose tongue you had in your mouth this afternoon."

"Oh, her." Cole puts the ice down and rests his arms on the back of the booth. *Jackass.* He knows exactly who I'm talking about. I don't understand what game he's playing.

"Explain yourself, now. Before I beat the hell out of you and make you wish you never touched a woman again."

"I thought you didn't care about Mila."

"I don't."

"Please. The only reason I found her, or tasted her luscious lips, is because I know you have a thing for her."

"I do not."

Cole ignores me. "I knew you wouldn't ask her out on your own, so I decided an intervention was needed."

"I was headed to find her five minutes after you left. That's why I saw the two of you swapping spit."

"How was I supposed to know?"

I growl.

"Fine, I knew you'd go after the girl."

"Mila."

"Mila. I knew you'd go after her, but I knew she wouldn't go for you."

"Why the hell not?"

"For one, your game isn't what it used to be. You've been out of practice for the last five years."

I shoot daggers with my eyes. But I pick up my drink to sip and let him finish.

"Two, you got her suspended from college with your kiss, so she hates your guts."

I drink. I can't argue with that one. I royally fucked that up.

"And three, she's still totally hung up on me."

I slam my drink down and about climb over the table to get to him.

"Whoa, chill. She's not into me anymore."

I sit back. "How do you know?"

"The kiss."

I growl again. "Don't remind me."

"She kissed me to avoid having to talk to you, but I know she's secretly wanted to do it since she saved my life."

"She didn't save your life; I did when I pulled you out of the burning car. Although I don't know why I did that now, you butthead."

He smiles. "Butthead is tame."

"Well, you're my only friend. I don't want to piss you off too much."

"How do you know she's not into you anymore?"

"The kiss."

I groan, *again with the damn kiss.*

"There was no spark. Chicks care a lot about if there is a spark on the first kiss."

I narrow my eyes. "Chicks always find a spark with you, although I have no idea why."

ELLA MILES

He shrugs. "There wasn't one. I even gave her my best kiss to piss you off thoroughly. Nothing happened though."

We both sip our drinks in silence as I process what Cole said.

"Nothing happened?" I repeat.

"Well, I offered her a job because she is desperate now that you've made her destitute."

"What kind of job?" I growl, hoping the job is in his legal department or something.

He glances behind me. "Mila's here, right on time for her job interview."

"What?" I snap my head around and find Mila. She seems both out of place and precisely in the right place. She's wearing a skirt and suit jacket two sizes too big for her frail body. Her shoes are dark pumps that also appear too big. Her hair is up in a high ponytail, and she's wearing red, fuck-me lipstick. I don't know whether she is looking for a job in a law office, or if this is part of her act when she goes on stage and strips.

"No, she's not fucking working here. She's not becoming a stripper, or escort, or whore. Not even a waitress here."

Cole smirks as he relaxes into the booth.

"I'm going to kill you. I'll give you another shiner to match the one you already have."

"No, you won't. Now, I can offer her a job, or you can. The choice is yours."

I grab my drink and down it, hating that he's calling my bluff and forcing my hand.

This is what I wanted though. A chance to make Mila mine. An opportunity for her to agree to my plan.

She spots me the second I stand. I'm not hard to spot. I don't exactly fit in at this club. I'm not a suit with a hard-on for young girls.

I see her eyes, and I know what she's thinking. She should turn and walk out the door. But Cole's right. She's desperate. I could probably convince her to spread her legs for half the men in this club if it

392

paid well. I don't know what's happened to her, but I hate seeing her this way.

"Mila, I didn't expect to see you in a fine establishment like this."

"I didn't expect to see you again, at all."

My cock is instantly straining against the zipper of my jeans when she speaks. I've never heard a voice like hers.

Thankfully, she doesn't notice. *Or maybe, unfortunately.*

"Here for a job?" I ask.

"No."

"Oh, then I guess you're here to watch the women dance. You could have told me you were into women; I would have left you alone."

She glares. "I'm not into women."

I circle behind her as she stares ahead, trying to pretend like the naked women in front of her don't bother her.

"I know."

She shivers.

I touch the nape of her neck. "Your body responds to my words, my touch, my presence."

"Don't flatter yourself. I don't want to talk to the asshole who kisses me, gets me fired, and gets me kicked out of college. How could you?"

I see the pain in her eyes when I move back in front of her.

"I'm sorry."

Her mouth drops. She wasn't expecting me to apologize.

"I thought I was helping you."

"How could kissing me be helping me?"

"Your supervisor walked in when you purposely tugged on my IV. And I think she saw you throw my pain medication in the trash, although I can't be sure. I thought if she saw me kiss you, she'd realize I'm a bastard that had been sexually harassing you, and she wouldn't punish you for what you had done previously."

Her mouth forms the perfect 'O.' And I can't help but wonder if that is her same look when she orgasms. I don't say that though. I'm already in the doghouse with her. And as much as she hates me, I need her help.

"Well, that backfired badly."

"I know, I'm sorry. I talked to the dean, but he had already made up his mind. Although, I think I can help you."

"I don't need your help."

I cock my head. "You sure about that, pretty girl?"

She rolls her eyes. "I'm sure."

"It seems I owe you a job after what I did."

"You own this place?" she gasps.

I shrug.

"Of course, you do. Only sick bastards like you would own a strip club."

"It's not just a strip club. It's also an escort service and every man or woman's fantasy. It's a club for the elite, and can become whatever they need."

She scans the crowd, realizing everyone here is in an expensive suit. Well, everyone but her and me.

"Do you want to talk about the job or not?"

I see the beads of sweat dripping down her neck. She licks her lips trying to moisten her dry mouth. I can hear her heart beating wildly against her cheap suit jacket.

She's considering what she will do or not do for money. No, not for money, to survive. It's obvious she's been through enough to be a survivor. She will do what she has to.

I admire that about her, but it won't protect her. She will still end up hurt in the end if she agrees to my plan, no matter how I try to protect her.

"I'm listening."

I don't know whether to smile or frown. As soon as I tell her my proposal, she will say yes. I still don't know entirely what I'm proposing, but I know it won't be good for her. It might even destroy her.

I turn and walk toward one of the private rooms. I stop Chrissy to get her to bring us drinks. I don't turn to see if Mila is following me, I know she is.

I've seen desperation. I've felt it. It's how I'm living. I will do anything to fix my current predicament. So in that regard, we are the same.

I hold the door open for her to the private room, and she steps inside cautiously, like a lamb walking into a lion's den. She takes a seat on the chair while I spread out on the couch.

I don't speak until Chrissy has brought us drinks.

I take them both from her. "Tequila or vodka?"

"Vodka," she answers.

"Good," I say handing her the vodka drink.

"That doesn't look like tequila."

I sip my whiskey. "It's not."

"Then, why did you offer me a tequila drink?"

"I knew you'd want one or the other. I guessed, but if you'd asked for tequila, I would have gotten that for you."

"Why do you think I would prefer vodka?"

"Because tequila represents your wild, carefree, fuck it side. Vodka is just as strong, but you feel more in control when you drink it, which is what you think you need around me."

She doesn't answer, which means I guessed correctly.

"I think you dressed incorrectly for the job, though. I don't think you're capable of what I need in that."

She frowns and sets her drink down.

"You don't think I'm capable of stripping in front of a bunch of horny men?"

"No."

She stands up suddenly, pulling her shitty phone with a shattered screen from a pocket in her skirt. She presses a button and music begins playing. These rooms are soundproof. They have to be to ensure the utmost privacy.

Slowly, Mila begins moving her hips to the music. I'm mesmerized. I can't move or think. All I can do is watch.

She slowly moves her hands over her body, until it gets to the button on her suit jacket. She undoes the button and lets the jacket gape open. She's not wearing a shirt underneath, just a red, lacey bra.

Fuck me.

Her boobs spill out of the bra, even though her body could use more meat on her bones.

She sways again, as her hands move to her back. She begins unzipping her skirt, and then it's a puddle on the floor.

I know I'm drooling; I have to be as I watch her. And my cock has never been this hard.

She's wearing nothing but a lacey, red thong and bra with her black pumps. She takes a step toward me, then another and another until she's right in front of me.

She hesitates for just a second, and then she's on my lap. Her body is gyrating over my crouch. *Why the fuck did I wear jeans? Sweatpants, always wear sweatpants.*

She reaches up and pulls the hair tie from her hair. Her hair cascades around me in long, thick strands.

"Fucking, beautiful," I curse.

She pauses, not expecting my words.

"Still think I can't strip in front of a room full of men?" she asks, as she caresses my neck and moves her lips inches from mine.

"No." I grin.

She glares. She immediately rolls off me and starts dressing again. "I just stripped in front of you."

"Stripping in front of *me* is different than stripping in a room full of men. And you didn't fully strip anyway."

Another scowl.

"Close enough," she whispers.

I grab her wrist and pull her back onto my lap. "No, not close enough. But that's not why you can't strip in front of a room full of men." Our faces are inches apart, and I want nothing more than to kiss her again.

"Why?" she breathes.

"Because I can't stand to watch you strip in front of anyone but me."

She gasps.

It takes her a while, but she finally finds her words. "I'm not sleeping with you to make money. I'm not a whore."

I frown. "You are definitely not a whore. And I'm not going to fuck you."

She narrows her eyes. "Then what do you want with me, Knight?"

I love the way she uses my last name as my first. I know it's supposed to be her way of teasing me, as I do by picking out random nicknames for her. She doesn't realize I've never gone by Ace though. I've only been Ace to one person. Knight is who I am. And it's sexy as hell for her to figure it out on her own and call me that.

"I want you to do whatever I say, no questions asked."

6 MILA

Knight wants me to fuck him. That's what he means when he says he wants me to "do whatever I say."

I can see it in his eyes, his voice is dripping with it, and even though he's wearing jeans, I can feel his erection press against me. Hard as a rock, begging to be inside me.

Right now, I don't know whether to regret that I'm straddling his lap almost entirely naked or to be thankful. *How did I get myself into this mess?*

My cheeks blush as his eyes rake up and down my body. I felt bold when I stripped for him even though he didn't ask me to.

I thought it would give me the upper hand.

I thought he'd be distracted by my body.

I thought he'd be speechless.

I thought he'd realize I'm capable of *anything*.

Instead, I'm horny and embarrassed, and can't do a damn thing about either.

I consider trying to move off his lap again, but his hands are firmly gripping my waist. I'm not going anywhere until we finish this conversation, no matter how uncomfortable it makes us.

This conversation is going to happen eye to eye, lips inches apart, with all of our lust on full display. Both of us completely vulnerable to each other.

Except, I feel a lot more vulnerable than he seems. Because I'm practically naked.

I grab the hem of his shirt.

He raises an eyebrow but doesn't protest as I lift the shirt over his head. I immediately regret it. I forgot how insanely hot he is. He's all abs, tattoos, and muscle. Even the few scars and bruises now covering his body do nothing to make him any less attractive.

"Are you trying to get me to fuck you?" he asks.

"No, just want to level the playing field."

"So, will you do anything I want?" His lips curl up as if he knows I'll do anything he wants for free, and more than that for money.

"No, I'd rather strip for strangers than give you whatever you want."

He shakes his head. "Stripping won't pay the bills." And the darkness in his eyes says he won't let me anyway. Even though I don't need his permission. We aren't dating. We aren't anything except two strangers who have kissed and are clinging to each other while shirtless.

"What does *anything* mean?"

He narrows his eyes but doesn't speak.

"If this isn't about sex, then what? You want me to pretend to date you?"

"I don't want you to *pretend* to do anything."

I gasp. I wasn't expecting that. I wasn't expecting any honesty in whatever it is we are doing.

"Why?"

"Because nothing I do will ever be pretend. I will always be honest with you, with my actions and words."

I believe him; I do. He will be candid with me when he speaks, but that won't stop him from hiding things from me. He is hiding the truth.

"I have a delicate situation I need your help with," Knight says.

I study him, but he gives nothing away until he's ready to. And I have a feeling I could work for him for years and never know what he's hiding.

His hand tucks a strand of hair behind my ear, and I shiver. Our eyes lock, and I want nothing more than to fuck him. I don't care if I have enough money to feed myself. I don't care if I have a place to live. I'll live off the high and afterglow from the orgasms he will give me.

Knight notices my reaction and removes his hands, placing them gently on the couch. My eyes are glued to his rough hands, capable of playing me like a guitar. And then I spot the tan line where a wedding ring used to be.

"You're married?"

"Separated. Soon to be divorced."

I lean back. "That's what you want my help with. Making your ex jealous?"

He chuckles, leaning back on the couch. I like his smile. I like everything about him almost as much as I hate him.

I fold my arms across my chest. "Why was that funny?"

"Because you don't know my ex. She doesn't get jealous. She has no reason to. When we were married, I loved her with everything I had. I didn't notice other women. I wouldn't let myself. It was her and me against everything."

"But not now?"

"No. Now I just want this over."

His voice changes when he says *over*. It's dark, deep, and broken. It's final.

"Messy divorce?"

He doesn't answer, which means yes.

"What do you want me to do then, if not make her jealous?"

"Anything I tell you."

My cheeks blush as his cock twitches beneath me, making his words dirtier than they should be. I look away and try to compose myself. I gently blow air out of my pursed lips, and I expect him to make a dirty comment about how we should fuck, he knows it's what I want.

But when I look at him again, he's serious. His lips thinned, his cheeks plain, his eyes focused.

"What does *anything* mean? Can you give me some examples?"

"You will come to my office every day. Your formal title will be my assistant. I will then have you do *anything* I need. Bring me coffee, retrieve my dry cleaning, attend events with me."

"Dry cleaning?" I eye his jeans and T-shirt. I doubt he even owns a suit.

He ignores my snarky remark.

"That's it? I just get your coffee and go to a few events with you, and you will pay me—"

"I'll pay you $250,000 over the next five months."

My mouth gapes. I've never had that kind of money before. I knew he had money. He said millions.

"I never realized the strip club business was that lucrative," I say when I get my voice back.

He chuckles and leans in like he's going to kiss me but stops short. "It's not."

I suck in a breath. Never have I been so breathless. I need to go to the hospital when this is finished and get hooked up to some oxygen until I can breathe again.

"I will also guarantee you can continue your nursing degree in the spring."

My eyes widen. "You can't guarantee something like that."

"I can with the donation I will be making to the school."

Holy shit! He is rich, and he must really want me to work for him if he's willing to donate money to the college.

"Shouldn't you be doing that part for free since you're the reason I got suspended in the first place?" Is what my smart mouth says instead of thanking him.

"No, *you* ran over my motorcycle. You denied me pain medications. I think if anything, you owe me."

He's right, but I'll never tell him that.

"Why me?"

"You don't think you are capable of getting me coffee?"

"I can get you coffee, but that is not what this job really entails. It's not about getting you coffee. It's about doing what you ask without question. And I'm sure most of the time I will just be getting you coffee, until..."

"Until?"

"Until the real reason you want to hire me. Until you ask me to do something illegal, dangerous, or sexual."

"I would never ask you to do anything illegal."

We stare at each other, neither of us blinking. *But he would ask me to do something dangerous or sexual?*

"Why me?"

"Because you are perfect for the job."

"That's not an answer."

"That's the only answer I'm giving you."

"What happened to honesty?"

"I'm being honest. The job pays well, and you will hate me by the end of this, but you will have your life back."

I frown. I don't want his honesty anymore. This is a bad idea. The last time I dated a bad boy, it almost destroyed my entire family and me. I know he's not asking me to date him, but he's asking for me to be vulnerable, for me to trust him.

I'm not sure I can trust him, not when he isn't honest with me. His words are the truth, but he's hiding something. Something he isn't saying. The real reasons he wants me to work for him. Something to do with his soon to be ex-wife.

"You're young to have a wife."

"I'm young to have millions sitting in my bank account too."

I nod. "You're not secretly a fifty-year-old man or something?"

"I'm twenty-four."

I study him. He's only two years older than I am, but somehow life has taken us on very different paths. I'm broke and about to do anything for money. He's rich but desperate to get out of a bad situation. Money doesn't fix anything; it just makes life more complicated. I should know.

"I'll agree on one condition."

He perks up, his eyes open more fully, and his lips purse like he's going to kiss me if I say yes.

"You already said you'd never ask me to do anything illegal."

He nods.

"And I can live with a little danger." *I already have enough danger in my life.* "But no sex."

"No sex?" he asks slowly.

"Yes, no sex. I won't fuck you for money."

He smiles when I say fuck.

"I'm not asking you to fuck me for money. I don't pay for sex. I'm not going to pretend with you, Mila. Everything that happens between us will be real. I won't fuck you if you don't want me to."

I will just break your heart. He doesn't say the words, but they are implied. If I do this, I will end up broken.

It's not possible to be more broken than I've been. He doesn't know about my past.

"Last condition."

He chuckles. "You said that last time."

"Whatever." I roll my eyes. "I need an honest answer."

He leans back, waiting for me to continue.

"What do you want?"

"I want you to work for me."

"No." I shake my head. "I mean, what do you want from life?" I can't work for a broken man who is just out for revenge. He doesn't have to be a saint, but I need to know his life is more than making his ex's life a living hell.

Knight looks away, and I don't think he's going to answer me. It's a personal question, and I need a truthful answer to agree to do this.

403

He's not going to be honest. He's going to let me go. I'm not going to get this job.

"I want freedom."

Our eyes meet, and I realize the truth. It's what we both want.

Freedom from our pasts.

Freedom to be ourselves.

Freedom to be happy.

Freedom to have a future.

"I accept your job offer." I hold out my hand, even though I'm not wearing a shirt or pants.

Even though he's shirtless.

Even though we've kissed.

He smiles and shakes my hand. "Miss Burns, I think we are going to make a perfect team."

7 KNIGHT

"Now what?" Mila asks, her eyes big with fear about what's coming, but also a tiny bit turned on. I know if I reached between her legs right now I'd find her wet. I haven't let my eyes glimpse her cunt that's wrapped in sexy lace. If I did, I wouldn't be able to keep my promise of not fucking her without her permission. I'd turn into an animal who wouldn't be able to stop.

"When does my job start? What hours do I work?"

"Immediately, and any hour I want you."

She shivers on my lap, which doesn't help my hard on. It's been too long since I've wanted a woman this badly.

I want to tell Mila to give me a lap dance. To see how far she will take her new job responsibilities. I want to torture her, but I'm not sure who I would be torturing more.

"What does my bad boss want me to do now?" she teases in her sultry voice.

"Get dressed."

Her eyes widen further into big green orbs.

"And never talk dirty again. It doesn't suit you. Your voice is more than enough."

"I wasn't trying to—"

I give her a look, and she stops. She was teasing me, trying to get under my skin. I know she thinks I'm nothing but a bad boy. She probably thinks I stole the money I've earned. Or earned it off of young women who dance for me. She doesn't know I've barely earned a penny from this club.

Mila climbs off of me slowly, like she's deliberately trying to drive me crazy as she rubs her body against mine. But I know it's not deliberate. She just doesn't realize how sexy she is.

She pulls her skirt on and buttons the jacket over her bra. She picks up the hair tie and ties her hair up high on her head into a ponytail again. And I'm left wondering if she was sexier in her lingerie or now fully dressed. I don't have an answer.

She stares at me, and I smile smugly as she eats me up.

"Are you going to get dressed?"

"Huh?" *Oh, I forgot I wasn't wearing a shirt.* I grab my T-shirt and throw it over my head.

"Have you eaten dinner yet?" I ask even though I know the answer. *No.* And if she did eat, she needs to eat a second dinner; she's far too skinny for what is healthy.

"Eat dinner here, at the club?"

"No."

"Okay."

"Okay?"

Mila frowns not understanding my words.

"I think a more appropriate answer when your boss gives you an order would be yes, sir."

She laughs. "Not happening, Knight."

I pout, and she laughs harder almost knocking herself off balance on her heels. I stand up and grab her hand, just before she crashes to the floor and I have to take her to the hospital. As much as I enjoyed our first kiss at the hospital, I don't want to have to go back to the hospital with her anytime soon.

"You sure, Mila? I could make you."

She stares down at my arm where I'm holding her. "You could, but you won't. You may be an asshole, but you won't force me."

"How do you know?"

She frowns and shakes her head. "I don't know how I know. I just do."

I nod, understanding completely.

I take her hand and walk her back out to the world of dangerous men, sex, and money. A world I want her far away from.

I lead her quickly out of the club, and then to my motorcycle that is waiting for us.

"Do you always park your motorcycle illegally?"

"No, it's the club manager's job to know when a client wants to leave."

"I don't care how expensive this motorcycle is; I'm not getting on it."

I let go of her hand and collect two helmets and hold one out to her.

"No." She stubbornly crosses her arms.

I sigh. "The agreement was that you do whatever I tell you to do. Without argument."

"I don't think that was the agreement."

"Read the fine print."

"There is no fine print. We didn't sign anything."

"Exactly. Your job is to do what I say without question or our deal is off. I won't pay you. I won't ensure you have a diploma waiting for you in May." *It's not true. I've already donated the money, and she's already enrolled next semester. She would be re-enrolled this semester if I didn't need her help first. And I won't let her starve or live in her car, which is what she'd do without my money.*

Mila huffs but then takes a step forward. "I will ride on this motorcycle tonight, but if we are to travel together in the future, I kindly ask you consider a different form of transportation. I'll even ride the bus."

"Why? What do you have against motorcycles?"

"They are dangerous."

I grin. "All the more reason you should ride them."

She snatches the helmet out of my hands and then straddles the bike behind me. I don't give her time to grab my waist before I jolt us forward. I love the squeal that escapes her as her hands squeeze around my waist.

I whiz around a corner, and she screams louder. I don't want to push her too far in one night, so after having a few moments of fun, I slow down.

"Faster," she whispers in my ear.

My mouth gapes. She can't be seriously asking me to speed up. So I test her. I rev the engine and step on the gas after the next stoplight.

"That isn't fast." She breathes on my neck.

Fuck.

I pick up speed, pushing both of our limits this time as I round another corner.

"Yes, Knight!" she cries out like she just came from the excitement of having black shiny rumbling metal between her legs. *Damn, why did I think this was a good idea? Now I want to be between her legs, spreading her, giving her a real reason to be screaming my name.*

I zoom through the city, the stars sparkling overhead somehow shining through the fog of the night. I zip between cars, not caring that what I'm doing is illegal and dangerous, as I hug the middle line to speed between two cars. One guy flips me off as I drive by.

I always drive fast, but I haven't felt this good on my motorcycle. I like teasing women on my bike, but this is different. More than I expected.

We reach our destination too fast, and I slow down, parking it on the side of the road in an actual parking slot this time.

Mila lets go of my waist, and I hear her removing her helmet as I do the same. Then, I turn and stare at her with disbelief.

"What was that?"

"Huh?"

"I thought you said you hated motorcycles."

"No, I said I shouldn't ride them because they are dangerous for me."

"Meaning?"

"I like them too much. The only dangerous things are those that we love. Even if motorcycles weren't inherently dangerous, it wouldn't matter, because I love them. Loving something is the only danger."

I nod, agreeing with her completely. "So you want me to pick you up in this again tomorrow?"

"I'm pleading the fifth." She smiles and tucks a loose strand of hair behind her ear. *That's a hell yes.*

"Where are we going to eat?" She searches the restaurants around us. "Ooh, are we going to that one?" She points at a restaurant on the third floor overlooking much of the city across the way.

"No."

"Where are we going then?"

I point in the opposite direction. A tiny little place that looks like a hole in the wall.

"Ramen? I'm going out with a millionaire, and he's taking me to get the only food I can afford on my own."

I laugh.

"Come on; it's one of my favorite restaurants in town."

"I doubt that."

I take her hand and start leading her across the street to the restaurant.

"What are you doing?" She stops dead in her tracks and stares down at our hands like she's holding onto a spider instead of my hand.

"Holding your hand. Since I've already seen you basically naked, I didn't think you would have a problem with me holding your hand."

"I have a problem."

"Noted."

I release her hand and place my hand instead on the small of her back. She shivers. "I don't need you to guide me to the restaurant. I know where we are going."

I nod. "Just trying to get you more comfortable with me."

"Why?"

I shrug. "Because I want you to like me."

She shakes her head. "That will never happen."

"We'll see."

"Knight, we weren't expecting you," the male host, Joni, says.

"That's okay; we don't mind waiting." I drop my hand from Mila's back and immediately notice her squirm. She can pretend all she wants that she doesn't want me to touch her, but I know better. I know she wants me to touch her, hold her, even kiss her again.

Mila glances around at all the people waiting for a table.

"It must be at least an hour wait."

"Two hours, actually, but we will move you to the front of the line. Just don't tell anyone," Joni smiles at Mila and winks. If I were on a normal date, I would pull her to me in a protective manner. I would let this asshole know that Mila's mine. It takes everything in me to resist the urge to touch her.

She shivers again and looks up at me with her big eyes.

"You need something?" I raise an eyebrow, but my lips frown. *I can't stand this.*

"Nope."

"Right this way," Joni says, leading us to a small table toward the back.

We both take a seat, and I make sure to keep my hands to myself. I don't even pull her chair out for her.

Mila looks around the room suspiciously.

"What are you thinking?"

"That I don't know what I'm doing here."

"I told you. I need dinner, and I hate eating dinner alone. I want us to at least be civil toward each other."

"No, you want to butter me up and make me fall for you, so

when you are finally ready to ask me to do the one thing you actually hired me to do, I'll say yes, instead of calling you a bastard."

I sit back in my chair. "So sure you have me figured out, huh?"

She nods.

I don't disagree with her. She has me figured out more than she realizes. But in other ways, she doesn't have a clue.

We both order a stiff drink, and I know I won't be driving my motorcycle home after this.

"I think I know why you like this place. They treat you like a god here, and nicer restaurants have much higher clientele they need to take care of than a place like this. You don't have to dress in a suit to go to dinner here. There is a dispensary next door for you to grab a joint from on your way home. And you don't have to spend much money on your 'dates' you bring here."

I stare at her as I take a drink, not letting her know how close or far away she is from the truth. She needs me to be a bad boy, so I will be.

"And the food is delicious; you are forgetting that part."

She rolls her eyes, not believing me.

"Tell me about yourself."

She frowns, downs her drink, flags the waiter for a second one, then responds. "No."

"You need to find a different word; you aren't allowed to tell me no."

"I will tell you *no* as often as I want."

"I will dock a thousand dollars from your pay every time you tell me no."

"Asshole."

"Somehow, you don't seem to have a problem using curse words anymore."

"You bring out the best in me. Am I not allowed to call you an asshole either, without you docking my pay?"

"No, call me whatever you want."

She rolls her eyes. "I have two siblings, both older. My sister is a pediatrician in Aspen. My brother is a lawyer in Cincinnati. My parents died when I was in high school, a freak accident."

"I'm sorry." *She doesn't know how sorry I am, but no words will make the pain go away, so I keep silent.*

She stares into space like she is reliving something, something dark I can't see. She quickly comes back to reality though.

"I bounced around to various community colleges and jobs until I got a full scholarship to CU Denver. I'm not as smart as either of my siblings, so I thought I would go for a less challenging degree, nursing. I was supposed to graduate this winter, until you happened. And now here I am, what about you?"

I stare.

"You seriously aren't going to answer after you demanded I answer? I don't think that's fair."

"Get used to things not being fair."

She glares at me, and I don't know whether to keep holding back to keep getting that adorable glare or start talking to get her to pout again.

"I don't have any siblings. My parents are very much alive last I checked, although I haven't talked to them since I was five. I lived with my uncle until I turned eighteen, and then he kicked me out of the house."

"I'm sorry."

"Don't be. I was a terror or a 'bad boy' as you would say. I was always in trouble. I spent high school drinking, smoking, and fucking."

Her lips twitch as I speak. *Jealousy perhaps?*

"I got accepted into Harvard. I was going to go. Get a law degree and stick it to my parents, but then I met Abri."

Her auburn hair and brown eyes float through my head. I hate thinking about her.

"We decided to take a year off before starting college. Go travel the world. We ended up eloping and started a million dollar company instead."

Her mouth drops. "You never went to college?"

"Nope."

"You got married at eighteen?"

"Nineteen."

"And you are a millionaire?"

I nod. "You already knew that."

She swallows. "I guess I did, but I'm still not sure I believe it."

"You will when the money hits your bank account."

"I'll know that you have $250,000 to spare, not that you are a millionaire."

Two bowls are placed in front of us.

She stares wide-eyed at the glorious bowls that look nothing like the ramen you get out of the little packets.

"Wait a second." I pull out my phone and get ready to take a picture.

"What are you doing?"

"Proving you wrong. Take a bite."

She gently takes the spoon in her hand and dips it into some of the broth, slowly lifting it to her lips like she thinks this might be a trap. She drinks the liquid and then smiles contently as she moans.

I snap a picture of her face. *Blissful.*

I hold out the phone to her.

She blushes.

"Fuck you, Knight."

I cock my head, not sure why she's cursing at me.

A tiny smile forms and she tries to hold it back. "This is the most delicious thing I've ever tasted."

I grin. "I know."

She looks to either side of her bowl. "How do I eat the noodles? There's no fork."

I grab two sets of chopsticks from the container at the end of the table and hold one out to her.

She eyes them like it's a snake about to bite her but hesitantly takes them.

"Do you know how to use chopsticks?"

She carefully breaks them apart and then attempts to position them in her hand, but instead of holding them correctly she holds it like a knife. She tries to stab the noodles with them.

I laugh.

"Fine, I have no idea how to use chopsticks. I have never been to a restaurant that uses them."

I position them in my hand. "Like this."

She studies my hand, trying to mimic the position of my hand. She dips her chopsticks into the ramen bowl, scoops up some noodles, and they immediately fall back into the bowl.

She growls.

I laugh before lifting some of my noodles into my mouth.

She stares at me with a gaping mouth, watching me slowly slurp the delicious noodles. I purr quietly, reminding her of just how good the food is.

"You're an ass."

I shrug and keep eating.

She licks her lips and then scoops more of the broth into her mouth. If she keeps doing that she won't have any left to eat her noodles with.

"Fine." She slams her spoon down.

"Yes, princess?"

She glares. "Will you please help me?"

"Of course, pretty girl."

I reach across the table touching her hand lightly so that I can see the goosebumps on her arms. And then, I move her top chopstick slightly in her hand.

"That's it?"

I nod. "Try now."

She clasps a noodle and brings it to her mouth. She chews the noodle slowly with her eyes closed. When she swallows, she opens her eyes.

"I've changed my mind. Knight, you have just become my favorite person in the world."

I chuckle. "I'm sure you'll change your mind again soon enough. But I'll take the compliment for now."

We both eat more of the ramen, slowly enjoying the best food in Denver.

"Tell me something no one else knows," Mila begs suddenly.

I think for a moment, trying to come up with something good.

"I pretend to hate my parents for leaving me, but I secretly wish they would come back every damn day. Even though I'm a grown man now, I still wish they would come back and be my parents."

Noodles fall out of her gaping mouth.

"I also have only ever loved one woman. Only had one serious girlfriend who turned into my wife. One love and now I think love is overrated."

She drops her chopsticks. She's going to regret that because she's not going to remember how to hold them correctly when she picks them back up again.

"Oh, and I've never been to a concert before."

"You've never been to a concert before?"

"Nope, I've listened to bands play in bars, but never bought a ticket and gone to an actual concert before."

"Why not?"

"Because I'm afraid I'll leave disappointed when I realize the band isn't as good as they are on the radio. That they are just normal guys playing instruments, and the only reason their voice sounds like that is autotune."

She frowns. "I'm taking you to a concert."

"What about you? Tell me something no one knows about you."

Her eyes sear into mine. "My favorite movie is 10 Things I Hate About You, my favorite musician is Taylor Swift, and my favorite food is tacos."

"Really? I poured my soul out, and you tell me your favorite food is tacos? That's not telling me something no one else knows."

She wipes her mouth on a napkin, her eyes not meeting mine. "Yes, it is."

I tilt her chin to look at me. "No, it's not."

She sighs. "I don't have many friends. My roommate is all I have, and we don't have time to talk about our favorite anythings because we are always working and trying to scrape by with enough money to even feed ourselves. And my family…"

"What?"

"Well, they hate me."

I narrow my eyes not understanding. "Your family can't hate you."

"They do. They put up with me, but they don't like me. They only care about making sure I don't put our name back in the newspaper again. They don't care what I like."

Our waiter returns, and I hold out my credit card, unable to take my eyes off Mila. I don't know what happened to her. I don't know what pain she's felt, but from the look in her eyes, it rivals my own.

She thinks we are polar opposites, but I think we are exactly the same.

I hold up my bowl and motion for her to do the same. Both bowls contain a few remnants of broth. We clink our bowls together and then drink until it's gone.

We both smile at each other when we are finished. I no longer hear the music playing in the background, I no longer feel the heat of the other people in the room, I no longer smell the soup. All my senses feel is her.

The connection I feel to her is instant. And I regret saying I won't fuck her. Because right now it's all I can think about.

I hold my hand out to her, sure she's going to brush me off and say she can walk without holding my hand, but to my surprise, she takes it.

I pull her to her feet and lead her out through the restaurant. The cool evening air hits us as we both reach outside, and I breathe in sharply like I haven't taken a breath in hours.

She leans into my chest as I jerk her closer, needing to feel her body against mine until our lips are inches apart.

Her eyes are doe-eyed, her mouth parted, and her tongue traces around her lips. Kiss me, she begs with her body.

I step back. *I can't. I will ruin her and any chance of her helping me.*

"Ever smoked a joint before, pretty girl?"

"No."

"Good, I want to be your first."

She gasps at the words I whispered in her ears.

I grin. *Damn, I'm not going to be able to resist her.* I thought I could, at least until I got what I needed from her. But my smart-mouthed girl won't open up easily. I need more time with her. Time without fucking her. But my dick disagrees.

Maybe my plan can work if I fuck her once? Maybe my plan can work even if she hates me?

8 MILA

I hold his hand in the backseat of an Uber like we are sixteen and being driven by our parents. Neither of us makes a move, but I know it's only because we have an audience. I know the second we are in his apartment we will be humping each other against a wall.

Knight is a bad boy, just like I always knew, but he's also incredibly broken. More than I realized. He thinks he's opening up to me, and being honest about his past, but he's not. It shows me that he's hiding more.

I know because I'm hiding plenty, even from myself.

The Uber stops, and Knight kisses my hand. *Yep, we are definitely fucking if I agree to go up. And I'm definitely staying at his place because I don't have any other place to stay unless you count sleeping in my car. That's the only reason I'm going up,* I tell myself the lie over and over. *Not because I want to fuck him.*

We step out into the night and walk into his building holding hands. We enter the elevator our fingers still intertwined. I expect him to kiss me. I expect fire and his hands to grab my hips and push me against the wall. I expect to be panting and begging to come within seconds of entering the lift.

Instead, nothing happens. Sure, the electricity continues to pass back and forth between us where our hands touch. And yes, I have butterflies swarming in my stomach. And my panties are wet from the dirty looks he keeps giving me. But other than holding my hand, Knight doesn't touch me.

The doors open and he pulls me into his apartment.

"Of course you have an apartment on the top floor. Can you be any more predictable?" I tease.

He shrugs. "Would you prefer I have a loft on the second floor?"

He opens the door, holding it open for me as I step inside. *No, I want him to have this apartment and let me have my own room here. Because damn.*

"That's what I thought," he smugly whispers behind me.

I don't even care. I'm afraid to step further inside for fear I will break something, and I know I can't afford to fix a lamp let alone replace any of the furniture if I accidentally spilled a drop of wine.

He places his hand on my lower back and leads me around. To the living room, dining room, kitchen, piano room, five bathrooms, and four bedrooms. *He has room for a fucking piano! That's crazy!*

"Do you play?" I ask, suddenly wanting to hear him play me something.

"No."

"Then, why do you have it?"

He shrugs. "Doesn't every fancy apartment have a room just for a piano? What else would I put in here?"

"A bar, a pool table, a man cave, I don't know. Normal guy stuff that you would actually use."

He blinks but doesn't say anything.

"Oh...sorry." I realize my mistake when I see the pink throw pillows on the couch next to the piano. This is the place him and Abri shared. I suddenly like it a lot less.

"Why haven't you re-decorated, if you hate her so much?"

He shrugs.

I'm getting tired of his shrugs.

"Knight?" I press again.

"I don't know. It doesn't bother me. I'm used to it the way it is. I'll change it when the divorce is final."

I frown. *Does he think there is a chance that they will work things out and she'll come back?*

I don't want to know the answer to that question.

"So that's it," he says leading me back to the kitchen where he starts pouring us drinks. Except he hasn't shown me the whole apartment. He never showed me his bedroom. I consider asking him to show me, but maybe he thinks we'll end up there in a few minutes anyway.

Knight pours himself a whiskey and me a vodka with a splash of lime.

"Let's go out on the patio."

I nod and follow him outside onto the patio. He takes a seat in the single chair while I sit on the couch. He hands me my drink, and I make sure to let our fingers brush together as I take the glass from him.

Knight frowns, seemingly displeased with the touch. *Maybe because he wants more? But why would he sit by himself instead of the couch if that is what he wanted?*

He pulls out the joint he bought before coming home and lights it. He takes a hit and passes it to me.

I take it from him looking at it curiously. Trying my best to seem like this is my first time smoking a joint. I try to fumble with it and cough as I take the hit, but it's like home in my mouth.

He eyes me suspiciously. "You've smoked before."

"What? No, I uh—"

"You've smoked a joint before."

I blush. "Yes, how did you know?"

"I didn't, you just confirmed. After watching you with the chopsticks, I can tell when you are trying something new and when you aren't."

I avert my eyes, trying to think of what to say. I don't want to tell him about my past. That's not what tonight is about.

He doesn't ask though. Instead, he takes another puff before passing it back to me. We continue like this, alternating between smoking and drinking.

I spent my high school years smoking, drinking, and fucking, his words play in my head. We've done two of the three. Now it's time for the last one.

Knight doesn't realize everything he is doing is turning me on more and more. I may know a good guy in a suit with a fancy job is better for me, but deep down I only like fucking bad boys like him. And I'm growing impatient and more attracted to him by the second.

I set my drink down on the glass table slowly, careful not to break the table or the glass.

Knight chuckles.

"What?"

He shakes his head, still smiling at me.

I don't know what he's laughing at. I'm not too drunk; I'm just being careful. Then I spot the joint. *Oh yea, the weed. I'm being paranoid.*

I stand up and remove my jacket revealing my lace bra again. I should have worn a shirt underneath the jacket, but I didn't have a nice shirt to wear, and I couldn't afford to buy anything. *It makes the outfit sexier,* I remind myself.

I step between Knight's legs, pushing them apart to fit my slim frame.

He eyes me, still holding his glass in his hand as he stares. He doesn't have to say anything. I know from his low growl, from his intense eyes, from his thinned lips that he wants me.

I grab the hem of his shirt again, pulling it off carefully so as not to spill his drink. Revealing the abs, scars, and tattoos again. I haven't had time to study the ones on his chest, so I take my time doing that now. I kneel in front of him and begin kissing his stomach.

His eyes burn into me, but still, no words leave his mouth. I kiss the first ripple, then the next, then the next. I make it to his chest and kiss the Chinese words, the dragon, the bottle of whiskey, the swirling lines, and then I stop.

The letters A-B-R-I are across his heart.

My eyes swell looking up at him. He loved her. He still loves her. *What the hell am I doing?*

He grabs my wrist and pulls me up.

"Stop."

I bite my lip. I don't have to ask what he means. *Stop thinking that he still loves her.*

He puts his drink down and pulls me to his lap until I'm straddling him. Our breaths come hard and fast, and our eyes lock together in a dance, trying to decide who is going to make the first move.

We both kiss at the same time. I moan as he nibbles on my bottom lip. Then he sweeps his tongue into my mouth. I open, letting him in. I might never let him into my heart, but I will let him into my body anytime.

This kiss is hard, full of a passion and desperation that wasn't there the first time we kissed. This kiss is rough, primal, exactly what I would expect from a bad boy who knows his way around a bedroom.

I grasp at his chest as he grabs my waist, not letting the kiss end. One kiss rolls into the next, then the next, then the next. Our moans bounce off each other in one endless sound. Our tongues find the innermost part of each of our mouths.

I've never been kissed like this. Not like I'm wanted. Not like I'm the only person in his universe.

"Just one taste," he mumbles under his breath.

"Wha—" I gasp as he pushes my bra aside freeing one of my breasts so he can take my nipple in his mouth. He nips at it gently before lapping his tongue over it. Teasing and taunting the hardened point.

"Yes, Knight."

He doesn't stop. He gives me more than a taste of what his tongue is capable of. *Yes, yes, yes.* It's been forever since I've had a man that knows what he's doing with a woman's body.

He grabs my legs and lifts me up as he attacks my other breast. My head falls back as he carries me inside.

I attack his mouth, his rough stubble brushing against my cheek with each kiss. *More, more, more.*

I grab his thick hair, keeping his mouth on me even as we ascend stairs.

Wait...stairs? I don't remember climbing stairs on our previous tour of the house.

He smirks against my lips. "I have my own, private staircase to my bedroom."

"Oh."

He pulls on my bottom lip, sucking it into his mouth and nipping roughly.

I growl, it only makes him suck more forcefully.

Knight pushes the door open, and I want to scan the room. I want to know everything about him. What makes him tick. What secret he's hiding. Maybe there is some clue in his most personal of spaces.

But I can't let go of him. I can't stop kissing him. I can't stop staring into his deep eyes or smelling his manly cologne long enough to care what his room looks like. It could be covered in dirty clothes, the sheets unwashed, with an odor of a pig and I wouldn't care. I want Knight too much to let anything stop this from happening.

Knight's eyes leave mine long enough to spot his bed behind me. *Yes, bed!*

He tosses me onto the warm sheets that have clearly been washed; the fresh linen smell trickling up to my nose. I hold onto his neck as he tumbles on top of me.

"Umpf," he moans.

I laugh. "Not expecting that, huh?" I like it rough when I'm not in a relationship and whatever Knight and I are doing is not a relationship.

How can we have a relationship when all we've done is lie and hide things from each other? We can't. But we can have hot sex while we 'work' together. That is something we should do a lot of from the way his thick length is pushing into my stomach. I can already tell how impressive he is and he hasn't even undressed yet.

Knight grabs my wrists and pushes them to the bed over my head. He wants rough too. There won't be anything sweet about this.

His eyes scan mine, searching to see if I want this. I purr and let my eyes turn to red-hot slits, begging to be fucked.

"I want this," I whisper.

He closes my eyes with a hand, and I can't help but get the feeling that he's shutting me out.

"Go to sleep, Mila." He used my name. He only does that when he's being serious and not teasing.

"What?" I try to sit up, but he continues to hold me down, his body pressing over mine.

"You heard me. Sleep, Mila. I'm not going to fuck you tonight."

My eyes are wide open now.

"We have work in the morning. You need to be well rested." He slowly lets me go and stands up.

My fingers automatically go to my lips, where seconds before he was kissing, gnawing and tearing his way into me with promises of what he was going to do to my body. Now, he's telling me to sleep. *How can I sleep with him in the bed next to me?*

But he's not walking to climb in the bed. He's walking toward the door. He won't even be sleeping in the bed with me.

"It's because you still love Abri?"

Knight's eyes darken, and his body stiffens. "No. This has nothing to do with Abri."

"Then, why? Why won't you fuck me? Why won't you even sleep in the bed next to me? Your bed, by the way."

"I only fuck sober women who want me and aren't using me to deal with their own problems."

I feel like he slapped me. He was the one who started us down this path, not me. I hate him. I won't ever fuck him.

Knight walks to the door, lingering in the doorway. "Sleep Mila, or tomorrow you'll hate me even more."

9 MILA

Buzz, buzz, buzz—

What the hell?

My eyes shoot open as the most annoying sound in the world hits my head. It feels like someone is repeatedly pounding on my head.

I roll over, find the obnoxious alarm clock and hit it off. *Sleep, I need sleep.*

I roll over, closing my eyes only for the alarm to sound again.

I slam it off again, and that's when I notice the note lying on the nightstand.

BE ready to leave at seven. Your day will usually start earlier, but I let you sleep in today because I'm nice. I'll meet you at the office. My driver will be downstairs waiting.

—Knight

SEVEN IS SLEEPING IN? What kind of crazy man thinks that? I sit up before I realize the room is spinning. And my stomach...

I run to the bathroom as the contents of my stomach come up. I spend the next five minutes heaving over Knight's toilet.

What would he think if I called in sick on my first day? I don't even have his number to call in sick though. I'm sure his driver would though.

I wash my face in his sink surrounded by granite counter tops and a mirror five people could easily use to get ready at the same time. And then I walk to the bedroom and find my phone to read the time. Five 'til seven.

Shit.

I race through the room, searching for any clothes I can change into. I find nothing but men's suits. He kept the pictures of Abri but got rid of her clothes, terrific.

I pull open a drawer and smile when I see women's jeans, but when I pull them out I know I would never fit into them. They are tiny. And I don't even know what I'm supposed to wear to this job. All I know is Knight owns a strip club, and I'll be his assistant. I assume it doesn't matter what I wear.

But I don't have time to stop by my car I parked just off campus to change my clothes, and there is nothing here for me to wear other than my clothes from last night. I pull on the jacket and skirt and stare at the wrinkles in the mirror. I look like I was just fucked. And I was, only not in the way I wanted.

I run my fingers through my hair and then tie my hair up in a high ponytail before slipping my heels on and racing downstairs.

I walk out into the crisp morning air. "Hello, Miss Burns."

I stare up at a man in a suit standing outside of a blacked out Audi sedan.

Knight really meant driver, not Uber.

"I picked up a coffee and a bagel for you. It's in the back, but if you'd prefer tea or—"

"Coffee is great. Thank you…"

"Gallagher."

"Thank you, Gallagher."

I climb into the back seat of the luxurious car and spot the coffee and bagel. I sip the coffee, and although I'm going to have to suffer through my massive headache all day, the coffee helps.

Gallagher begins driving in the front seat, singing along quietly to the music.

"Where are we headed? Are we going to the strip club again?"

Gallagher chuckles, raising an eyebrow.

"Oh sorry, I meant gentleman's club."

He shakes his head. "Why would we go there?"

"Because Knight owns it. He said I would be his assistant for the next couple of months. Does he have separate offices away from the club?"

Gallagher smiles gently. "Something like that."

That's rather vague.

"Tell me about Knight. Is he a good boss?"

He nods. "He compensates me very well."

Vague again.

"Did you ever drive him and Abri?"

Gallagher stills, but nods.

Does he still love her? Is that what he's hiding from me? I don't ask my questions though. It's clear Gallagher won't answer me anyway.

I eat my bagel, trying to anticipate what is going to happen when I arrive, but I have no idea what to expect. If I weren't desperate for the money, I would have quit after last night. I need to talk to him about a payment schedule or getting an advance so I can find a place to live instead of sleeping in his bedroom or in my car. I need to formulate a plan like I always do for the rest of my life.

Gallagher stops the car in front of a high rise. Before I can open the door, he has it opened for me. No one has ever opened a door for me. Not even past boyfriends.

"Thank you."

He smiles and holds out his hand to help me out. I grip his hand as I stumble out, still clutching my coffee in my other hand. I'm going to need more when I get inside.

"Here's your security badge, Miss Burns. Mr. Knight's offices are on the top floor. He's waiting for you."

I nod and take a step forward, feeling like Bambi learning to walk for the first time.

"Would you like me to accompany you up, Miss Burns?"

I smile and take a deep breath to compose myself. "No, I got it. Thank you though."

"Of course, Miss Burns."

"Gallagher, will you be driving me every morning?"

He nods. "Most likely. I usually drive Mr. Knight, but he has made you my assignment for the foreseeable future."

"Then please call me Mila."

"Mila, I would suggest you hurry inside. Knight isn't a patient man."

He drops the mister from in front of Knight's name as well, and I start to think the 'mister and miss' was just an act Knight requested him to do, and not how he usually behaves.

I know I should hurry inside, but after what Knight pulled last night I don't care. He's an ass. I don't care how much money he is paying me. He can wait.

I walk inside, flashing my card to the security guard. I wait at the elevators with a dozen other people all sipping their coffees in their expensive suits and heels.

I glance down at my wrinkled mess of clothes. I thought I looked okay for going to a strip club, where I expected it to be mostly empty. This place isn't empty. It's full of sharp looking business people.

I swallow hard and stare at the doors, begging them to open so I can get this hell of a day over with. The doors open, and we all cram inside. I can't even see the buttons to tell if my floor is pressed or not. It takes forever to climb the more than twenty stories as the elevators stop on almost every level to let people on and off. But finally, it's just a woman left and me.

"First day?" she asks.

I nod.

The doors open, and she smiles knowingly. "Good luck, working for Knight is a tough job. You're going to need a tough skin to survive here."

I blink, not understanding. *How did she know I was working for Knight?*

"Good morning, Mila," Cole says when I step off.

I smile. "I didn't expect to see you here. Do you work with Knight?"

"Something like that."

Ugh, again with the vagueness.

"I thought I'd show you to your office and get you set up. Knight is currently in a meeting."

Cole's eyes rake up and down my body. "I'm glad you and Knight seem to be getting along."

I frown, realizing now why Knight ensured I would show up in this outfit. To make Cole think Knight fucked me. *Bastard.* Knight wants to claim me without really claiming me.

"I still can't believe you and Knight get along well enough to work together."

"We get along better than that. We are best friends."

I stop, not believing him. "What?" I snap.

"I've known him since high school. He's my best friend. I would die for him."

I doubt that. I follow Cole and watch as he limps. Scars still cover his arms and face. Knight has healed faster than Cole.

"Here's your office," Cole says holding a door open to a small room.

A door! I've never had an office before. Most people here don't have an office; they have cubicles.

"Why do I get an office? I figured I'd be stuck in a cubicle somewhere. I'm only Knight's assistant."

Cole bites his lip like he wants to say more, but can't.

I step inside and run my hand over the bookshelf covered with books. Over the white desk that looks like it was designed for a

woman. I look out the large windows that have a view of the mountains. I could work here forever. I'm not even sure I want to be a
nurse again if the pay is this good and I get a view like this.

"So what is the name of this company? What does it do?"

Cole eyes me like he can't believe Knight hasn't told me already.
We were a little busy not fucking.

I sit behind the desk and drink the last drop of coffee. Cole walks
over to where a coffee maker sits in the corner of my office. He pours
me a fresh cup and hands it to me. "You have your own coffee maker
so you can make coffee at any time, but there is also a coffee shop two
floors down that your employee card will get you access to for free
coffee."

I sip the coffee that tastes even better than the cup Gallagher got
me. I don't think I'll ever need to leave this office.

"The company is called Perfect Match. We help match
people up."

"Doesn't that already exist? Tinder, Match, Ok Cupid?"

Cole frowns. "Yes, those exist, but that isn't the goal of Perfect
Match. We're not just a dating site, although some of the users are on
the app to find dates. Most people are looking for more than dates.
They are looking for companionship. They are looking for people to
go to baseball games, people to share a room, people to start a
company, travel the world or work on saving elephants. You get the
idea. The app has you answer questions about your life, and then it
matches you to people it thinks you need in your life. You may not
even realize you care about saving the elephants, but the app will
realize you do and match you with a similar person who also cares
about elephants so you can go save the world."

"Huh, I've never heard of it."

"Not surprising since it looks like your phone barely functions as
is." He glances at the phone on my desk.

I grab it and throw it in the top drawer of my desk.

"So what does Knight do here?"

Cole's lips curl up. "Knight—"

"Needs you in his office," Knight says standing in the doorway.

I stand nervously looking Knight up and down. He's wearing a suit that fits like a second skin to his muscles and is far more expensive than the suit Cole is wearing from the look of it. Knight's suit is tailored to fit him, while Cole's is nice, but doesn't fit quite as well.

"I'll let you two talk. It appears you have a lot to talk about," Cole says turning to walk out. "If I could be a fly on the wall," he mumbles and then disappears.

"My office. Now."

I jump to my feet at his harsh words and then chase him the two feet to his neighboring office.

He takes a seat at his sizable black desk.

"Shut the door."

I jump again but shut the door behind me. I'm taken aback by his voice and his outfit. I'm baffled. If I were to look at him now, I'd say he is the opposite of a bad boy.

"I need you to move my nine o'clock meeting with Jacob to ten. I don't care what he says, make sure it's ten. I need you to schedule a meeting with Catherine Scully for one this afternoon. Check over the rest of my schedule and confirm with my driver we can travel to the one o'clock meeting in time. I need you to drop off my dry cleaning at the building on Anaheim and have it picked up by seven tonight. Order lunch to be delivered from Tony's at one sharp."

"I thought you had a meeting at one."

Knight smirks. "You are listening. It didn't appear that you were since you aren't writing anything I'm saying down."

I blink. "I have a perfect memory."

"I doubt that."

I sigh. "Nine o'clock with Jacob move to ten, no matter what. Meeting with Catherine Scully for one this afternoon. Confirm schedule with Gallagher. Drop off dry cleaning on Anaheim and make sure it's ready by seven. Lunch from Tony's at one although you have a meeting then so I'm not sure if it's a lunch meeting or a mistake."

He smiles. "I knew I chose well."

I nod. "I didn't realize you were serious in needing an assistant. Who was your assistant before?"

He doesn't answer. *Another secret.*

"The lunch order isn't a mistake. I will eat while he talks."

I nod.

"Shall I continue?"

I sigh as he continues spouting about meetings, emails, and errands he needs me to run. I'm barely listening. He frowns the whole time, assuming I'm not listening. But if I hear it, I won't forget it. It's a blessing and a curse. Every time he thinks I'm not listening to him, I repeat the last few sentences, and he growls before continuing.

That's when I spot it. His nameplate. Ace Knight, Founder and CEO.

Holy shit!

"Wait, you own Perfect Match?"

Knight stands up and walks around to the front of his desk.

"Yes."

My mouth gapes open. "Do you own the strip club?"

"No, Cole does. I'm a minor investor, mainly because I'm his friend, nothing more."

"You own Perfect Match, not a strip club?"

He nods again.

I cock my head to the side like I'm seeing him for the first time. *Maybe I am? How could I have gotten the men so wrong?*

"You're still an asshole." I cross my arms and stomp my foot to accent my point.

"You still have a smart mouth."

I glare. "When do I get paid? I don't have any money to afford rent. Can I get an advance?"

"Add meeting with HR to your agenda today. I'll cover your living expenses while you are working here, and I'll make sure you get an advance on your paycheck. You will get your checks in regular increments until you are finished, with a bonus in the end." *When he asks me to do the thing that will cause me to hate him, and possibly myself.*

I nod.

"You're dismissed, Mila."

I bite my lip to hold my tongue. I want him to use a nickname. I don't like him calling me Mila. It's like he's scolding a child.

I turn and walk out of his office and return to mine. I won't think about Knight. He's a dick. I don't think about figuring out whatever task he really hired me for either. I have a job that is going to pay me six figures in less than six months. I have a job that will keep my mind occupied and ensure I never have to worry about money again when I get back to finishing my nursing degree.

Just as I open the shiny laptop on my desk, the phone on my desk rings.

I hesitantly pick up, "Hello?"

"That's not how you answer your phone. You are the voice of Perfect Match. The first voice anyone hears when they call our offices. Try again," Knight snaps.

I sigh. "Hello, you've reached Perfect Match, Mila Burns speaking. How can I help you?"

"Better, but don't speak like you are having phone sex."

"I don't talk like—"

"I have more tasks for you."

Shit. I listen as he rambles a dozen more tasks. I don't know what my hours are, but there is no way I will get all of this finished by seven when I'm supposed to pick up his dry cleaning and when I assumed our day would be done. I'll be lucky to get everything done in time to sleep at all tonight.

※

I HATE Knight more than I thought was possible.

He's yelled at me more today than I've ever been yelled at before. And my siblings like to chastise me, a lot.

I got yelled at when his lunch was two minutes late. I got yelled at when Jacob didn't show up for his meeting. I got yelled at when I took a pee break and missed Odette's call. I'm beginning to think whoever had my job before me didn't last long. I don't care how much it pays; if I weren't desperate, I would have quit already.

And more than anything, I've realized Knight has a split personality. I think I prefer when he wears the tattoos and biker outfit. That version of him isn't dangerous. He's nice, kind even, compared to the jerk in a suit sitting in his office.

"How are you holding up?" Cole flashes me a knowing grin as he steps into my office without knocking.

I smile, happy he's not Knight. I'm not sure I can handle another demand from him. If he asks me to do one more thing for him, I'm likely to quit.

I bite my lip when Cole approaches me. It's hard not to show my appreciation for the man that looks like dessert in a suit. Although I no longer want Cole, I can still appreciate his charming smile, his tight ass, and the warmth he brings with him when he enters a room.

My phone rings and I pick it up and slam it back down without answering, already knowing it's Knight. If he wants to talk to me, he can get off his ass and come to my office to have the conversation face to face. I won't deal with his scolding over the phone.

"That bad, huh?"

The phone rings again, and I again pick it up and slam it down.

I shrug. "It could be worse I guess. I could be working as a stripper in your club."

Cole walks behind my desk, and I turn in my comfy executive chair to face him. Cole's eyes drop to me, and he turns me toward the desk as he steps behind me and starts massaging my shoulders.

"Mmm."

"If you worked at my club, you would be treated like royalty, not like a dog who constantly disobeys."

I close my eyes and lean into his hands. I didn't realize how tense I was until Cole's hands touched me. If I'm going to survive five months at this job, I'm going to need to hire a masseuse to make it through.

"I didn't realize Knight could be more of an ass than he already was."

Cole chuckles. "He's been going easy on you. It's going to get worse from here."

I sit up, and Cole drops his hands. "What? How can it get worse?"

Cole rubs his neck like he's trying to decide what to tell me and what to keep private. "Knight is intense. He cares a lot about this business as much as he pretends not to. His first assistant was amazing. She had the same level of passion he did. He didn't have to ask her to work crazy, ridiculous hours, she just did. She was the other half of his brain. They were able to communicate without speaking. They were a perfect team."

"Why did she leave then if she was so perfect?"

Cole looks out the window instead of looking at me. "She fell in love."

I nod, realizing who he is talking about. Abri. Knight's first assistant became his wife. Then his ex. There is no way I'll be able to live up to whatever he had with her. I can't fuck him in his office when he's upset like she could.

I sigh and kick my feet up on my desk. I have five minutes until I need to leave to pick up Knight's dry cleaning.

"It will get easier. Knight will realize what he has with you. He'll realize that you are different than Abri. In a way, you are exactly what he needs right now."

"Knight told me the same thing. That I'm perfect for him. I'm exactly what he needs, but I don't understand. I'm anything but perfect, and I haven't met this Abri yet, but she sounds like his perfect match. I'm just here because Knight thinks I can help him hurt her."

Cole frowns and tugs my hand, forcing me to my feet. I sigh, silently cursing my heels as I stand up. *Tomorrow, I will not be wearing heels.*

"You're not perfect for Knight because you can help him hurt Abri, although I have no doubt that is why you are here. You are perfect for Knight because you challenge everything in his life. Abri made his life easier; you will make it harder. She fell into his lap, but he will fight for you."

I blink several times, not understanding, but then his wet lips press against mine, and I'm even more confused. I thought he was done kissing me after the last time. And as much as I might like Cole, I'm not sure I can trust him after he kisses me.

I push him off me as I hear a familiar creak in the door. Cole's hands are wrapped around my waist despite me attempting to push him off me, and Knight is standing in the doorway to my office.

Knight looks at me like he hates me. And I thought he was supposed to be making me hate him, not the other way around.

I have nothing to apologize for. I didn't kiss Cole. He kissed me. If anything, I could file sexual harassment charges against Cole. And Knight and I are nothing more than boss and employee. He made that clear last night.

"The deal is off," Knight says as he turns to leave. I'm not sure if he's talking about his deal with me or if he has a deal with Cole.

Cole chuckles. "No, it's not."

Apparently, Cole thinks Knight is talking about him. Knight stops walking and then storms back into my office, punching Cole in the face on the same spot that he punched him before. Then, he turns to me.

"Don't talk to Cole again, or you're fired."

He's gone in an instant while I'm left gasping for air.

Finally, I regain my breath and glare at Cole. "What was that for?"

"Don't worry; I didn't kiss you because I like you, although you are hot as hell. I kissed you to help you both."

I narrow my eyes not understanding.

"How the hell does kissing me and almost getting me fired help me?"

"Because it reminds you how much Knight wants you. I've never seen him punch anyone. I've kissed countless of his girlfriends and dates before. He never cared that I kissed them. He just ended the relationship. He wants you, even though he will never admit it because he has an ulterior motive. And he thinks fucking you will get in the way of that."

"Why are you telling me this?"

"Because I think him fucking you is exactly what you both need. He needs to forget about his past and find his future."

Cole adjusts his tie and touches the side of his cheek where a bruise is forming. I don't know whether to thank Cole or punch him.

So I slap him across the cheek.

"Jesus, woman. What was that for?"

I storm toward my door. "For kissing me. Don't do it again. Ever. Or I'll do a lot more than slap you."

"Fine, no more kissing."

I pause in the doorway. "And for the record, I can fight my own battles. I can decide if I want Knight to fuck me or not. Knight might need to get laid, but it's not what I need. I need the money. I need to finish my degree. Graduate and get a real job where I take care of myself. I don't need a man to help me with that."

I leave my office. My body shakes to my core. I'm furious. And turned on. Not because of Cole's lackluster kiss, but because of the look in Knight's eyes when he saw what happened. I'm a fucking mess, and all I've done is kiss Knight.

I meant everything I said to Cole. I can't fuck Knight. I'm here to get paid and then move on with my life. That's the plan I'm sticking to. No matter how charming, or good-looking he is. No matter what naughty words are whispered in my ear. I won't give in. I've let one bad boy ruin my life before. I won't do it again.

10 KNIGHT

Why does Mila keep fucking kissing Cole?

He's not that good-looking, he has the personality of a sloth, and he's the ringleader of bad boys. The opposite of everything Mila claims to want.

I stare at my computer screen, angrily scrolling through my various emails and appointments for today. I can't work, not when I can't get the image of Mila and Cole kissing out of my head.

My door opens without a knock. I don't look up. I don't care if it's Cole or Mila coming to beg for my forgiveness. I don't want to see either of them right now.

"I updated your schedule so you can fit in the Thompson meeting tomorrow at nine between your eight-thirty and ten o'clock meetings," Mila says.

I don't look up. I'm sure my devil eyes would scare her off if she saw what was going through my head right now.

"I also want to assure you that I'm a professional. I will keep my private life private from now on. It was unacceptable what happened, and it won't happen again."

I shake my head but keep my mouth shut.

"Knight?"

I can't take it anymore. I look up and see her standing across the desk from me glowing. I haven't called her into my office for the last three hours because every time she leaves it, clearing her body from my mind takes twice as long as her voice to leave my head when I talk to her on the phone. I can't have my productivity hampered that much.

"I'm on my way to pick up your dry cleaning. Is there anything else you need before I go and then head out for the night? I talked with HR, and they said you would write me a check for my advance so I can get an apartment."

"Yes," I hiss. "There are some things I need you to do for me before you are done for the night."

She sucks in a breath but otherwise doesn't flinch.

"I need you to generate July's P&L, prepare an update for our investors, read the ten articles that were submitted to be included in the company newsletter, give me summaries of the spreadsheets Daniel sent me, find a place to host the fall party and finish answering my emails."

Her eyes get big, but she doesn't argue. She was expecting me to add more to her plate. I want to threaten her job if she so much as looks at Cole again, but I don't want to bring up my bastard of a best friend again.

"Done." Her eyes narrow and her lips thin. "My advance?"

I smirk. "I don't think you have earned your advance yet."

She raises an eyebrow. "I've worked my ass off for you today."

"Liar. You did the minimum needed. And then you kissed and would have most likely fucked, my best friend in your office. That doesn't sound like someone who is a hard worker."

She frowns.

"You're really not going to give me an advance?"

"No, but don't worry. My bedroom is yours until you get paid at the end of the month. Although, I have a strict no men allowed rule that I doubt you will be able to follow."

"Fuck you."

"I'm letting you stay in my condo for free. I think you should be thanking me."

"Thank you, Knight, for ensuring that any feelings I had developed during our drunken and high night together have completely vanished. I will work hard and earn my money. And then I'll be out of your life, forever."

"Good, you've finally learned."

She leaves without another word. *It's for the best,* I remind myself. I'd rather destroy her now than later.

"I'm leaving for the day," Cole says sticking his head into my office.

I growl. "Get the fuck out, Cole."

Cole doesn't leave. He steps inside with his smug ass expression.

"Dammit Cole!" I slam my computer down, and it breaks. "I thought you kissed her the first time to mess with me."

"I did."

"Then, what the hell was that?"

"You are holding back. You aren't going to pursue her beyond whatever stupid thing you hired her to do. I was helping."

"I don't need your fucking help, Cole. I need you to get out of my life."

"Don't worry. I'm done meddling. It's clear I'm not helping anyway."

"You were wrong. Mila likes you."

Cole laughs. "That's what you think? Mila slapped me. It stung worse than your weak ass punch too."

Mila slapped him. *Shit.* And I pushed her away even further.

"Mila wants you. Although, I'm sure you were an ass to her and now you'll be lucky if she keeps working for you."

I was, but he doesn't need to know that.

"I meant what I said about our deal. I'm selling my company to someone else. You don't deserve it."

Cole shrugs. "I have more than enough money. What are you going to do about Mila?"

"Nothing." *Not a damn thing.* I shouldn't have even hired her. She can't help me. No one can. It was a gut reaction. I thought she could help, but she can't.

Cole shakes his head. "Tell Mila now that you broke your computer and she needs to get you a new one, rather than waiting until later when the Apple store has closed." And then he's gone.

I need to lock my damn door. I get up to do just that when Abri steps inside.

"You talking to me yet, Ace?" Abri asks with a smile on her face. She brushes her hand over my chest, and it takes everything in me not to grab her wrist and throw her out of my office. But that's precisely what she wants.

"No, not after what you did."

She cocks her head to one side and twirls her auburn hair. Anyone else would think she looks like an innocent teenager, not a dangerous twenty-four-year-old.

"What did I do?" Her smile grows larger, and she bats her eyelashes like she couldn't have possibly done anything wrong.

"Nevermind," I mumble under my breath. I step back and watch as her hand falls into the space between us. I want to retreat behind my desk again, but it would be a victory for Abri. I'm not going to let her win. Even for a second.

Abri knows me too well though. She skips over to my desk and takes a seat like this is as much her office as it is mine. It was once. It's one of the many reasons I want to sell this company and start over.

"I heard you hired a new me and gave her my old office."

I clench my teeth together to keep from growling. I hate her behind my desk, and I don't want her to notice Mila. I should have never brought Mila here. I keep my expression blank and indifferent. Abri doesn't need to know Mila is a weakness.

"I did. You weren't exactly cutting it as my assistant anymore."

Abri rolls her eyes. "Partner, if I recall. My title was partner."

I shrug. "You seemed like an assistant to me."

"If the new girl isn't up to the job, all you have to do is ask me nicely, and I'll take my job back. I'll even let you call me your assistant."

I snicker. "You haven't had a hard day's work in months. I doubt you even remember how to work hard."

She tucks her hair behind her ear revealing the curve of her neck, my favorite place to kiss her. She knows it. It's why she always exposes that spot of soft skin around me. To distract me and remind me what I can never have again.

She doesn't realize the spot no longer attracts me to her. My cock no longer responds to her advances. You couldn't pay me enough money to touch her or even kiss her.

"We could try to keep it professional this time. You know I'm the best assistant you've ever had. The others haven't even lasted longer than a week."

I narrow my eyes. The others haven't lasted because of Abri, not me. She's tortured them. I'm not the best boss. I work all of my assistants hard, easily working them a hundred hours or more a week. But I pay them well, really well. When I hire them, they understand what is expected, and I know that no one will stay at a job for more than a year, two max. But none survive even a year; the money isn't enough to deal with Abri.

"Miss Burns will last longer than a week." I hate calling Mila, Miss Burns. It sounds too formal, not at all like Mila truly is.

Abri pouts and then pulls out a tube of red lipstick from her purse applying it slowly to her lips like that is going to make me want to kiss her or something.

"Are you finished? Some people have work to do."

She slowly puts the tube back into her purse. "You should get the A/C checked. It's scorching in here, Ace."

She slowly removes her jacket and hangs it on the back of my chair. My chair will smell like her Chanel No. 5 perfume the rest of the day.

Dammit.

I know she's pushing her boobs up in her lace tank top, but I don't notice. I'm tired of her damn games. She started this, but I'm going to finish it.

"I think I'm going to check in with your new assistant tomorrow. Miss Burns, is it? Show her some pointers to ensure she lasts."

"I don't care what you do as long as you get out of my damn office."

Abri licks her lips. Her last move at trying to seduce me. She forgets I'm more than aware she's a manipulative bitch.

Abri runs her hand through my hair. "I miss your long locks, Ace. You look too grown up with this haircut."

I grab her wrist this time. I can't help myself. "I'm not a teenager you can play games with anymore without consequences, Abri. If you play with fire, you are going to get burned."

"Maybe, but so far I think I'm winning. And you haven't even seen what I have planned for my grand finale yet. It's good, Ace. I would surrender now while you still have something left you love. Otherwise, I'm taking everything. You don't get to fuck with me and get away with it."

I drop her wrist. "Out."

Abri leaves without another word, but she makes sure to sway her hips in hopes I will watch her go. I watch her leave, not because she looks sexy, but because I need to make sure she's actually leaving.

I walk over to my desk, grab the jacket, and toss it in the trash. Then I text Mila to have a cleaning crew clean out my office ASAP. I don't want it smelling like Abri tomorrow. I won't get any work done.

I want to tell Abri to stay the hell away from Mila, but I can't. It will make it worse on Mila. Mila wants to fight her own battles, here's her chance. Mila can hate me all she wants, but I'm not the devil. Abri is.

11 MILA

I storm upstairs to my bedroom in Knight's apartment. He isn't home yet, but the driver gave me a key to his apartment. Well, apparently *our* apartment until I get paid. I kick my heels off revealing the blisters on my toes and then fall onto his large bed.

I've never been this exhausted before. I love working hard. I've pulled twenty-four shifts at the hospital. I thought nothing could top that, but working for Knight does. Not just physically, but emotionally and mentally. I can't keep doing this every day. No matter how much money he is paying me.

I need a bath and a change of clothes. I stand up and walk to his closet again to try and find some sweatpants or something of his I can force to fit me after my bath.

I gasp when I open the closet. My clothes are hanging neatly next to his. My duffel bag, backpack, and books that were in my car line the bottom row. *How did he find my car? Did he break into it?*

And there are more clothes in my size next to mine. Mostly work clothes it seems. Heels I will never wear line the bottom of the closet.

Who did this? It sure wasn't Knight. I've had to do everything from getting his coffee to answering his phone. I'm surprised he didn't want me to wipe his ass when he takes a shit. There is no way he did this. *How many other assistants does he have? And why does it seem he dumped the most work on me?*

Questions for later. Right now, I need a bath. I grab my sweatpants and a T-shirt and carry them to the bathroom where a large tub sits in the corner. The tub could easily fit four people, and I'm going to have it all to myself.

I turn the water on as hot as it will go and add soap so that bubbles form. Then I strip and step into the tub, and everything else disappears. I close my eyes and doze in the tub. When I'm finished, I'll order some pizza or something and then collapse in the bed. I don't have time to argue with Knight tonight. Not if I have to do this again tomorrow.

Everything melts away. The hate. The pain. The aches. The lust. All of it. I don't think about Knight. I'm lost in my own world until I take a deep breath. My stomach growls as flavors of Mexican food drift up to the bathroom.

I'm starving. I haven't eaten since breakfast, and it's almost midnight now. I couldn't afford anything in the cafe downstairs, and I didn't want to ask Knight to pay for my lunch.

Please let Knight still be at work or already in whatever bedroom he's sleeping in now. Please don't let him be downstairs.

I get dressed quickly and creep downstairs, careful of what I'm going to find.

"You like tacos, right?" Knight says smiling, pleased with himself as he sits at the bar where he has two plates of food. One sitting in front of him, the other in front of an empty chair for me.

"Good job, you remembered I like tacos," I say sarcastically as I approach the bar slowly like it's a trap.

Knight hasn't changed out of his suit. He's removed his jacket and tie, and his sleeves are rolled up. Otherwise, he still looks all business.

He pulls the chair out for me, and I take a seat. I stare down at the glorious tacos, my mouth watering.

"Eat," Knight commands.

I sigh. He likes bossing people around. We are going to have to work on that.

But I'm too hungry to fight him right now. I take a bite, and it's like heaven exploded in my mouth.

"Oh my god! This is the most delicious thing," I say with my mouth still full. I take another bite and then another.

"Did you order these from somewhere or did your cook make them?"

He raises an eyebrow. "I didn't order them, and I don't have a cook."

"Then who cooked these?"

"Me."

My mouth gapes as I stare at Knight. There is no way he made these. The tortillas are homemade, along with the green chile sauce, and the pork tastes like it's been stewing all day.

"Liar. I thought you would always be honest with me. There is no way you had time to make these. I bet you can't even cook toast without burning it."

"I don't lie. At least not to you."

I blink rapidly, not understanding. But when I examine his kitchen, I notice the dirty pots and pans stacked in his sink. I notice the spilled sauce on the counters, and when I look at his shirt, I spot the drops of grease on his shirt. He cooked this.

"Thank you."

He smirks. "Don't thank me. I would have cooked something whether you were here or not. It's my time to destress."

"You don't go to the gym for that?"

I blush when he realizes I'm talking about his hot body.

"I do, but cooking helps me wind down before I sleep."

I nod and eat more of my tacos.

"I still hate you, you know."

He stills, then nods. "I know."

"It's what you wanted though, isn't it? You want us both to hate each other."

Again, he nods.

"Well, mission accomplished. We hate each other. You don't have to worry about us developing feelings for each other."

"Good."

I wipe my mouth on the napkin next to my plate. He even remembered to give me a napkin. No other guy I've dated before would cook for me or even remember something simple like a napkin.

"But if you want me to keep working for you, which I know you do, I have some demands. I've already heard most of your assistants don't last the week."

He nods slowly.

"Then you have to treat me nicer."

"Nicer? Are you serious?"

"Yes, you can be a bit of an ass."

"I've heard." He smiles like he's proud of it.

I sigh. "Yes, if you want me to keep working for you it wouldn't hurt to say please and thank you. Or to give me all of my tasks at the beginning of the day, as opposed to throwing random tasks at me throughout the day so that I can plan. I'm a bit of a control freak and like to have my day planned in advance."

He turns and stares at me, and suddenly my heart is fluttering. "That's not what you want. You want me to go easy on you. Give you less work."

"No, I like work. I will earn the money you are paying me. Just say please and thank you."

"Fine."

"Fine?"

"I will say please and thank you."

That was too easy. Something is up with him.

"And I would like my own place."

"Then get your own place."

"I can't afford it without my first paycheck."

"I don't see how that's my problem."

I sigh. *Just take the first win for today and move on.*

We finish eating in silence although if he saw what was going on inside my body, he wouldn't be silent. Because every time he takes a bite it draws my attention to his lips, and then I want to kiss him. I shouldn't want to kiss him. He treated me like a slave today. He lectured me for a kiss that wasn't even my fault. I should hate him, but hate isn't that far away from love. They are both strong emotions that make people do stupid things.

I will not kiss him. I excuse myself quickly when I eat the last bite of my tacos and then race upstairs. I fall into his cushy bed that smells like him. Rough, manly, and bad boy.

I want to leave, but I also want to stay. His bed is incredible, better than anything I can afford. That's the only reason I want to stay, I tell myself. *That and the cooking. His scent. And the way he stares at me like I'm the most important thing in his world.*

Maybe I am? Why else would he make me my favorite food for dinner?

Because he was trying to apologize for being an ass without having to say I'm sorry. That's all. Tomorrow it will go right back to how it was before. The more we work together, the more I will hate him. Then I won't want to kiss him anymore.

I take another deep breath and get a whiff of his shampoo from his pillow. I'm just going to steal this pillow when I leave.

My phone buzzes. A message from Lana.

LANA: Are you living on the streets yet?

ME: No, I'm living like a princess in the highest tower.

LANA: Explain, NOW.

. . .

ME: Too tired. I'll call you tomorrow before work at six AM.

LANA: That's too early! Tell me now.

ME: Sleeping...

I GLANCE at my watch that says a quarter 'til seven. Knight usually gets here by seven, sometimes earlier, which is why I got here at five. He thinks I don't want to work hard. He believes I haven't earned my advance yet, but today I will prove him wrong.

The elevator doors open, and Knight steps out in a dark grey suit and piercing blue tie. I step out of my office to greet him before he enters his.

"Good morning, Knight."

He narrows his eyes at me. "Morning," he mumbles.

He opens his office door, and I follow him inside. Sitting at his desk is a large coffee and the oatmeal breakfast he requested. He takes a seat behind the desk.

"I already made sure to confirm your schedule for today, I've answered all of your emails, and made summaries of your emails and voice messages. I also wrote out some thoughts about the meeting with Gerard. He left a detailed email, and I don't think you should merge with Wayfinder. Their business is floundering and will take your company down with them."

"Thanks for your advice," he says snarkily.

"I know you are new to this, but that's not how you thank someone."

I wait for him to say something but he doesn't. So I take matters into my own hands.

"Thank you, Mila, for getting here early, making sure my coffee and breakfast were sitting here waiting for me, and going above and beyond in your work," I say in a deep voice mimicking his.

Knight doesn't even look up from his breakfast.

"You're welcome. If you have more tasks for me to complete today, please compile them and call me into your office or send me a detailed email, instead of calling me every five minutes," I say in a higher pitched voice.

I deepen my voice. "Of course, Mila. Oh, and here's your advance."

Nothing. No response.

I sigh, running my hand through my hair before shifting my weight in my heels. I wasn't going to wear heels, but I couldn't resist these sparkly Gucci heels that were in the closet. They match so perfectly with this light grey and blue dress. I've lined all of the outfits up for the next week in the order of my favorites so I ensure I can wear them all. It seems Knight and I decided to match today.

Something catches my eye, and I turn my head toward the trashcan in the corner where a woman's jacket lies on top.

What is a woman's jacket doing in the trash?

It hits me quickly. That is why Knight wanted his office cleaned last night. He fucked someone in his office and didn't want it to smell like sex this morning.

I turn to leave but stop.

"And please give me a heads up today if you are going to bring a woman into your office to fuck. My office is right next to yours. I don't want to interrupt or overhear anything accidentally."

Knight's head shoots up, and he stares at me for the first time this morning.

"What makes you think that I would fuck someone in my office?"

"Because you did last night."

He licks his lips and glances at the evidence in the trash. "I didn't fuck anyone last night."

"Liar."

He rolls his eyes. "I thought we've been through this. I won't lie to you."

"Why is there a woman's jacket in the trash? Why did I have to hire an emergency cleaning crew to come in last night?"

Knight takes a second and then slowly stands up and walks to me, but at the last second instead of touching me, he leans against his desk.

"Abri left her jacket here. She has the strongest perfume in the world. I hate it. I knew I wouldn't be able to stand to work in here this morning if the room wasn't clean."

"Oh."

"And make sure you fire the cleaning crew. They should have taken the trash out along with cleaning."

I frown and walk over to the trash can to throw out the trash. I snatch the bag containing the jacket up and begin to storm out, but Knight blocks my path.

He steals my breath with just a look. And I hate myself for letting him affect me so.

"And just so you know, Mila. I don't plan on fucking anyone in my office. Not unless you are offering. Why would I want anyone but my hot, sexy assistant?"

"I'm not fucking you."

"I've already got you sleeping in my bed. You'll be begging me to fuck you by the end of the week."

"I hate you."

"I know."

He's right. If I keep letting him get to me like this, then I will do more than beg him to fuck me. I will jump him and let him fuck me here on his desk, no matter who hears.

He moves out of my way, and I storm back to my office, determined to start thinking of him as nothing more than my asshole of a boss.

MY WATCH TURNS to seven in the evening. I've finished every task Knight has given me. I might get to do something fun this evening. Something to distract me from Knight. I should text Lana and see if she wants to go to a movie or get drinks with me tonight. I have a twenty dollar bill I can blow since Knight is providing me with food and a place to live.

A knock on my door startles me.

"Dammit, Knight. I finished everything you asked me to do; I'm going out."

The door opens. "Sorry, I'm not Knight. Well, I am but not the Knight you are thinking of. I promise not to put you to work." A gorgeous woman says as she pokes her head into my office.

I open my mouth, but no words come out.

"I'm Abri Knight. I'm a partner here at Perfect Match. I thought I should introduce myself and give you some tips, so you don't get fired on your first week."

She steps inside and closes the door behind her. She's tall, slim, perfect. Her dress is tight, but not too tight for people to think of her as anything but professional. Her hair hangs in loose curls, and her makeup highlights her face instead of overwhelming it like it does when I wear makeup.

"I'm Mila Burns. I'm uh...Mr. Knight's newest assistant."

We shake hands cautiously, and it feels more like she's sizing me up rather than being friendly.

She takes a seat across from my desk without being invited to do so. I take a seat behind my desk.

"How has your first couple days been?"

"Um..."

"That bad, huh?" She smiles. "Don't worry; I wanted to quit my first week too. Ace can be intense, but he seems to like you. So maybe he'll go easy on you and keep you around."

I shake my head. "Knight... I mean, Mr. Knight doesn't like me. He just thinks I will be good at this job."

She studies me carefully. "Anyway, I know it's only your second day here, so I'm sure you still have lots of work to finish, but I wanted to see if you wanted to take a break."

"Actually, I've finished for the day unless Mr. Knight adds any more tasks."

"You are the best assistant he's hired, then. Well, since me." She smiles. "You want to go work out with me then?"

"Um...I was going to go meet a friend for a drink."

"We can do that afterward. Earn our drinks." Damn Abri and her perfect fit body and tight ass. My rail-thin frame with no muscles can't compete with hers. I'm a stick; she's a goddess.

"I don't think—"

"I won't take no for an answer. Besides you may need me to defend you to Ace for leaving early on your second day whether you finished the work or not." She winks at me like we are best friends.

"I don't think Mr. Knight would mind."

She walks over to me and hooks her arm in mine. "He would. Trust me; you don't want to get on his bad side."

She yanks me up. Her body is much stronger than mine.

"You can call him Ace you know. He hates being called mister."

I nod. "I know, but I prefer to call him Knight. Sometimes, asshole."

She smiles at that as she drags me out of my office.

Knight's door opens like he was coming to talk to me, but stops when he sees us together.

"Oh Ace, you won't mind if I steal your assistant away. She finished all her work for the day."

Knight's face tenses, his jaw thins, and I know he wants to tell her no.

"It's up to Mila, what she wants to do."

I look at him, but he isn't looking at me, he's looking at Abri. I can't find any sign if he wants me to get close to Abri or not. I don't want to go with Abri, but if I go with her, I might be able to learn more about Knight. Why they broke up and what he has planned for me to do to help him.

"Do you have anything else you need from me? If not, I'd like to go with Abri."

Knight's jaw twinges.

"Yay, I'm so excited to have a new friend," Abri exclaims, not giving Knight a chance to answer as she drags me toward the elevators. I don't look back at Knight. I know that scowl on his face and the pain in his eyes. He doesn't want me to go. But I need to figure out why.

⚬

I REGRET MY DECISION IMMEDIATELY. "I thought you said we were going to the gym, Abri."

"No, I said we were going to work out. What fun is going to the gym?"

"Um, it's safe and air-conditioned."

"Where is your sense of adventure? Nothing fun will ever happen to you running on a treadmill."

She opens the back of her jeep, one of the last cars this well-dressed woman should be driving. She changed into a sports bra and leggings, while I'm wearing a T-shirt with the arms cut out and shorts. I'm not prepared for this.

"Grab the ropes," Abri says swinging a bag over her shoulder.

I grab the ropes and stare up at the massive mountain we are climbing. *I can't do this, but I'm not backing down.*

Abri starts setting up the equipment. And every time she opens her mouth, I think I've heard it before. I'm missing something. She's familiar, but not too familiar. I may have met her before, but only in passing. And after the entire twenty minutes I've known her, I don't know whether I like her or hate her.

"Have you climbed before?"

I frown. "No." This feels like a competition. Like I should be able to do anything she can do. Which is silly. We aren't competing for Knight. He's her ex, and I'm his assistant. We can be friends.

"No worries, this one is an easy climb. We will do it together, and Jamal and Blake will spot us."

Two men arrive as Abri says their names. Both attractive men are going to watch me fall on my face. Abri gives me a very quick tutorial about the equipment and then we are strapped in and slowly climbing up with the men spotting us from the ground.

"So how did you and Knight meet?" I ask trying to seem interested.

She smiles. "I'm not sure I can get used to hearing someone call him Knight."

"Sorry, I mean Ace."

"We met in high school. He was the popular football player. I was the prom queen, cheerleader type. We fell in love and started a company together. Next thing you know we are married and running a million dollar company together."

"That's incredible."

"It was a fairy tale come true."

"I'm sorry it didn't work out."

She pauses, and I have to move my handhold higher to get even with her again. That's when I see the tears staining her cheeks.

"I'm sorry. You two seemed perfect for each other. But sometimes, things don't work out."

Abri shakes her head and releases her hold on the rock, which completely freaks me out. Even though we are connected to ropes, I'm still petrified at any moment we are going to slam into the rocks below.

She climbs higher, not speaking to me, and I do my best to keep up, although at a slower pace. Finally, she stops again and looks at me, her eyes almost dry.

"I know I'm the ex, and you and Ace are keeping things professional, but I feel now that we are friends, I should tell you the truth. That way you can make your own decisions about Ace. I don't want you to fall for him like all the rest of his assistants and end up hurt."

I suck in a breath, not sure if I want to hear what she says. And I'm definitely sure we aren't friends.

"We were in love. We had passion. We were everything to each other. But then..."

"Abri? What happened?"

"We were too passionate about everything. The love turned to constant fighting."

I nod, understanding.

"The bickering turned to physical fighting. Ace has a temper, and he..."

More tears fall, and I need to know what happened. I need to know how he hurt her. I need to know the truth.

"Abri? Please tell me."

"He hit me. Hard across the face. And then..." Her voice trembles. "Then, he hit me until I passed out."

I gasp. I know it's not what she needs, but I can't help myself. It doesn't fit what I know about Knight. But then maybe the Knight I know and the Ace she knows aren't the same people.

I want to say I'm sorry, but my words would be empty, meaningless.

"I'm sorry," she says. "I need to go."

"What?"

She quickly descends. I stare in awe at how quickly she moved down the side of the cliff. She detaches herself from the rope and runs to her car. Both men chase after her, most likely worried and wanting to hit on her.

Shit, both men!

I look down at high up I am. I'm gripping the wall tightly. And I can't repel down like her; I have no one belaying me. I have to climb down. My legs are suddenly jello, and my hands are sweating as I try to grip the rock. I'm high enough up I'm sure if I fell I would die or at the very least break several bones.

My entire body is shaking now. I need help.

"Abri! Help!"

Nothing.

"Help! Someone, please help!"

The wind blows, and I grip the rock tighter. *That bitch.* The longer I'm up here, the more I replay the conversation in my head. Some of it might be true, all of it even. But the way she spoke, waited until we had reached the top before climbing down makes me believe she deliberately trapped me up here.

I shake my head. *Now I'm just paranoid. I can do this. I'm not that high up.*

But I try to move my foot lower, and it slips.

Shit. I can't do this. I'm going to die.

"Mila?"

I close my eyes and take a deep breath. *Knight.*

"My knight in shining armor, coming to save me again," I say nervously.

"I can leave if you prefer."

"No! I need your help."

I swear I hear him chuckle, but I don't look down to know for sure.

"I need you to let go, Mila."

"What? I'm not letting go. I'll die if I let go."

Now I know he's laughing, but it's an anxious laugh.

"Look down."

I hesitantly do and see him holding the rope.

"I got you. You aren't going to die."

"I can't let go."

"I can come up, but then no one will be belaying you. You're safer if I'm here, supporting you."

I take a deep breath. *He's right.*

"Trust me; I've got you."

His words again. *Dammit.*

I slowly let go and grab the rope as he carefully lowers me down. When I almost reach the ground, he cradles me in his arms as I start bawling.

"Shh, you're okay. I've got you. I won't let you go."

It doesn't stop my bawling.

"How did you know where to find me?"

He wipes my eyes as my tears begin to slow. "There is a reason most of my assistants quit. Abri is a bitch. You especially threaten her, so I knew she'd up her game."

"I could have died. You saved me. You're always saving me."

"No, if it weren't for me she wouldn't have pulled this crap in the first place."

"Oh my god, Mila. I didn't realize you were still up on the mountain. I'm so glad you are okay," Abri says running up behind us.

Knight's body stills, holding me tighter against him like he's a shield between Abri and me.

"Just leave, Abri."

"I need to apologize. I was just a wreck after I told her how we broke up. I thought Blake tied the rope up before he left. You were perfectly safe."

"Go, Abri."

"I need to talk to you first, Ace. We need to talk about our meeting tomorrow and—"

I can't listen to her talk one more second.

I know Knight doesn't want anything fake to happen between us. He doesn't want me to make Abri jealous, but there is nothing fake about what I do.

I grab Knight's neck and kiss him firmly on the lips, letting my tongue slip into his mouth. He tastes my desperation and terror and pulls me further in showing me how horrified he was in return at seeing me on top of a rock and unable to get down. Our hands tangle in each other's clothes, and I know this isn't going to end here. Once we get home, this is going a lot further. Neither of us will be able to stop.

Abri said passion turned to love and then hate. Our hate turned to fear and desperation.

I don't know if Knight did all of those horrible things to Abri or not. I know if I asked him, he would tell me the truth. But I can't ask. Not now. I need to find out my own truth. Ace may have treated Abri like shit, but Knight is my savior. I just hope my knight doesn't turn back into the asshole I thought he was this whole time.

12 KNIGHT

Mila's kiss knocked all of the air out of me. It took me completely off guard. It suffocated me and set me free at the same time.

I didn't think I would ever taste her again. I thought that ship had sailed after the way I treated her. I thought her hate for me was stronger than any desire she felt.

I've never been happier to be proven wrong.

"If we didn't have an audience, I would fuck you against the rocks right here," I whisper against her ear.

She blushes and bites her lip. "I have no objections."

Now I'm biting my lip, trying to hold back from fucking her into oblivion, while Abri and her boy toys watch. As much as I want to fuck Mila, I'm torn. Because I want to kill Abri just as much.

I tried to downplay how unsafe it was for Mila. Abri claimed Blake tied the rope off when he abandoned Mila, but the rope wasn't tied up. It was dangling freely in the air as Mila clutched to the face of a steep rock over a hundred feet up.

One wrong move and Mila would have fallen. To her death, most likely. Abri could have killed Mila.

I don't know if what Abri did was intentional or not, but I want to hurt Abri all the same for what she did to Mila.

I've never been so terrified. I've looked death in the face before. I've been helpless before, but this was different. Mila could have died because of me. That guilt would have never left me, and the pain of losing a woman I wanted, but who was never really mine, would have gutted me.

My body trembles, holding onto Mila, as the tears begin burning my eyes.

Mila wraps her arms tighter around my neck, and I grip her closer to my body.

"It's okay. You saved me," she whispers, but her voice is shaky.

"I'm never letting you go again."

I see the tears in her eyes again. I was strong before when she cried, but I can't be strong again. The reality of the situation has sunk in.

"Ace, I need you to talk to me," Abri pleads, trying to grab my shoulder to turn my attention to her instead of Mila.

"Fuck off, Abri," I say, carrying Mila toward my motorcycle.

I set Mila down gently on the back of my motorcycle and hand her a helmet. When she puts it on, I ensure it's fastened securely. Then I kiss the tears on her cheek, even as my own tears stream down my face.

"Take me home, Knight."

I feel a knot in my stomach and an ache in my throat as she says *home*. My place is her home. She has nothing else. No apartment, no dorm room. Only a rusted out Subaru to return to because of me.

I need to fix that, along with everything else I've fucked up in her life, but for now, I need to make her mine.

I climb on in front of her, and she wraps her hands tightly around my waist without protest. Then we are gone. I drive just fast enough to get us home quickly, but not enough to scare her. That's the last thing I want.

We ride in silence, only the wind and sound of engines purring around us to keep us company. It doesn't matter that we can't speak. Our bodies say enough.

We are broken.

We are hurting.

Only the other person can heal us.

I pull in front of my building, not caring there isn't a parking spot. I don't wait for the valet to take my motorcycle. They will get it or they won't. I have more than enough money to buy hundreds of motorcycles if I want. I don't care if this one gets stolen.

All I care about is getting Mila, naked and writhing underneath me in my bed. I take her hand, a gesture that a couple of nights ago would have scared her off, but tonight is more than welcome.

I don't know what has been going on in her head on the thirty-minute drive from the mountains to my building. I don't know if she wants me. I don't know if she wants to take a hot bath and be left alone. But I'm not sure I can leave her alone if that's what she needs. It will take everything inside of me to leave her for even a moment.

It's not about sex, although I'm desperate to be inside her. Feel her wet walls clenching around me as I make her come. Knowing that the pleasure I'm giving her helps ease the pain she's feeling. I need her close by. I need to know she's still breathing, her heart still beating. I need to protect her at all costs.

We enter the elevator with another couple. I grip her hand tighter, needing my lips on her, but afraid to scare her away. Neither of us has spoken since we got on the motorcycle.

Our eyes meet, and I see the desire mixed with the fear. I wish I could take away the fear, but I'm afraid it's going to stay with her a lot longer than the desire ever will.

Mila moves her body in front of me, she grabs both of my arms and drapes them over her shoulders. I pull her body flush against mine as she leans into my body. It's the most intimate thing we've done, and she's sat half naked on my lap and kissed my stomach. But this moment is different. She's letting me in even though she knows I can hurt her.

And I no longer want to hurt her.

The only way to not hurt her is to leave. Get out of her life. Because if I stay, she's doomed.

I'm a selfish bastard though; I can't leave.

The couple gets off, and Mila pushes her ass against my swollen cock.

"Mila," I warn. She's lighting a fire, and I won't be able to stop if she goes much further.

The elevator doors open on my floor.

"I need you, Knight. Don't hold back."

"You sure? Your smart mouth won't be able to save you once we start."

She takes my hand lifting it to her mouth and kisses the palm of my hand sweetly like the innocent girl she is. Then, she has my pointer finger in her mouth, sucking viciously, swirling her tongue over the tip.

"I'm sure."

Fuck.

I grab her hips at the same time she jumps, wrapping her thin legs around me. She's a stick. I don't know how she was able to hold onto the rock as long as she did.

I slam her body against the door of my apartment and curse as I try to dig my keys out of my pocket as her lips suck on my neck. I regret not taking up the building manager's offer to install a keyless entry for me. The key finally grants us entry before I do something stupid, like fuck her against my door.

We burst inside in a tangle of arms, legs, and nerves. I've never been so nervous and so excited at the same time.

Mila pushes my suit jacket off my shoulders before she starts on my tie, as I kiss every part of her body my lips can reach without putting her down. Her lips, cheeks, neck, and ears. I get acquainted with every part of her skin. When I kiss her neck in Abri's favorite spot making Mila purr, I don't think about Abri like I thought I might. The sounds Mila makes are more angelic than anything I've ever heard.

Mila's raspy sounds. The purring, the moaning, the growling makes my already hard cock tighten with each sound. I think I could come from her voice alone.

Mila gets my tie off and starts working on the buttons on my shirt, quickly getting frustrated by how hard it is to get the shirt off.

"Slow down, pretty girl. We've got all night."

"All night isn't enough," she whispers back.

And I know it's the truth. I can fuck her all night long. Over and over and over. It won't be enough. Not enough to heal us. Not enough to rid ourselves of the desire in our core. Simply, not enough.

But it has to be. This has to be a one-time thing. I can't ruin her.

Neither of us speaks the truth though. We both know that this *is* a one-time thing. That's why she's so desperate. That's why there is sadness in her eyes.

So I give in to her. I race upstairs to my bedroom and toss her on the bed.

"You're never going to forget this night, sweetheart."

She grins at my nickname.

"Neither are you, asshole."

I lick my lips as I rip my shirt open, not caring about the expensive buttons that will need replacing. The look on her face makes it worth it.

"It's good to know you still hate me."

I kick off my shoes and remove my pants and underwear, freeing my cock that points in her direction, leading me into a dream I never thought I'd have, knowing, in the end, it will turn into a nightmare when I have to leave her.

Her eyes sear through my body. My arms and chest, covered in tattoos, over my abs, to my straining cock.

"Yep, definitely hate you."

It's a lie. She doesn't hate me, that's the problem.

She grips the covers on my bed like she's trying to hold herself back, but it makes her look innocent. So, so innocent. An angel that isn't capable of wrong.

And I'm the devil that soon will be taking her wings.

I slowly move to the bed as her legs move wide, inviting me in. But not wide enough to fit my frame. So I push her legs open further as I kiss every inch of flesh I can find. I remove her shoes slowly along with her socks until I'm kissing her feet, then calf, then inner thigh.

She writhes against me, both wanting me to kiss her in the most intimate of places and not ready for it yet.

I grin before jumping over her shorts and moving to her stomach. I push her shirt up as I kiss her concave stomach. Even with three good meals a day, she is still too skinny. I need to feed her more. She deserves to have everything she needs and more.

Even though I can see her ribs, she's still beautiful. More than beautiful. There needs to be a new word to describe how gorgeous she is. It's not just her body that has me entranced. It's her mouth, the words that leave it. It's her mind, the way she already understands my company on her second day. It's the way she pushes me to be better.

She raises her arms, and I lift her shirt over her head.

"When was the last time?" I say.

I return to kissing her stomach slowly as I inch my way up to her bra. It takes everything in me not to flip her over and fuck her roughly in my bed. But it's not what either of us needs.

"Um..." she moans as I kiss her.

I lift her bra off her body and then twirl my tongue slowly over her nipple.

"How long?" I demand.

"Over a year. Five if you're counting the last time I was in a relationship. Or the last time..."

"The last time?"

I gently bite down on her nipple making her cry out.

When I stop, she answers. "The last time a man has made me come. But even then..."

"It wasn't fucking amazing," I finish her sentence.

"No, I doubt you are capable of better, but usually I prefer my B.O.B. to what any man is capable of doing. Men are selfish."

She's not wrong. Most men are selfish. I'm selfish, but not when it comes to pleasing her. I'll put any battery operated boyfriend to shame.

"You sure about that?"

"Yes," she squeaks out.

I hook my thumb under her shorts and panties and jerk them down. Instantly reversing our positions, I grab her hips and roll her on top of me.

She gasps, but I haven't even started yet. I pull her hips forward until her glorious pussy is staring me in my face.

Her eyes are wide as she stares down at me, unsure of what do to.

"Just enjoy this, sweetheart. Enjoy the ride."

I move to kiss her and stop short when I see the tattoos on her hips, covered by her panties before. They aren't tattoos to honor a lost family member. They aren't words of encouragement or something sweet like I would have expected from my innocent girl. No, the tattoos are of fire. She's on fire, burning. She's dangerous, possibly more than I am to her. But it won't stop me from diving in.

I pull her on top of my face, as my tongue carefully swirls around the lips between her legs. I take my time, learning her body. Figuring out how her body responds to my touch. Which places are more sensitive, and which can handle a sharper attack.

My tongue darts inside of her, feeling how tight and wet she is.

Her eyes close at the intrusion. Her hands grip my head though, telling me to never stop.

"Jesus," she mutters.

"Jesus has nothing on me."

And she hasn't even begun to feel pleasure yet.

I slip a finger in her cunt, then a second. Slowly torturing her with my fingers as I find her G-spot deep inside.

My tongue finds the spot that I know is the key to making her scream my name. And then I'm relentless. My tongue dances faster and faster against her clit. Her thighs tighten around my head, begging me to keep going and to stop at the same time. I keep going, loving the mix of sweet and salty that is pouring off her onto my mouth.

I lap it all up. Needing more. Needing to milk her entirely of all her pleasure. I'm selfish in that I want this to be the best she's ever had. I don't want any other man ever to have a chance to compare to what I'm doing to her body. I want it all.

"Knight," she cries out. "Fuck, Knight."

I feel her clenching, her coming over my face. Her voice, singing my name. I'll never get enough of seeing her like this. Completely at my mercy. And completely *mine*.

She rocks her hips back gently as she comes down from her high until she's resting against my chest.

"Thank you," she breathes.

I smirk. "Don't thank me yet, that was nothing compared to what I have in store for you."

I roll us over again, placing her beneath me while I do everything I can to hold back from thrusting inside of her without getting protection first.

"Knight?" her voice is sweet, raspy, and needy.

"Yes, baby?"

I reach over to the nightstand and find my stash of condoms. I pull one out and sheath myself, hoping to God she isn't about to say she's changed her mind and doesn't want me to fuck her.

She closes her eyes and then opens them, like the time closed was needed to give her the strength to say her next words. "How long?"

I move all of my attention back to her. I hate seeing her this vulnerable. Her eyes, so full with fear of what my answer will be. Knowing I could break her with my answer.

I tuck her hair behind her ear, and stroke it slowly, my eyes and body trying to be as vulnerable in return to her. Because of all the things I've told her. All the honesty I've given her, she needs to know, this is the most honest I've ever been.

"More than a year."

She exhales like that was the answer she needed. It is also completely the truth.

"Even longer if you only count the last time I was in love and felt anything real."

She touches her fingers gently to my lips. "This is real. I may hate you, and you may despise me, but what we are feeling now is real. It may not be love, but it's something more. A passion and connection we will never experience again."

I lower my lips to hers. Kissing her carefully and passionately. "It's more than anything I've ever experienced."

And it's the truth. I've experienced love, passion, pain. But whatever this is, it's greater than all of it.

It's pleasure, and safety, and need, and love, and pain, and passion, and hate, and honesty. It's everything combined. It's what Mila and I are together. A connection that can't be tied to a time or place. A link I haven't been able to escape since the first time I saw her.

We both open our eyes at the same time, and I push inside her both gently and all at once. I fill her, just as quickly as she filled my heart. I can't escape Mila Burns, ever.

Her mouth opens wide in a cry of pain as I push her open. I kiss her, my tongue whisking her away to a place of pleasure as her body adjusts to my size inside her.

Our fingers intertwine together as I slowly pull all the way out of her, before slamming into her again. Her back arches as she pulls me inside her deeper. I could get lost in the depth of her. Mila has so many layers, and I've barely explored the surface. But it's now that I realize she will let me in all the way, even though she knows she will get burned. We both will.

"Come on me, pretty girl."

She does, and I follow suit.

I collapse on top of her, but I'm nowhere near finished with her.

I pull us both off the bed and carry Mila to the bathroom, into the shower. I turn the water on that chills us at first before slowly turning to heat.

I spin her around, so her back is to my front, as I let the water stream down her front. My hand hooks around her stomach and down to her most sensitive bud, playing with her slowly and torturously.

Mila started opening up to me before, but I'm afraid she may close to me now.

"What happened with Abri? What did she tell you?"

Mila leans her head back against my chest as I strum her further.

"She told me the man she married was a monster."

It's the truth. I was a monster. Mila is telling me the truth, without saying exactly what happened. I taught her that move. And I don't get to push her further. Mila is hiding the truth while being completely honest.

"What do you think of me?"

"I think my knight isn't the same person as Abri's husband."

I nod and push Abri out of my head as I make Mila come in the shower. Then in my bed two more times before I know she is spent and can't handle another.

I tuck Mila into my bed as I sit on the edge. Mila is hiding what Abri said. And if I can't learn the truth from Mila, I'm going to have to get it from Abri.

"Stay," she whispers.

It goes against everything in my body to leave her. I want to hold her against my body all night. Memorize her scent and the sounds she makes as she sleeps. I want to protect her all night long, and then let her ride me in the morning.

But the only way to truly protect her is for her to hate me. She'll hate me more if I leave her. I need to stay as far away from her as possible. Keep her as far away from Abri as possible. Before I end up hurting her like I did Abri.

13 MILA

Knight is easy to fall for. He's handsome, charming, and he saved me. *What's not to love?*

But maybe the reason my heart flutters around him is I don't really know him, and he doesn't know me. Not knowing the truth about each other's pasts makes it easy to love someone. If he knew my truth, it would be hard for him to love me. Our pasts are the key to letting each other go, but even though Knight left me alone in his bed, letting each other go right now is the last thing either one of us wants.

I saw the pain in Knight's eyes when he left me tucked in his bed. He didn't want to go. He thought he was doing the right thing. Saving me as always, this time from himself. He thought I would hate him more if he left. But I don't think hating Knight is possible anymore.

How can I hate someone that made me feel alive for the first time in years? How can I hate someone who saved me? How can I hate someone who loves me?

I can't.

Knight may not realize that he loves me, but he does. I never thought you could fall for someone so quickly, but I think we've been falling since the first moment we met weeks ago. And in some ways, I feel like the universe has been conspiring to bring us together for a lot longer than a few weeks.

I close my eyes. My body is sore. It will only be worse tomorrow. But it was more than worth it. That may be the last time Knight kisses me or touches me. The love that formed may only last one night, but I wouldn't trade it away. Even if I knew how our story would end. I would do it all over again.

Sleep, I need to sleep. Tomorrow, I will go back to reality. Tomorrow, we will see if there is enough hate to return to how we were living before or if something stronger wins. Tonight, I will dream of Knight and the future we could have together if our pasts weren't so painful.

*

NO.

Stop.

No!

"Mila, shh, it's okay. I got you. I'm not going to let anyone hurt you," Knight's voice says.

Knight?

He's not here. He's not the one hurting me.

"Mila, no one is hurting you."

No one is hurting me, I repeat the words in my head.

I feel his arms wrap around me, but it takes me a while to convince myself to open my eyes. I'm not where I thought I was. I'm safe in Knight's bedroom. In his arms.

Knight strokes my hair with worry in his dark eyes. The same concern he had, holding me in his arms, after rescuing me from falling to my death.

"It was a nightmare. That's all. I won't let Abri or anyone else hurt you."

I nod. I know he won't let Abri hurt me.

"Do you trust me?"

"Yes," I whisper. I trust him, but he shouldn't trust me. I'm not even sure I can trust myself, because Abri wasn't who I was dreaming about.

"Do you need anything? Water, food, more covers?"

I stare out at the darkness. *No one is here. It's just Knight and me. I'm safe.*

"No, I'm okay."

He pulls the covers back over me, and I think he's going to leave me again. My body shakes at the thought of being alone again. My heart beats rapidly, but I try to keep from moving, so Knight won't realize how badly I need him.

"Thank you for coming. I'll be fine now. It was just a nightmare."

He lifts my chin to stare at him. I can't hide, not when he stares at me like this. "It wasn't just anything. Hearing your scream like that was one of the scariest moments of my life. I thought..."

He thought someone was hurting me now. *Does he believe Abri would break into his house and do that?*

I stroke his cheek and kiss him very lightly on the lips. "I'm okay. I promise. I used to get nightmares all the time. Today must have triggered one again. I'll watch TV or something for a little bit, and then I'll fall fast asleep again. You wore me out. I won't have a choice but to sleep. Go back to bed."

"You think I'm going to leave you again?"

I freeze. I don't know how to respond. *I did think he was leaving.*

"I'm never leaving you again."

He wraps his body around mine to make his point. Then he reaches over me to grab the remote on the nightstand. He flicks the enormous TV on and then hands the remote to me. I pick a station with puppies playing on the screen. I can't go wrong with puppies. And then I lay my head against Knight's arm. He tightens his grip around me. He's not wearing anything but his boxer briefs. His bare chest is pressed against the thin T-shirt of his I'm wearing. I need to be closer though.

As if he has the same thought, he moves the T-shirt up my body, and I pull it over my head. It's not sexual. It's the intimacy we seek. Our skin presses together. And Knight kisses my shoulder.

"Mine," he whispers.

I let his words float through me. I would give anything to be his beyond tonight. My nightmare granted us a few more moments of being together, but it won't last. When we wake up, we won't be anything but employer and employee. We will do our best to let the hate back in and guard our hearts. It's the only way either of us will remain safe.

"GOOD MORNING," Knight says still holding me.

"Morning," I say, smiling and blushing at how naked I am. He stares down at my breasts that are no longer covered by his silk sheets. I know what he wants. To taste them. I feel his cock at my ass, begging for entrance.

I can think of no better way to start the day then a good morning fuck.

"How did you sleep?" he asks.

"No more nightmares." *Because of you.*

He nods solemnly and presses his cock further against my ass. *Yes! Fuck me.*

An alarm blares, and Knight rolls off of me toward the alarm he must have set on his phone. I glance at it. Five in the morning. *Ugh, why does Knight have to get up so early?*

He gets up, and I know our moment together is over. *Stupid alarm.*

I move to get out of bed too, but Knight stops me. "You don't have to be into work until seven. Sleep for another hour. I set another alarm to wake you then."

"Sleep with me," I say, not keeping the double meaning out. *Fuck me and then snuggle some more. Or just fuck me until the next alarm goes off.*

"I can't. I have an early morning meeting."

He kisses me dismissively on the forehead and then goes to the bathroom. I consider just getting up and showering, but I know Knight will protest. He wants me to sleep. So I do my best to sleep.

I get into work at a quarter after seven, sore and unsatisfied after not getting morning sex.

"Work starts at seven," Knight's voice booms as I set my purse down.

I haven't seen him since he left my bed almost entirely naked. Now he's dressed in a dark suit, with a burgundy tie that matches the dress I'm wearing.

"I understand. Starbucks was slow with your coffee this morning." I hold up the coffee to him.

He stares down at it blankly. "I already got my coffee. You should have left earlier."

"What? You set my alarm! I left when you thought I should leave."

But he looks at me, and I know for sure our time is over. He's back to playing the jerk of a boss, and I'm left feeling confused and lonely. *It's for the best.*

"I'm sorry. I won't be late again."

"There is a list of things on your desk I need you to do. They are of the utmost importance. Don't bother with your usual tasks until after they are complete."

I frown and snatch the list off my desk. Try out ten different restaurants and report back which food is the best for the luncheon next week. Then stop by six different dessert places to find the best cake. Interview new laundromats, he's not happy with his current one. He wants a new bed for his guest bedroom. Pick one out for him. And he needs new patio heaters before it gets cold.

It's obvious what he's doing. Trying to keep me out of the office as much as possible. Away from Abri, and him. He's not even looking at me now. He's inspecting the floor like he's reading a story off it or something.

"If I eat at all these places today I'm going to be sick or fat," I tease.

His eyes go to my body that is far too thin. I need to eat more. He doesn't know I've been skipping lunches because I can't afford them without my paycheck or him paying for them.

I sigh. "Anything else?"

"Report to me when you are finished, I'll have a new list for you."

He disappears, and I'm left with a fake list of tasks that don't even matter. Last time he talked about the luncheon, he just wanted me to pick any restaurant that could hold the fifty people invited. He didn't care. Now I have to taste the food and select a separate dessert place.

A knock rattles me before it's opened.

"Wow," Cole says staring at me.

"What?" I snap, not able to deal with his crap.

"Whoa, I'm sorry. Didn't mean to intrude. I promise I won't kiss you. I know you aren't in the mood."

"I'm not in the mood because Knight's psycho ex-wife almost killed me yesterday." *It's only partially the truth.*

"And now I have to do these stupid errands for Knight. He's trying to keep me out of the office so I won't kill him." I hold up the list.

Cole frowns. "I'll do some of the tasks with you, and then you and I can talk and get to know each other better. I'm hungry and could use twenty lunches today."

I laugh. "I don't think that's the best idea."

"I will not kiss you again. Well, unless you ask, but I'm pretty sure you've been kissed plenty since the last time I saw you."

"Why do you say that?"

"Because Abri has been sulking all day, Knight is more pissy than usual, and you are glowing in an outfit that matches Knight's."

I frown.

"Don't worry; you two look adorable in your matching outfits."

"I don't know how that happened. We didn't plan it, and he was awake before I left."

Cole grins. "So you were together last night then?"

"Ugh, I'm not talking to you about my love life or lack of one."

"Fine, don't talk, but I promise I'm only looking out for you and Knight."

I roll my eyes. "Yep, I'm sure that kiss was just a way to bring Knight and me together."

"It worked, didn't it?"

I huff. "What are you doing here anyway, Cole? Don't you have a strip club to run?"

"The strip club runs itself. And I'm going to be the owner of Perfect Match soon, so I need to spend more time here."

"What did you just say?"

"Um...nothing. Don't worry about it."

Is Cole planning a coup? Should I tell Knight about it? Is Cole trying to take over now that he sees Knight is weakened?

My phone buzzes and I answer it automatically.

"Yes," I snap because I know it's Knight.

"You haven't called your driver yet, don't worry, I did your job for you. He's downstairs waiting to take you to the first restaurant."

I end the call without a goodbye. I snatch the coffee meant for Knight along with my own nearly empty cup. I'm going to need both to get through this day.

⟡

KNIGHT HASN'T SPOKEN to me all day. He's texted me a few more work things to do, but otherwise nothing. There was dinner waiting for me on the counter when I got back to his place, but otherwise no sign of Knight. The food smells delicious. Some homemade pasta dish Knight must have fixed before he disappeared again, but I'm too stuffed to eat anything after the day I had.

So instead of eating, I slink upstairs and into the bed. I don't even have the energy to shower or undress. I flick the TV on, ready to get lost in some drama to put me to sleep. I only make it twenty minutes into a rerun of Scandal, before the door opens.

My eyes shoot open as Knight steps into the bedroom.

"If you think I'll fuck you after how you treated me today, you're wrong."

He takes a step inside, closing the door behind him.

"I hate you," I spat.

He keeps walking.

Dammit, if he touches me, kisses me, or even speaks a word I will jump him.

He does none of those things though. He slowly removes a T-shirt and sweatpants he must have changed into after work and then climbs into the bed next to me.

"No," I say because I won't fuck him. *I can't.*

"I'm not going to hurt you. I just want to help you sleep." He doesn't say the words, but he means help him sleep too, to know I'm safe.

"Okay," I whisper. His hands go around me, and within moments he's snoring.

That's how the next two weeks go by. Knight yells at me during the day, giving me ridiculous tasks that all involve being away from the office. I dog walked for his neighbor. A neighbor he doesn't even know or care about. I did Cole's dry cleaning at a separate dry cleaner's than Knights. I got Knight's motorcycle and cars washed, even though they didn't need it, twice.

Every day I showed up, somehow in a damn matching outfit to what Knight was wearing, and he'd bark orders at me. It was our only interaction during the day, but somehow those moments meant to drive us apart brought us closer together. The words we spoke to each other were fake, the heat between us the only truth.

But the days weren't as bad as the nights. Every night we developed the same routine. Knight would cook dinner, and we'd eat together in silence. Then we would go our separate ways for a couple of hours before Knight would find his way to my bedroom to hold me all night and keep the nightmares away.

Somehow we exchanged truth for hatred and sex for keeping the nightmares away at night. I'm not sure we made a fair trade.

And in two weeks, everything could change. That's when my first paycheck is due. *Two weeks.* In two weeks, I will have enough money to move out and get my own apartment. But I'm not sure that's what I want anymore. But I have to. It's the only way to keep my sanity.

I sit down at my desk to enjoy a sandwich on my lunch break, one of the rare times I've been in the office the last two weeks. But instead of eating, my door gets thrown open.

I growl. *I need to get a lock installed on the door ASAP.*

"Hey bestie," Abri says. "I wanted to see if you were available to have lunch with me."

Despite Knight's attempts to keep me away from Abri, she has still found me. She pretends nothing has happened between us, that we are best friends now. She's delusional.

"I'm already eating my lunch, but thanks."

"Oh, well good thing I brought my lunch today." She sits down across from me and pulls her own sandwich out of her purse.

I sigh.

"I'd rather eat alone, Abri. It's been a long week."

"We are eating alone. That's why we aren't in the cafeteria silly."

I eat my sandwich, pretending she isn't here as she speaks nonsense.

"Did you see the new secretary Knight hired? He'll be fucking her by the end of the week."

"Did you see the way Knight looked at me yesterday? He was pining bad."

"Did you hear him talking to Jessica? I think he's been fucking her."

Ignore her, I repeat. Her conversations don't even make sense. *How could Knight be attracted to so many people at the same time and be fucking them all?*

I smirk to myself. Abri doesn't know I'm the one sleeping in Knight's bed every night. Even if it's just sleeping, it doesn't matter. I'm still the only one that gets him. *At least for two more weeks.*

My phone buzzes, and I grab it to turn it off. Knight knows I won't answer on my lunch break. It's not Knight though. It's Ren, my sister.

"Hello?"

"What the fuck, Mila? You didn't tell me that you got expelled! What the fuck are you going to do?!"

"Suspended, not expelled. It wasn't my fault. And I'm enrolled for next semester, so it's really fine. I found a job in the meantime. I'm good."

"You are coming to Aspen this weekend! We need to have a long talk."

"Ren, I'm fine. Really. I work most weekends, so it will be tough for me to get off."

"Mila Kay Burns, you get your butt to my house this weekend!"

"I'll talk to my boss, Ren. But no promises."

I end the call. *Shit.* I'm sure Knight will let me go, it means I'm away from Abri for the weekend. But I don't want to spend the weekend with my sister.

"How is Ren?" Abri asks smirking at me.

"My sister is fine," I say hesitantly.

"Good, I've meant to call her again. It's been a while since we spoke. How are the kids? What are their names again? Oh yes, Bailey and Camden."

I freeze. "Wait...you know my sister?"

Abri blinks in confusion. "Of course, I do, silly. I remember you too, although it took me a while to remember you. You've changed so much. You used to have red and blue and green hair."

"Purple and blue."

"Oh right, purple and blue. You used to follow your older sister everywhere. It was very annoying."

And just like that, one truth comes flooding back. Abri and Ren were close friends in high school. I was going through a rebellious stage and didn't see my family or sister much, but who could forget Abri. The few conversations we had she would tell me how awful my hair was, and that I had horrible split ends and needed to wear a hat or wig instead of dying my hair.

Was Knight there?

I search my brain trying to bring up a memory of Knight. I find none. No, I couldn't have known Knight back then. I only knew Abri for a year at most before she graduated with my sister. And my parents would have never let them bring boys over.

I never hung out with Abri or Ren outside of the house. I was in middle school still when they were in high school. There was no way I knew Knight.

But we were so close. We could have met back then. Before life damaged us both. *Could we have been together then if our pasts hadn't ruined us?*

And how could I have forgotten, even a moment of my past?

14 KNIGHT

I need to talk to Abri, but for once, she's been avoiding me. I need to threaten her with her life if she so much as talks to Mila again. I've had Mila run ridiculous errands to keep her away from this building. Away from Abri, and if I'm honest, me.

I don't know who's more of a danger to Mila, Abri or me. But being gone keeps Mila safe.

But more than threatening Abri, I need to find out what she told Mila. I need to know how much Mila knows. So then I can figure out how to share my secret.

A loud knock pounds on my door, and I know it's Mila. There is nothing soft about her. She's fierce, independent and even though she has no business experience, if I spent a week teaching her how my company runs, I have no doubt she would take over with full energy and bring our profits up to an all-time high. Even the stupid tasks I've given her she's tackled full on with all of her strength.

She found the best restaurant in all of Denver to host our luncheon at. My motorcycle and cars have never been cleaner. My schedule has never made better use of my time. And she saved me money while finding a better dry cleaner. Not to mention the countless clients she has persuaded to use our app with a simple email or phone call. She's like a machine that doesn't stop until she's shut off.

Mila has a fire I can't find a way to extinguish. Maybe she's strong enough to survive the storm headed her way.

I don't answer. I know Mila's routine at this point, and she knows mine. She waits for exactly three-seconds for a response to her knock. One that I never give her. And then she walks in, not caring who is in my office. She's walked in on countless meetings. The women I'm meeting with, look up at her with jealousy. The men with lust.

Mila doesn't even realize she's bringing attention to herself when she does it. She's just pissed enough at me that it doesn't matter.

"Good afternoon, sweetheart."

She growls at me as she stomps into my office. I guess it's not a good afternoon.

But I can't take my eyes off her. She's wearing a light gray jacket with a hot pink shirt underneath and bright pink pumps. Her hair, which was once curled, is disheveled on top of her head instead of her usual high ponytail that stays in its perfect place throughout the day, no matter what happens.

She takes a seat across from me, crossing her legs forcefully as her arms come crashing down on the armrests of the chair. I'm surprised she didn't break the chair.

"Yes? I thought you were on your lunch break?"

She growls again.

I lean forward so I can stare down her shirt. I'm a bastard, but she doesn't give me a snide remark for being a horny prick.

"Are you going to growl at me all afternoon, or are you going to tell me why you stormed into my office, even though you said you would never shorten a lunch break for me?"

She opens her red lipstick stained lips. I've never seen her reapply lipstick throughout the day, but somehow her lips are always red. Just like her eyeshadow is always a little smudged. Not enough to make her look unprofessional, just enough to make her a real woman, instead of a pristine plastic doll like my soon to be ex-wife.

"Uh..."

I laugh at her speechlessness.

"What's wrong baby? Do I make you speechless?"

"No. Yes. Stop talking."

I cock my head and force my eyes to leave her breasts as her cheeks heat into pink circles. I love Mila when she's full of confidence, storming into my office to chew me out. But I also love her like this, disheveled, embarrassed, and speechless. She's not weaker at this moment. She's just affected. I like simply being near me can make it hard for her to breath.

"I like your outfit." I let my eyes travel up and down her jacket and skirt lazily, knowing it's going to take her a while to find her voice again.

When my eyes meet her gaze, all I see is dark fire.

"How do you always match my outfit? Every fucking day we show up in matching outfits. How? Why? You always leave before I even get out of the shower. Do you have a closet here where you change after you see what outfit I've chosen?"

I lean back in my chair as she stares at my pink tie.

"That's really what you came in here on your lunch break to ask? Why does my tie match your shirt?"

"Yes," she hisses not revealing the truth of why she's here.

I stand up, not intentionally, but because I need to be closer to her. I walk around my desk and snatch her hand off her lap. She tries to pull her hand back, and I let her.

Our eyes lock, and words flow from my mouth. "I match you because even though you hate me. Even though I push you away. Even though I bark orders at you and treat you like a slave instead of a woman more capable than any other employee in my office, of not only being my assistant but running my company. Even though I can't have you. Even though you will never be mine. Even though you deserve so much more. I need to feel like you are mine. I need to be connected to you. I need the world to know that I've claimed you. And matching you, wearing something similar makes me feel close to you, even when you are scowling at me and hating me."

Her mouth falls open as she processes my words. I pick her fallen hand up again and kiss her hand, then her fingers, then her palm. I try to keep my kisses chaste. I'm kissing her to bring her back to life, not to take things too far. But I can't help but pour everything into her with each kiss.

"How?" she barely whispers.

I take one of her fingers in my mouth, taking my time as I lick the length of it, knowing it's a direct connection to her core. I've just lit the flame I don't know how or want to put out.

"You're a planner, Mila Burns. You may pretend you left that part behind you when you got suspended and started working for me, but it's still there, hidden in everything you do.

"I know at night you've already planned out both of our schedules for not only the next day but the next few weeks. I know you have already planned and found two apartments you can easily afford once I start paying you in two weeks. One close to me and the office, the other close to campus in case you need distance from me. I know you already have your top three companies you will apply to when you graduate. I know you plan on paying your brother and sister back in January when I finish paying you. And I know you order all the suits in your closet in the order you plan on wearing them. All I have to do is look at what suit is next in your closet and match you."

Mila bites her lip, and I don't know if it's to scold me or be happy with me. It doesn't matter, either way; this isn't the reason she's in my office.

And the longer she's silent, the more I can't help but kiss her. So I kiss every part of her hand she will let me while the turmoil spins inside of her.

Please don't hate me anymore. I can't stand it.

"Your ability to plan everything lets you see your future. It lets you live it before it even happens. It's a skill that will let you go far in life. But it's also something that will hinder you from truly living. If everything is always planned, then you will miss out on some of the greatest moments."

Mila's eyelashes flitter up from her lap. Her eyes brighten, and her teeth slowly release her lip.

"Like getting fucked on the desk in your boss's office?"

I grin. "Yes, that's exactly what I mean."

My hands grab her neck as she pounces into my body, our lips colliding together like they are meant to be together. Like they can't function without being pressed together.

Her legs wrap around me as I stand, our lips still attached to each other's, desperate to never part again. My office is far away from most of the others on this floor other than Mila's. But I'm not taking any chances. People in my office prefer to storm inside rather than knock before entering. Cole and Abri especially don't honor boundaries.

I slam her body against the door grabbing her chin to separate us for a second so she can catch her breath, and I can find the lock on my door as quickly as possible.

"I hate being interrupted," I say against her lips.

"You seem to love my interruptions."

I growl and nip at her bare neck. "You are the only one who is allowed to interrupt me. In fact, I may make it part of your daily tasks to interrupt me more."

She bites my lip teasingly, but it draws blood.

I smack her ass in retribution, making her squeal.

"Quiet, baby or the whole office will hear you. I don't mind, but you might not enjoy the entire office knowing you are fucking your boss."

She shrugs. "I could care less who hears me. I'm not that close to anyone in the office anyway. You've made it impossible with all the stupid errands I've been running, Cole and Abri are about the only people I talk to. Cole already thinks we are fucking. And Abri..." She freezes.

I set her down on the edge of my desk, trying to understand what is going on in her head. Fear, regret, loss. Her eyes grow big then small.

Shit.

I kneel in front of her, pleading with her to listen to my truth before she freaks out.

"I've never fucked Abri in my office before."

She stills more if it's possible. "Why not? Didn't you build this company together? This was your baby? You can't tell me you two didn't fuck in the heat of an argument? Or after winning a new client?"

I sigh. "We did, but not here."

"Where?"

"A hotel room. Abri didn't want the other employees to hear us. She was more private than you realize."

She exhales, but I can tell her mind is still twirling. I kiss the inside of her thigh trying to bring her back to me. I see the chills run up and down her leg as she shivers, but my touch isn't enough. She needs more words.

"I've never fucked you in the same place as Abri."

"Your apartment?"

"I've fucked Abri in my apartment, but not the bed. The bed I bought new after Abri moved out." I can see the jealousy in her eyes, and I don't know whether to love her more for it or hate her jealous streak. Instead, I choose to understand her feelings. I would be jealous as hell if she were with another man recently. If she were married before or shared anything special with another man.

"Then I'll happily be your first," Mila teases.

"Thank God." I bury my head between her legs and dig my teeth into the thin, flimsy piece of fabric between her legs to pull her panties down. I grab her pink panties that, of course, match the rest of her outfit and stick them into my pocket.

"I'm getting those back, Knight."

I laugh before my tongue dives inside her. *Unlikely.*

She grips my head as I flick, tease and twirl over her sensitive, swollen bud. She responds to every touch like she's never been touched here before. I love that I'm the only one who has made her come from oral, but it also pisses me off that she hasn't had this pleasure before. It pisses me off that I've let two weeks go by without pulling an orgasm from deep inside her core.

The more I lick, the wetter she gets. The harder she grips my head until she can't hold on anymore and grabs the desk instead. True to her word, she doesn't give a fuck who hears us, which only makes me work harder to make her screams louder until I'm sure our entire floor, plus the ones above and below, hear her moans.

"Knight, Knight, Knight!" She screams at the top of her lungs, her body convulsing in an orgasm that rips through her body before rolling into another when I don't let up.

"I can't..."

I smirk. She thinks her body can't handle more, but I'm just getting started.

I slowly stand up, "You deserve more, better. You deserve the world, pretty girl with the smartest mouth."

She blushes in her innocent way.

I snatch her off the desk, spin her around, and push her against my desk until her hands are gripping the desk and her legs are spread wide.

I kiss against her neck, keeping her wet and ready for me as I undo my pants, freeing my cock. Seconds pass, but it feels like hours as I find the condom in my back pocket and slip it on. And to think I almost left my condoms at home so I would behave.

I grab her hips and push inside her.

"Jesus," she cries as I fill her.

"I would fuck you all day just to hear that beautiful, raspy sound."

"I would fuck you all day because—"

She never does finish that sentence. We are both too impatient to wait until she finishes speaking. I thrust, and she gasps.

I thrust, and she pushes against me, meeting me, begging for more.

I thrust, and she purrs.

I thrust, and she screams.

I thrust, and I can't imagine my cock in any women's cunt but hers.

Shit, I'm fucked.

Her skirt is hiked high as I fuck her, but I need more skin. I push her shirt up so I can kiss every bit of her skin. I try to slow myself down. I try to make this moment last forever, but with each thrust, she tightens around me more, and I know she's about to release her orgasm, and the sounds she makes then will leave me no chance of holding on.

One more thrust inside and she comes.

I come after. And I'm not sure if I'm broken because I don't know when or if that will happen again, or because I know that neither of us can deny ourselves this any longer.

I need more, but I can't collapse on top of her on the desk. I don't imagine it would be the most comfortable position for her. So I grab her, and we fall to the floor in a puddle of limbs. We can't move. We don't clean ourselves up or cover skin that shouldn't be exposed when we go back to work. We lay on the cold, wood floor panting like animals.

"I need more," she says between pants.

I roll to my side so I can see.

"More?" I'm not sure what she means. *Does she need us to date? Does she need us to be in a relationship?*

"I need more fucking."

I grin in relief. *I can give her more of that.*

"I'll trade fucking for nighttime snuggles," she whispers.

I frown as I stroke her face; her hair is going to be even more disheveled than it was before.

"No."

She pouts.

"I mean, how about both? Fucking and snuggles to keep the nightmares away. I think we need both."

The light reappears on her face as her lips curl upward. "I think both would be great. I can fuck you and snuggle and still hate you."

I twirl the end of her hair between my thumb and fingers. "I know you can." She can hate me in her mind, but it won't stop her heart from falling for me.

"Butyouhavetodoonefavorforme," she says in a flush of words all scrunched together, barely comprehensible.

"Slow down, baby and try again."

She takes a deep breath. This is what she came here to tell me.

"I need to go to Aspen this weekend."

I sit up abruptly not expecting her to say she's leaving tomorrow. I can't stand her gone for two whole days without me.

"My sister, Ren, she...well...somehow she found out I got expelled."

"Suspended, because of me," I correct her hating how losing her schooling makes her feel, even if it means I get to have her in my life a little longer.

She nods. "Ren wants me to come to see her in Aspen this weekend and make sure I'm okay. That she doesn't need to put me on suicide watch or something."

I swallow hard. I have to let her go. We usually work the weekends, but family is more important. She needs to show her sister how she's flourishing even without school.

"And..."

Shit, there's more. I can't handle more.

"And I don't know how I didn't make the connection before, but I know Abri. Well, I don't really know her, but I've met her a few times. Ren and Abri were friends in high school. I only saw Abri a handful of times, and we barely spoke the few times she was at my house, but anyway...it's probably not important, I just thought you should know..."

If I don't stop her, she's going to keep rambling. As much as I love listening to her talk, I have to stop her turmoil.

"I'm sorry you ever had to meet Abri. Now or in the past. She's not a nice person now. She was a better person before..." I can't finish that sentence. Abri was a good person before me. Before I turned her into the evil she is today.

Mila touches my arm, bringing me back to the reality.

"Of course you can go this weekend if that's what you want. I would love a chance to go to Aspen."

She grins. "Wait...what?"

"I'm going with you." I have to go. I might finally figure out the truth. I might find a way to get Abri out of my life. If Mila can't help me, then maybe Ren has a key to Abri's past to help me escape.

"No. Why would you want to go with me?"

"Because now that I've persuaded you to fuck me, I can't go two days without it." *It's mostly the truth, while still hiding my damn secret.*

Mila tries to hide her smile, but she can't. "You sure? My family is going to think we are dating."

I kiss her nose. "Does it matter if they think we are together?"

"No, it doesn't." She pushes her skirt down and sits up as she runs her hand through her hair.

"Good, when are we leaving?"

"Tomorrow, after work."

"I'll drive."

She shakes her head. "No, I'm not riding on your motorcycle for three hours. I'll drive."

"I have other vehicles than my motorcycle you know."

"I know, but I want to drive. My Subaru runs just fine. You can chip in for gas."

I grin like an idiot. "Fine."

She pulls her hair up into a ponytail, tying it off and getting rid of the most obvious evidence that we just fucked, although she's going to smell like me the rest of the day. Her body is going to glow and blush any time anyone speaks to her when they remind her of me. And when she speaks, everyone in the office will know it was her who I fucked, because no one could mistake her voice for anyone's but her's.

"I should get back to work."

"Yes, you should. Your boss won't like that you took an extra long lunch."

She raises an eyebrow. "He won't? I thought he would demand I take extra long lunches in the future."

I stand, tucking myself back into my pants and walking over to her. I kiss her firmly, ending our teasing game.

"Get to work before your smart mouth gets you into more trouble."

"Stop giving me ridiculous tasks to keep me away from you. I'm not getting your car washed again, or going to any more restaurants. I gained three pounds this week. I made sure to eat four meals a day. And I promise to lock my door, so Abri doesn't barge in."

I kiss her again quickly. "Good, now get your cute ass out of here before I fuck you again and lose all of my clients."

She rolls her eyes. "Yes, sir."

I shake my head as my cock comes to life again. "Of course, now you call me, sir."

She unlocks the door as she bats her eyelashes at me. We both grin like idiots until Mila disappears to do whatever stupid tasks I listed for her to do today.

I wait about three seconds before I decide I should run after her and keep her locked in my office all day. But when I chase after her, she isn't in her office.

Dammit, why did all of her tasks have to involve her leaving the office?

I change course and head to the bathroom to try to clean myself up so I might be able to get work done without smelling like her. I walk into the bathroom and head to the sink to wash her scent off my hands.

The door opens, and I don't acknowledge whoever enters.

"I can't believe you fucked her while still married to me," Abri says.

My face hardens along with my heart. I'm pissed at Abri, but I've needed to talk to her for the last two weeks. I'm not going to scare her off so quickly.

"Don't even, Abri. I know you've been fucking half the office and half the celebrities, athletes, and politicians in this town while we were still living together."

She smiles as she approaches me. "I'm still the best lay of your life."

"No, Abri, you aren't."

Her eyes narrow. "You'll get bored with your new assistant, just like you get bored with all women, then you'll come crawling back to me, begging me to take you back."

"No, I won't."

Abri places her hands under the water where I'm washing my hands as she brushes against mine and then splashes me with water.

"Oops, did I get you?"

I can't deal with this. "I'm going to be gone this weekend; you'll have to ensure the company still runs this weekend." Abri is ruthless when it comes to her revenge against me, but she won't destroy the company. She feels the same way I do about it. She'll sacrifice everything to ensure it's running smoothly.

She shakes her hands roughly, not caring she is splashing me with water. "What a coincidence, I happen to be leaving town as well. I guess you'll have to put your friend Cole in charge while we are both in Aspen."

I grab her shoulders and push her hard against the wall, harder than I probably should. "What are you doing in Aspen?"

"I'm going to visit an old friend, Ren Burns. I haven't spoken to her since I ran off with you after we graduated high school."

Fuck.

"Like hell you are."

She shrugs. "You can't control me as much as you wish you could, Ace."

I growl, even her using my first name pisses me off. I've never been Ace to anyone but her.

"What did you tell Mila? Why did you almost kill her?"

"Don't be dramatic. I didn't almost kill her. Just scared her a little. I wanted her to know she should stay far away from us. But isn't that what you are doing, sending her on endless, useless errands?"

I don't answer.

"What did you tell Mila?"

"The truth." Her eyes flicker down to where my hands are forcefully gripping her arms against the wall. "You are a dangerous man, and she deserves better."

I release her, and she walks to the door.

"We all do," she finishes.

15 MILA

We are supposed to leave for Aspen in fifteen minutes, as soon as Knight finishes his last meeting for the day. My stomach is in knots thinking about it. I don't want to go. I'd rather have a painful bikini wax. I'd rather do more of Knight's stupid errands. I'd rather listen to Abri pretend to be friends with me than face my family.

I've finished all my work today and more. I didn't do any of Knight's stupid errands. Instead, I spent my time maximizing his schedule to ensure he could get the most work done, answering emails, and writing my thoughts out about which markets they should target next.

And now, I'm stalling as I stare at the door, both wanting Knight to come through the door, and begging him not to at the same time. We both packed last night, after another fuck in his bed. I drove my car here this morning instead of having Gallagher drive me. All that is standing between Aspen and me is Knight's meeting and a three-hour car ride.

I blast the radio on from my laptop. I don't have the money to pay for Apple Music or Spotify. And I like listening to the commercials and the silly games the hosts play.

"Tonight is going to be a gorgeous night in Colorado. A perfect night to see a concert at Red Rocks. Tickets are still available for..."

Knight has never been to a concert. Here's my chance to fix that.

I pull up the Red Rocks site and grab Knight's credit card I use to run all his errands. I've been tempted before to use his credit card to get back at him. Use it to rent an apartment. Buy a new car. Or even something simple like buying myself lunch. But I never have.

I decisively click the touchpad on my computer. *Tonight that changes.*

My door creaks open, and I turn down the radio station.

"You ready to go, beautiful?"

I smile at the nickname from Knight's lips.

I nod, closing my laptop and grabbing my purse.

I walk out of the office with Knight close behind me but not touching me. He nods at his employees in their cubicles on the way to the elevator. Everyone's eyes are on us. Even though I've worked here for two weeks, I hardly know any of their names. I haven't had time to connect when Knight has been sending me on wild goose chases. They all know what happened yesterday in Knight's office. They all look at me with wide eyes and whispered comments. It will take a lot to win any of them over as real friends.

I expect my cheeks to flame when I realize that everyone knows I fucked our boss. I expect not to be able to meet their gaze. But it makes me hold my head higher because Knight isn't really my boss. Well, not in the same way as he is to everyone else. Me working here is just a way to pass the time until he asks me for a favor I don't want to give. And I'm afraid that time is growing near. He made it clear it wouldn't come until closer to December, but nothing about our relationship goes slowly.

We step into the elevator, and I expect Knight's hands to be all over me. He doesn't jump me. Our fingers brush together, and my breath catches as I gaze at him out of the corner of my eye. He's in a dark blue suit with a grey tie. He matches me, even though I purposefully picked an out of order outfit. Somehow we are in sync, even though the rest of the world thinks we should be apart.

The elevator doors open in the parking lot below the building, and Knight motions for me to step out. I do, and he follows me toward my car. I climb into the driver seat as he climbs in the passenger seat. I should have spent the day cleaning my car. It smells like fast food and old books. The fabric seats are faded and covered in dust and hair. Knight looks out of place in my car until he takes my hand and squeezes tightly.

"You sure you don't want my driver to drive? We could have a lot more fun that way."

"No," I say smiling.

His phone buzzes, and he frowns at the number. "I don't have to take this."

"Answer." I already know it's Peter from his last meeting calling to take Knight's offer. The clients always call when the meeting is over, jumping at a chance to work with Knight.

He holds my hand tighter as he answers the phone.

I push everything out as I drive with one hand on the wheel and one hand holding Knight's. *Tomorrow is going to suck, but tonight is going to be fucking amazing.*

Knight ends his call after thirty minutes. "Um...Mila, do you need directions to Aspen? I've only gone a couple of times, but I don't think this is the way."

I smile. "It's not the way to Aspen."

"Are you trying to kidnap me?"

"Something like that." I turn onto the side road that climbs up the mountain.

"I don't think now is the time to go hiking again, either."

"We aren't hiking."

"Then what are we doing?"

"We are going to your first concert."

"Who's playing?" he asks grinning far too wide.

"Does it matter?"

He laughs. "You don't know. You bought tickets for a concert, and you don't even know who's playing."

I wince. "Actually, you bought tickets for our concert. I don't have any money, remember?"

He frowns and pulls out his wallet. He starts pulling hundred dollar bills out, counting them quickly, he hands the wad to me.

"Your advance."

I blink rapidly as I take the money. "I earned it?"

"More than earned it."

I put the money in my purse as we both step out of the car. People have parked on either side of us and are walking toward the concerts in jeans and T-shirts.

I pause suddenly.

"What's wrong sweetheart?"

I frown. "We can't go in like this." I glance at his expensive suit and my skirt, jacket, and heels.

"Then, what do you suggest?"

"You packed a T-shirt and jeans, right?"

He laughs, and we head to the trunk. After five minutes of digging through our bags, we finally find something suitable to wear.

Knight removes his jacket, as I help him with his tie. We both stare at each other silently, as I slowly undo the buttons. He shrugs out of his shirt and places the items into the trunk.

"You should, uh, climb in the back seat to change," I say.

His eyes stay on me as his lips curl up. I try to keep my eyes on his face instead of his tantalizing muscles. He sits back into the car, grabs my hand and pulls me inside as well.

I giggle uncontrollably as he pulls me on top of him in the back-seat. The door shuts behind me, trapping us inside.

"Knight, we can't! People will see," I squeal in a high pitched voice as he kisses down my neck to my breasts.

"We can't what? Change?"

My eyes roll back in my head as he kisses above my breast again. I would fuck him in front of the entire world and feel no embarrassment. I just want him. All of him. Even the parts he won't let me have because he's afraid I'll hate him for real.

I take control, kissing down his chest stopping when I reach the V that disappears into his pants where a bulge is waiting to be freed.

He slips my jacket off, and slowly unbuttons my shirt, as he pulls me up to his face and buries his head between my breasts, carefully keeping me covered while he kisses me.

"Yes," I moan as he twirls my nipple in his mouth.

"Fuck, we should have taken my car. We could have done so much more."

I nod in agreement, but then his fingers are under my skirt, pushing aside my panties, and then finding the wetness that has already soaked them. He moves the juices around my clit as he punishes my nipple for not agreeing to take his car.

I try to reach down between my legs to give him pleasure too, but he swats my hand away.

"If you pull me out, I won't be able to stop until I'm inside your beautiful cunt and I can't, not here. You're mine, and I won't let anyone else see how amazing you are."

I fist my hands in his hair to keep myself from grabbing his cock.

He slips one, two, three fingers inside me as I gasp and pant, riding his fingers as if they were his cock.

More, more, more.

He does. His tongue laps faster around my nipple, teasing me with his teeth as he nips at me, and his fingers move faster in my pussy. I'm sure his fingers and pants are drenched in my cum, but it doesn't make him stop.

Just as I'm about to scream his name, his mouth comes down on mine, and I scream his name into his lips.

I've never felt more alive than when I'm with him. I've never felt more taken care of or more free to be me.

This is just about sex. There is no us. This isn't a relationship.

Knight gives me an I-just-rocked-your-world smile when I finally come down off my high.

"What was that for?" I ask.

"I couldn't resist. And you needed to get out of these clothes anyway." He leans forward nipping at my ear. "Although I would suggest changing your panties as well, these are soaked."

I laugh, and then we both change into jeans. I pair a gray tank top with mine, and he wears a gray T-shirt.

"Always matching," I laugh as he takes my hand.

"Always connected."

We walk into the venue, hand in hand. I buy the beer with the new money I got paid with, despite Knight's protests. And then we find our seats in the middle.

"Wow," he says when he gets the view of the city below, twinkling in the dark night.

"It's perfect, isn't it?"

Knight moves me in front of his body and wraps his arms around me, pulling me tightly to him. "Now it is."

We hold each other as the music plays, drinking beer, and pretending we know the lyrics to the music even though we don't.

It feels like a date, and I constantly have to remind myself that it's not.

"Tell me something I don't know," I whisper into his ear.

He doesn't miss a beat as if he was anticipating my question. "I never met Ren. I know you want to ask, but I've never met her. Abri never introduced me to her friends. She didn't like me hanging out with other girls. I guess she thought I would find someone better."

I cock my head so that I can look him in the eye. More truths from my bad boy with the dark eyes. It also means if he didn't meet Ren, he never met me. I don't know if I'm happy we never met, and therefore don't have to feel bad about forgetting him, or sad we don't get to have some epic love story that transcends time.

"Your turn, pretty girl."

"Cole told me he wants to take over the company. I think he's planning some sort of overthrow."

Knight laughs and kisses my lips softly. "Don't worry about Cole. He's a good man; he'd never hurt either of us."

"The kiss wasn't hurting us?"

Knight shrugs. "Cole thought if he kissed you it would piss me off enough to claim you. It worked."

I nod. He's probably right.

"Now, tell me something real, not about Cole."

"I've never been fucked in a bathroom at a concert."

Knight laughs. "Now that I can make happen."

※

IT WAS late before we decided to leave the concert and head to Aspen. And now it's almost three in the morning as we arrive outside my sister's house. A house that used to belong to my parents.

The drive was peaceful and tranquil. We didn't talk much, occasionally sharing a random fact about ourselves. Other times we would listen to music. And sometimes we wouldn't say anything at all.

Knight didn't complain about me driving. He let me take control. Something I haven't felt in a long time.

Knight is currently fighting sleep in the passenger's seat. He usually wakes up in two hours and isn't used to being awake this late.

"Knight, we are here. Time to wake up."

"I wasn't asleep," he mumbles.

I kiss his lips. "I know."

I park the car in the driveway of what most people would call a mansion. My sister just calls it home.

We both climb out, and Knight grabs my duffel bag, along with his spinner bag, and we march toward the garage. I enter the code to open the garage.

"The guest bedroom is on the second floor. Third door on the right. We have to be quiet, so we don't wake Ren or the kids." The guest room used to be my room. It holds too many memories. Most of which I'd rather run away from.

Knight nods and follows me inside. I texted Ren earlier that I would get in late and just use the code. I lied and said Knight's meeting ran late, and I had to stay. I didn't tell her Knight was coming. I didn't want to upset her further until I knew for sure he was coming.

Knight curses in a whisper as he stubs his toe on the corner of a kitchen counter.

I hold back a laugh until the lights come on.

"Ren, you're awake," I say as my sister stands in her robe in the kitchen.

"Of course, I'm awake. I couldn't sleep until you got here. I wasn't sure if I was going to have to rescue you if you got lost or stuck in a ditch somewhere."

I walk over and hug her. "Sorry you were worried," I say even though I know her worry has more to do with not wanting me to be in the news than her fear.

"And who are you?" Ren asks Knight.

Shit. I'm not prepared for this. It was the one subject Knight and I didn't bring up on the car ride over.

"I'm Ace Knight, but you can call me Knight."

Knight extends his hand to Ren, and she takes it hesitantly.

"I'm her boyfriend."

I freeze. I want to stop this. Tell Ren he isn't my boyfriend, he's my boss, but Ren is smiling brightly like I finally did something right. Ren looks to me like she has a million questions, but I'm not staying awake to answer any of them.

"It's been a long night. We should get to sleep."

"Of course, you guys can sleep in the guest bedroom. Third door on the right." She doesn't even call it my bedroom, even though it is.

Knight smiles and carries the bags up the stairs with Ren and me following. I tell Ren goodnight and then head into our bedroom.

"I thought we weren't pretending," I say.

"We aren't."

"Then what was that crap about you being my boyfriend? You could have just said friend or boss or something."

Knight smirks. "Because I wanted to go with the truth. You're mine, Mila, which makes me your boyfriend."

16 KNIGHT

Boyfriend. Why did I say that?

I can't be a boyfriend. For one, I'm still technically married, though separated. And two, I just can't. My heart can't love again. I can't be the man Mila deserves.

But when I look at Mila leaning against the door of the bedroom, completely broken herself, I know I want to be her boyfriend more than anything.

I'm willing to try again. Willing to risk it all for her. I just have to convince her and my heart of it.

Mila looks down at her feet instead of at me. She's nervous. It's clear from the way she twists the end of her hair. The way she shifts her weight back and forth on her feet. But there is a smile there, buried beneath the worry.

I don't know how to do this. I don't know how to be the boyfriend she wants and needs. All I know is I can't be apart from her.

I should say those words to her, but I can't find my voice.

Instead, I find myself looking around the room. This isn't a guest room. This is Mila's room. Or at least, it was. But this room isn't like the Mila I know now. The Mila who occupied this room was a free spirit. Posters of various bands I've never heard of line the walls. Sketches of tattoos she never got are mixed between the posters. There is a lava lamp in the corner and glow-in-the-dark stars on the ceiling. A pile of CDs is piled high in the corner, and a desk sits under the window still covered in textbooks and papers as if she were still studying in high school.

My eyes keep scanning the room of her youth, but I find no pictures of her family. Only one of her and a guy that looks to be in college, while she seems to be about fifteen. Her hair is blue and purple. Her makeup is dark and heavy. And her outfit looks like she is about to run away with the band. The guy next to her is covered in tattoos with long dark hair. He looks like me if I hadn't met Abri.

My eyes scan to her bed that can't be more than full-sized and is covered in a dark comforter with red throw pillows.

I laugh. "I think you are going to have to sleep on top of me because there is no way we are both going to fit side by side."

She looks at me. *Finally.*

I can't read her expression though. I don't understand her lack of smile, her breathless expression, or her stillness.

Finally, she says "This is me. I'm not innocent. I'm not a planner. I'm not sweet. I prefer dark over light. I prefer heavy metal over pop. I prefer tattoos over bare skin. I prefer wild over easy.

"I'm not your sweetheart. I'm not your baby. I'm not your pretty girl. I'm a wild flame who never wanted to be tamed. But I followed orders. I changed. I became what everyone wanted me to be. The girl who finds a normal life. Graduates college and settles down with a man who can take care of me. It's not what I wanted, but I'm not sure I can go back to this." Mila holds her hand up motioning to the items in her room.

"I can't be the untouchable girl again with the bad boy boyfriend. And yet, I can't go back to being the nurse who waits for her knight to come save her. I don't know who or what I am anymore."

Tears threaten her eyes. She's trying to give me an out. A way to take back my words about being her boyfriend.

Instead, her words make me want her more. I walk to her, even though I want to run. I pull her into a deep hug as she releases the tears.

"I want all versions of you, Mila. I want the smart mouth version who calls me out on all of my bullshit. I want the sweet, innocent version who wants to be a nurse to take care of people. I want the wild version who's a free spirit and prefers tattoos to getting her nails done. I want all of you, Mila. The good, the bad. Your future, your past. It doesn't matter. I want you."

She blinks, and the tears slowly disappear.

"I can't date a bad boy again. No matter how badly I want to."

I kiss the wetness on her cheek. "Good thing I'm not a bad boy then. That version of me died years ago, just like this version of you. The version you prefer to keep hidden."

She smiles. "You are a bad boy, but you are also kind, and strong, and fierce, and loyal, and stubborn, and mine."

Her lips crash into mine, knocking me backward as she slings her arms around me. This kiss is different than our previous kisses. Sure our tongues push into each other's mouths, exploring with such a passion our lips can barely stay together from the force of the kiss. And yes, our hands grip each other exploring each other's bodies through our clothes. And of course, Mila moans and whimpers while I growl into the kiss.

But none of those things are what make this kiss different. This kiss connects us in a way that will be painful to break. She agrees to date me with this kiss. Agrees to be mine. She gives herself to me, and I give myself to her. Whatever happens from here on out is either going to be the most wonderful thing either of us has experienced, or it's going to wreck us. There is no in between.

"We are really doing this?" Mila asks between kisses.

"Well, we were doing this, but then you stopped to ask me a question."

She laughs and hits me playfully on the chest, knocking me back onto her bed.

She releases her hair from her high ponytail, letting her locks frame her face. "Yes, we are definitely doing this," I growl.

She licks her lips, then grabs the hem of her shirt and lifts, revealing her black bra. Then she slowly undoes her jeans like she's trying to strip for me again. I'm mesmerized with her body. With everything she does. I have to be hers. I've been hers since she climbed on my back after she injured herself on that hike. But I'm not sure she's been mine until this moment.

It feels like she has a vice grip on my heart, and if she squeezes too hard, she's going to obliterate me.

"Strip," she commands looking at me with flirty eyes. She stands confidently in front of me in nothing but her underwear and bra. Another reason I'm falling. No matter which version of herself she is, she's confident.

I quickly rid myself of my shirt, jeans, and underwear until I'm naked on her bed with a condom I pulled out of my jeans pocket lying next to me.

She eyes the condom but doesn't take it initially. Instead, she slowly climbs up the bed between my legs as she eyes my rock hard cock.

When she reaches me, she kisses the tip far too sweetly.

I groan. This is going to be torture if we continue moving this slowly.

She smirks as she lazily rolls her tongue around my shaft, barely touching me at all, but driving me insane all the same.

"That's not fair; I never tortured you."

She laughs. "You've tortured me every day I've worked for you."

I frown.

She grips my cock firmly in her hand as she wraps her mouth around the tip. *Damn, I about come with just her touch.*

She smiles like she knows the power she has over me. She's always had it over my body, but now she has it over my heart too. That scares me far more than what she is capable of doing to my body.

She pumps her hand up and down my shaft with her mouth moving in unison. My eyes roll back in my head as pleasure fills every crevice in my body. I never want this to end, and yet, I want more.

This isn't enough. Not for tonight.

I grab her hand, forcing her to stop, and pull her face toward mine to kiss her.

"Let me finish."

"No."

"I owe you after what you did for me in the car."

I chuckle, shaking my head. "This isn't about owing me anything. What I did was as much for me as it was for you. You don't owe me anything. Ever. Remember that. But right now, I'd really like to fuck my girlfriend for the first time."

She smiles and grabs the condom. She rips it open with her teeth and pushes it over my shaft. I rip her panties off and unhook her bra until she is fully exposed to me. I grab her hips and pull her on top of me, but I let her make the final movement on top of my cock.

She does, sliding over my cock with ease and desire I've never felt from her before.

"I want you so badly, Knight."

Her body slides up and down on top of me, making it hard for me to speak as her breasts bounce in front of me.

"You have me. All of me."

Our lips collide again as she rides me like she's been doing it her entire life. Faster and faster she moves until I'm lost in her. Her red lips, marking me. Her breasts bouncing for me with her nipples erect for me to torture. Her pussy clenching as she slides up and down my length. Everything she does makes my decision more concrete.

This is what love should always feel like. *This.* Passion, courage, strength, desire, want, need, lust. But I've seen the other side of love. The dark side that is all pain, jealousy, horror, and heartbreak. If love was always this, no one would ever break up.

"I want this to last forever," I whisper seconds before I know she's going to release. My words aren't a proposal or a promise. They aren't even a declaration of love. But it is the truth. A wish I know is impossible to come true.

"Then take this moment with you forever, Knight, and it will," she whispers back softly before digging her nails into my back and kissing me like it's a competition.

We both climb higher and higher trying to hold out from coming so this moment can last longer. On any other night we would fuck numerous times, but not tonight. We are too exhausted to go another round. It's after three in the morning. This is our only shot tonight.

I bite her lip. She nibbles on my ear.

I growl, and she moans louder.

"Come, Knight," she commands, finally knowing if one of us doesn't stop this it will literally continue forever because neither of us wants to stop.

"Not without you." My thumb presses over her clit rubbing as I buck into her harder. Pulling an orgasm from her as I find my own.

She falls on top of me and falls asleep almost instantly. I smile, loving her on top of me with my cock still inside her. I hold her in my arms and no matter if my arms fall asleep, my muscles ache, or my body begs me to roll over I won't. I'll hold her all night. Because for the first time, I have someone worth holding onto.

LAST NIGHT WAS the greatest and worst night I've had in a long time. Great because Mila is amazing. I've never felt so connected to anyone. And worst because Mila has never had so many nightmares in one night. I would wake her up and try to calm her down. Remind her that I'm here. That she's safe. But as soon as she fell asleep again, she would have another nightmare.

True to my promise, I held her all night long. Through every terror but nothing I did helped her. It was as if this house brought her back to her worst place. And not even I am strong enough to bring her out of it. *I need to tell her the truth.*

"Coffee will help," Mila says still curled up in my arms.

I nod.

Both of us are going to struggle to make it through today. Both of us lie in bed for a while longer until we hear Ren's voice yelling. Until we hear kids feet running, and we know if we don't get out of bed soon, it's going to be worse.

Mila climbs out of my arms and walks over to her duffel bag. She pulls out a sundress. I'm surprised she's wearing a dress when she prefers jeans anytime she's not working.

"I should probably shower first."

She shakes her head. "We don't have time."

"What?"

"My sister will start yelling at us to get out of bed in about five minutes. It's already after eight. That's sleeping in, in her view."

I frown, understanding why Mila doesn't get along with her family a little more now.

I pull out a pair of jeans and a T-shirt that matches the blue in Mila's dress. We need to be a united front to make it through today.

Mila bites her lip looking at the clothes I'm holding.

"What's wrong?"

"Did you bring anything nicer? A suit or khakis or a shirt with a collar?"

"No, I thought this weekend would be casual."

"Did you bring a long sleeved shirt?"

"No? Why would I? It's eighty degrees outside."

She frowns. "Sorry, it's stupid. My family isn't a big fan of tattoos, but you know what. It's fine. They need to see the real you. We aren't going to hide."

I grab the nape of her neck and kiss her trying to take her worries away.

"Mila!" Ren's voice rings through the house.

We both exhale and finish getting dressed quickly before heading downstairs for the trap awaiting us.

"Good morning," Mila says to her sister who is standing in the kitchen with a cup of coffee in her hand and a scowl on her face. She's dressed like we are going to a luncheon. In a curve-hugging dress, nicer than Mila's. Her hair is curled, and her makeup is full on. I don't know what Ren's plans are for today, but I feel very underdressed.

"More like good afternoon," Ren snaps.

Mila ignores her and walks to the coffee pot. I sneak behind her as she hands me a coffee. I whisper in Mila's ear, "Protect me."

Mila giggles.

Ren snaps her eyes at us like she just caught us making out in her car or something.

"I'm going to give Knight a tour of the house. Then we can talk," Mila says.

Ren narrows her eyes at us in a glare I'm sure is meant to persuade us to stay and talk now.

But Mila doesn't back down. She takes my hand and pulls me out of the impressive kitchen that despite its large size, felt tiny because of her sister's stare.

"Don't worry about my sister. She's a bitch to everyone," Mila says.

I hook my arm in hers. "I see why you avoided driving here as long as possible yesterday."

She nods.

"I'll try to come up with a good excuse for us to leave early. An emergency like my app crashed. Or my dog is missing."

"You don't have a dog."

"I could have a dog."

Mila laughs. "Thanks, but I don't think it will work. It's only two days. We can last that long."

I raise an eyebrow in fear.

She laughs again. "We can."

I don't think we can, but I let Mila lead me through her mansion of a house. It's beautiful. I don't understand how someone who came from so much money couldn't afford college or a place to stay.

"My parents were broke when they died. Us kids just didn't realize it. My brother Henry and Ren found a way to save the house. And now Ren can easily afford the mortgage on this place," Mila answers my unspoken question.

"How do you feel coming back here?"

"Like I don't belong here. All my demons come back when I'm here."

I pull her close to me. "Let me help you escape them by creating new memories here."

She nods and continues the tour, leading into the children's playroom.

"This is Bailey and Camden," Mila says as two kids come running toward me. "This is Knight."

"Cool name," Bailey says.

I smile, at least the kids are cool. "Thanks."

"Can you teach us to play chess? You can be the Knight!" Camden says.

"Sure," I say. I don't have a clue about chess, but I don't think I get to be the knight. I'm positive that's not how the game works.

I look over at Mila who mouths *I'm going to talk to Ren.*

I nod even though inside I'm yelling *Fuck, fuck, fuck.*

I don't want her anywhere near Ren. I want her with me, *always.*

I start making up rules for chess, trying to stay focused on the kids, instead of on the voices carrying from the other room. But each word I hear pisses me off more.

"Mila, how do you get kicked out of college in your last semester? I'm not letting you live here rent free."

"Mila, he's married to Abri. Abri is one of my closest friends. How could you do this to her? You're a home wrecker! A slut! A whore! Can't you see you are headed down the same path as before?"

I can't take it.

I move the knight forward on the chess board, and Camden captures it.

"Oh no! I lose." I mock getting stabbed and defeated. "I'll be right back. I need to ask your mother a question. Keep playing."

I get up off the carpeted floor and head to the kitchen where Ren is yelling at Mila, and Mila is frozen.

Shit.

I walk over to Mila, ignoring Ren's fierce stares and put my arm around her. "Mila isn't a home wrecker and she sure as hell isn't a slut or a whore. I was divorcing Abri long before Mila came into my life."

Ren shakes her head, ignoring me.

"How could you? After what happened with Nasser?" Ren asks staring at Mila.

I have no idea who Nasser is.

"That was five years ago. I've changed since then. Knight isn't Nasser."

Ren eyes me up and down. "He looks exactly like him except older."

She's talking about the boy in the picture. The same one I thought I looked like.

"How could you do this to Abri? She was our friend."

"No, she was *your* friend. I barely knew her. And I didn't even remember her until she reminded me of that fact."

"That's crazy; you have a perfect memory!"

Mila's sobbing now, but her voice is stronger than ever. "I have a perfect memory *now*; I don't remember anything from before. It's all a blur up until that night."

Ren shakes her head, and I pull Mila tighter, backing her up without saying anything. Just letting her know I'm here for her.

"And you!" Ren turns her attention on me. *Good, it's me she should be focused on.* "How could you do this to Abri? You loved Abri. I saw it the night our parents died."

It's like a ghost returned at that moment. A past none of us realized we were hiding from each other. The one thing none of us have spoken about because we weren't ready to share. It's also the one thing that can set me free.

Mila steps out, away from my grasp. "Wait? You were there?"

"I can explain."

"No, you told me you've never met Ren."

"I haven't."

Mila looks to Ren who clearly disagrees with my statement.

"I never spoke to Ren. I might have seen her at the hospital when I was there to support Abri who was supporting Ren in her loss, but I never spoke to Ren, and I don't remember her. Trust me, Ren is someone I would remember."

"Did you meet me?" Mila asks. All of her fury now focused on me instead of her sister.

I can't lie. I promised I would never lie. She never asked me before, which is the only reason I didn't have to tell her.

"Yes."

Mila's eyes drop in disappointment.

"Let me explain."

Mila's eyes slowly drift back to mine with wide eyes.

I don't wait for her to give me permission to explain, I just start talking.

"We talked for only a moment. And I didn't realize I had met you before until—"

The doorbell rings, stopping my thoughts.

Ren's kids start yelling.

The world doesn't stop just because I want it to.

"I need to make sure the kids haven't killed each other. Answer the door, Mila. It's probably Henry. I told him to get his ass here as soon as I realized who Knight was. He's no knight. He's Ace the asshole."

Ren leaves Mila and me alone in the kitchen.

I try again. "I didn't realize I had met you until—"

Mila ignores me and walks to the front door. She opens it, and I expect to see her brother. Instead, Abri is standing in the doorway looking smug and gorgeous in a black dress.

I didn't realize I had met Mila until I kissed her in the hospital.

Mila turns with a glare in her eye. "I'll leave you and your *wife* to talk."

Shit, now I'm fucked.

17 MILA

I lock myself in my childhood bedroom. I'm not speaking to Knight or Ren or anyone until I remember. If I'm going to have a chance to recall it, this is the best place to try. *Where the darkness started.*

I need to remember that night in order to have a shot at figuring out how I feel about Knight.

I sit cross-legged on the center of my bed. A bed Knight became my whole world in. And today, he became my nightmare.

I push Knight out of my head as I close my eyes. Tears have been staining my cheeks since I realized Knight knew me before. He knew me five years ago, and although he never lied, he refused to tell me the truth.

I wipe the tears on the back of my hand, keeping my eyes closed. *Remember I plead with myself, please remember.*

"NO!" I scream. My screams mean nothing though. My voice isn't loud enough to stop it from happening.

"Nasser, please," I beg for him. But it doesn't stop.

. . .

I SEE the bright lights shining at me, almost blinding me. I'm flying. Or falling. I can't tell the difference.

I scream, or maybe it's someone else. Or maybe it's both.

BEEPING from the machine next to me as I'm lying completely broken. Pain is consuming me. Pulling me into a dark hole, I'll never be able to escape.

"THIS IS YOUR FAULT, Mila. All of this is your fault. I will never be able to forgive you," Ren's voice says over and over.

I OPEN my eyes as I shake on the bed. No memories of Knight flooded my head. I don't remember Abri visiting me. I don't remember anything except the pain of what happened, and the guilt of what I caused.

I could ask Ren to remind me of all the details. Or as many as she remembers, but her story would be confounded with her own pain.

Knight.

He's the only one who can tell me the truth. What he remembers. How we met. Nothing else from that dark day matters, just how Knight and I met.

Once I know his truth, then I can decide what my next move is. If we can still date after this. If I can still work for him. If we can have any relationship at all.

Maybe we can start over with full honesty.

I can't remember my past, but maybe he can.

I go to the door, surprised Knight or Ren isn't already on the other side waiting for me, but the house is eerily silent.

I walk downstairs and find a note on the counter from Ren.

· · ·

TOOK the kids to go pick up Henry from the airport. We will all talk when we get back. And you will fix this before it becomes a bigger problem.

—Ren

I LEAVE the note on the counter and search for Knight and Abri. Hopefully, he kicked her out so Knight and I can talk. I search the living room, office, and kitchen but don't find Knight anywhere. I've been in my bedroom for over half an hour. Abri should be gone.

But as I walk toward the front door where I left Knight, I know she isn't. They are yelling, and Knight has Abri pinned against the wall.

I gasp when I see her through the window beside the door.

I walk closer because I need to know the truth. Even if this is the only way, I'll get it.

I should run away. That's what the voice in my head says. *Run away. Keep your heart from more pain.*

But I can't move.

I watch their lips move. I watch the anger explode. And then I hear the words that break me.

"You killed our baby," Abri screams as tears roll down her face. I wait for Knight to deny it. I wait for him to yell, scream, argue. It doesn't happen. Instead, he pulls her to him, and he hugs her as she grows limp in his arms.

I stumble backward. I hit the glass end table behind me, and we both shatter to the floor.

"Mila Burns! Can you do..."

I don't listen to Ren yelling. It doesn't matter what she says.

I can't be in a relationship with Knight.

I can't date him.

I can't work for him.

I can't be friends with him.

I have horrible judgment in men. I always pick the bad boys. The ones that hurt me.

I thought Knight would tell me his story, and we could find a way to heal together.

But Knight doesn't get to talk to me.

He doesn't get to apologize.

I'm pulling back my soul, but I'm afraid I've already given away my heart. I'm afraid I gave it to him five years ago.

18 KNIGHT

I didn't get to talk to Mila. I was never let back into the house. Eventually, Henry came out and yelled at me to leave after throwing my suitcase on the front porch.

I tried calling Mila. Texting. I tried stopping by the house, but she never answered me.

So instead, I rented a car and have been sitting in it down the block from her sister's house. Waiting. It's only been a few hours since I was kicked out of the house, but I know Mila won't last long in that house.

I spot Mila's beat up Subaru barreling down the road. She doesn't notice me; she's too focused on leaving. I don't blame her. She wasn't kidding when she said her family didn't know her or appreciate her.

And I became the asshole she always thought I was right before her eyes. I don't know what Mila's siblings told her. Or what Abri might have said. Or what nightmare Mila has come up with in her head. I deserve all of her wrath.

I start my rental car and zoom after her. I watch her the entire time back. I make a note to fix the bump on the back of her car where she backed over my motorcycle. But mostly, I just watch her drive away from me and hope, despite the tears I assume are continuously falling from her eyes as she drives, that she will give me a chance to explain.

I'm surprised yet happy to see her park her car in front of my apartment building. I take my time following her inside. If she knows I've been following her the entire time she might run off.

I open the door to my apartment cautiously, as if a lion might attack if I open it too quickly.

"Mila?" I say as I step into the bedroom.

She slowly steps out of the closet.

I suck in a breath when I see her. She's wearing one of my T-shirts along with a pair of jeans. Her face is puffy but her eyes determined.

"I'm sorry," I say, knowing those are the first words that need to leave my mouth.

She holds up a hand, stopping me from moving or speaking.

"I'm leaving."

I close my eyes to keep my pain in. "Mila, please. Can we talk first? Give me a chance to explain why I didn't tell you we've met before. Then you can decide what you want to do."

"No, I don't want to talk. I've talked enough. I've heard enough. I quit, and whatever it is we are doing, dating or fucking, we are done."

She steps back into the closet, and I can't help but fight for her. I would do anything for her.

I stop at the closet's edge as I watch her throw her clothes into her duffel bag.

"Stay, please. I'll sleep in the guest bedroom."

She continues packing.

"I'll sleep at Cole's place."

She starts throwing shoes into the bag.

"Let me pay for a new place for you to stay."

Her head snaps to me. "So you can keep tabs on me and know where I am?"

"No, I'll give you the cash. I just want to make sure you're safe."

"I'll be fine."

She picks up her duffel bag, slings it over her shoulder, and storms out of the closet to the bathroom.

She starts tossing various other toiletries into the bag. Hairbrush, straightener, toothbrush. But then she stops and faces me.

"I can't remember."

My eyes widen. "I know. You have a perfect memory of everything else. You remember phone numbers, statistics, names, and spreadsheets. I know you would have remembered me, no matter how short of a time we met. I know you can't remember." *Even though I wish you would. Or maybe I wish she could forget.*

Her eyes pierce mine, and I stop talking. I don't get to talk. Only her.

"I only remember bits and pieces in my nightmares. Never the full story. I only know what the newspapers wrote about that night and what my family told me. I know I fucked up then, but I'm not going to repeat my mistake by falling for another asshole."

I nod, understanding but wishing I could help her fill in the gaps. The problem is I have gaps too. Not because I forgot, I could never forget her, but because I wasn't there. And she never told me what happened. All I know is I'm the one that fucked up, not her.

"I can't remember," she repeats. "It's like my brain shut everything off before that night. And my perfect memory now is a coping mechanism to flood out the memories from before. If I'm preoccupied with remembering my present, then I don't have enough space left to remember my past."

Mila looks at me like she wants me to talk, but when I open my mouth, she shakes her head and moves past me. I follow her as she heads downstairs to the kitchen. She walks to the fridge pulling out a bottle of water and drinks it like it's her life savior. The only thing keeping her alive. Finally, she stares at me.

"I heard you and Abri."

I swallow hard, the lump in my throat growing large as her words penetrate through me.

"Abri told me you beat her."

I close my eyes, wishing there was something I could say to make her realize the words Abri said weren't true. But I don't deserve to get to defend myself.

"She said you killed your baby."

I close my eyes. There is nothing I can say to refute those words or make my own pain lessen enough to be able to talk.

"Goodbye, Knight."

Mila walks to the door, but I can't let her leave. Despite the pain I feel every time I think of losing my child, I can't let that pain overwhelm me and cause me to lose another person I love.

"Wait," I run to the door and put a hand on it, stopping her from leaving.

"No words I say will be enough to make you change your mind about Abri and me, but I can tell you one truth. I didn't realize who you were until I kissed you in the hospital and from that moment on, I realized you could help me. I was selfish. I wanted your help to take down Abri. I created a plan to sell the company to Cole to ensure she got nothing. But I thought you could help me take more from Abri because you had a connection to her when you were younger through Ren. I'm so sorry for using you. I never wanted to hurt you. I thought I could help you."

I suck in a breath.

"But I don't care about any of that anymore. I don't care about hurting Abri. I don't care about my company. I don't care if I go completely bankrupt. All I care about is you. I lo—"

"Stop."

"Mila please, let me finish."

"No. Most women could give you a second chance, but I can't. Not with my past. I can't afford to give out second chances."

I'm frozen watching her leave. I consider chasing after her and forcing her to hear my words. I consider locking her in my bedroom to know she's safe.

I do neither. I've made too many decisions about her life without her input. I cost her her career. I forced her to live with me. To work with me. And brought up a past she clearly needs to keep hidden. Whatever happened that night, it's worse than I thought.

I need to let Mila Burns go. I need to give Abri whatever she wants to ensure she stays away from Mila. Then I need to get drunk and forget the last five years ever happened.

I don't know how long I stand in the entryway staring at the door. Five minutes, an hour, or ten hours. But eventually, I realize I should have gone with the option that involved forcing her to stay. Because I realize too late where she's most likely sleeping tonight. In a cheap motel room or her car. I gave her a couple grand, but that's all the money she has. She doesn't have another job, although I will gladly give her the money I promised her if she will take it. But even the couple grand I gave her she won't spend out of principle.

She'll sleep in her damn car.

I jerk my phone out of my pocket and dial Lana's number. She's the only friend Mila has that she keeps in contact with.

"Hello? Who's this?" Lana answers.

"Lana, this is Ace Knight. I'm Mila's um..."

"I know who you are. And no, she's not here. She's not allowed on campus because of you."

"I know, and I'm sorry. I fucked up. I want to make things right, but I can't do that if I don't find her."

Pause.

"Her favorite place to sleep in her car was on Walnut Street, by the Old 17th Avenue Bridge."

"Thank you, Lana."

I drive to the spot Lana gave me, but I don't find Mila. I drive to the office and question everyone I can, but she's not there. I get desperate and call Abri, but she doesn't answer me.

Cole.

I dial his number.

"Hello," Cole answers.

"Is she there?"

Cole swallows.

"Fucking, answer me, Cole. Is Mila staying with you?"

"Yes."

"I'll be right there."

"No, Knight. You won't."

"You're not fucking my girlfriend."

Cole sighs. "Go to sleep, Knight. Give Mila some space."

"No, I need to be there for her. She can't sleep without me."

"She's sleeping just fine. I'll watch out for her though, and make sure she doesn't get any nightmares."

"Cole! You fucking bastard."

Silence. He ended the call.

I slam my phone down. Cole's my friend. He won't hurt Mila, but Mila might try to use him to hurt me. To make sure things end permanently between us because she knows I can never forgive her if she sleeps with my best friend. And she can't forgive me for keeping the truth from her.

I'm fucked no matter what happens.

19 MILA

I open my eyes slowly like I've been asleep all night. I don't think I slept more than five minutes at a time without a nightmare impeding my sleep. I've been lying in Cole's bed for the last hour awake, but unable to convince myself to get out of bed or even open my eyes.

I swing my legs over to the side of the bed to force myself up, taking a break from trying to sleep.

"Umf."

I retract my legs as I hit a lump on the floor. I turn on the lamp on the nightstand and look down to see Cole lying on the floor.

"Morning," he says rolling over.

I tuck my legs underneath me as I sit on the edge of his bed.

"You shouldn't have slept on the floor."

He cracks his neck as he sits up. "You were having nightmares. I didn't want to leave you alone."

"You could have slept in the bed with me."

Cole shakes his head as he laughs off my statement. "No, I couldn't. Not if I wanted to keep breathing after Knight found out."

"He wouldn't find out."

"Knight is my best friend. I would never betray him. Even if he deserves it."

Cole stands up.

"You're a good man. I'm sorry I ever thought differently."

Cole shrugs. "Don't worry; I can be as much of an ass as Knight is."

I smile.

"Breakfast?"

"Sure, what do you have?"

He frowns. "I think I have cereal, although I don't think I have any milk."

"Do you have coffee?"

"Yes, that I have."

"That's all I need."

Cole smiles and starts walking toward the kitchen in his low riding sweatpants and T-shirt. I wait until he leaves to climb out of bed. I'm still wearing Knight's T-shirt. I don't know why I put it on in the first place other than I needed to feel close to him. I needed to smell him. I needed to know we still share a connection despite how much I hate him.

I'm wearing shorts underneath his T-shirt, but they aren't visible since his shirt fits more like a dress than a shirt on me.

I walk into the kitchen, and Cole only stares at my bare legs once before he sets a cup of coffee in front of me. He also pours me a bowl of Cinnamon Crunch cereal.

"Knight would kill me if he found out I didn't feed you."

I sigh and pop a couple of pieces of the sweet cereal into my mouth. I should have snuck into Lana's dorm room. Then I wouldn't have had to talk about Knight.

"You're staying here until you can afford your own place. I'm not arguing about it. And if you think Knight is bad, I'm worse when it comes to being a controlling prick. If I find you sleeping on the streets, I will drag your ass back here and lock you up in my bedroom."

I smile. I don't plan on sleeping on the streets again. I only did that once during the summer between freshman and sophomore year. My scholarship didn't cover summer dorm rooms unless I was taking summer classes. I was stupid and thought I could find a job and a cheap place to live easily. I was wrong on both accounts.

"Don't worry, I'll find a job soon, and you won't have to worry about making sure you have breakfast for me."

"Work for me," Cole says, his bright eyes suddenly serious.

"Really? You would do that for me?"

"Of course, you're Knight's girl. I would do anything for you."

I shake my head. "I'm not Knight's anything."

"Fine, but regardless of what happened, he loves you."

I'm not sure he does. Not after I saw him with Abri. I think he might still love her.

"How about being my assistant? I know you are qualified for the job."

I groan. "Really? Can't I waitress or bartend or something?"

He opens his mouth, and I can already tell what's going to fall out of it. Knight would kill me if he found you waitressing in the skimpy outfits and getting ogled by men.

"Fine, I'll be your assistant."

Cole grins.

"When should I start?"

"I could use some help when I go into work in an hour or so." He wiggles his eyebrows as he says it.

It's Sunday. I know he doesn't work on Sundays. He's just trying to distract me. But I'll take it.

"Give me two hours. I want to go for a run and then shower."

"Deal," he says.

I get up and head to Cole's bedroom, which has now become mine. I tried to use one of his spare bedrooms, but he wouldn't let me. He said his bed was the best and it had the only functioning shower.

I walk to the bathroom to change into something I can run in and brush my teeth, but I forgot my toothpaste and can't find any in his cabinets. I walk back out to the kitchen.

"Cole, where is your toothpaste?" I freeze. Knight is standing in the kitchen next to Cole. *Traitor*, I mouth to Cole who shrugs and slinks away, leaving Knight and me alone.

Knight's eyes take all of me in greedily, unlike when Cole looked at me. He doesn't hide his lust when he stares at my bare legs. He doesn't pretend he isn't looking. His eyes burn into my skin with a passion I can't escape.

Finally, Knight's eyes trail back to the room I just left: Cole's bedroom.

He exhales deeply with a grimace as if his words are going to fight back and hurt him. "You fucked Cole." His words aren't a question. He doesn't say them accusatorially. He says them sadly like his words are fact.

I cross my arms across my chest. "I don't think that's really any of your business. We are broken up."

He nods, dropping his head. He doesn't look like he slept much either. I figured he would be hungover, but I'm not sure he is. At least, he doesn't smell like alcohol or vomit.

He's wearing another gray T-shirt, matching the one I'm wearing. *Always matching.*

He reaches into his back pocket and pulls out a check. He holds it out to me. I stare at it skimming it quickly. It's made out to me for $250,000.

I shake my head. "I don't want your money, Knight."

"I'm the one who fucked up and caused you to want to end our contract. You should get paid for your time."

"No, we never signed an official contract. And like I said, I don't want your money. I found a new job."

"Oh." He slips the check back into his pocket before pulling out another piece of paper and holds it out to me.

"You're enrolled for next semester. The school also wrote you an apology for your suspension after realizing I was the one at fault."

I take the piece of paper confirming my enrollment for next semester. I'll take it because I deserve to be able to finish school. It was his fault I'm not currently finishing my last couple of months.

He grabs the nape of his neck as he stares at me with sad eyes. He looks completely broken and helpless.

"Is that all?" I ask.

"No, it's nowhere near all. I know I fucked up in an unforgivable way. I broke your trust in me. But know I'll wait forever for you. For you to come back to work or be my friend, or my girlfriend. I'll take whatever I can get. Even if it means we can only be pen pals. I don't care. I just need you in my life."

I close my eyes because his words sting. Nothing he does should be able to hurt me. He shouldn't be able to pierce through my armor, but he does. It's why I can't be in his life.

"I won't replace Abri. It's clear you aren't over her. You comforted her. Held her like you were still together. You still have pictures of her scattered throughout your apartment. You had me do her job. I'm not Abri. And I never will be."

Knight's mouth falls, and I think it might hit the floor and shatter, much like my own heart. He carefully chooses his next words.

"I hugged Abri because I'm the only person in her life who understands what it's like to lose a baby. The pain is indescribable. I keep the pictures to remind me of the pain I caused us both. And I had you be my assistant because it was the only way I could think to have you in my life. I don't love Abri. Not anymore. I could never love Abri again. We've been through too much. Abri will confirm that for you. She hates me as much as I used to love her."

I nod, but it doesn't change anything. He doesn't love Abri, but I can't love him.

"I'm not ready to talk about losing Gideon yet. I wish I could. It might be the only thing that can bring you back to me."

Gideon. The baby had a name. And it breaks my heart. Even if I could forgive him, I'm not sure I want to be in his life. I will have to carry his heartbreak along with my own. I'm not strong enough to handle that burden.

"I'm not sure anything you say will help me to forgive you."

He stills like I just slid a sword through his chest. A low groan pours through him like he can't stand to continue breathing.

And I can't help but ease a tiny bit of his pain. "I didn't fuck Cole."

His eyes widen as a tiny part of him comes back to life.

"You think I would put your shirt back on if I fucked Cole?"

Hope. I just gave Knight a tiny drop of hope. And now I regret it because there is no hope.

I turn and walk back to Cole's bedroom leaving Knight alone in the kitchen.

I want to know Knight's story, despite how it could hurt me. It's clear he blames himself for the death of Gideon. And knowing the truth could hurt me more than knowing he hid it from me.

But can I blame him for the death of his baby when I'm the reason my parents are dead?

20 KNIGHT

I try to open the door, but it won't budge. I'm trapped in this cage of metal, rubber, and glass. I kick the door, but nothing happens.

I look over at Cole who is coughing profusely, trying to rid his lungs of the smoke burning its way through his body. We don't have much time left. Cole tries to push his door open, but his attempts are weak.

It's up to me.

I kick harder and harder, but it's not helping. I have to focus on the glass; it's the only way. I start kicking the glass and then use my elbow to try and penetrate it.

The smoke is filling the car now. I can't escape it. I can't breathe. We are going to die.

I need something sharp. My foot is doing nothing to the window. I feel around but don't remember anything sharp I keep in the car.

My head falls back against the headrest. I'm exhausted. I need a break. But there is no time for breaks.

The headrest falls down from the weight of my head. The headrest!

I turn around and yank as hard as I can against the headrest. It breaks free, and I see the two sharp metal prongs that usually hold the *headrest into the back of the seat. I start slamming the ends of the headrest into the window.*

Crack.

The glass begins to break.

Fucking yes!

I hit the glass over and over with the headrest. Each time I hit the glass, more cracks form. Until it shatters.

"Cole!" I shout, prepared to pull him through the window.

He doesn't stir.

Shit.

He needs out, now.

I hook my arms under his armpits and pull with everything I have, coughing every second as I suck in smoke along with a tiny bit of oxygen.

I climb through the window, pulling Cole with me. His body thuds against the asphalt as I yank him out of the car. I wince, watching the blood spill from his head where it hit the street. But he's safe now. He's free. I hear the ambulances. We are going to live.

"You can't save everyone. You saved Cole. You saved yourself. But you can't save Mila. She's mine."

ABRI'S WORDS wake me up. *Fuck, it was just a nightmare, but it felt so real.* Probably because the first part was true. The car accident, the smoke. But I've never heard Abri threaten Mila's life, but now that I've dreamt it, I know she will. It's her next move to hurt me.

If I do nothing, then Mila is as good as dead. Abri half attempted to hurt her before while they were rock climbing. She will try worse. She will ruin Mila or kill her. She knows how much Mila means to me. She will do anything to hurt me.

It's four in the morning. I should wait a few more hours and make sure this is how I'll feel in a few hours. But saving Mila can't wait.

I pick up my phone and dial Abri's number. She answers on the second ring. "Yes, Ace?"

"I'm ready to sign the divorce papers."

I can feel her smiling on the other end of the line. "And what makes you think I'm ready to sign?"

"Because I'm giving you everything you want."

IT TAKES a week to get the paperwork figured out and a time where everyone can meet. I thought waiting a week would be hard, but I know Mila is as safe as she can be with Cole. And I took the week to begin to adjust to my new found freedom. I don't know why I didn't do this in the first place. Making sure Abri paid for her crimes isn't worth it.

So I did everything I love. I hiked, I rock climbed, I rode my motorcycle too fast. I drank, I smoked, I ate fried food. I slept in late and went to bed even later. I should have felt more alive than I have in years. But I didn't.

Instead, I feel a calmness because I'm a hundred percent sure I'm doing the right thing.

My lawyer told me to wear a suit and tie to the meeting, but in about thirty minutes, I won't own any suits anymore, so it felt wrong to wear one now. Instead, I'm wearing a black T-shirt with dark jeans. I'm in mourning. Not at the loss of anything other than Mila.

I walk into the building and my lawyer, Doug Lundy, sits on a bench waiting for me. He's dressed in a blue suit. He eyes my clothes but doesn't comment. *Good, you fucking work for me. You don't get to dictate what I wear or what I do.*

"You sure about this? We can get you a much better deal. That's why you hired my firm," Lundy says.

"I'm sure. I was an idiot for not doing this months ago."

Lundy sighs.

"Don't worry, Lundy. I made sure the agreement calls for you getting paid well for your work."

"I'm not worried about getting paid. I've been a divorce lawyer for a long time. I've won several cases and lost others. But I've never felt more like justice isn't prevailing than in this case. You deserve better, Knight."

I shrug. "It doesn't matter what I deserve." *I'm protecting someone who deserves the world, and all I gave her were a bunch of half-truths.*

Lundy opens the door, and we step inside the mediation room. Abri and her team of three lawyers are already sitting on one side of the long table. She's wearing a suit. She's all business.

Lundy and I take a seat opposite them.

"I didn't think you would show," Abri says.

"I'd rather get divorced than be rich."

She smiles. "Good."

Lundy pulls the papers out of his briefcase and lays them on the table. "I know everyone involved has had time to review the settlement, but let's review all the terms and ensure everyone still understands and agrees. If there are any objections, we can discuss them and decide if we can reach an agreement today."

I already know we will easily reach an agreement today.

"First item, Abri will—"

"Please call me Mrs. Knight, as that is my name," Abri says.

Lundy looks to me, and I nod. Abri probably won't even change her last name after we get divorced. She will keep my name just to piss me off for all of eternity. But I won't let her know that now. She's won enough. I won't give her any more than what is already stated in the document.

"Mrs. Knight will get the apartment and all of its contents," Lundy says.

Everyone nods.

"Mrs. Knight will retain all of the vehicles acquired during the marriage with the exception of Mr. Knight's motorcycle, which was acquired after the two separated."

More nods.

"Mrs. Knight will receive all of the money the couple acquired throughout the almost five-year marriage."

My eyes burn into Abri. I am giving her my money. She may have earned half of it, but half isn't enough for her. She's greedy, and I couldn't care less about the money.

Lundy sucks in a breath before he states the last line of the agreement. He looks at me one last time to ensure I haven't changed my mind. I haven't. I could give her everything but this one thing and Abri would still be pissed. She would still try to hurt Mila. I won't let that happen.

I nod my head for him to continue.

"Mr. Knight will turn over complete and full ownership of his company Perfect Match. He will give her all of his stock and board membership roles, including any rights to make any decision about the company's future endeavors."

Abri's smile turns into a devilish grin. She thinks I will back out. She thinks I will object to her getting my company. The one thing I cared about almost as much as I did Abri when we were married.

I love Perfect Match. I loved starting something and building it to an incredible place. But I don't love having it used as a bargaining chip. I don't love that no matter how much I love the company, it will always be tainted with thoughts of Abri.

"Do all parties agree to the terms written out?" Lundy asks.

Abri's lawyers lean in to whisper in her ear.

"We agree to the terms if Ace does," Abri says.

Lundy leans over and whispers. "It's not too late to change your mind. You don't have to give her the company."

"I do."

"Since you are giving up everything, which isn't required under the law, I also advise you to add a clause where she can't take you to court or file criminal complaints from the time during your marriage.

It's clear she wants to make you pay for the separation, and I could see her taking additional steps to ensure you pay. And at that time, you won't have any money left to fight her with," Lundy whispers.

I stare into Abri's bright eyes. "Thank you for your advice, but I'm ready to sign the divorce papers as is."

Lundy reluctantly hands me a pen as he slides the papers to me. I sign my name, more sure about this decision than I was on the day I married Abri. That day I was so certain. Today, I know what certainty feels like.

I slide the papers to Abri who signs them as fast as I did.

"Congratulations, we will file the papers today, and you will be legally divorced."

I stand and walk out before I have time for anyone else to say anything else.

Cole is standing in the hallway when I exit. I should have known he would find out about the divorce today.

"You divorced yet?"

"Yes."

"Good, I never liked that bitch."

I raise an eyebrow. "I thought you cared about her? I thought you thought I was treating her unfairly? I thought you thought she was my perfect match?"

Cole shakes his head. "I was trying to be a good friend. She always gave me a bad vibe. So what did she get?"

"Everything."

Cole gasps. "You fucking idiot. She shouldn't have gotten anything."

"You're right. I guess she didn't get everything. I'm able to walk away with my heart and body still intact."

"She did something to the car, didn't she?"

"I think so. I think she did something to the breaks, which is why I couldn't stop the car."

"And you let her get away with it! You let her take everything!"

"Yes, to protect Mila."

Cole stops screaming. "You're still an idiot, but I would have done the same thing."

I'm glad Mila has him. He's been a good friend to me over the years. But it kills me she will talk to him and not me right now.

"Are you afraid she will do anything now? To hurt Mila or you?"

"No, I'm not afraid if she does because I didn't do anything wrong. At least not to her. The truth would come out. But she won't. She thinks I have proof she tried to kill us."

"Do you?"

I shrug. "I'm not sure." Mila was the only one who could have evidence Abri tried to hurt me. But Mila hates me. She wouldn't do anything to help me, and I wouldn't want her to. Because helping me involves remembering a past that is darker than I realized. And above everything, I don't want to hurt Mila.

21 MILA

My stomach growls as I step into Cole's downtown apartment. It's not as nice as Knight's, but it's still larger than anything I will ever be able to afford. I'm tired, but not because working as Cole's assistant is exhausting. Being his assistant is the easiest job in the world. His club runs almost flawlessly. Everyone knows their job and does it without question.

Cole gives me a few tasks he needs help with each day. I answer a small number of emails and then follow Cole around and help him. Which mostly means I get to listen to Cole talk about Knight.

I now know too many random facts and stories about Knight. I know Knight let Cole sleep on his couch when Cole was broke. I know Knight gave Cole the initial investment to start his club. I've heard the story about how Knight got his first tattoo of a rubber ducky on a dare when he was fifteen. He has since covered it with a dragon tattoo.

I've heard too many stories of when Cole and Knight would fight over girls and how Knight would always win. And I know Knight once saved Cole's life when they were sixteen. Cole was drunk at a party and fell into the pool. He was knocked unconscious, and nobody around the pool attempted to help. Knight jumped in and saved him, then kicked everyone's asses for not helping.

"We should order pizza tonight. I'm starving," I say to Cole.

"I can cook."

I frown. "No, you can't."

"Fine, then you cook."

I laugh. "I can't cook. I've never had a kitchen of my own before. I have no idea how to cook."

"I can cook," Knight says, sending chills down my spine. I turn and face him for the first time in a week.

"That would be great." Cole walks over and hugs his friend.

I don't respond. I just walk into my bedroom. Well, Cole's bedroom I now sleep in. Cole has made himself a cot on the floor so he can be there for me when I have nightmares.

I slam the door behind me as I enter.

The door opens a second later. "Knight, I don't have time to deal with you—"

"It's just me," Cole says.

I turn. "What is Knight doing here? I thought you were on my side? I thought you said Knight was in the wrong?"

"He was."

"Then what is he doing here?"

"He's moving in until he finds a new job."

"What?"

"He divorced Abri and gave her everything."

I gasp. I don't know what I was expecting, but this isn't it.

Shit. I need to move out. I can't live here with him being here.

"You're not leaving, Mila. You promised me you wouldn't leave until you found someplace safe to go."

"I'll sneak into Lana's dorm. I can stay with her."

"No, you can't."

I pout. "I'll think of something."

"Until then, you are staying here."

"Fine," I growl.

Cole's smile is faint on his lips. "I have one more story I need to tell you. I know you are tired of my stories about Knight, but I promise after this one, you can get his stories directly from him."

I roll my eyes and sit on the edge of the bed. Waiting for another Knight-is-amazing story.

"Knight is an asshole."

My ears perk up at his words. Maybe this is a we-hate-Knight story.

"He was an asshole to my girlfriends. He never thought any of them were good enough. He teased me constantly when we were kids. He's punched me in the face at least six times. He's gotten drunk too many times where I had to come save his ass. He wasn't a perfect boyfriend or husband to Abri. Even though he loved her, he kept up his guard too much. But no matter what we've been through, Knight has always been there for me."

I nod. "Are you done?"

"No, that wasn't the story. I want to tell you about the car accident."

"The one that caused you both to end up in the hospital?"

He nods. "I didn't know the truth about what happened until recently. It was a sunny day. But somehow, our car ended up crashing into the median on the highway at almost eighty miles an hour. It was the scariest moment of my life. Although, I'm not sure if it even makes the top five most terrifying moments for Knight.

"Somehow, we both stayed in the car when we crashed. I guess the airbags did their job. But the car caught on fire. Smoke filled the car, and I was too beat up to be able to get out."

Cole takes a second to compose himself before continuing.

"Knight wouldn't give up on getting us out. He broke the window, but by then, I was passed out and dead weight. Knight should have climbed out and saved himself. He could have died, the smoke was that bad, but instead of saving himself he made sure he got me free."

I feel a tear at his words, but I won't let his story affect me.

"Afterwards, I was thankful he saved my life, but also suspicious of what caused the accident. I couldn't come up with anything that would have caused it. I thought maybe he had been drinking, but I hadn't noticed."

I blink, not understanding.

"Abri caused the accident. She messed with the breaks."

I gasp.

Cole walks up to me and strokes my hair. "Don't hate Knight for trying to keep you out of his messed up life. Don't hate him for keeping secrets. It's the only way he knows how to protect the people he loves."

I nod, drinking in his words.

"Knight gave Abri everything to protect you. She got his money, his apartment, his company, his life. He was ready to fight for what she did to him. To us. But he wasn't willing to risk you."

Cole leaves, and I cry until there is nothing left but sobs. *What do I do now?*

My stomach rumbles, reminding me of how hungry I am. I splash water on my face in the ensuite's sink, so I no longer look like I'm crying, and then I walk to the kitchen.

"You're just in time. Knight fixed enchiladas," Cole says.

I smile at Knight who gives me a knowing look. "It was the closest thing I could come up with to tacos without pissing you off by actually making your favorite food. But don't complain if it's bad. Cole has no food in this place."

"Hey," Cole says throwing a chip at Knight.

We fix our plates, and I take a bite. *Damn, it's delicious.* Cole and I both moan as we eat.

"What have you been feeding her, Cole? You both look like you've lost weight since I last saw you," Knight says.

Cole frowns. "Um...mainly macaroni and cheese. It's the only thing either of us can make without burning the house down."

"You were the one who burned the pizza, not me."

"And you caught our last package of macaroni on fire because you forgot to add water, genius," Cole teases.

I smile. I would love living with them if it was just like this all the time. No drama, just us teasing each other.

We all eat, listening to Cole trying to make jokes to ease the tension. Except I don't feel a lot of tension with Knight around. He seems happier than I've ever seen him. No, maybe happy isn't the right word. He seems content. Ease and calm I wouldn't have expected to see from someone who just lost everything.

Cole's phone buzzes. "I need to take this. Don't kill each other." Cole gets up and heads out through the front door.

"Don't expect Cole to come back until later tonight. He's still betting on us getting back together," Knight says.

I nod. I guessed the same.

We begin gathering the dishes, and Knight washes them while I dry. We are about halfway through before Knight starts talking.

"Abri was the perfect girlfriend. She was smart, funny, beautiful. She understood me. That although I dressed like a bad boy and got into constant trouble, there was more to me underneath. She believed in me when I couldn't."

"We don't have to do this." *I don't think I can hear him talk about Abri.*

Knight doesn't stop though. "We ran away together after high school. Like I told you, we eloped and started a company together. I was the CEO, and her title was officially assistant, but she was my partner in every way. Three plus years later, the company was worth millions. We had it all. We were young, happy, and successful. But then I got Abri pregnant."

Knight's voice catches, and he stops washing the dishes and turns to me. His eyes are already burning with tears.

"It wasn't planned. The condom broke. I thought she was on birth control, so I didn't mention it to her. I didn't want her to worry. But she was pregnant, and it was the best news I ever heard. Even

Abri who was skeptical at first, she thought we were too young, was ecstatic."

Knight swallows hard as he convinces his lips to keep moving and tell the rest of his story.

"The first couple of months went by quickly. We found out the baby was a boy, and we started buying everything. Decorating a room in the apartment. We went all out. But then the fights started. The worry set in. I felt Abri was working too much, and she didn't want to give up her dreams for our baby. I told her I would take time off when the baby was born. We'd hire help. It would be fine."

His tears fall hard and fast, but I can't comfort him. I can't make them stop, not until he finishes the story.

"Then, one night, the fighting got worse. I don't even remember the words we were fighting about. Abri fell. I didn't touch her. I tried to catch her, but I couldn't. I raced her to the hospital. She gave birth a few hours later to Gideon. They said stress and anxiety caused her to go into labor early. It was far too early. The doctors couldn't save him. He died in my arms as he attempted to take his first breaths."

Tears are flooding our eyes now. "It's not your fault."

"It is. I got her pregnant even though she wasn't ready. And I fought with her when all she wanted was help. Abri was perfect before I ruined her. She wasn't the same after she lost the baby. Neither of us was."

I want to comfort him. I want to make the pain go away, but it's impossible. No words will help. No touch will soothe. This is his pain to bare.

"I should have stopped it before it came to this. You gave me a chance to stop it, and I didn't listen."

"Huh?"

Knight wipes his tears and then brushes mine away with his thumb. "Can I hold your hand?" His breathing is erratic, his chest rising and falling too quickly.

He's asking permission to hold my hand. I want to hold his hand.

It's the first step toward forgiveness if I hold his hand. *Am I ready for that?*

I stare down at his hand, and before I realize what I'm doing, I reach out and take it.

He exhales at my touch like he wasn't whole until I touched him.

He gently pulls on my hand, leading me out to the patio where a small loveseat sits. He motions for me to sit and I do, pulling him next to me. I've never wanted to be closer to someone as I do right now.

He tries to pull his hand away, but I hold it firmly. His eyes widen, and his pupils dilate. But his breathing calms at the gesture.

I open my mouth, but no words come out. I need him to finish talking. I need him to tell me how I tie into all of this.

"Abri and I were close to graduating high school. It was a Thursday night, and I picked Abri up from her house. We were going to go to a movie, but we never made it past my car. We parked in the parking lot of the movie theater and made out in the back of my old Crown Vic.

"It was an ordinary night. We were making out, and whenever we came up for air, we talked about skipping college and running away. Traveling the world and starting our own life together."

His eyes meet mine again as he traces the lines on my palm with this thumb.

"Then Abri got a phone call. Her mother would sometimes call and demand she come home early, but it wasn't her mother. It was Ren."

I suck in a breath, both from his words and the way his fingers feel on my palm.

"Ren said it was an emergency. She needed Abri to come to the hospital.

"I'd never met any of Abri's friends before. She was afraid if I did, I would like them better than her. She was the jealous type back then."

"Still is," I mumble.

Knight pauses before continuing. "We got to the hospital, and it was chaos. Nurses and doctors were running around frantically. Ren and Henry were there with tears and fear in their eyes. Their bodies frozen with shock.

"Abri tried to comfort Ren. And soon I was lost to the shadows. No one even remembered I was in the waiting room. No one talked to me or looked at me. Everyone was too occupied with trying to save the three lives that stood on the edge between life and death."

"My parents," I whisper.

He touches my chin. "And you."

I nod, needing more.

"I needed an escape. I had never faced death before. And it felt wrong to take part in someone else's worst moment when they had no clue who I was. So I made some excuse about getting them coffee, and then I slunk away. I walked down the hallway aimlessly just trying to find a place to cry like a baby in the corner.

"I found what I thought was an empty room. No nurses were hovering around it, and when I knocked no one answered. So I opened the door and pushed inside, but the room wasn't empty."

"I was there..."

⁂

"PLEASE, Nicole, I'm not ready to face Henry or Ren yet. Please, just tell them I'm still unconscious, and I can't have any visitors yet. At least until I find out how my parents are doing," I say.

Nicole looks at me with sad eyes. "Rest Mila, don't worry about your siblings. Just try to rest. We will give you an update as soon as there is one."

"Thank you," I whisper as she leaves.

My body is riddled with pain. My head is on the brink of explosion. My chest feels too tight. But my core and legs hurt the most.

I feel tears, boiling up inside me, but I won't let them out. I won't cry for myself. I won't cry until I know the outcome of my parents' surgeries.

The door opens before I even have a chance to close my eyes. And a man walks in. He's tall, muscular, and sad. A few tattoos are scattered along his arms and the way his chiseled jaw moves and his five o'clock shadow seems to grow as the seconds pass seem to indicate that he is a few years older than me.

I grab the covers harshly and pull them up to my chest.

"Did Nasser send you?" I ask nervously.

The man's eyes flicker to me slowly as if he didn't realize I was here. "Who is Nasser?"

I shake my head. "It doesn't matter."

"I'm sorry I should go."

"No, stay. I could use the company."

"Don't you have family waiting for you?"

I nod. "I do. I'm sure my family is in the waiting room frantic to talk to me."

He stares at me longer, then says, "You're Mila Burns."

I nod.

"I'm Ace Knight. I should talk to your brother and sister and let them know you are awake. They are worried sick."

"No, please don't. I can't face them yet."

He frowns. "Why?"

"Because this was all my fault."

His frown deepens until he's red with fury. "I don't know what happened, but I can assure you, it's not your fault."

"That's kind of you to say, but you don't know the whole story."

He sits down in a chair next to my bed. "Tell me what happened then."

"How about you tell me about your night instead? I need something to distract me." I wince as I move and my cracked ribs sting.

He takes my hand almost instinctively, comforting me as I deal with the pain.

"My story isn't very interesting."

"Just tell me. I could be dying for all you know. You could fulfill my final request."

He laughs and strokes my face lovingly. "It would take a lot to kill a spirit like you. You've been hurt, but you aren't going to die. I won't let you."

"My knight in shining armor will save me?"

He laughs again. "Yes, I'll save you."

"Good, now tell me a story, Knight."

He smiles again. At least I can make his sadness go away, even if there is nothing that can erase my own. Even if my parents survive, I will live with the guilt forever. The pain is too much to survive.

"Ok, my pretty girl. This tale is a happy tale. It starts with a princess, who didn't realize she was a princess, and a knight."

I smile, liking him too much. To some he might seem like a bad boy, but not to me. I've met a real bad boy. The kind who hurts you to your core. Knight is just playing one with his tattoos and mischievous grin.

Knight is the kind of man I could fall for if I got rid of my purple and blue hair, risqué clothes, and heavy metal music. And most importantly, if I started behaving and playing by the rules. I think I've finally realized why I will always follow a plan. I'll never risk my life, or anyone else's again.

"This princess was locked away in a castle, surrounded with white walls," he glances around at the walls around us.

"Every day she laid in bed alone, waiting for a prince to come and save her. And every day she was disappointed that none came."

I bite my lip. "Go on."

"But then after waiting for years, a knight came. This was no ordinary knight. He was tall, dark, and handsome of course, but he was better than the other knights, for he had the strength to defeat the evil dragon guarding the castle gate.

"He knew not of the prize that awaited him when he defeated the dragon, but he hoped the greatest treasure would befall him if he bested the beast. So after an arduous, vicious fight, the knight risked his life for a chance to see the beauty beyond the white castle door.

"And when he entered, he found a princess so beautiful, so smart, so sexy that he fell at her feet, unworthy of such perfection.

"In his fall, he injured his heart, and it shattered into tiny pieces. So torn was he that he knew he could never stand again.

"But the princess was strong. Even stronger than he, she found all of the tiny pieces of his heart and quickly put it back together. She saved him, as he had saved her. And then they lived happily ever after."

His grin is contagious.

"Lame," I half moan, half tease.

He laughs. "Sorry, I'm not the best storyteller when put on the spot."

"And you're taken."

He nods.

I sigh. If only he were truly my knight.

"Who's the lucky girl?"

His eyes don't meet mine anymore. "Abri. Her name is Abri; she's friends with your sister."

I gasp. I knew Abri had a boyfriend, but I didn't listen when she talked about him. I hardly listened to anything Abri said.

"Break up with her."

He laughs, thinking I'm joking and teasing like we have been all night.

"I'm serious. Break up with her."

He frowns. "I'm planning on marrying her."

"No."

The memories all come back. Flooding me with the entire night. But I can't keep reliving them. I can't go any further.

"Mila?"

Knight. My thoughts come back to the present.

I realize now why he hired me. Why he wanted me in his life. He wants me to tell him why I told him to break up with Abri that night. Was it just a hunch or did I have a valid reason? One he could have used against her in the divorce filings?

I can't help him now. It's too late. But it won't stop the memories from coming back. I need it to replay more in my head, but right now, I need Knight more.

"I forgive you for not telling me," I whisper.

Knight inhales like he's taking in every word of my forgiveness. Then he kisses the palm of my hand.

"I thought I needed you to tell me why I shouldn't have married Abri, but I'd rather you not have any more pain. I love you, Mila. I would have loved you that night if my heart wasn't already taken. But when I found you again on the mountain, I fell harder than I've ever fallen. I used you and don't deserve your forgiveness. After Abri, I didn't think I could love again. That I could trust someone again. But you changed that. And regardless of what you want next, know I will love you forever pretty girl."

Knight destroyed my heart, and I don't know if I have enough left to love him with. Just like his story that night, he shattered my heart into tiny pieces, and it will take both of us to find all of the shards.

But I want to try again with Knight. Because he is the best and one of the worst things that ever happened to me. He's had my heart since that night in the hospital. I tried to save him then, but he wouldn't let me. He couldn't see the danger coming. But maybe I can save him now.

22 KNIGHT

I told Mila I love her.

I never thought I would be able to say those words again. After what happened, I didn't think she would ever forgive me. Staying with Cole was never about getting Mila back. Sure, I thought maybe I'd get her to talk to me, eventually. But the words started spilling out of me. Words I've been holding back from everyone, even Cole. And Mila listened.

I thought she would run away or storm out. I thought it would take months of begging and pleading to get her to even sit at the same table as me. But that's what makes Mila so special. She's able to look past people's flaws to find the beauty within. It's a blessing and a curse. Because it makes her vulnerable. Bad people can take advantage of her forgiveness. She will let people in who don't deserve to be let in.

If I wish for one thing in the world, it would be to protect her. That's all I want.

But I'm getting more than the ability to protect her. I'm getting a second chance.

She forgives me. She remembers. I don't want her to dive too far into that dark place. If she does, I'm not sure she'll find her way back out. And I'm selfish; I want her all to myself.

I'm still holding her hand, but I don't dare do more. I won't push my luck. I want her completely. I want to feel a connection again I haven't felt since we were in Aspen, but I don't deserve it. Tonight, I'll take her forgiveness and pray we can be more at some point.

Mila's breathing is fast like she's just ran a marathon and is about to pass out.

"Mila? Are you okay? Do you need water or something?"

She shakes her head, but she doesn't look at me or say anything. She hasn't spoken since I told her I love her.

"You don't need to say I love you back. You don't need to say anything back; I just needed you to know."

Her long eyelashes flicker up as her gaze focuses on me. She pulls her hand away, and I reluctantly let my hands fall to my lap. She's pulling away from me, and I have to let her go.

But then her small body turns to face me. Her hands tremble in her lap.

"Mila, please tell me what's wrong. If you are remembering something bad, please let me in. Let me help you."

She takes a deep breath in and out, and I sit on my hands to keep from touching her. Don't push her away. She will come to you when she's ready. For now, simply sit until she asks for help.

If she passes out from not breathing enough, I'm never going to stop touching her to make her better.

Her hand reaches out toward my hair. She gently takes a few strands between her fingers, pulling gently, as if she's remembering my much longer hair before. Her fingers slip down to the side of my face. I want to close my eyes at how intense it feels for her to be touching me again, but I don't. I don't want to miss a thing with Mila. Because I'll never know when it will be the last time she touches me like this.

Her eyes pierce through my pupils into my soul as she strokes my cheek. What she sees, I don't know. But I implore my heart to show her the love I feel for her is true.

I always thought Abri was the one for me. Perfect in every way, but my heart lied to me. Mila is who I love. I thought I would do anything for Abri. I would have died protecting Abri. But I'll do more for Mila. I will let her go to keep her safe. And the difference between Abri and Mila is Abri would ask me to take a bullet for her; Mila never would.

Her gaze and hands drop over my black T-shirt. To my biceps, then forearms covered in tattoos.

She smiles when she finds a dragon on my forearm.

"This used to be a rubber ducky?" she asks.

I laugh. "What has Cole been telling you?"

"Everything."

I don't doubt it. He's been trying to get Mila and me together since the first moment I told him about her. If I had told him about Mila all those years ago, he would have persuaded me to date her then.

She traces her fingers over the outline of the dragon. "They did a good job covering it up. I can't see the rubber ducky anymore."

I swallow the lump in my throat. "I got the dragon to remind me of you. Of the story I told you that night. I realized after I left you are no princess. You are more of a dragon."

She nods.

"I don't need a knight to save me."

"I know, but maybe I need a dragon to protect me," I whisper.

Her hands hold onto either side of my face. She holds my head steady as she lowers herself until our lips are inches apart. "I'm sorry for forgetting you. If I had remembered, I would have saved you earlier."

"Save me now."

She closes the gap and our lips touch so gently I have to keep my eyes open to ensure we are, in fact, kissing. And then we are really kissing. Her lips crash down roughly, kissing me in one long kiss trapping me beneath her.

I give her everything with this kiss. I tell her how sorry I am as I slip my tongue into her mouth.

She forgives me with a sob and moan as I nip at her bottom lip.

Her hands tangle in my hair as I kiss away her tears and continue down to her neck.

We both apologize profusely.

For everything.

For forgetting.

For remembering.

For not telling the truth.

For hiding.

For hurting.

"Touch me, Knight. Hold me, kiss me, fuck me."

I realize I'm still sitting on my hands, not sure if any of this is true.

But at her words, I grab her desperately, sliding my hand beneath her black jacket. A jacket that matches my dark shirt.

"We've always been connected, even when we were miles apart. Even when we didn't remember. Or tried to hide from our past. Even if our connection isn't healthy," she whispers.

Her words are true. I doubt we wore the same outfit every day for the past five years. But I know there wasn't a day that went by I didn't think back to her. When I didn't think of my pretty girl and what she was doing. It wasn't love. At the time, I gave my whole heart to Abri. It was a connection to a woman I thought would never be mine.

"Fuck me," she says again.

I take her mouth with mine and kiss her with everything I can give her.

She moans and grinds her body on top of mine. I know if I let her, she'd fuck me right here and come from the grinding she's doing alone. One week is too long for us to go without being with each other when our connection is so passionate.

"I'm not going to fuck you on this tiny couch," I growl into her lips.

I lift her up and carry her back into Cole's apartment. *Bed, I need to get to a bed.*

But Mila starts unbuttoning her jacket and I know I won't make it to her bed. I need to see her breasts. Need to kiss and torture them. Now.

I set her down on the edge of the kitchen counter and quickly help her rid herself of the jacket and black tank top she was wearing beneath it. I see the black sparkly bra drawing me in with promises of what lies beneath its pretty lace and sparkles.

I'm not patient enough to find the clasp on her back, so I push the bra up until her breasts fall out for me.

She gasps as I lean down to taste her nipple, hard and begging for me.

Her body falls back against the counter as I lick the hard point. Her body shivers against the cold air and my heated touch. I move quickly to her other nipple, needing both at the same time and cursing that I only have one mouth. My hand does its best to give her other nipple attention while my tongue is focused on the other.

Her legs tighten around my waist and I know her wetness is pooling between her legs. Everything about her makes me want her more. Her whimpers, how she arches her back, how she begs me for more while wanting this to last forever.

Suddenly, she grabs the hem of my shirt and pulls herself back up. She grabs fistfuls of my shirt and yanks it off. Her eyes dilate as she drinks my body in. I see the drops of drool as she stares at my tattoos. Her lips start kissing me places, and I can't focus on what I want to do to her body anymore.

She kisses each muscle, each spot of skin, each tattoo claiming it all as hers. She hesitates when she gets to my heart where the words

Abri are written. I need to change that. It's not fair to either woman, but then Mila drops her lips to kiss over the words and my heart.

"Mine," she purrs.

I suck in a long, hard breath. "Yours forever."

She smiles, and I lift her off the counter, regaining my focus on getting her to a bed as fast as possible.

She kisses me hard on my lips, and I close my eyes as I carry her, getting lost in the desperation and love pouring out of her. I stumble, and we fall onto the couch in the living room.

She giggles as I fall on top of her. She grabs my jeans as her eyes suddenly grow heavy.

"Off," she moans into my lips as she pulls at my jeans.

I'm desperate for her. I would do anything for her. But getting out of my jeans while still holding her is an impossible task, and I can't decide which is more important. Getting out of my jeans or kissing and holding Mila.

She laughs. And finally pushes me off her body. I reluctantly stand up, and she follows after. She starts kissing me roughly, sucking on my bottom lip while I work on my jeans.

It's never taken me so long to undress, but I've also never enjoyed undressing more than I do with her lips pressed against mine.

When I'm finally naked, I grab her hips, and we stumble back toward the bedroom. I work on finding the zipper to her skirt, but I can't find it. It doesn't matter. I slip my hand up her skirt and pull her panties down as we stumble onto the bed.

My head moves between her legs, kissing every sweet part of her. Her sensitive bud, her lips, and then I dive inside her, filling her with my tongue.

"Knight," she moans as he grabs my hair roughly, pulling me from her pussy.

I pout, but she tosses a condom at me.

I grin. *How could I have forgotten to bring a condom when I came over to Cole's apartment? Good thing Cole has his own stash here.*

I rip the condom open, slip it on and pause, waiting to push inside her. *What the hell is wrong with me? Just fuck her.*

But I can't. I need more than fucking. If this is all she wants, I'll kill myself when I pull out and know it's the last time. *Man, I've turned into a pussy.*

Her eyes brighten as she reads my mind. "I want more too."

I kiss her tenderly and then pull away.

"But I swear, if you don't fuck me now, Knight, I'm going to kick your ass."

I grin and slide into her slick entrance. She moans and curses as I fill her. Her body readjusts to me after going without me for days.

"Damn, I've missed this," I moan.

"Not as much as I have," she purrs back.

I grab her hips and slam harder. Her body writhes beneath me, angling her body to let me reach deeper than I've ever been inside her.

She doesn't tell me she loves me with words. She doesn't tell me she wants to start our relationship again. But I can feel it with her body. She needs me as much as she needs air to breathe.

So I fuck her, harder, faster, longer. I watch as her face turns from pleasure to bliss. Her mouth goes from panting to screaming. Her body goes from sensitive to exploding.

We come together, now in sync. And I hope we never lose this connection again.

We aren't a perfect couple. We are broken and tragic. Our lives have always intertwined, but we were never headed toward a happily ever after together. But now might be that time.

I pull out of her, lie down next to her in the bed, and pull Mila to me as her eyes begin to drift close. Neither of us has slept much since we've been apart. And as much as I want to fuck her again and again, I want to protect her while she sleeps more.

The door opens, and light floods in as Cole stumbles in, presumably to sleep on the cot he made for himself on the floor. He spots me, stops, and smirks.

"You know that's my bed right?"

I nod.

"Ugh, fine, it's your bed now. You owe me a new bed, Knight."

I stroke Mila's face. *I'll buy him whatever fucking bed he wants. I have Mila back.*

Cole leans down and picks up his blanket and pillow off the floor. "I'll go sleep on the couch. Glad I'm not on nightmare duty anymore. She sleeps better with you than me."

I growl at Cole, and he laughs before leaving us alone. It's been years since I didn't know what my future held when I closed my eyes at night. But I welcome it. My greatest adventures always came when I didn't know what was coming next.

23 MILA

I love Knight. I've always loved Knight. One of the reasons my mind forgot that horrible night was to forget about him choosing her over me. I tried to stop him. I tried to warn him. But he was loyal to a woman he loved, even if she didn't love him back.

I glance at Knight who is holding me close to him in Cole's bed. Knight thinks he saved me from Abri. He thinks losing Gideon was what caused her to deteriorate. To hate him. He's wrong. We aren't safe. I remember everything. I won't let her ruin us. Even if we deserve it.

I ease myself off the bed, cautiously, so I don't wake Knight. He doesn't move. I don't think he's slept since Aspen.

I quickly put a pair of jeans and a T-shirt on and leave before I change my mind. It's six in the morning. Knight is usually awake by now. The only thing keeping him asleep is his exhaustion.

I tiptoe toward the front door, smiling when I see our discarded clothes strung about the apartment.

"What are you doing?" Cole asks, sitting up on the couch.

I stop and smile, pretending nothing is wrong. "What are you doing sleeping on the couch? You have a spare bedroom."

"The spare bedroom shares a wall with my bedroom. I didn't want to listen to the two of you all night."

"Sorry if we kept you awake. And for stealing your bed."

"Don't worry; it's your bed now."

"I'm just going to run and get breakfast for us. Do you want something?"

He stands and walks to me. "I want to know what you are doing sneaking out at six in the morning."

"I'm getting breakfast. I can't cook so this is the only way for me to do something nice for Knight."

"You and I have become good friends, Mila. I know you pretty well. And you are a horrible liar. What's going on? Are you and Knight broken up again?"

"No."

Cole studies me a moment and then grabs my arm. "You are going to Abri."

"If I don't go, we will all die. Knight thinks he fixed the problem. He just doesn't realize what she threatened me with before. She's not done. She may have all of his money, but it's not enough. If you don't let me go, we die."

My words may be a little harsh, but it's the truth. Abri will do anything to survive, to get revenge.

Cole releases my arm and steps aside. I run to my car and begin driving as fast as I can toward Knight's old apartment that Abri now owns. It's a long shot that she is there, but it's my only hope of finding her quickly. Even though Cole let me go, I have no doubt he will wake Knight, and they will be right behind me.

The elevator ride up to the apartment is quick. Faster than I remember. I try to think of the words I'm going to say to fix this, but I'm not sure I can. I just know I need to confront Abri.

I fidget with my phone as the elevator opens, and I walk to the front door. I still have a spare key Knight gave me, and I doubt she has changed the locks on the door quickly. I knock once, and when no one answers, I use the key to get inside.

"You know, I could shoot you for breaking and entering," Abri says, standing in the entryway.

"So shoot me then, it's what you want. To hurt Knight and punish me for the pain we've caused you."

She narrows. "Since when do you know anything I want?"

"Since I remember that night."

Abri studies me a moment and then turns toward the kitchen. I follow her and watch as she pours us each a glass of whiskey.

I take mine, thankful we might be able to have this conversation woman to woman. Or we will get drunk and turn this into a cat fight.

"Why are you here, Mila?"

I take a sip of the whiskey for encouragement. Abri is in a robe, and it's clear she's not wearing much underneath it.

"Because I want to apologize."

She raises an eyebrow as she laughs. "You want to apologize?"

"Yes." This is my only chance to protect Knight.

"I hurt you that night. I knew you and Knight were together. I knew you were in love and I hurt you anyway, and I want to say I'm sorry."

"Your apology is five years too late."

"I know, and I'm sorry for that as well."

She drinks all of her whiskey. "It doesn't matter. I don't accept your apology."

Shit.

"What do you want then, Abri?"

She paces back and forth as if no one has ever asked this question. "I want to be happy. I want to never worry about feeding myself again. I want to be with someone who loves me back. And I want you and Knight to pay for what you did."

I wince at her last words.

"You were a princess, Mila. While I was trailer park trash. You had everything while I had nothing. I fought even to find enough food to live. I shivered in my bed at night because we didn't have any heat while you had everything. Why did you have to take my boyfriend too?"

"I didn't take him. And I wasn't a princess. It was all an illusion. My parents were broke. I've slept on the streets. I've done unspeakable things for food. I understand. You're a survivor, just like me. You would do anything to survive."

"I did anything to survive."

I nod.

"I don't blame you for dating Knight. He was set to make a lot of money. You saw your chance, and you took it," I say.

"I was happy. I had choices. I could divorce him and take half, or find a way to fall in love and live happily ever after."

I still. "I get it. But you can still be happy now. You have the money. You don't need to hurt us anymore. We've suffered enough."

She laughs. "I've suffered for five years. I will suffer more from the memory of losing my baby. You haven't known suffering."

I catch my breath. *This was a mistake. I won't convince her to change her mind.*

"Five years ago, when Knight stumbled into my room, I fell for him, but he didn't fall for me. I kissed him, but he didn't kiss me back. I begged him to stay, but he chose you. He loved you. You could have been happy."

Her sob catches in her throat, and I realize the pain she carries. From seeing me with Knight. From losing her baby. From losing Knight's love.

I walk over to her and hug her. She cries into my chest.

"I'm sorry. I'm so sorry," I say.

Finally, she pulls away, wiping her tears. The moment is gone, and anger fills her eyes.

"You should still pay."

"We did. You have everything. Money, the apartment, the company."

"And you have *him*."

I suck in a breath. "You never loved him, only the idea of him."

She slaps me, and I deserve it, but it's the truth.

"I remember hearing you and Ren talk about Knight. You weren't in love. You said he was a way out of your trailer park life. You planned on getting a divorce. You even said if it looked like you wouldn't get enough money in the divorce, you'd kill him and get the insurance money."

Abri stills at my words.

"Is my memory wrong?"

"No."

"Did you try to kill Knight in a car accident?"

"Yes."

"Did he ever hurt you? Beat you?" I suck in my breath, waiting for her honest answer. I love Knight; I might be blind to his faults.

"No. I lied to try and keep him away from you."

I exhale all of my pain in that moment.

"That kiss destroyed me. Even though I never loved Knight, it hurt. Not as much as losing Gideon, but I can't forgive you for it either."

I nod, and then I see the flash of metal.

I hold my hands up cautiously. "Abri, relax. We are just talking."

"Abri, what are you doing?" Knight asks from the hallway. His hands are up as well, showing caution. But his eyes are all fear.

"You both hurt me so much. And yet, I was the one punished. I lost my baby," Abri cries again.

Shit. What did I do? This isn't going to end well.

"You will find happiness again. You have money now. You have a company you love. You can adopt a baby or find a sperm bank and have your own. You don't need a man to be happy. Or you can find a man and fall desperately in love. You can have anything you want, Abri. I want you to be happy. I just don't want to spend my life wondering if you will come after us," I say.

Abri raises the gun, and I turn to Knight. We both freeze, unsure what is going to happen. *I love you,* I mouth to him.

I love you too, he mouths back.

It probably isn't the smartest thing to do in front of Abri. It makes her pain worse and gives her more reason to shoot us, but if this is my last moment on this earth, I want to leave it loving Knight.

I turn back, and instead of the gun pointed at my head, Abri holds out the gun for me to take. I do, hesitantly.

She looks at me. "I won't come after you. I won't think of you again after today. I'm starting a new life. This is my surrender. Be happy. Just know that Ace isn't a saint."

"Thank you. We won't press charges. We won't take our evidence to the police unless you force us to, but know if either of us ends up hurt, this entire conversation will be played in front of a court."

"It won't come to that," Abri says.

I nod and watch as she walks to Knight. "I'm keeping everything. You still deserve to suffer some for what you did, you asshole."

"You deserve to be happy, Abri. For what it's worth, I loved you and would have loved you forever if I could. And I'll love our time together because it gave me a brief moment with our son." Knight pulls Abri into a tight hug, and they both cry into each other's shoulders.

I walk out of the apartment giving them a moment alone together. I take the gun and put it in my back pocket. I've never held a gun before and will never hold one again. Hopefully, Knight or Cole knows how to get rid of it.

I take my phone out of my pocket and stop the recording. I'll keep the evidence, but I don't think I will really need it.

Knight comes out of the apartment a few minutes later. "Thank you," he says.

"For what?"

"For forcing us to talk and saving my life."

His lips crash down on mine.

"I love you, Knight."

"I love you, pretty girl. Let's go back to Cole's place."

I smile. "We can, but first, I need to tell you what happened that night. The whole story. Abri is on her way to healing. Now I need a chance to heal."

24 MILA

Five Years Ago

"YOU ARE GROUNDED, and that's final," my father's voice booms through the whole living room.

My mom sits idly by on the couch, not bothering to give any input. I know she hates my boyfriend as well. But she won't even bother to talk to me. She hates him and thinks I'm already a lost cause. Her efforts would be wasted, she thinks, so why bother?

But my father, he's too stubborn to ever give up. He wants to control me. What color my hair is, what I eat, when I sleep, where I go to school, and what I do. Even who I date.

"What am I grounded for? I didn't do anything wrong?"

"Your hair is the color of the sky, your clothes are ridiculous, and as I've already said, you aren't going anywhere with that boy!"

I glare at him. He's stubborn, but so am I. I won't give up so easily.

"Fine, I'll just stay locked away in my room forever."

I storm upstairs, not bothering to listen to anything else. I slam my door shut, and sit on my bed with my phone, prepared to text my boyfriend, Nasser, that I won't be able to meet him.

The wind gusts and the screen over my window shudders against the sill. I stare at it for only a second before I make up my mind. I'm leaving. I can't stand to stay in this house another second. I'll drink my frustration away tonight, and tomorrow I will make a plan to leave town for good. I can graduate from high school early, get a job, and then decide if I want to go to college. I don't care if I have money. I'll be free.

I tiptoe over to the window. My room is on the second floor, but it overlooks the covered deck. I push the screen off and watch it blow away with the wind. I text Nasser.

ME: Meet me at the end of my block in five minutes.

AND THEN I CLIMB OUT, sliding onto the roof. My body glides to the edge. *It's not that far; I can make it.*

I let go, and my body falls to the grass below with a loud thud. I look back at the house, expecting someone to have heard me, but no one comes out.

I start running down the street to meet Nasser even though my heart is begging me to stop. I don't want to stop. I want to move faster. I want to escape the nightmare that is my home.

If I were to return now, I would get my ass kicked. I would be grounded for real. I would know a whole new level of punishment.

Nasser is the lesser of two evils. He may not be my ticket out of this town, but he is my ticket to freedom tonight.

Nasser's car is parked at the end of my block. I spot his Camry two houses away. This block isn't the nicest in Aspen, but it's nice. Too nice for his old Toyota.

I climb in the passenger seat, and we drive off before I have a chance to say anything. Nasser doesn't ask me any questions about my family, and I don't offer up what happened.

He plays his loud music and drives. That's what I like about him; he gives me space. Doesn't pressure me to be anything the way my family does. We've only been dating two weeks now, and I don't see a future. But I like that I can be free when I'm with him.

Nasser pulls into the driveway of the house he shares with his three other roommates. It's a large house, but it hasn't been updated since the fifties and could use some work. But I'm not here to critique the decorations.

Nasser doesn't open my door. He just turns the car off and gets out. I follow him at a leisurely pace. By the time I'm gone, he's already disappeared into the basement.

I head downstairs where the music is blasting. I find Nasser with his roommates and their friends drinking and passing around a joint.

I walk over to the bar and grab a beer before joining them. When the joint hits my lips, I'm in heaven. Finally, I can let go.

Hours go by as we listen to music, drink, and smoke our worries away. No one asks me to be anything but who I am. I don't have to change my hair color or remove my tattoos or pretend I want to go to law school. I'm just me.

I lean against Nasser's chest as he strokes my hair.

"Let's go for a walk. I want to show you my favorite part of the house," he whispers against my hair.

I smile and nod as he takes my hand and leads me to the door of the basement. We haven't had sex yet, and tonight won't be that night. I'm too drunk to think properly. But I'm fine with some heavy making out and sleeping in his bed while he gropes me all night.

He slides the glass door open, and we slip out into the night.

"You look beautiful tonight."

I blush at his compliment. "Thank you."

He leads me to a gazebo. "Dance with me."

I giggle as he wraps me in his arms and we dance to a silent melody. My head starts spinning from the movement, and if I'm not careful, all the alcohol I've drunk will come back up.

"I need to sit down," I mutter.

"How about lie down?"

"What?"

Before I can respond, Nasser is lying me down on the couch in the gazebo. *Yes, I need to lie down.* My head already feels better.

But then Nasser is on top of me, kissing me harshly.

"Slow...down," I mutter between kisses.

He doesn't slow down. Instead, his hands slide up beneath my skirt.

"No, I too drunk."

"Shh, you won't remember this."

He pulls my panties down before I can stop him. My body tries to push him off, but the alcohol and drugs make it feel like I'm fighting in a fog. I can move, but slowly. I can think, but only one step at a time.

"No," I say again as his fingers slip inside me.

"You want me."

I try to say no again, but my words don't leave my mouth. I'm paralyzed now as I hear him undoing his zipper. *He's going to rape me.*

You deserve it, my dad's voice says in my head.

You were asking for it, my mom says.

If you would have just listened to us, Ren says.

If you dressed in jeans instead of a short skirt, Henry says.

No.

No.

NO.

The word never leaves my mouth again. I feel his slimy cock against my entrance. I don't want this. I need him to stop.

But I'm frozen. I can't move.

You're a fighter, a new voice says. *You can fight this.*

I can fight him. I won't let him win.

His lips come down hard on me, and I bite as hard as I can.

"Fucking Christ," he cries out as blood spills from his mouth.

I push him off of me with everything I have, and then I run toward his house.

Suddenly, I've never been so sober as I run. My skirt is ripped, my panties gone, but nothing will stop me.

I run up the steps to the deck leading into the kitchen. The doors to the walkout basement are closer, but I don't trust his friends.

I get the back door open, and I slip into the house, but I'm not safe. I need to be safe.

His car keys lay on the stand by the door. I grab them and run out into the night again, as much as it scares me to be out in the dark. I don't pause to see if he's following me. I run straight to his car, jump in, and start it all in one movement.

Then I'm backing out of the driveway. I just need to drive a few blocks away, then I can call for help. Then, I will be safe.

I've been drinking; I should stop. But when I reach into my pocket, I realize I don't have my phone. I can't stop. I need to find someplace safe. I need to find a police station.

So I keep driving. My heart beats erratically, and my foot hits the gas harder.

I close my eyes to keep the tears back, and when I open them, I see lights coming straight at me. I try to swerve, but it's too late. The light hits the car, and I'm jolted back into the cold night.

Pain. My entire body aches as I shiver in the cold. I feel lights on me and hear sirens in the background, but I don't know what's happening. And then I see her. My mother is lying on the cold concrete next to me.

"Mom?"

She doesn't respond.

I sit up, but the second I do, the world spins out of control around me. I blink, but the world doesn't stop spinning.

I see another car. My parents' car with the front smashed in. My father sits in the driver's seat with blood pouring down his face.

What did I do?

I close my eyes and open them again. When I take in my surroundings again, I'm in the back of an ambulance. *How did that happen?*

"She's conscious again," a man over me says.

"Where does it hurt?" he asks.

"Everywhere."

"Do you remember what happened?"

The images of Nasser trying to force himself on me flash through my head. But I can't make the words leave my mouth.

"Driving drunk," comes out instead.

The man nods.

And I can't keep my eyes open anymore. I have to close them.

When I open them again, I'm in a room. It's white and cold. A woman is standing over me.

"Try to rest. You have a lot of injuries."

"My parents?"

"They are in surgery. We will update you with their condition soon."

My parents are in surgery because of me. Because I drove drunk.

It was to escape, the voice says.

What if I hadn't escaped? What if I had let him rape me? Then my parents wouldn't be dying in a surgery room.

I close my eyes again, and the guilt comes, but I don't see images of my parents' lifeless bodies. Instead, I see the look in Nasser's eyes. The aggression as he takes what he wants from me.

I escaped, and because of that, my parents might die.

I open my eyes to escape the nightmare.

"You're awake. Your parents are still in surgery. But your siblings are here. They will want to see you. I'll go get them," Nicole, according to her name tag visible on her chest.

THE TATTOOED OLDER BOY AT the end of my hospital bed insists on marrying Abri to my total dismay.

I spot Abri coming around the corner. He can't marry her. She'll destroy him. She's only looking for a rich man. She will take all of his money in a divorce, or kill him if his life insurance policy is worth enough. She will do anything to survive. Those were the words she spoke.

Anything to survive.

I understand now. After what Nasser did, I will do anything to take away the pain I feel.

I won't let Knight feel a similar pain.

I yank on his hand until he falls forward toward my bed and then I kiss him. As soon as our lips touch, I'm lost. I don't know if it's the drugs I'm on or him, but I've never felt so desperate. I want him. His lips are soft and perfect. And when I push my tongue into his mouth, he moans softly before he realizes what's happening.

He pulls away with a stunned look.

My eyes drift behind him to Abri, who looks like she's going to punch someone or throw up.

Knight turns to her. "I love you, Abri. She took me by surprise. I think she thinks I'm someone else. She's on a lot of painkillers."

Abri looks at me, and a gracious smile covers her face as she turns back to Knight. They walk toward each other, meeting in the middle. He kisses her with a passion I wish he would kiss me with. Their kiss kicks my kiss' ass.

Their kiss is between two people who love each other.

Maybe I was wrong. Maybe Abri truly loves Knight if she's willing to look past a mistake like this so easily.

They are a perfect couple. They have what I want.

And my life is in shambles. My family will blame me for tonight, and they will be right.

I need to tell someone about Nasser.

I need to tell Knight what I know so he can make the best decision about Abri.

I need to...turn all the pain off.

I close my eyes and shut off the world.

I shut off Nasser. I shut out my parents' corpses. I shut out Ren, Henry, and Abri. And I force Knight's kiss from my lips. This night didn't happen. I will not remember.

※

PRESENT

"THAT NIGHT WAS MY FAULT," I whisper.

"No, it was Nasser's fault. You never pressed charges against him?"

I shake my head. "Until recently, I didn't even remember the details of what happened. Only the newspaper clippings and stories my siblings told me."

Knight kisses my cheek as we sit in my car. "You shouldn't have kissed me that night."

I look at him with sadness. "You shouldn't have kissed me and gotten me fired, either."

"I thought you would remember you tried to save me with a kiss."

I smile. "I couldn't remember you without remembering the pain."

He kisses my lips again gently.

"Both of those kisses were so perfect, yet so destructive," I whisper against his lips.

We kiss again.

"If I had felt anything less than love for Abri, I would have been mesmerized with you after that kiss."

"And if I hadn't lost my scholarship and ability to finish school after your kiss, I would have fallen for you then."

Another kiss unites us, each of us promising we will let nothing come between us.

"How could I forget you?" I whisper.

"Because you had to survive the pain and guilt. It wasn't your fault."

I nod. It will take me a while for the guilt of what happened to vanish completely. And the pain of everything I lost that night will only ease with time. But in the meantime, we have each other.

We get out of the car in Cole's parking lot.

"You realize neither of us has any money or a job now," Knight says.

"Speak for yourself, I have two hundred dollars in my bank account, and a job as Cole's assistant."

Knight laughs. "That's more than I have."

I pull him to me. "I would live on the streets with you if it means I get to have you."

He smirks. "I don't think I would survive sleeping on the ground. I'm a bit of a germaphobe."

I laugh. "You're right. You wouldn't survive."

"I guess we will be living with Cole then."

"You get to be the one to tell him."

He kisses me. "I think you should tell him. He'll punch me in the face. He owes me a few punches."

I smile. "Fine, I'll tell him."

We kiss again, and I know we won't be able to stop kissing for the rest of the night.

"Our relationship won't exactly be perfect then, will it?"

"Perfect is overrated."

I smile. "Kiss me and make me forget."

I fell in love with Knight with one kiss, and with one kiss I brought him from the brink of despair.

"No, I'll kiss you, so you never have to forget again."

EPILOGUE

KNIGHT

"Hey, Knight?" Mila shouts from the couch of our living room.

Why she's shouting, I don't know. I'm cooking in the kitchen three feet away from her. The apartment we occupy is tiny. Less than five hundred square feet. But it's ours.

"Yes, baby?" I stir the marinara sauce.

"How accurate were the results at Perfect Match?"

I raise an eyebrow as I glance her way. "You would know better than me."

"You had a hundred percent guarantee. And when you matched couples, you had less than five percent report incompatibility after they started dating."

"Then I guess we were pretty good."

She frowns.

"What's wrong?"

"I just filled out both of our profiles, and it says we are incompatible. That we shouldn't be together. Do you think Abri knows it was me filling out the questionnaires and rigged it just to mess with us?"

I laugh and turn off the burners before walking over to Mila on the couch. I stand behind her, rubbing her shoulders gently that have tensed from reading the results.

"We are incompatible, huh?" I ask, ignoring the part about Abri. Neither of us brings her up often, but last time I checked, she had grown the company by ten percent and was dating a finance guy from Manhattan. She seems to be doing just fine.

"Yes," she groans.

I lean down and kiss the top of her head, then trail my kisses down to her ear.

"What do you think now? Are we still incompatible?"

She nods. "Yes."

"Hmm." I move my lips to her neck, sucking her sweet skin.

She moans.

"What about now?"

"Still incompatible."

The top of her scrubs gives me a fantastic view of her chest. I let my hand gently glide down her chest until I squeeze her breasts, letting my thumb trace over her nipple.

"And now?"

"Mmmhhh, still incomp—"

My lips land on her mouth as I tilt her head to me. Her tongue sweeps into my mouth and then I'm gone. I forget about making dinner. It will have to wait. I can feel her desperation and mild heart-break, and I won't ever let her feel that way again.

I climb over the couch, so I don't have to end the kiss and kneel in front of her feet. With one last kiss, I pull her pants and underwear down, burying my face between her legs.

"Yes!" she cries at my touch.

"Yes, we are compatible?"

She pants. "Ahh, almost."

I laugh and then drape her legs over my shoulders as I go to work on making her feel like mine. I should have had her the second she got off her twenty-four-hour shift.

My tongue licks, finding her clit with ease as I trace circles just the way she likes. I slip a finger into her tight cunt, and within moments, I feel her clenching around me.

"What about now?" I smile against her leg before kissing her inner thigh.

"I think we are perfect for each other."

"Good, now get dressed before dinner gets cold."

She pouts.

I laugh. "I'll fuck you more after dinner."

"Or you could fuck me while eating dinner."

My eyes darken. "Dammit, I love you."

TWO HOURS later we are fucked, our tummies full, and we've showered and changed.

"Where are we going?"

"To one of my favorite places."

She climbs onto the back of my motorcycle without any more questions. Today is the anniversary of her parents' deaths. The anniversary of when we first met. Most of the day she's been distracted with work, but now she's mine.

I drive quickly away from our tiny apartment to our destination, loving how her hands feel wrapped around my waist. I could spend the whole night driving, but then I wouldn't know what is going through her head. I wouldn't be able to see if she's having nightmares or dozing peacefully behind me. And I can't stand not being able to save her from any pain if I can.

So I pull up in front of the tattoo parlor, and Mila takes my hand as we get out.

"We are getting tattoos?" she asks.

"Yes, I thought what perfect way to mark you as mine?"

"I love that idea."

"That is if you can afford it, my sugar momma."

She laughs. "I'm not your sugar momma."

"You make all the money saving people's lives at the ER. You pay all our bills. That's the definition of a sugar momma."

She rolls her eyes. "You just got investors to invest over five million dollars in your latest app idea. I don't think I will be paying for anything for long."

I kiss her hard. "I won't see any of the money in my pocket for years. In the meantime, I'm in your debt."

She kisses me back before running into the parlor.

I chase after her.

"What tattoo do you want to get?" Mila asks as she looks at various designs in the office.

"I want your name, here," I say, pointing to ring finger of my left hand.

She gasps.

"What tattoo do you want?" I ask.

"A dragon."

I raise an eyebrow. "Really? Where? I think that tattoo will take more than one night."

She laughs. "Kidding. I want your name here." She points to her own ring finger.

We've talked several times about it. Marriage may or may not be in our futures. It's not something that is important to either of us right now. But I want her to know she's mine, and I'm hers. This is the way to show it.

We both take a seat in chairs next to each other as the artists begin needling the ink into our skin.

I've already gotten one tattoo since I met Mila. A cracked heart around Abri's name. Mila wouldn't let me erase her or mark over her, but she agreed to let me have a broken heart.

Mila's phone buzzes and I glance over just catching Ren's name as Mila silences her phone. Mila is meeting her siblings tomorrow for brunch. Things haven't completely healed between them yet, but they are all working on mending their relationships with a lot of therapy sessions and brunch meetings. Something about how none of them can yell if they are eating brunch.

"What's going through your head, pretty girl? What's your plan for the rest of our lives?"

She smiles as she thinks for a moment. "I don't have one. I had a plan for a perfect life to replace my horrible life, but I found you instead."

I laugh at her jab against me.

"You sure you don't have our entire life planned out yet?"

She smirks. "I guess you'll have to wait and see."

The End

Thank you so much for reading *Finding Perfect*!
I hope you enjoyed the entire Hate Me or Love Me Collection! Read more of my contemporary steamy romances in Pretend I'm Yours & Pretend We're Over.

JOIN ELLA's NEWSLETTER & NEVER MISS A SALE OR NEW RELEASE → ellamiles.com/freebooks

Love swag boxes & signed books?
SHOP MY STORE → store.ellamiles.com

ALSO BY ELLA MILES

Dirty Revenge

Dirty: The Complete Series

ALIGNED SERIES:

Aligned: Volume 1 (Free Series Starter)

Aligned: Volume 2

Aligned: Volume 3

Aligned: Volume 4

Aligned: The Complete Series Boxset

UNFORGIVABLE SERIES:

Heart of a Thief

Heart of a Liar

Heart of a Prick

Unforgivable: The Complete Series Boxset

MAYBE, DEFINITELY SERIES:

Maybe Yes

Maybe Never

Maybe Always

Definitely Yes

Definitely No

Definitely Forever

STANDALONES:

Pretend I'm Yours

Finding Perfect

Savage Love

Too Much

Not Sorry

ABOUT THE AUTHOR

Ella Miles writes steamy romance, including everything from dark suspense romance that will leave you on the edge of your seat to contemporary romance that will leave you laughing out loud or crying. Most importantly, she wants you to feel everything her characters feel as you read.

Ella is currently living her own happily ever after near the Rocky Mountains with her high school sweetheart husband. Her heart is also taken by her goofy five year old black lab who is scared of everything, including her own shadow.

Ella is a USA Today Bestselling Author & Top 50 Bestselling Author.

Stalk Ella at:
www.ellamiles.com
ella@ellamiles.com

9 781951 114